"If Austen w... might be som... edly witty and superbly satisfying romance."
—*Chicago Tribune*

"Believable and captivating . . . an outstanding and memorable tale." —*Publishers Weekly* (starred review)

The Summer of You

"How many romances really, and I mean *really*, stir the heart? This one did." —*All About Romance*

"Vivid and touching . . . Something new, something real, something genuine, something special and alive. It is worth savoring and appreciating." —*Smart Bitches, Trashy Books*

"Will touch your heart and wring your emotions until you find yourself laughing and weeping simultaneously."
—*TwoLips Reviews*

"Sharp, clever, and adorable . . . Those who are big fans of Julia Quinn, Laura Kinsale, and Tessa Dare will want to pick this one up." —*Babbling About Books, and More*

"A work that will touch your heart [and] make you laugh."
—*Night Owl Reviews*

continued . . .

Revealed

Compromised

If I Fall

KATE NOBLE

BERKLEY SENSATION, NEW YORK

THE BERKLEY PUBLISHING GROUP
Published by the Penguin Group
Penguin Group (USA) Inc.
375 Hudson Street, New York, New York 10014, USA

Penguin Group (Canada), 90 Eglinton Avenue East, Suite 700, Toronto, Ontario M4P 2Y3, Canada
(a division of Pearson Penguin Canada Inc.) • Penguin Books Ltd., 80 Strand, London WC2R 0RL,
England • Penguin Group Ireland, 25 St. Stephen's Green, Dublin 2, Ireland (a division of Penguin
Books Ltd.) • Penguin Group (Australia), 250 Camberwell Road, Camberwell, Victoria 3124, Australia
(a division of Pearson Australia Group Pty. Ltd.) • Penguin Books India Pvt. Ltd., 11 Community
Centre, Panchsheel Park, New Delhi—110 017, India • Penguin Group (NZ), 67 Apollo Drive,
Rosedale, Auckland 0632, New Zealand (a division of Pearson New Zealand Ltd.) • Penguin Books
(South Africa) (Pty.) Ltd., 24 Sturdee Avenue, Rosebank, Johannesburg 2196, South Africa

Penguin Books Ltd., Registered Offices: 80 Strand, London WC2R 0RL, England

This is a work of fiction. Names, characters, places, and incidents either are the product of the author's
imagination or are used fictitiously, and any resemblance to actual persons, living or dead, business
establishments, events, or locales is entirely coincidental. The publisher does not have any control over
and does not assume any responsibility for author or third-party websites or their content.

IF I FALL

A Berkley Sensation Book / published by arrangement with the author

PUBLISHING HISTORY
Berkley Sensation mass-market / April 2012

ISBN: 978-0-425-24711-2

BERKLEY SENSATION®
Berkley Sensation Books are published by The Berkley Publishing Group,
a division of Penguin Group (USA) Inc.,
375 Hudson Street, New York, New York 10014.
BERKLEY SENSATION® is a registered trademark of Penguin Group (USA) Inc.
The "B" design is a trademark of Penguin Group (USA) Inc.

PRINTED IN THE UNITED STATES OF AMERICA

10 9 8 7 6 5 4 3 2 1

ALWAYS LEARNING   **PEARSON**

To my brother-in-law Andy, who has instilled in my nieces and nephew the importance of intermittent swashbuckling.

And to my writing friends, my partners in caffeinated desperation, who frequently kept me from throwing my laptop across the coffee shop.

Prologue

January 1823

SHE liked the ring on her hand. She liked the emerald glitter; she liked the weight of the gold band. She liked the way it felt there, solid and right, and the fact that her sisters and all her friends admired it with enthusiastic jealousy. But more than the ring, Sarah Forrester liked the man who gave it to her, and what he had said when he did.

"This belonged to my mother," he'd rasped, looking up at her lovingly from his kneeling state—or at least she assumed it was lovingly, her vision was a bit watery at the time. "She wore it every day of her marriage. Over thirty years." He smiled, with a charm that was rakish and kind all at once, and lowered his voice to a conspiratorial whisper. "Do you think we can match that?"

And now, as all of their family and friends, acquaintances, and people she didn't even know but her parents wished to gloat to were gathered in the house in London, dressed in their finest silks and satins, cooing over her ring, Sarah Forrester only wanted one thing to make the night perfect: the man of her dreams standing by her side.

Amid all the music and dancing, she spotted him. He

looked bemusedly harried, as if he, too, was a little over-whelmed by the whole thing. Jason. Her heart did that strange, happy flip she was slowly becoming accustomed to every time she saw him. His red hair made him easy to spot, as did the crowd of people that naturally gravitated to her future bride-groom. His easy, befuddled charm endeared him easily to all around him. And to those who it did not, his dukedom surely did the trick. A fact he knew, but rarely capitalized on. Really, most of the time Jason was . . . just Jason. Teasing and kind, occasionally melancholy but he came out of it quick enough. Whenever she came over and smiled at him, he would smile back. He was, admittedly, a little bragish, but held in check by those whom he loved.

A number that now included Sarah, she thought with a thrill.

"Oh, let us see it again!" Amanda cried, her round face lit up with glee. Sarah's youngest sister may not have grown into her full, remarkable height yet, nor had she lost all of her youthful plumpness, but she was already getting eyes from several young gentlemen. At fifteen, she was on the border of acceptability to be out in society, and since it was her sister's engagement ball, Amanda had wheedled and argued with their parents that *surely* there was no harm in letting her at-tend.

"Mandy . . ."

One desperate look from her burgeoning-on-adulthood sis-ter had Sarah correcting herself. "I mean, *Amanda*. You are being ridiculous," Sarah replied through a smile. "You've al-ready seen it a thousand times!"

"But Miss Brooks hasn't, and neither has Miss Croft, have you?" Amanda turned to the two young ladies beside her. They were marginally older than Amanda, but eager to follow the enthusiastic girl in her demands, and shook their heads vigorously.

Sarah sighed, and proffered her left hand. The emerald was oohed and aahed over; Miss Brooks even gave a dutiful squeal. Strange. Utterly strange, the way this ring affected everyone around her. Including herself.

Because of its size. Because of its sparkle.

Because of what it meant.

She looked up again, sought out the red hair in the menagerie of the guffawing gentlemen across the room, only to find it missing. She scanned, searched . . . there he was, by the terrace doors. He looked to be making an escape, but before he could, he was looking over the crowd, scanning, searching . . . and found her eyes.

He waved a hand in front of his face. *I'm hot!* his gesture said.

She rolled her eyes and repeated the gesture. *Goodness, me, too!*

Come on, then. He nodded toward the terrace door with a mischievous smile.

Lord did she want out of this pack of young girls and into his arms, but . . .

"Look how the emerald flashes blue in the candlelight!" Amanda said as she took Sarah's hand and raised it up to the candle, eliciting more oohs and aahs.

Sarah jerked forward slightly as she was pulled, but held her ground. Tolerated her sister's enthusiasm. Amanda could be irrepressible in a terribly kind way.

Sarah held up her other hand to Jason, fingers spread. *Five minutes*, it said.

He held his hand back in the same way. *Five minutes*, he replied.

I love you, she mouthed, with a laughing smile, but he missed it, as he was already out the door, providing a cool rush she could feel from the other side of the room. She frowned slightly, unhappy that he was so uncomfortable that he rushed out the doors.

"Oh, when will the wedding be?" Miss Brooks pounced on her.

"And where will you honeymoon?" Miss Croft asked at the same time.

"What about the gown? And have you seen His Grace's estates yet?"

Then again, Sarah thought, she could not begrudge Jason his speed out the door. For in four minutes and forty seconds, she would join him.

❧

It was actually closer to six minutes, as once she had extracted herself from Amanda and her friends, Sarah had been waylaid by her mother, Lady Forrester, who had no fewer than three of the gentlemen she had been aiming toward Sarah in a circle around her. Sarah waited patiently as Lady Forrester made sure they all knew what a loss it was to them that Sarah was no longer available. The gentlemen looked appropriately aggrieved— mostly for Lady Forrester's sake, Sarah thought privately.

But finally, finally, she made her way to the terrace doors, and greeted the cool winter air with a smile of relief.

"Winn, wait—" she heard Jason say from somewhere in the darkness of the terrace. She turned toward his voice, and narrowly missed being bumped into by a shorter lady trying to make her escape.

"Oh, excuse me!" Sarah exclaimed.

But escape the smaller woman did, slipping past Sarah without so much as a nod of acknowledgement.

Sarah's head whipped around to follow the petite woman's movements, watching as she quickly folded herself into the overcrowded room. There were many people here that Sarah did not know personally—her parents had decided it was far more important for *their* friends to be invited to her engagement ball than her own, and Sarah had smiled and allowed it. So it was not surprising when she did not recognize a guest. But the woman who had skirted past her, with what almost looked like tears in her eyes . . . she was oddly familiar. . . .

And then suddenly her brain placed the woman. From an editorial cartoon that had appeared in the papers about six months ago . . . an etching of a small woman, standing in a crowd of scandalized men, and facing down the enormous belly of Lord Forrester, Sarah's father, as she attempted to gain admittance to one of the most exclusive learned societies in Britain, the Society of Historical Art and Architecture of the Known World.

"Was that Winnifred Crane?" Sarah asked, turning to Jason, who looked unnaturally pale in the moonlight. At his nod, Sarah could not help but smile.

"Where is she going? I so wanted to meet her!" Sarah could not help but gush. Miss Winnifred Crane's adventures of the past summer were now the stuff of legend. She had challenged

Sarah's father, as head of the Historical Society, to a dare—if she could prove a painting's authenticity, or lack thereof, he would have to allow her membership. She had apparently had to run all over Europe to do so, but prove herself, she did. And even though Lord Forrester had been depicted as the obstacle in the editorial cartoon—really, the exaggeration of his belly was most unkind, her father was only a *little* fat, Sarah had groused—her father was a great friend of Miss Crane's late father, and consequently her.

"My father told me he wanted to invite her, but didn't think she'd attend as she's been traveling through Europe—" Sarah continued breathlessly. But her admiration of Miss Crane was cut short by Jason's sharp interruption.

"You knew?" he said, almost accusingly. "You knew she would be here?"

Sarah was taken aback—there were no other words for it. Jason's normal teasing persona had fallen away as absolutely as gravity. His face—the pallor she had barely noted before began to take on new meaning.

"Yes," she replied, cautiously, gauging his reaction. "I did not realize you were acquainted with her, however."

She watched as red spread over Jason's face. "Only . . . only a little," he stuttered. "Her father was one of my professors at school . . . and then when she wanted to get into the Historical Society, I was there, and . . ."

Relief fell in waves over Sarah's stiffened shoulders. For a moment, she had thought that she had seen . . . something else, in his frame.

"I remember now," Sarah cried happily. "You helped her get inside Somerset House, and to her audience with my father." Although he was not depicted in the editorial cartoon, she remembered it being mentioned that the Duke of Rayne had shown gentlemanly grace when confronted with a woman claiming she wanted entrance to the Society, reacting the only way he could—by escorting her in. Of course they were acquainted. There was nothing else to it.

So why would this unease not abate?

"I hear she's writing a book, you know," Sarah continued blithely. "All about her misadventures, trying to gain admittance to the Historical Society." Her father had told her—and while other members of the society were decidedly miffed, her father had simply chuckled and said he couldn't wait to read it. A sudden thought struck Sarah, and she turned her inquisitive gaze to her fiancé. "Do you think you'll be in it? You did play an instrumental part in getting her through the door—"

"No!" Jason cried, shocking Sarah to her toes. He began to pace, like a man consumed. "That's just it! She's writing me out of it. How can . . . how can someone do that? *Literally* write someone out of their lives?"

And, as he paced in front of her, his brow furrowed and his gaze at his feet, Sarah felt the earth fall away beneath her feet. Felt the cold of the air around her, chilling her to the bone. Felt her limbs turn to stone, as the still world rushed past her, and her entire being focused on the dawning truth.

She didn't know what had given him away—his angry speech, his mask of joviality fallen away—but it was plain as day on his face. And Sarah knew—knew as surely as she did her sisters' names, or the color of her own eyes—that Jason, her fiancé, felt something deep and raw for the small woman who had slipped past her just a moment ago. In a few bare minutes, Winnifred Crane had provoked strong feelings in Jason . . . stronger, Sarah realized, than she likely ever could.

"Jason," she rasped, unsteady, "I, ah . . . that is—how well do you know Miss Crane?"

To his credit, Jason tried to recover.

"I told you, when I was a student . . ." But his voice fell away when he saw her slowly shaking her head.

"No, I think you know her better than that."

He was silent for a moment, met her steady gaze. She could see him turning over thoughts in his head: *Should I lie? Would she believe me? What is best?* But each question fell pitifully away as he ultimately made his decision.

"Yes, I do," he whispered.

And suddenly, the last vestige of hope, of denial, slipped away and was lost to the cold night. Sarah felt her knees start to buckle.

"I think I should like to sit down," she said, looking to her left and right, seeking anything, anywhere, that could buoy her before she fell.

She felt his arms come around her. She should hate him right now. She should push him away, but oddly, she welcomed his support. He guided her to a small bench, a few steps farther away from the noise of the party beyond the doors.

She caught a glimpse of his face then, as he settled himself beside her. He looked so stricken, and earnest—he knew full well that whatever pain existed now, he was the cause of it. She felt so bad for him in that moment! But, *but*, she shook herself . . . She had to know. Everything. And she couldn't ask him her questions while seeing the concern on his face.

She looked away, her eyes roaming the darkness beyond the terrace, and found the strength for honesty there.

"When?" she asked in a surprisingly clear voice.

"When?" he replied, uncomprehending.

"When did you come to know"—her tongue tasted sour at the name—"Miss Crane? Was it at school?"

He hesitated. "After."

"Before we met?" she asked. Somehow, it would be better if it was before they had met. It would not change the current circumstances, but it was better . . . surely.

"No," he replied, resignation in his voice. "This summer, when I went to the Continent for a few weeks."

And with that solemn confession, suddenly the last piece of the puzzle fell into place. Jason had abruptly left town last summer, just disappeared for a few weeks of fun in Paris, he had explained. They hadn't been engaged then, of course. He had never even spoken of his intentions, but his deference to her had been marked. And then, when he came back . . . something was different. The attentions toward her were the same in quantity, but—and she may have sensed something then, but could only see it now—*he* had been different. And as much as he had been everything kind and accommodating, there were times when she caught him looking out the window, or into a glass of wine, and . . . he was somewhere else.

And apparently that somewhere else had not been Paris. It had been cutting across Europe, as Miss Crane's companion on her adventures.

She tried to speak, tried to ask and accuse, but the only sound that she managed to create was a small, pained, "Oh."

"Sarah, I am going to marry you." Jason began in a rush,

turning his body toward her, grasping her cold hand in her lap. "Don't worry. And we'll . . . we'll be happy. What she and I have . . . *had*—it was a matter of circumstance. It's over between us."

"No, it's not." Sarah focused her eyes toward the light of the party. Beyond those windows, there were her family and friends, and they were celebrating *them*. They were celebrating their future.

"I have made a study of you, these past months," she breathed. *How was her voice not shaking? How was she not crying?* "You have been my favorite subject," she admitted, somewhat sheepishly, only now realizing that it was true. She had wanted to understand him, so very much. "And you have been many things with me—jovial, joking, pleased, content . . ." Those moments when his mind had been far, far away came back to her with such frightening ease that she had to wonder if they hadn't been resting right under the surface the entire time. "But never happy. Not . . . not truly. Nor have I ever seen you as stirred up as you are after a mere few minutes in the presence of Miss Crane."

Jason shook his head, desperate in his urgency. "That doesn't mean you and I won't—"

She pulled her hand from his, and finally sought his gaze. "Jason, look at me."

He did, meeting her eyes. She saw her own pain reflected back at her. Her own resolution.

She said the words she had to say.

"If you are going to break my heart, do it now. Not three months from now, after we've made vows. Not even tomorrow. Do it now. Have the strength to say what you want. And to go after it."

He stood up then, looking as if he would jump away at any second. But he did not move. His face was lit by the light from within the house, his gaze entranced. He was searching . . . for someone that wasn't there.

He looked down at her then, and she couldn't help it: her breath caught. Just the slightest hitch, but it was a betrayal of all she was holding back under her well-bred mask. She stifled it . . . She just had to keep the tears from spilling down her cheeks for a little longer . . .

"I'm sorry," he whispered.

It was the only sound on the cold night air.

She let out a long, unsteady breath. She felt her body ready to crumble, but she would not let it. Not here, and not now.

She heard him ask the time . . . She knew she responded. He asked what she would tell her parents. She replied that she would tell them in the morning. But her voice was so far away from her, dull to the ears.

She watched him take her hand and kiss it. But it was as if she could feel nothing.

She wanted, needed to be alone.

"You should go," she whispered, putting a smile on her face. She did it to hurry him along, because if he didn't go now, she would burst, and if he was here for that, he would not leave. But the sadness in the smile—that was real.

He turned, finally. But before he faded away into the darkness, he turned again, his voice cutting through what was left of her numbness.

"Sarah," he breathed, his voice cracking in a way she knew she could not allow in herself, "please believe, I know I would have been terribly happy with you. If only . . ."

"If only," she agreed.

And set him free.

She sat there for some minutes, alone in the dark. The coldness had begun to seep through her skin, but she could not move. She could not go in and face her family and friends yet. They would see, on her face . . .

It was the hardest thing she had ever done.

It was the only thing she could do.

Her chest tightened over her heart. It became unbearable to breathe. She clutched her hand over her mouth so as to not make a sound.

If only . . .

But no—there was no use in "if only." Because as the tears began to fall, ugly drops running down her face, across the ring on her hand, Sarah knew one thing with absolute certainty.

Everything was broken, and nothing would be right again.

One

I T was over.

Everything was all right again.

Sarah closed the door to her bedroom, sinking back against it with an audible sigh of relief. Finally, the horrendous night had ended, and she was safe again.

It wasn't meant to be a particularly taxing evening. After all, it had only been a card party, with supper and some light amusements thereafter, Bridget on the pianoforte. Just close friends, her mother had said. No one there would dare mention . . .

The Event.

And to their credit, no one did. No one would think to do so in the Forresters' own home. But that didn't stop them from staring. And whispering.

Sarah pushed herself off of the door, giving herself the smallest of shakes. "Close friends." What a laughable conceit. When your father is consumed by antiquities, and your mother has one daughter entering her third Season and another daughter her first, the term "close friend" becomes muddied. What Lady Forrester considered a close friend was, apparently, the wife of the man whose personal collection of Roman statuary Lord Forrester was trying to acquire. And said Lady's sons—who happened to have been among the men who danced with Sarah more than once last Season.

Although, that had been before.

She pulled her weary body over to her silly little scrolled dressing table and sat on the small velvet stool that had always reminded Sarah of nothing so much as a tuffet. Which, of course, was why Sarah had picked it out when she was twelve.

No one should be held accountable for his or her adolescent tastes.

The dressing table was fluffy, if a wooden object could be described as such. There were cherubs, and clouds, and other white-painted rococo touches that made the twenty-one-year-old Sarah certain she had been a slightly ridiculous child.

She took off the pearl drop earrings, the pearl pendant at her throat, placed them aside.

She glanced at her left hand. Now naked. She quickly looked up, moved her gaze back to the fat woodwork of the silly dressing table.

Somehow, today, the silliness was a comfort. Because she could recognize it. It reminded her of herself . . . before. Though as she turned her face to the dressing table's mirror, she could not recognize the face that stared back at her.

It was not twelve.

It was not one-and-twenty.

It was ancient.

The face did not smile. The eyes were hollows of exposure in the moonlight. If she went so far as to light a candle in the dark room, she would see herself, true. She would see the pearl pins in her golden hair; she would see the light green eyes that bespoke her Anglo-Saxon ancestry, and her pale un-lined skin that attested to her youth. But the old woman with hollow eyes would still be underneath. Because . . .

Because that's who she truly was now.

A swift knock at the door, and the curt entry of Molly, her maid, snapped Sarah to attention.

"Ah, miss, quite the party tonight!" Molly said, efficiently straightening her cuffs before she approached Sarah and struck a flint to light the candles at the mirror.

"Yes," Sarah said, again painting her face with the serene smile she had tried to adopt all night. She was certain it had only fallen a few times over the course of the evening, and that she had quickly recovered. "My mother does love to have her *friends* over."

Molly, whose professionalism belied her youth—she couldn't have more than a few years on Sarah herself—hummed a noncommittal reply, as she began pulling the pins from Sarah's hair.

But the sweet relief of having her thick straight hair give in to gravity's pull was negated by the truth Sarah knew, and Molly was too smart to say.

"Be honest, Molly." Sarah finally broke the silence that had been filled only by the brush being pulled through her hair. "Tonight was a disaster."

"It was no such thing, miss!" Molly declared, the brush never stopping. "The courses were all served on time. None of the china was cracked. And we could all hear her Ladyship's laughter all the way in the kitchens."

It was true. Her mother's laugh did carry—especially when it was forced.

"I suppose your definition of success differs from mine." Sarah sighed.

"It might at that"—Molly shrugged—"but don't think we didn't see you standing up to dance with that Lord Seton. He seemed a jolly sort."

He seemed the sort to report back the answers to any and all of his probing questions to the nearest gossip columnist, Sarah thought wearily, recalling his pointed queries and his short breath, due to too-tight stays. Worse still, he was the only one to have asked her to dance. Maybe she no longer looked the type to wish for a dance.

Maybe that was one of the times the ancient woman who lived beneath her skin had slipped through the surface.

"Now, would you like to dress for bed, miss?" Molly asked, taking the pearl-headed pins and placing them precisely in the case, next to the matching jewelry. "Your parents are still in the drawing room, having a bit of cold cheese before retiring. Perhaps you'd wish to join them first?"

Sarah saw herself blanche in the mirror. But while the

thought of rehashing the evening with her parents was bad, the idea of lying in bed with nothing to do but rehash the evening to herself was even worse. She needed a distraction.

A warm glass of milk. A lurid novel. Anything that could remove her from herself.

From what they called her in whispers.

"Thank you, Molly, I can see to my dress. The kitchens must need an extra hand this evening."

"You have the right of it, miss." Molly smiled kindly as she curtsied. "Good evening, miss."

"Good night, Molly," Sarah replied distractedly.

A novel. From the library. She could slip down the servants' staircase, and avoid the possibility of her parents hearing her on the main stairs. On the way back up, she could retrieve a glass of warm milk from the kitchens while enjoying the distracting comfort of their bustle and hum.

A novel. That should do the trick.

Unfortunately, while one could in theory avoid the drawing room doors if one were, say, leaving the house, it was impossible to cross to the library without passing said doors.

It was luck that had them closed.

It was bad luck that they were thin enough to hear through.

"It could have gone worse." Sarah heard her father's gruff voice as she tiptoed across the foyer. His usual booming jubilance was countered by a certain reserve. As if he were asking a question instead of knowing his own opinion.

"Not much worse," Sarah heard in a feminine grumble of reply. She would have continued on past the drawing room doors; she would have nodded and smiled curtly to the servants bent over pails to clean as she headed briskly to the library, shutting the door behind her.

She would have done so—except for one thing. The voice that responded to her father had not belonged to her mother. It instead belonged to her sister, Bridget.

"Come now, my dear," Lady Forrester replied this time, the weariness apparent in her voice. "I thought the evening went . . . as smoothly as we could expect."

"Smoothly?" her sister scoffed. Sarah, via some previously

unknown gift for subterfuge, silently went to the door and knelt at the jamb, half concealing herself behind a potted plant. She briefly locked eyes with a footman, who was busy dusting footprints from the marble tiles in the foyer. He looked back down again and quickly resumed his work.

"*Smoothly* would have been if Sarah hadn't looked like she was about to faint the entire time," her sister replied in that lecturing tone she took on when she thought she knew better than everyone else. "*Smoothly* would have been if Rayne's wedding announcement hadn't been printed just yesterday."

Sarah could feel the blood rising to her face. It was silent beyond the doors, Bridget's pronouncement simply hanging in midair for the barest, longest of seconds.

The announcement. God, what horrific timing.

It had been almost four months since that terrible night, when Jason Cummings, the Duke of Rayne, had dashed everyone's hopes and called off their engagement. Shortly thereafter, Lord and Lady Forrester had retired with their daughters for the spare remainder of the Little Season to Primrose Manor, the family seat near Portsmouth. Four months should have been plenty of time for people to forget. For Sarah to forget.

It had been peaceful at Primrose. Comfortable. There, Sarah had room to breathe.

But it was also quiet. And the quiet only let the memories slip in.

As such, she had been determined to return to London for the Season proper. New gowns, new plays, new people. It would be, in her estimation, a fresh start.

She had expected some questions. Some whispers.

But not like this.

It hadn't helped that Jason had been so bloody *good* about the matter! Once the engagement was called off, he told everyone who would listen that absolutely no fault lay at Sarah's door, that she was nothing if not a kind and deserving young lady. And then, blessedly, he left town for an extended stay on the Continent.

But when Jason left London, he left the gossipmongers behind.

The day after they first arrived back, the gossip columns

noted their arrival. Strange, as no one really noted the comings and goings of the Forresters before. They were proper young ladies of good family, of course, but not high ranking enough or scandalous enough to pique a newspaperman's interest. For heaven's sake, her father was president of the boring, stuffy, academic Historical Society. The Forresters could not have been less salacious if they tried.

But there it was. In bold print.

"The Girl Who Lost a Duke Returns to Town."

After that, Sarah avoided the papers.

So she hadn't known about the announcement. Until yesterday, when one of her mother's "friends" told her.

"Oh, my dear," Lady Whitford said, coming over to clasp Sarah's hands in a show of sympathy early in the morning. Too early, really, to be paying calls. And far too early to be wearing such a ridiculous silk costume of patriotic ribbons across her bodice. But there she was, her round face shining with predatory concern, the feathers from her striped turban flopping into her earnest eyes. "How can you stand it? How can you go on?"

And then she told her. The Duke of Rayne had been married last week in Provence, to noted historian Winnifred Crane. Sarah tried to feel something. Anything. Other than a wistful sort of dread.

Because, while Sarah had been certain that she would be quite able to go on, contrary to Lady Whitford's opinion, it seemed more and more people were just as certain that she wouldn't. She couldn't, they'd said. Enough people repeated the same thing to her with wide, sad eyes, and thus she began to question herself.

Will I be able to go on? . . . Should I even try?

She held out a small hope that something, anything would happen to distract the population. A global catastrophe, a declaration of war, anything. But sadly, the only bit of gossip involved some gentleman who got caught in, and then managed to escape from, Burma—and since most people could not locate Burma on a map, it was not nearly of enough interest to waylay the ogling of the "Girl Who Lost a Duke."

Therefore, the dinner party that Lady Forrester had planned for weeks, as a casual reintroduction of herself as a hostess, while also easing her daughters into society again, had been a clamorous game of expectations. People had been expecting her to break. To make some sort of comment about the situation.

And the whispers and stares had made her want to do nothing more than oblige them.

To give in to gravity's pull.

Bridget's imperious voice broke the silence from within the drawing room, and broke through Sarah's racing thoughts. "And *smoothly* would have been if anyone had bothered to remember that they were there to meet me, too."

"Bridget!" her mother admonished, shocked.

"It's true, Mother!" Bridget replied, adamant. "Any woman that spoke to me made sure to ask, 'Oh, and how is your sister?'" Bridget's voice took on a quality of mock concern, her pitch eerily like that of Lady Whitford. "And any man who thought to talk to me could barely put two words together, as if they were afraid that I was tainted with the same man-repelling stain!"

"For heaven's sake, Bridget—" her mother tried, but Bridget would not be stopped.

"This was to be *my* Season. How am *I* supposed to catch a husband when Sarah looks like she's going to break into pieces at the idea of a dance? She should have just married the Duke—even if he did not love her. Everything would have been better!"

"Bridget, that's enough!" her father interrupted. "Such petulance is ugly."

Sarah could have heard a pin drop. Their father usually left the set downs to their mother. If such words from him landed heavily on Sarah all the way through the door, she could only imagine her sister's expression.

"Ugly it may be," Sarah finally heard Bridget say shakily, "but it is the truth. And if you don't do something, we may as well all dye our clothes black to join Sarah in mourning her lack of husband!"

Sarah barely scooted back behind the potted palm in time to avoid the swinging door as her sister made a dramatic exit, unknowingly marching past the object of her fury and up the stairs without a backward glance.

The door slowly creaked closed, a million years passing before the latch caught. Sarah caught the eye of the scrubbing footman again, but this time, before he looked away, Sarah knew the blush that crept up over his face was a mirror to hers.

The young footman might feel for her, but Sarah was alone in her humiliation. Of all people, Bridget! Of her whole family, Bridget had been the most supportive, the one who had propped her up the most through the winter months in Portsmouth with little to do but watch the ships sail in and out of the harbor. The one who had immediately sworn a lifelong vendetta of hatred against the Duke of Rayne, as all good sisters do. The one who had their trunks packed to come back to London before the decision had even been made.

Foolishly, Sarah had thought she was doing so in support of her. The fact that it was to be Bridget's debut Season had completely slipped her admittedly preoccupied mind. But obviously, it had not slipped Bridget's.

So now, not only was Sarah miserable and wretched, but her mere presence was destroying her sister's Season, too.

Brilliant.

Bridget—who had declared undying hatred of the Duke of Rayne—would marry her sister off to him, because that would be less miserable for everyone. Bitterness flooded Sarah's mouth. So much for sisterly affection.

Sarah was so caught up in her own burning frustration, she almost missed her father's voice when it rumbled forth again.

"I received a letter from the Portsmouth steward," he began, his voice hesitant and careful. "He has asked that I return to oversee the installation of the new well. It shouldn't take me more than a few days."

"Darling, I really would prefer if you didn't leave just now," her mother's voice was honey and lemon—soothing but stern, the way it always sounded when she negotiated for what she wanted. "Or if you must, make it as short as possible. The Season has only just begun, and if Sarah is to endure, she needs the support of the family behind her."

"I was thinking I would take Sarah with me," her father

replied, much to Sarah's own surprise. And her mother's, apparently.

"What on earth for?" Lady Forrester asked.

Her father paused a moment before answering.

"I didn't think it would be this bad."

There was a pause, heavy in the air.

"Neither did I," her mother finally said softly. "But we'd hoped . . ."

"Hoped, but not prepared," her father countered.

In her mind's eye, Sarah could see her father. He was likely sitting on the edge of her mother's favorite stuffed settee, looking down at his interlaced fingers, twiddling his thumbs the way he always did when he was thinking.

"I don't know if she's ready for this. I don't know that I am."

Sarah's heart, dampened under layers of her own effort, went out to her father. Outside of herself, he had been the one most hurt by the Event.

Her father had loved Jason. They became acquainted as members of the Historical Society, and Lord Forrester (father of three daughters) had been practically giddy at the idea of not only a son-in-law, but also one with whom he could converse for hours and hours about antique pediments and arcane painting techniques.

"Oh, my darling." Her mother's voice came through the thin door, placating her husband. "Maybe we can find a way to take Sarah's—and your—mind off the troubles."

"I would have him removed from the Historical Society if I could," her father stated, his voice muffled by what Sarah had to assume was her mother's shoulder. "But I cannot allow personal feeling to belie—"

"I know, I know," she soothed. "But for now, let us be thankful that Rayne had the good grace to remove himself to the Continent. And let us hope he—"

And that was the point that Sarah decided she had heard enough.

Because as hard as it was to think and hear about her parents' disappointments in her—it was infinitely more difficult to dwell on the Duke of Rayne, where he was, and what he was doing.

She stood up abruptly and crossed the foyer as fast as her feet would carry her to the library, without concern that her footfalls were too loud or rapid to be mistaken for a servant's. Without care for the eyes of the footman following her. And without any idea for whom she would meet inside the library's doors.

"Oh my God!" Sarah cried, coming to a sudden halt.

"I'm afraid not, Miss Forrester," the elegant figure that lounged with a volume of poetry in her hand said. "It's just me."

"L–Lady Worth," Sarah breathed, as breeding won out over shock, and she curtsied. Phillippa, Lady Worth, the unofficial but undeniable reigning leader of the ton, did not smile and stand in return. Instead, she flipped the book shut and regarded Sarah with a bemused expression.

"Oh, so you do know who I am. I was beginning to wonder if you remembered me at all from last Season."

"Lady Worth, of course I remember you," Sarah replied, blushing to the roots of her hair. "I attended your garden party last year, and of course you were at . . ." *my engagement party*, she stopped herself from staying. Instead she shook herself. "I apologize, let me fetch my parents. It is quite odd hours for calling, but—"

"Yes, I am aware it is quite odd hours for calling," Lady Worth replied as she stood to her full height. She was dressed in easily the most beautiful evening gown Sarah had ever seen, but to Lady Worth, it was likely just her Tuesday ensemble. "Your butler may seem stern, but entry was fairly simple. I just told him I had been here for your supper party and had left a reticule behind. He allowed me to search on my own." Lady Worth suddenly frowned. "I am going to recommend to your mother that you reinforce the need for security with your staff. After all, I could have been a thief—or worse yet, a newspaper reporter."

"My mother," Sarah repeated, latching onto a solid form throughout Lady Worth's bewildering speech. "Yes, allow me to fetch her, she's just across the hall . . ."

"Never mind that." Lady Worth waved her hand in dismissal of the idea. "I have come here to see you."

"Me?" Sarah squeaked.

"Yes, child. For heaven's sake, when did you become such a mimic? Last Season you seemed to have more brains that that."

Sarah, not having an answer to that, prudently remained silent.

"How long have you been in town, Miss Forrester?" Lady Worth asked, as nonchalant as if she had asked the question in full daylight in a room full of society ladies.

"A fortnight, ma'am," Sarah answered, her eyes following Lady Worth as she gently paced the carpet.

"And in that fortnight, how many invitations have you received from me?"

"Ah . . . I am uncertain . . ." Sarah hedged.

"As luck would have it, I am entirely certain. Two. You have received two invitations from me to come to tea. I know this because I rarely ask anything of anyone more than once."

"Oh," she replied, knowing she sounded stupid and out of her depth . . . because in truth, she was. "I think, ma'am"—she tried valiantly—"that my mother thought—that is, she didn't want us to accept any invitations until after we had settled . . ."

But at that, Lady Worth stopped pacing, and simply stood with her hands on her hips. "I have always preferred the truth to pretty lies, my dear. But if you insist upon continuing with that sentence at least speak it with conviction."

Sarah's head came up sharply. She met the challenge in the taller lady's eyes. And decided to rise to it.

"How could I visit with you, Lady Worth, when your family is connected to Jason's?"

Sarah had thought to shock Phillippa Worth. And she had. But not for the reasons she had imagined. Because while she read surprise in that lady's eyes, she also recognized not horror, but applause.

"Yes, my husband's brother is married to the Duke of Rayne's sister." Lady Worth waved her hand in the air again, seemingly waving away anything that she did not consider important. "But that is exactly why you *should* have accepted my invitation."

"Lady Worth, I . . ." Sarah tried, but suddenly, she felt very tired. The weight of the party, overhearing her parents and sister's conversation, and now the mad assault on logic and propriety that was Lady Worth being in her library, settled over Sarah, and she could no longer stop her shoulders from slumping.

"Do you mind if I sit down?" she asked, already half seated on the settee.

Lady Worth, to her credit, immediately sat down with Sarah and, in what she must have thought was a sympathetic gesture, patted Sarah's hand.

"Would you like me to call for some tea? Or perhaps sherry?" Lady Worth inquired kindly.

Sarah let out a small, exhausted laugh. "Lady Worth, we are in my house. I should be offering tea to you."

"Oh," she replied, with a smile. "I nearly forgot. And I think this will be simpler if you take to calling me Phillippa, and I call you Sarah."

"What will be simpler?" Sarah asked hoping to finally understand . . . anything.

Lady Worth—Phillippa—regarded her quietly for a moment.

"It's too early in the Season for you to be this tired," she finally observed.

Sarah thought about denying it, thought about making excuses . . . but somehow, she couldn't fight it any longer. She couldn't pretend to be even and fine. The only thing left to do was admit her failings.

To give in to gravity's pull.

"I don't know what to do," Sarah admitted. "Tonight, we had our first party—my mother was so excited to be a hostess again, and it's my sister's first Season, and it was just—"

"Terrible," Phillippa supplied. At Sarah's questioning look, Phillippa smiled in bemusement. "Really, you should simply assume that I know everything already. It saves time."

"Yes, but how—"

"At least three of your evening's attendees were at the Newlins' ball after your fete. Interestingly, no fewer than five people fought through the crush to rush to my side and let me know—as the only connection to the Duke of Rayne in town—just how unfortunate your supper party was."

Sarah started rubbing one of her temples. "Wonderful. Everyone will know."

"Oh, I'd expect that it will be in the papers tomorrow."

"So all of London thinks I'm a fragile mourner for a missing Duke."

"Where did you find that description?" Phillippa peered at her intensely.

"My . . ." not wanting to implicate her sister, Sarah changed tack. "I feel like I'm disappointing my family, most of all. And I don't know what I could do differently. I smile, and everyone thinks I'm covering my feelings. I frown, and everyone thinks I'm about to break down and cry. I don't know how to act under such scrutiny. I wish I could just go back to being one of a thousand girls. And not—"

" 'The Girl Who Lost a Duke'?" Phillippa finished for her.

Sarah nodded, then turned her gaze to her hands. "My father . . . I think he's planning to go back to Portsmouth soon and perhaps it would be easier—"

"Don't you dare," Phillippa intoned severely, her expression suddenly focused and serious. "Now you listen to me— first of all, do not concern yourself with how your family feels right now. I know it is curious advice, but you have been a dutiful daughter for your entire life. You have never given them reason to be disappointed in you, so do not let them make you feel as such now. Nor should you let the world make you feel as if you are somehow damaged goods. You are no such thing. In fact, when one takes a thorough accounting of your actions, one can only conclude that you have not only done no wrong, you have, in fact, done everything right."

"Exactly!" Sarah cried. "I did everything right. *Everything.* I got top marks from every teacher I had, I learned to play the pianoforte—a little—to sew, to speak French and Latin. I came to London, and only accepted dances from men my mother approved of. And then I met a man who was supposed to be the one I would spend the rest of my life with and I . . ." Her voice broke, an echo of the seam that still sat along her heart. "I did everything right. And somehow, I still lost."

"You lost a battle." Phillippa agreed. "But the war is long. And the enemy . . . changeable."

"What do you mean?" Sarah asked.

"Public perception," she said with a smile, "is a tricky thing. The world looks at you now as 'the Girl Who Lost a

Duke.' You have to change that. Else, no amount of time spent
in Portsmouth is going to kill that idea here. In fact, as more
time passes, it will be cemented as such. *You* have to make the
world stop looking at you with pity."

"How?"

"First of all, stop looking at yourself with pity. Tell yourself
a hundred times a day that it was Jason's loss, not yours, in
ending the engagement. Even if you don't believe it." Phillippa
gripped Sarah's hand. "Then, you take London by storm. Be
charming, vivacious. Just this side of outrageous. Flirt with
appropriate men and dance with inappropriate ones. Be the
person every hostess absolutely must have at her party. Put on
a mask and save your true feelings for when you are in private.
Soon enough, all of London will have forgotten the 'Girl Who
Lost a Duke,' and instead think the Duke of Rayne utterly mad
for having let you escape."

"I . . . I don't know if I can do all that," Sarah replied
breathlessly.

"*You have to.* It is how you survive." Phillippa's face suddenly shuttered with old memories. "It is how I did."

Sarah looked at the hand gripping hers. Then, she ran her
gaze up the elegant dress and stature of the queen of society
sitting in her library. But for once, it was not the extravagant
dress or the beautiful jewels at her throat that Sarah envied. It
was her posture. Her conviction. Her strength. Phillippa Worth
was everything a young lady aspired to be. And she knew it.

"How do I begin?" Sarah asked.

Phillippa's eyes lit with anticipation. "We already have."

Two

As sure as a gun,
We shall all be undone,
If longer continue the peace;
A top we shan't know
From a futtock below,
Nor a block from a bucket of grease.

—William Nugent Glascock, *The Lieutenant's Lament*

A little over a month later . . .

"WELL, what do we do now?" First Lieutenant Jackson Fletcher—called Jack by friends—asked, to no one in particular. But since he was standing on deck next to his second lieutenant Roger Whigby, he invariably was to receive an answer.

"We have to supervise the men, Mr. Fletcher. They still have a dozen duties on board before we can even hope to make berth," Whigby said through bites of cold salted ham that he had stashed in his pocket after breakfast that morning. Whigby was the type of kind soul who, for some reason, was eating something every time he spoke. "Although why the captain insists the old girl's brass fittings shine with the rising sun is beyond me."

Jack tried to refrain from rolling his eyes—instead he kept his gaze on the horizon. Normally, all he would see was an expanse of water, dotted with gulls, depending on how far from shore they were and how seafaring the birds. But now, as they headed up the Thames, they were surrounded not by water, but by farmland, that progressively gave way to towns. In a few hours, the small towns would give way to the colonnades and domed buildings that made up London's skyline.

"I expect it is a point of pride, Mr. Whigby." Jackson replied, but kindly. "Captain Healy wants the ship to be at her very best when she's seen by her judges."

From the quarterdeck, seven bells sounded. Half an hour until the noon meal and the watch change. Although really, there was no slacking today, no gadabouts. Even those men not currently on duty were on deck, including Whigby. Pulling into the port of London was too exciting, even the long ride up the river had the men jubilant, waving to the specks of people on shore, shouting at those that they thought might be wearing skirts. Jack had been forced to reprimand three seamen for their rowdiness already, halving their grog rations for the day. And they were nowhere near the city. The men had grumbled and shrugged. In their minds, they had already disembarked. It's not like they'd be dealing with the likes of him much longer in any case.

"Her executioners, you mean," Whigby snorted, swallowing another bit of ham. "If the *Amorata* is lucky, she'll find herself in ordinary, or as a prison hulk—"

"She's not big enough to be a prison hulk," Jack countered dismissively.

"Right then," Whigby grunted. "More likely, she'll end broken up and sold for scrap."

Jack shot his friend a look. "Do you really have so little faith in our girl?" He reached out and caressed the smooth, polished rail that ran the length of the HMS *Amorata*'s starboard side. She was a Banterer-class sixth-rate post ship, meaning she was small but fast. She had twenty-two guns, but an extra eight 24-pounders and two howitzers had been added during wartime. She was nothing compared to first- and second-rate ships of the line that fired cannons at the enemy from three different deck levels . . .

But then again, there were not a great deal of Royal Navy ships firing at the enemy at all, anymore.

"Captain Healy will never let her go to ground . . . like all her sisters," Jackson intoned to himself in a whisper. Almost a prayer, too low for Whigby to hear over the last of his chewing.

Indeed, the *Amorata* was the very last Banterer-class ship to be flying a British flag. A half-dozen others were ordered and built during the height of the Napoleonic Wars, but those that survived combat were deemed too small or too battle scarred to go on, and were broken up after the conflict ended. One was taken as prize by the Americans in 1815, and according to the Royal Navy's logs, now sailed under their banner and a different name. If she was still on the seas, she was likely somewhere off the coast of Africa, trying to regulate that ugly American trade.

Why the *Amorata* had been spared her sister ships' fates, Jack could only put up to timing, geography, and a lot of luck. Until now.

Jack had been on board the *Amorata* since he was sixteen, a Royal Naval College cadet coming to serve as a midshipman. It was 1814 when he first stepped onto her deck, his eyes wide with wonder.

He'd been in love with this little ship since that moment. The *Amorata* had been in Portsmouth to make some small repairs before going back out to sea, with intentions to join the blockade against the Americans in the North Atlantic. And he was assigned to it as his post.

It was a heady year. There had been battles, and prize money, and *adventure*. The exact thing he had been dreaming of for three years while learning to chart ship movements from a book. And for the two before that he had spent convincing his vicar father to let him join the Royal Navy.

But then . . . the battles, and the adventure, stopped.

"At least, we won't let her go without a fight," Jack concluded.

"True, Mr. Fletcher." Whigby smiled. "But then again, it may be the only fight left for us."

"Yes. I've sadly come to the same conclusion, Mr. Whigby." Jackson finally said, turning his eyes from the horizon.

Whigby looked at him quizzically. "What conclusion?"

"That peace is the worst thing for a navy man." He stroked the rail again. "And their ladies."

For the past few years, the *Amorata* had somehow escaped a dire, reducing fate, and rolled along with the waves once peace settled over the seas, its size making it useful for playing protective escort or scout for merchant vessels in the East Indies. In 1817, when Jack earned his lieutenancy, he knew he was lucky to do so. There were plenty of midshipman who would be forced to endure at that level because there were simply too many officers and, since the wars ended, not enough ships.

While other larger, faster, and stronger vessels were being decommissioned, the *Amorata* slipped through the cracks, due in no small part to Captain Healy's established friendship with the Board of the Admiralty. Now, several years had passed since the war ended, years regulated by bells and boredom, years during which several of Captain Healy's friends retired, and Jack had begun to question. Just how long could they slip past the eyes of the navy and remain at sea, free from the fate of so many of their friends?

Then, the answer came, as they ran up against Mother Nature around the Cape of Good Hope.

Where years before, cannonballs had missed the little ship due to its speed and size, now, in older age, it could not outrun a storm.

After that, they had no choice but to send word home of their plight, and for home to send for them to come back.

And so, now, they limped into London for assessment.

"Assessment." What a terribly unkind word for such a beautiful old girl.

And Jack could only fear that the assessment would be unkind.

The storm had whipped their sails practically to shreds, but they were patched as best they could be. (Never say a navy man had no practical training. Every single one of them could sew like the wind.) But the boom of the foresail cracked—it was currently being held together by the grace of God and some very strong rope knots.

Luckily their trip up the coast of Africa had been uneventful and blessedly quick.

Jack knew, intellectually, that Whigby's declaration of the old girl's fate was probably correct. The navy didn't require an excuse to decommission the *Amorata*, but one look at her current condition, and they would most certainly have one.

But he had to have hope. He had to. As long as there was a chance . . .

The *Amorata* was his home, after all. He had spent his entire life in pursuit of a career at sea. The alternative was . . .

Unthinkable.

What am I going to do now?

Even if the *Amorata* were to go down, it would be a different matter entirely if Captain Healy were to use his connections to seek command of another ship—he would be able to pick his men and no doubt would take Jack, as his right hand, with him. But ever since the storm, the captain seemed shaken, and kept mentioning a newborn grandson he had yet to meet. Retirement seemed his future.

So what would Jack's be?

"I may not have your faith, Mr. Fletcher, but then I have never had the same love of this ship that you do," Whigby said, seemingly nonchalant.

One, from afar, might think that Whigby had no sentimentality in his soul, but Jack knew better.

"How could you not?" Jack asked jovially, playing his role in the argument they loved to have. "She's a beauty down to her bones."

"Her leaky bones."

"A little water is . . .

". . . good for a navy man! Keeps him fresh." They finished together, quoting Captain Healy and one of his favorite sayings.

"Come on Jack, she's creaky and small."

"She's light and fast."

"I can name a hundred ships that are better than this one," Whigby declared.

"Really. You can name a hundred ships?" Jackson's eyebrow went up.

"I can." Whigby boasted, his chest puffing out.

"A hundred ships that have done you a better turn than the *Amorata*?" Jackson smiled. "You, who felt to your knees, crying in joy, when you managed to secure your post?"

"I was never worried about securing my post! I passed the lieutenant's exam well enough." Whigby smiled.

"I passed the lieutenant's exam with top marks, and I was damn glad to get to stay on this ship."

"That's only because you don't have—" But Whigby stopped himself, hesitant.

"It's all right, Mr. Whigby. I'm all too aware that my well-connected friends are few, and even then, have no influence with the Royal Navy."

"And I do," Whigby said quietly. "Jack," Whigby said, dropping the formalities that ruled on board. "I want you to know that if I get the opportunity, I'll speak well of you to my uncle. Surely finding a position cannot be as terrible as we've heard. It seems absurd! After all, I've already—"

Jack looked up at Whigby with slight shock in his eyes. Whigby had the grace to look down at his shoes, somewhat ashamed.

"I . . . the mail frigate that met us at the mouth of the river? It had a letter for me from my uncle. I'm to report to the *Dresden* when it makes berth in two months."

Jack felt the deck shift beneath him, and this time, it could not be attributed to the sea.

Of course. Thanks to his uncle, Whigby, who was second lieutenant under him and had two years less experience, was to be assigned a berth on a first-class ship of the line. Whigby wasn't going to have to live in the queasy dread of limbo, waiting to hear if the *Amorata* would sail again. Whigby wasn't going to face the horrible proposition of signing the affidavit quarterly, going on half pay. Unable to seek work outside of the navy without giving up that meager income, and unable, without a miracle, to receive work inside of it. Jack wanted to growl in frustration.

Instead of giving lease to that impulse, Jack shook off the gray cloud of worry that had overtaken him, and slapped his friend on the back. "I'm just surprised that you gave up on our girl so easily. You'll have twelve superior officers to report to on the *Dresden*. I doubt they'll even let you wave me off when the *Amorata* sets sail herself."

"I'm sorry, Jack," Whigby said, nervously picking at his nails. "If it's any consolation, he made the arrangements without my asking."

"Don't apologize," he said, watching relief wash over his friend's face. "After all, it's not your fault your uncle is a rear admiral who retired with enough metal on his chest to make an eight-inch gun."

Whigby laughed at that, the buttons on his somewhat snug uniform waistcoat straining slightly. "I dare say he wouldn't allow that—it would deprive him of wearing his full dress uniform at any and every opportunity. Church," he intoned. "Every Sunday."

Jack clapped his friend on the shoulder. They stood silent for a moment, listening as, from the bow of the ship, Dingham, one of the carpenter's mates, whistled and clamored at a group of bonneted ladies far distant on shore. It was impossible that the ladies could hear Dingham over the wind and at that distance, but he insisted on making a fool of himself anyway.

"Oh hell, the bloody fool's starting up again . . ." Jack rolled his eyes, and took a half step in the carpenter's mate's direction before Whigby clamped a hand on his shoulder.

"Let me take care of it, Mr. Fletcher." Whigby said, his expression suddenly stern. "After all, I'll have a lot more men on the *Dresden* to command. I'll need the practice."

Jack would have glared at Whigby then, if the serious set of that man's brow hadn't been so comical. But suddenly, that serious expression cleared, and Whigby hastily felt through his pockets.

"I nearly forgot! There was a letter in the packet for you, too!"

Jackson took the small packet of paper with some surprise. He rarely received letters. He had gone away from home at the age of thirteen to attend the Royal Naval College in Portsmouth, and while he'd had loving and kind parents, they had lived in Lincolnshire, and his chosen path had made visits home difficult. He'd sent them letters when he could, but life at sea made the ability to post anything erratic at best. Receiving mail was just as difficult, if not more so.

In fact, there was only one person he received letters from with any regularity.

He turned the packet over in his hand, a pleasant sensation spreading through his chest when he saw the handwriting.

It was the same handwriting that had surprised him twelve years ago, as a young cadet in Portsmouth. The same handwriting that kept him apprised of life in England for the past nine years. The same handwriting that had tearfully informed him of his parents passing. The handwriting that had become his only tether to a home.

"Lady Forrester," he murmured, as he broke the wax seal.

The letter was dated a little over a month ago—which to a man at sea was practically of the moment.

My Dear Jackson—it began, sounding in Jack's head the exact same way Lady Forrester would pronounce it, with the sugar and starch she reserved for her own children.

My dear Lord Forrester and I send you greetings. We are well here, as are the girls . . .

The letter continued on in this manner for a few paragraphs, speaking of nothing beyond the everyday life of a family about town, undergoing the rigors of the social Season. Pleasant as it was to hear of his friends, Jack's brow did not pick up until he read down the page, to the heart of the letter:

We read in the Times *of the* Amorata's *sad circumstances. I also understand that you will be docking in London while the ship awaits word of her fate.*

(Jack took some small hope at that—even with the British navy being reduced at an alarming rate, the fact that the *Amorata* was not pronounced dead in the *Times* was good news, surely.)

As we are in London as well, I would invite you to pass your time with us. I may know little of the modern navy officer's preferences, but I do know that you, Jack, would much prefer Cook's currant scones to that any boarding house could supply. Add to that, I know my dear Lord Forrester suffers mightily from what he has termed "feminiaphobia"—that is, a fear of being overrun by all the females in his household. He would welcome your presence as readily as I.

Also, it would be of the utmost kindness to me—I hesitate to mention this, but you will come to know the circumstances at any rate: our dear Sarah has lately suffered a severe disappointment, and I am at a loss as to how to distract her from it. I saw the notice of your ship in the paper, and thought it fate. You always managed to keep her in good spirits as a child, and I can

*only hope that some stories of adventure on the high
seas can do the trick again. Do come to us at your ear-
liest convenience. Not only would you be allowing us to
keep a promise made to your father (wherein he made
us swear to look after you), but you would be doing us
a great service.*

> *Yours, etc.*
> *Lady Forrester*

Jack stared at the neatly written pages for a full minute
before he snapped back to the present. He had been lost in a
sea of memory, of school holidays spent in the company of the
Forresters at Primrose.

But then his mind began racing with questions: It had been
years since he had seen the Forresters. Would it be awkward?
What was the nature of Sarah's disappointment? And lastly . . .

What would they think of what he had become?

Jack was, admittedly, a proud man. But that pride had
never been unfounded. He had been a top student at the Naval
College, a person upon whom expectations were placed, and
met. The bright future of the British navy. He remembered the
pride and joy in Lord and Lady Forrester's eyes when he first
boarded the *Amorata* more than he remembered his own parents'. They had, for a brief period of time, become a second
family to him, and now . . .

Now he was a first lieutenant of a sixth-rate post ship that
was about to be decommissioned. Much like he himself was.

Too many officers. Not enough ships.

No. He would not let them look on him with pity. He would
not allow himself to do so, either.

But while he worried about the long weeks ahead, awaiting
his ship's fate, all of that took a secondary position to one central tenant:

Here, was a place for him to go.

And something for him to focus on.

Something for him to do while awaiting word of the *Amorata*'s fate.

At the very least, he had the answer to his initial question.
He knew what he was going to do next.

Three

"**B**LOODY hell," Whigby breathed, as their hired hack pulled up to the address that had been written on Lady Forrester's note. "Are you sure this is it?"

The town house on Upper Grosvenor Street was much the same as the others that surrounded it—pristine white, four stories above level with columns that lined the doorway and supported the upper-level balconies. Wrought iron fencing lined the property along the more public sidewalk, protecting the pansies and tulips that sprung up in wide Grecian urns that sat as centurions guarding the steps up to the heavy front door.

The main difference between this town house and the others that surrounded it was the half-dozen gentlemen in their best black coats that bickered with the butler for entrance.

"It *is* number sixteen," Jack said, his eyes flicking automatically to the letter in his hand, checking once again.

"Maybe it was written ill?" Whigby asked, but Jack shook his head. No, there was no mistake, this was the house.

"Maybe someone died and they're paying respects!" Whigby cried.

Jack shot his friend a look.

"Of course, that would be terrible," Whigby was quick to amend.

"I suppose we best find out what's going on," Jack said, opening the door to the hack and letting himself down, while the coachman disembarked from his seat and helped unload Jack's trunk. Whigby alighted as well.

"Do you want me come with you?" Whigby asked. "You know . . . to pay my respects?"

"No one has died, Mr. Whigby." Jack assured his friend (at least, he hoped no one had died). "Go on to your uncle's, I'll be fine."

"You have my direction if you need it," Whigby extended his hand, and Jack shook it.

Then Whigby, in a show of emotion not uncommon to that larger fellow, pulled Jack into a fairly rib-cracking hug. "I'm so sorry for your loss."

"Mr. Whigby . . ." Jack wheezed, "It's not a funeral . . . And you're crushing me."

"That's right!" Whigby replied, releasing Jack so quickly that the air rushed back into his lungs. "Keep hope!"

And then, Whigby turned to reenter the hack to convey him to his uncle's, a few spare blocks away. But perhaps he should not have been so free with his condolences, because the hack had already started to rumble down the block, with Whigby's trunk still up on the back.

"Oy!" Whigby yelled after the coachman, breaking into a run. "Wait for me!"

Jack, shaking his head, turned to the front door of number sixteen. And the men there that blocked his path.

They were a variety of ages, from just down from school to those with white hair. But all the men wore their money: Jackson saw at least three gold cravat stickpins and seven watch fobs. They eyed his rumpled naval uniform with severe distaste.

Jackson narrowed his eyes, and stepped into the gauntlet.

"They come fresh off the boats now?" one man murmured to a friend. "I'm amazed they get the gossip sheets out at sea."

"What's amazing is that he thinks he stands a chance," his friend replied, sniggering.

Jackson kept his eyes straight ahead, ignoring these men.

Their talk made no sense to him, but their manners did. They didn't think much of him. Well, the feeling was mutual.

Jack reached the butler, who stood guard at the door with a hulking giant of a footman. Normally, the door would be opened with the butler standing inside, but here, they had gone so far as to stand outside the door, keeping it barred.

"I'm sorry sir, but the Forresters are not receiving today," the supercilious man said, his nose in the air.

"Then why is everyone else here?" Jack asked before he could think better of it.

He was met by chuckles from the peanut gallery behind him.

"We are staking our place in line!" one of the younger ones cried.

"Making sure people see us here," one of the others drawled.

"Besides, they have to come home sometime," another— the sniggering one—said, clamping his hand on Jack's shoulder, trying to pull him back.

One look from Jack had that man removing his hand forthwith.

"I have an invitation," Jack said, directing himself only to the butler.

But that sentence elicited raucous laughter from the men behind him.

"Of course he does!"

"And I've a recommendation from Prinny himself!"

"We all do!"

Jack reached into his pocket and produced the letter from Lady Forrester—as he did, the men behind him grew quiet for the first time.

The butler perused the letter with an unseemly amount of leisure. (Jack felt certain that the old servant took no small amount of pleasure in the power he wielded.) Then, with a curt nod to the burly footman beside him, he handed the missive back.

"If you'll follow me, sir," the butler said, as the door behind him opened with silent efficiency.

Cries of outrage came from the assembly.

"What?"

And . . . "You can't mean to admit him! I'm a viscount!"

And the deferentially desperate . . . "Er, I'm with him! We came together!"

But of course, these were ignored and shortly silenced by one flex of the footman's muscles, as he took up the central position, while Jack, hauling his own trunk, followed the butler inside.

"Wait here," the butler intoned, leaving him to go seek out his mistress, Jack assumed.

Jack removed his tricorn, shaking out his sandy hair into something resembling neatness. He pulled at his cuffs, straightened his coat, like the nervous schoolboy he used to be.

Alone in the foyer of the Forresters' London home, he was immediately struck by a sense of remembrance. He had never been in this house before, but he had been in this position before, long ago.

There is little more frightening to a thirteen-year-old boy than being removed from all you know, he thought, letting himself drift into memory. Even the horrific, tantalizing prospect of thirteen-year-old girls compares little to no longer being in the daily presence of your parents, the paths you know to the village where everyone knows you. Even when one begs their father to let him go to sea seeking adventure beyond those well-trod paths, those faces fading away makes a thirteen-year-old boy feel like nothing so much as a thirteen-year-old man, but without any means by which to handle the transition.

Luckily, Jack's father knew something of being alone in the world, and wrote a friend for help.

❧

He tugged nervously at his cuffs again. They were already beginning to come up short, even though his mother had sewn his Naval College uniform not three months ago. He was already a tall boy, as a first-year cadet towering over most of the second years and even some of the thirds . . . and in a career where he was constantly told to stand up straight, he could do little to hide it.

When Jack crossed the entrance of Primrose Manor, the

Forresters' country residence not five miles from Portsmouth, he had been expecting an inspection. Therefore, for the whole week leading up to this moment, he had been very careful with his uniform. His white pantaloons were spotless—a feat in and of itself for any thirteen-year-old boy, let alone one who had grown so increasingly nervous over the course of the week that he had spilled his food not once, but twice, at mealtimes. But somehow he had managed to keep everything from the top of his hat to the heel of his shoes in good order. Which was of the utmost importance, as he was to meet his possible future patron today.

Jack did not know what a future patron might want to know of him. He only knew that when he finally convinced his parents to allow him to attend the Royal Naval College—a compromise, as it would keep him on land until he was sixteen instead of a midshipman at thirteen—Jackson's father had written to his old school friend Lord Forrester, and asked him to look in on the boy every once in a while, as he was unable to do so in Lincolnshire. As Jack's father was always writing to great men asking for patronage for any one of his and Mrs. Fletcher's charitable causes (for Mr. Fletcher refused to yield to expectation of being a retiring country vicar, instead choosing to involve himself vigorously in the cause of war orphans and widows), Jack thought nothing of it.

He'd expected, at most, a letter from Lord Forrester. Instead, he had received an invitation.

As he was admitted to the hall, he tried very hard not to be awed by the grandeur of the house. But how could he not be? Marble and oak lined the massive room, making even the smallest sound, from his footsteps to a gasp he hadn't managed to contain, echo across the space. When the butler went to fetch his master, Jack couldn't help but poke his head around the corner, and peer into an even larger room! Why this one room must have been bigger than his entire house! After a few moments, Jack decided it must be the sitting room, for receiving callers. And there were plenty of places to sit, he thought, making sure to keep his mouth from hanging open. There were dozens of sofas and chairs and things that looked so fine they would surely break if he touched them. He briefly glanced at the ceiling, two stories above. How did the ceiling stay up in so massive a space? Churches had flying buttresses and the like, reinforced columns, but this ceiling just seemed to soar high above.

He wondered for the umpteenth time that week just what on earth was expected of him. Surely, people that lived in a house this intimidating would look down at him as nothing more than . . . charity.

He was edging his foot into the sitting room, when he heard it. It sounded like a fork striking a glass, but somehow . . . human. It must have been the echo, he thought, but it almost sounded like a giggle. He immediately straightened to attention. But when no one emerged, his curiosity won out again, and his gaze returned to the sitting room. Where, if he was not mistaken, one of the heavy velvet drapes was twitching.

Unsure if his mind was playing tricks on him, Jack thought it best to ignore the twitching curtain, and instead remain at attention. Surely, that's what a man like Lord Forrester would want out of a cadet he sponsored. Someone who obeyed the rules, and stayed where he was told, and . . .

And there was that giggle again!

Finally, he couldn't help it any longer. Perhaps some ruffian had sneaked in and was hiding until he could thieve everything out of this room in the dark of night. Which Jack could not allow.

And so, he went over to the window, and drew back the curtain dramatically, his hand going automatically to his side, searching for his sword . . . which of course was not there, as he had no sword.

Instead of a thief, however, Jack found two girls. One far littler than the other.

When he drew back the curtain, the taller girl stumbled— she had been holding on to it for support, as the littler one was latched on to her leg. Jack caught her arm before she could fall, and was about to make some sort of exclamatory statement, such as an, "I say!" or even the practically-a-swear "My God!" but the smaller child beat him to it.

"Hide-and-seek!" cried the littlest, who could not have been more than three, with dimples and curly blond hair that bounced when she shrieked with laughter.

"Not yet, Mandy!" the elder girl said in a hushed voice, as she straightened herself, blushing up at him. She looked about nine or ten, and whereas her hair matched the youngster's in shade, it was straight and plaited down her back. She looked up at Jack with the biggest green eyes, twinkling with mischief. "We're hiding, don't tell," she whispered to Jack, as she gave him back his arm.

"Hiding from what?" he asked.

"Will you be quiet?" came a hushed whisper from the other side of the room—a brown, curly head popped up, freckles gone mad upon her nose and cheeks. "Papa will find us without any trouble when he hears you stumbling and making a racket. And Mandy, you're supposed to hide somewhere by yourself!"

But little Mandy just shook her head, and inched closer to her sister.

"She couldn't find any place to hide," the elder girl whispered back.

"Of course she can, Sarah. You just baby her. Mandy, you're small enough to fit in the cabinet, go over there."

But Mandy simply shook her head and burrowed further.

"Wait, are you playing some sort of game?" Jack asked, utterly bewildered.

The eldest—Sarah—blinked back in surprise. "Of course we are. Haven't you ever played hide-and-seek?"

"Well, I . . ." Before Jack could appropriately answer that question, which would have been embarrassingly in the negative (A vicar's child, he had been taught, did not play games where nothing was learned or made useful. Was it any wonder he sought the adventure of the sea?), footsteps were heard in the hallway beyond.

"Come hide!" Sarah whispered. But when he hesitated, she sent him an exasperated look. "It will be an adventure!"

But again he hesitated just a moment too long, and as the door handle on the far side of the room turned, all three girls went rigid with excitement, and popped back into their hiding places.

Just then, a barrel of a man came thudding through the hall, his posture that of an ogre about to attack.

"I know you're in here!" he cried, a stern expression on his *brow. When he saw Jack, however, his expression cleared and he straightened.*

"Oh! You must be Dickey's boy!" he cried, his face no longer that of an ogre, but now with an easy smile. "Forrester. Very pleased to have you in my home."

"Er . . . yes, sir," Jack said—straightening to attention and bowing at the same time, which ended up as merely awkward. "My father is Richard Fletcher. I am Cadet Jackson Fletcher, and . . . they told me to wait in the hall, but I—"

"Happy to have you! How is the Naval College treating you?"

"Good," Jack said, unable to keep his voice from breaking embarrassingly. And then, when Lord Forrester made no reply . . . Jack couldn't keep himself from rambling. "It's different than I expected: I wanted to go to sea first, but my father didn't want me on the ocean with no training and two wars going on—and it seems we would not have been able to obtain a King's Letter in any case. But my years at the college count toward my required six as a midshipman, so it's not lost time. . . ."

But Jack saw that Lord Forrester's attention had wandered from himself to just over his shoulder.

And the curtain that twitched ever so slightly there.

And suddenly, Jack found himself playing the game, too.

"Ah, Lord Forrester," he said, inching himself ever so slightly to block the view of the curtain. "I am so terribly honored that you have invited me to dine. Indeed, I did not expect such kindness. . . ."

"You didn't?" Lord Forrester asked, his surprised attention back to Jack. "Nonsense, my boy. I knew your father at school. And how is the good reverend? We were all shocked to learn he went into the church instead of the law . . . all the way up in Lincolnshire, of all places! He would have made an excellent politician."

"Yes, well, my father always says he would much rather be doing than telling everyone else what to do." Jack quipped, and turned red in the face before he could stop himself. After all, Lord Forrester was a peer! He was one of the tellers, not the doers! He had just insulted his possible future patron!

Luckily, Lord Forrester just leaned his head back and gave a hearty laugh.

"That sounds like old Dickey. And it goes without saying that I would see his son properly fed for at least one Sunday dinner." Lord Forrester nonchalantly sidestepped Jack, so he was now standing next to the curtain. "And I think you'll be pleased with the menu. We will be serving that rarest of all delicacies . . ." He reached his hand back behind the curtain. "Little girl!"

Lord Forrester whipped the curtain back, revealing Sarah and Mandy who began to shriek and run. While Sarah ran with direction and aplomb, little Mandy could do barely more than run on short legs in a circle.

Lord Forrester trotted after her, making sure to not catch her too easily. Because as she shrieked, she giggled, and Lord Forrester kept saying, "I'm going to get you and serve you up!" and she simply shrieked more. Then Mandy ran behind the couch, and the other brown-haired girl had to get up and run, lest she be discovered, too. Soon the entire room was filled with running girls, chasing father, and hysterical laughter.

No, he had not been expecting this at all.

⁊❧

Jack shook his head ruefully. Had he ever been that young and frightened? Waiting in a hall and surprised to learn that young ladies of rank played hide-and-seek with their fathers. Although the pit that existed in his stomach when he had been thirteen and waiting in a Forrester foyer was uncannily similar to the one that rested there now.

He scuffed his toe on the marbled floor, the squeaky sound echoing off the marble tiles. Given the clamor of well-dressed gentlemen—"holding their place in line"—who existed just outside the front door, it was alarmingly quiet in the Forrester's town house, with only the tick of a grandfather clock to keep him company. He did not expect a reception by any means. He hadn't written a reply to Lady Forrester's letter, as they had docked in London before any such note would have arrived. But as that damned grandfather clock ticked on, he did begin to wonder if the supercilious butler had forgotten him.

"Perhaps he stuck his nose too high in the air, and it got

caught on a cobweb," Jack mumbled aloud, mollified by the echo that followed.

Jack was just about to try one or the other of the heavy doors that stood on opposite sides of the main hall, when the thudding of adolescent footsteps broke the silence, and a gasp floated down from the top of the stairs.

"Jack!"

And before he could formulate a thought, Jack found himself practically tackled by the young lady as she ran down the stairs and threw herself into his arms.

"Sarah?" he asked, disbelieving. The last time he had seen Sarah Forrester, she had been twelve, and just beginning to gain in height and womanly virtues. But this young lady that wrapped her arms—tightly—around his waist . . .

"La! Do be serious, Jack! It's me! Amanda!"

"*Amanda?*" he couldn't help but cry. Jack immediately pulled away and stared down into her face. "But Amanda's the youngest!"

She laughed at that, which was followed by a decidedly unladylike snort. She covered her mouth quickly.

"My governess keeps telling me I have to *not* laugh if I'm going to laugh like that—but it's too funny, you thinking I'm Sarah!"

Once given the benefit of a longer look, Jack recognized the blond curls down the back and slightly shorter dress style that exemplified youth. And he recognized the dimples that had been ever present on the child Amanda shining forth on the cheeks of the young lady in front of him.

"Well, you'll have to forgive me, Miss Amanda," he teased as he gave a smart bow. "The last time I saw you, you barely reached my waist. I didn't expect anyone quite so tall."

Amanda immediately hunched her shoulders, trying to make herself smaller. "I can't help it," she said mournfully. "Mother is afraid I'll be taller than any gentleman who might wish to dance with me. Miss Pritchett—our governess, you know, although, she's only my governess now—has recommended they restrict my food so I stop growing."

Jack refrained from shaking his head. Talking to females—especially fifteen-year-old ones—was trickier than one expected.

"Well, I still have some inches on you, so I suspect you should feel safe to keep eating for a few weeks or so."

Amanda giggled, and slowly her shoulders came back up to her full (remarkable) height.

"What brings you to visit?" Amanda asked, as she waved at the butler, who had magically reappeared and seemed to be eyeing Jack's trunk with distaste. "Take that to one of the guest rooms, please, Dalton," she instructed, before a quizzical look crossed her brow. "Whichever one my mother would say. You are staying, aren't you?" she turned her gaze to Jack.

"Your mother wrote me, and asked me to do so," Jack replied.

"She did?" she replied, then shook her head, making her curls bounce. "I wonder that she didn't tell me—but then again, no one tells me anything anymore."

"Anymore?" he replied as he offered Amanda his arm, which she took with girlish joy. They moved with absolutely no purpose whatsoever to the drawing room.

"Or ever, really," Amanda sighed.

The first, and indeed only thing, that he noticed in the drawing room was the overwhelming amount of flower bouquets, of every variety, on every surface. If Amanda had been wearing mourning clothes, he would have thought Whigby was right and there had been a funeral.

"Ever since *the Event*," Amanda continued, hardly pausing for breath, "everyone gets very quiet when I come into the room. I saw my mother elbow my father in the stomach when they *finally* started talking about something interesting!"

The Event. The importance with which Amanda imbued those words made Jack pause.

"And then, when we came to town again," Amanda continued blithely, "or, more accurately, after Everything Changed, everyone's been too busy to think of telling me what on earth is going on!"

Jack followed Amanda's conversation as best he could. Again, he could hear the emphasis she gave the words "everything changed." Talking to teenagers was like learning a new language, and Jack had to be careful to pick up on the cues.

Finally, he asked, "So you don't know why there are a half-dozen gentlemen loitering on your doorstep?"

"Oh, them." Amanda rolled her eyes. "They're *always* there. You would think they would take the hint, but panting after Sarah is something of a badge of honor, I gather."

"Panting after Sarah?"

"Mama likes to think I don't know of course, but Bridget constantly grumbles about how Sarah's swains have made it so she can't even get in our front door, and they should be shot as trespassers. But then Mama says, 'What a thing to say!' and Lady Worth says, 'It would certainly make the papers,' but she says it like making the papers is a *good* thing." Amanda paused long enough to ring for tea, frown quickly, and then smile again. "But maybe it is a good thing, because Bridget has *never* been mentioned, and I don't think she likes it. But enough about all that. I want to hear about you! You're so tan—were you in the West Indies? The East Indies?" She practically tore his arm off, she clutched him so tightly in her excitement. "Did you meet with any pirates?!"

Before Jack could answer—or even realize that Amanda had stopped her monologue and begun asking questions—a commotion could be heard in the hall they had just vacated for the comfort of the drawing room.

It was the sound of a half-dozen lovesick swains making their unhappiness known as feminine voices uttered sweet regrets . . . followed by a quick slam of the door.

"I'm telling you, that particular problem would be well solved with a short pistol," an acidic young lady's voice pierced the drawing room door.

"Oh, Bridget, it's sweet," came another voice, this one lighter, more relaxed.

"Besides, Viscount Threshing is out there. Terribly bad form to shoot a viscount." Yet another female voice, this one soft, but authoritative.

"Well, I cannot help but be glad that the afternoon is over—driving in the park is meant to be relaxing!" This voice he knew, Jack thought with a smile. It was undeniably Lady Forrester's. He and Amanda made a move to the door, edging it open wider, to peer out into the hall.

There, he was met with the sight of four colorful peacocks, doffing hats and gloves and spencers and handing packages to a number of mute ladies' maids, in a mad whirl of movement and color that blinded the unseen audience to little else.

But as the layers were shed, and four ladies emerged, their conversation did not stop, and Jack found his eye drawn automatically to the form of the golden-blond one in a pale yellow ensemble, but with the slightest shimmer. The color of a clear winter morning's sun.

She was stunning, elegant . . . but even given her dress's hue, cool. Frighteningly so, as if the world were on her string and she hadn't decided yet whether or not to cut it.

"That's Lady Worth," Amanda whispered in his ear. "But Sarah gets to call her Phillippa, they are *such* good friends. Even Mother takes her cue from Lady Worth. Everyone says she's the queen of society, but I don't think an actual queen would like to hear them say that."

Ah, that must mean that the grumbling brunette in green was Bridget (indeed, he would have recognized Bridget's freckles anywhere—as he did her dark curls, which matched Amanda's lighter ones), and the tall blonde in the smart violet was Sarah.

"If you're not going to shoot them," Bridget sneered, "why not invite them in? Or are you too disappointed that the Comte is not among them?"

Even though they stood in full view at the drawing room door, they had yet to be noticed. The women were too invested in their own conversation. It allowed Jack the opportunity to observe his fill.

He paid particular attention to the one in violet. Her face had turned out very angular, and she was quite polished. Funny, he never thought of Sarah as city polished. He thought of Sarah as twelve, hanging upside down from a tree, trying not to fall and yet retain her dignity.

Stranger, this Sarah didn't seem to be suffering from an extreme disappointment. Stranger still, she was the only one who did not remove her spencer and hat—in fact, she waved the footman away when he came to take them from her.

Surely he would have contemplated further—surely he would have figured it out . . . but at that moment, the lady in yellow turned and Jack saw her full face.

And he lost his breath.

She had a face made for whimsy, for mischief. But it had been schooled—or perhaps tricked, with rouge or powder or other women's secrets—into an expression of haughty superiority.

But . . . there was something familiar about those green eyes . . .

"The Comte has trampled through Burma and India, he is far too . . . interesting a man to wait outside of a door," the one in yellow—Lady Worth—said, as she turned to admire herself in one of the foyer's mirrors. "Really, Bridget, you shoot one of those gentlemen, you could very well be shooting your future husband, and then where would you be?"

That face full of freckles came up, a hot anger burning across her cheeks.

"I'll never marry a man who mooned after you, thank you very much."

A pretty pout crossed the taller woman's reflection. "You may not have that choice," she said sweetly. Too sweetly. Jack couldn't help but feel a little for Bridget as she huffed past the other women and stomped up the stairs.

But then . . . why would Bridget be so rude to a guest? And why would Lady Worth retaliate so?

"Well, I should be going!" said the lady in violet—although, why would Sarah be leaving?—as she took a few of the parcels out of the pile that had amassed in the hall. Hers, presumably. "I will be seeing you at the Langstons' card party this evening, yes?"

"Only if Sir Langston will let us play vingt-et-un, not just boring old whist," the yellow-clad Lady Worth replied to her reflection in the mirror.

"It is the only way we shall deign to attend," the violet one responded with air kisses, followed by prolonged good-byes.

"Amanda, who is the woman in the purple?" Jackson asked in a low whisper, trying not to attract attention.

"I told you, that's Lady Worth!" Amanda explained. "Look, she's almost as tall as me. Isn't her gown exquisite? When I'm of age, I'm going to wear a gown in just that color."

But Jackson didn't hear anything else. He was dumbstruck, because if the lady in purple was Lady Phillippa, the queen of society, that meant the one in yellow, with the face made for mischief but schooled into snobbishness, who was so absorbed in her reflection she didn't notice the way she wielded power—or more likely, didn't care—

"Sarah, you should be kinder in how you speak to your sister," Lady Forrester chided.

The one with the familiar green eyes . . .

"I'm sorry mother," the one in yellow replied on a sigh, "but I was merely stating the truth. If she is determined to be unhappy with life, then nothing I say or do will change that." Then she smiled brightly and turned from the mirror, her reflection having finally met with approval. "Now, we simply have to find a dress in my wardrobe to go with this reticule we purchased—I insist on using it this evening for my vingt-et-un winnings!"

Thus Lady Forrester was successfully diverted, and took her daughter's arm to begin a chatty stroll up the stairs to prepare for the evening's festivities.

"See?" Amanda said, a little sadly, as they watched their retreating forms. "I told you they don't realize I'm in the room sometimes."

Jack could only nod. His mind was too consumed by one topic: There was no way that that beautiful, snobbish, mean creature was the Miss Sarah Forrester that he had known.

Or, at least, that he'd thought he'd known.

Four

"I CAN'T believe you are staying with Sarah Forrester! *The* Sarah Forrester!" Whigby whispered to him a few evenings later, in the ballroom of some party or another—which one, Jack could not be bothered to remember.

There simply had to be two Sarah Forresters, Jack thought. There was no other way to explain it.

"They say she left a Duke crying her name at the altar. He was so devastated, he up and left for the Continent," Whigby continued blithely as he grabbed a small bit of exotic food off a passing tray.

The Sarah Forrester of old was from Jack's memory, a girl who led her sisters like a mother hen into childish mischief. The other Sarah Forrester was a jewel, sparkling, alluring, whose looks drove men to camp outside of her house in the hopes of a glimpse of her fair hair and green eyes, and whose acerbic wit bordered on cruelty.

Everyone at this party had no idea the former existed, instead falling madly for the latter.

Including Whigby.

"I need a drink," Jack mumbled, looking down into his cut-glass cup of orangey liquid. "A real one, not this . . . stuff."

"That's a plan!" Whigby cried, cramming the bit of food into his mouth. "We can forgo this madhouse for a better one—with drink and cards, and women who let you touch more than their hands . . ."

"A hell?" Jackson's brow perked up.

"Better than this mess."

"True enough—but I'm afraid that since I am lucky enough to be staying with a good family, I must act deserving of it."

"And you're the luckiest bastard in England because of it." Whigby said between chews. "I still can't believe it! Miss Sarah Forrester! The Golden Lady."

Over the past several days, Jack had heard the phrase "the Golden Lady" more times than he could count. Indeed, ever since he came to London, Jack had received a daily education on the life of Sarah Forrester.

It began almost immediately with Amanda announcing his presence to her mother and sisters seconds after they began to head up the stairs that first day. Amanda, of course, crowed with delight over having the information first for once, a full ten minutes ahead of everyone else. And then, delightfully, everyone else crowed over seeing him.

"Jackson!" Lady Forrester cried, her eyes taking on a decided sheen. "Oh, my boy, can it really be you? I hardly recognize you."

"Perhaps you should put your spectacles on, mother," Bridget piped up, exasperation in her voice. In years past, Lady Forrester had frequently gone without her spectacles, and it seemed her vanity had not changed.

Indeed, that good lady ignored her daughter's good advice, simply embracing Jack again. "You're so tall, and so dark!"

"Except his hair, mother," Amanda piped up. "Look, he's gone quite blond in the sun."

Indeed, he was soon to be embraced by all of the Forresters (even Bridget had a smile on her face where previously there had been only a scowl) when Lord Forrester stepped through the front door not a minute later.

"Demmed suitors, trampling my crocuses . . ." he grumbled as he passed through the door, his moustache twitching in a way that bespoke his frustration. But his grumbles changed markedly when he saw Jack enveloped by the sea of femininity, lighting up and pumping his hand with such vigor that Jack had to stretch his fingers afterward.

Indeed, everyone had surrounded and embraced him like the prodigal child he didn't know he'd been. Except for Sarah. She held herself back. Waiting for her moment.

Then, she slowly moved down the few stairs, and came to stand before—but still above him.

"Jackson," she said coolly, her lips curving up in the smallest of smiles. "Or should we address you as Lieutenant now?"

It was the oddest thing. Here he had been, caught up in the enthusiasm of being received by the family he thought of as his own, blushing with the joy of it, and suddenly, Sarah had floated in and sounded . . .

Seductive.

Controlled.

False.

It set his back up, and set off alarms in his head.

Instead of stuttering in her presence or blushing over her hand, like Sarah seemed to expect him to, he pulled himself up to his full height and gave the deepest of bows. "If you so desire, Miss Forrester. Or we could dispense with artifice that has never been there in the first place."

While Sarah stared into his face, visibly trying to discern his tone, Bridget nearly choked on laughter. Lord Forrester thumped Jackson on the back.

"Quite right! No artifice between the Forresters and Jackson Fletcher!" And then he threw his arm over Jackson's shoulders (well, he threw it as high as he could) and pulled him toward the library, saying, "Now, I'm very eager to hear all about life at sea—you've been in and around the Orient, correct? Have you come across any interesting features in architecture? If so, I would love to take them to the Historical Society."

"Perhaps that will allay some of the bad feelings between you and the society, father!" Amanda piped up.

Everyone in the room shot Amanda a silencing look. Sarah especially.

"What possible bad feeling could be between Lord Forrester and the Historical Society? I thought you a founding member?" Jackson had asked innocently. Innocently, because he did not know he was walking into a snake pit.

Sarah had turned her cool, assessing gaze back to Jack, while the rest of the room—her parents especially—held their breath.

Then, she laughed, a light happy trill. And everyone in the room exhaled.

"Oh, tell him about the Event, father. He'll know soon enough in any case. I have a dinner to dress for." And with that, she turned and flitted up the stairs. Escaping her family below.

So, he was told. Told of Sarah's engagement to a Duke who had jilted her on the night of their engagement party. A Duke who was a member of the Historical Society, and that Lord Forrester's loyalties had been divided between his family and his institution ever since the Event. Told that up until about a month ago, Sarah had been in such low spirits, the Forresters had considered taking her home to Primrose Manor.

Then, he was told of her miraculous change in fortune, and her rise in popularity.

"And I know we have Lady Worth to thank," Lady Forrester sighed, as she sipped her wine after dinner. Lady Forrester always said wine improved her eyesight—it certainly relaxed her perpetual squint. They had dined en famille, although, of course without Sarah, as her social engagements were far too pressing. The younger girls had been dismissed, and it was just Jack and the lord and lady of the house. "She made my girl sit up and sparkle."

"Yes, she is very well received now," Lord Forrester agreed with a grunt, as he took a box of tobacco and a pipe from a servant and began packing the stuff in.

"Very well received?" Lady Forrester repeated. "My dear, she's the toast of London. I have to say, I knew she would pull through. And of course a little motherly guidance never hurt anyone . . ." She paused when Lord Forrester cleared his throat conspicuously. Then, she turned to Jack. "And you need not fear, my dear. While the purpose for my invitation has altered, the invitation itself hasn't. We would love to have you come stay with us, my dear Jackson, for as long as you need. We were so sorry to hear of the *Amorata*'s fate."

Jack's eyes shuttered at the thought of his beloved ship, already written off for scraps by the people of London. Not wanting to dwell too much on it, he waved off the thought.

"Now how many times have I asked you to call me Jack, Lady Forrester?" he said with a charmed smile.

That good lady preened like a mother hen. "I like having something special to call you," she replied, then her face turned to a frown. "But really, Jackson, are you certain there is no cause for alarm—?"

"I'm sure the *Amorata*'s fate is not so dire as one might think. A few repairs and she'll be like new again." Then he turned the glass of wine on the table, and turned the conversation. "So you no longer worry about Sarah, the way you initially did?"

A look was exchanged between husband and wife. While Lord Forrester looked dubious, Lady Forrester was stern, commanding. Then, she—not he—answered with a bright smile. "A parent always worries about her children. But even you must see that Sarah has nothing in the way of depressed spirits, or low attitude." These words were spoken with force, as if she willed them to truth. "Why, she has transformed herself!"

Indeed, he did see. But how much had she changed? Not only from the enjoyable, precocious child she had been, but from the bright, hopeful, open young woman he knew intuitively that she had grown up to be? Because that person—the one he read about in the letters he received from Lady Forrester, the one who had enough poise and confidence at nine years old to talk him into playing pirates in a meadow, the one with an inner light of optimism and mischief—was nowhere to be found on Upper Grosvenor Street.

He decided to find out the next morning over breakfast.

He'd seated himself at the table, at what he considered a terribly luxurious hour—half past nine—and waited. And waited.

He read the paper cover to cover while waiting for any of the Forresters to arrive, but it seemed they had adjusted themselves very definitely to town hours. It was eleven o'clock before anyone made an appearance.

And surprisingly, it was Sarah.

"Oh!" she gave a surprised little sound. Then her brow came down, calculating. "Everyone thought you had gone."

"Gone? Where would I go?" Jack replied quizzically.

"To the naval offices?" she shrugged. "You do have a ship to check up on, do you not?" She smiled at him when he looked nonplussed.

Before disembarking, he had been taxed by Captain Healy—as Healy was headed to his daughter's home in Kent—to stay informed about anything related to the *Amorata*. Jack knew this meant checking in daily on the proceedings.

"The naval offices are right next to the Historical Society at Somerset House," Sarah continued, very polite, very correct. "Father would be more than happy to take you there after breakfast."

His eyes followed her as she filled a plate. "I know. He made such an offer last night. What do you mean, 'everyone' thought I left?"

Again she shrugged. "I suppose I just meant me. After all, why would you hang around here all morning? Surely you have better things to do."

"I intend to 'check up on my ship,' as you so eloquently put it. Other than that, I have few obligations." Then, deciding the niceties were enough, he began his first test. He slid the newspaper across the table to where she was seated. She slid it back.

"Since when do you not read the paper?" Jack asked, startled. "Did your mother's scolding finally take effect?"

When they were younger, Lady Forrester used to admonish Lord Forrester for letting the girls read the paper—it bordered on bluestocking behavior, and lead to bad eyesight. But Lord Forrester would always sneak Sarah the paper anyway. Sarah—the real Sarah—would have jumped at the chance to read the day's events.

But instead, Sarah threw her head back in laughter. "Goodness no! My mother never managed to break us of that." She smiled at him. And it was the first time since he'd arrived that he felt he'd seen the Sarah of old. But the new, cool Sarah came back before the clock could tick once. "I decided a few months ago that there was simply nothing worth reading in there."

His eyebrow went up, and she continued. "It's always something about British India, followed by something about parliament, and then you get to the society pages, and its ever so dull reading your name over and over again, recounting what you did yesterday. Especially when one has far too much to do today."

She looked at him then. He remained silent. And then he saw it. The moment that she realized she had lost control of the conversation, and had to get it back again.

Because that's what she'd had ever since he'd first seen her admiring herself in the hallway. Control.

"Have you any friends in town that you can call on?" she asked politely, turning the conversation back to an interview of him, instead of the other way around.

"I have a few friends . . . but having been on board a ship for as long as I have . . ." he replied, letting her draw her own conclusions from his dropped sentence.

And draw conclusions she did. "Well, I shall simply have to introduce you to some of mine. We'll have ever so much fun while you're in London. Let's see, there are the races in a few days. The Whitford banquet on Saturday. And oh, the boys— you met them, the ones that hang about the front door—they always make sport of themselves when we go riding in Rotten Row, trying to impress me."

"I'll likely be busy at the naval offices . . ." Jack tried, wanting to see what she would do when she was refused.

But what she did was not what he expected.

She leaned over in her seat, and placed her hand on his. Her shoulders came forward, vulnerably—not to mention emphasizing the neckline of her fashionable day dress. "Oh, but, Jack, wouldn't it be fun to spend some time together? You and me? Like old times."

She looked him dead in the eye as she spoke, her lashes only fluttering the slightest bit at the end. Jack felt an extreme reaction from where her hand brushed against his to his very center. She was flirting with him.

A slight smile reached the corners of her mouth. Definitely flirting with him.

Trying to seduce him into her control.

"Don't do that," he warned quietly.

She flinched back, blinking. "Do . . . do what?" she stuttered innocently, bringing her hand away from his.

But by the red that flushed up her cheeks, she knew the answer.

She *had* been trying to control him. She likely did it to all men and, given her beauty and notoriety, met with uncommon success. But by her reaction, she was new enough to the gambit to be embarrassed by failure.

However, whatever recovery she might have made was to remain a mystery, because just then Lord Forrester entered the breakfast room, and her face went stony once more.

"Ah, there you are, my boy!" he declared heartily, as he made his way to the sideboard of egg, sausage, and kipper-based dishes. "I was afraid you had left without me."

"I, too, thought he had vacated the premises, Father," Sarah replied, her voice coming back up to that place where it held only sharp wit and ice. "Perhaps there is something about him that makes one overlook his presence."

No one remarked on that little dig—Lord Forrester barely glancing at his daughter's impertinence. She simply smiled and returned her attention to the eggs on her plate, and gave them each a little smile.

"Now, Jack, my boy," Lord Forrester addressed him, "I'm afraid I am not acquainted with many military men, but I will introduce you to who I know, and do my best for you. But in the meantime, you should have some fun in London, don't you think?"

"I don't know if Lieutenant Fletcher is adept at fun," Sarah interjected again. "But by all means, do try."

"Well, I can think of one thing fun," Lord Forrester said, rubbing his hands together with glee. "Coming to see the new Holbein the Historical Society has acquired!"

As Lord Forrester waxed rhapsodic about his idea of fun, Jack tried to meet Sarah's eyes, but she studiously avoided his.

Over the next few days, Jack found enjoying London was no easy feat, for one simple reason: He was too adept at reading the weather.

And he could tell that the wind had shifted.

Long days on board ship, having to deal with the insular politics of commanders and men, and Jackson knew one thing for certain: The men with the highest ranks weren't always the ones in charge.

And in the Forrester household, it became very clear that Sarah was the one dictating their lives.

She was the one in control.

She decided that they would not forgo Sir Leighton's card party for a family meal at home, and so they went. She dictated that her mother should not wear a certain shade of green the next night out, and so she did not. She dictated that they attend this Whitford banquet for no other reason than it was the Whitford banquet and she had decided to go. So . . . they did.

In fact, over the last few days, without intending to, Jack had begun to catalogue all of Sarah's interactions, whims, and behaviors, much like the naturalists who flocked to Brazil to study life in an untouched setting. (Pure observation was aided by the fact that she found herself irrevocably busy, with little time to engage with him.)

He watched as she laughed and cajoled her somewhat awe-struck parents into letting her stay out at never-ending parties with only Lady Worth as chaperone.

He watched as she cruelly cut down a suitor, whose hair might have been a shade too gray, by asking after his grandchildren.

He watched as that man was reeled back into her fold with a smile and a caress, thanking him for punch.

Perhaps it was his unique perspective that kept him from falling under her sway—he was, after all, the only man in London who had opportunity to observe Sarah Forrester at home and in the wild. Perhaps it was his own worries that fogged his mind and didn't allow him to be diverted. But either way, the idea that she had the entirety of London under her spell completely baffled.

"Do you think you could introduce me?" Whigby asked suddenly, his eyes alight. "Then my aunt might forgive me for breaking that vase . . . although who leaves a vase on a shelf in a hallway, honestly?"

Jack looked up at his friend, his eyebrow cocked in disbelief. Apparently Whigby was one of the spellbound.

"I didn't mean to break it. I sort of bumped into it—" Whigby began, and Jackson decided not to correct his assumption as to what he found unbelievable.

Before Jack could even begin to roll his eyes, he was jostled again, as another young lady with ever-widening sleeves tried to pass by him in the crush of the party. The young lady gave him a sparingly apologetic glance, before squeezing through the other people standing in the hall, turning her head as she did so—and hitting Jack across the cheek with a feather.

Slapping him out of his Sarah Forrester reverie.

"Take care, Mr. Fletcher," Whigby said, having been quick enough to dodge the offending feather. "A slap from a feather is akin to that of a glove—or so my aunt says."

"I can't imagine what I've done to be slapped by a feather." Jack drawled, leaning his frame against the wall. It went against his years of training to not stand at full height while in uniform, but it seemed easiest to getting out of everyone's way. "Other than have the gall to be in the hallway."

"In the hallway in uniform," Whigby drawled.

"What do you mean?" Jack sent him a questioning look.

Then, Whigby said something so practical, and so cruel, that Jack thought for a moment that his silly friend had been having a go at him for the whole of their acquaintance. "Only because it marks you as a fortune hunter." He shrugged, another little bite of food in his mouth—apparently he had grabbed a handful of them in the last pass.

"A fortune hunter?" Jack recoiled at the thought. "Just because a man wears a lieutenant's bars and happens to not have a position on a ship does not make him a fortune hunter."

"It does in this ballroom." Whigby wiped the crumbs from his fingers on his coat pocket.

And suddenly Jack could see only red around the edges of his vision.

He didn't want to be here. He wanted to be on board the *Amorata*; he wanted to be darting in between the islands of the East Indies, eating fruit, bored, and not worrying about his future any further than the next eight bells. But here he was, in a ballroom, being told with glances and feathers that he was not welcome.

"Lucky you have your position secured then, and can wear your uniform without being slapped by a feather," Jack bit out. But thankfully, good old Roger Whigby never seemed to notice his moment of jealousy.

"I'd have to, in any case!" Whigby said with a mournful sort of good humor. "My uniform is the only suit of clothes I have that fits—my aunt says I'd pop the buttons on my civilian coats, and she may have to have them let out."

That made Jack laugh. And he would have laid money it was the outcome Whigby had wanted, because he thumped Jack's shoulder with aplomb.

"Besides, you're not in so bad a situation—being in the same house as Sarah Forrester. Half the clubs' betting books have you married off to her already."

Jack felt for the barest of moments like his entire body was going to fall through the floor or pop out of his uniform or something equally horrifying.

"You cannot be serious."

Whigby smirked. "Of course I can. On occasion. I find being serious sets people back on their heels."

"Mr. Whigby—"

"Oh, all right," Whigby replied on a grin. "It's not half the betting books. But it *is* on the books in my uncle's club, he showed me." Whigby caught Jack's outraged stare and shrugged. "I would be lying if I said that your relationship with the Forresters was not a matter of speculation in certain quarters."

"Why?" Jack asked, frustrated. "Why would anyone possibly care about me staying with the Forresters? And what business is it of theirs?"

"Because you're a bachelor and she's . . . the Golden Lady."

Jack's gaze moved from where Sarah was holding court, to any of the other hundred people in the room. He could feel it now. Their gazes, their glances. Their suspicions and speculations. The movement of a fan over the wide-sleeved lady's mouth as she whispered to a friend and then laughed, as they very consciously didn't look his way.

For the entire course of the evening, Jack had been wishing himself anywhere else. But he'd managed to swallow the feeling, keep it at bay, letting it only eat at the edges of his resolve. But now . . . goddamn, but he was weary of this.

"How about that drink, Mr. Whigby?" Jack commanded more than asked. "I find myself compelled to forego this hell for a different one."

And being as Whigby had been second lieutenant to his first for so long, he replied with a hearty, "Yes, Mr. Fletcher," practically clicking his heels. "Just let me go tell my aunt," he said, scanning the crowd for the commanding diminutive presence of Mrs. Whigby. "Er, not to tell her that I'm going to a hell of course, but that I'm . . ."

"Yes, Mr. Whigby," Jack smirked, dismissing his friend from having to explain the obvious. As Whigby squeezed his way into the crowd to find his aunt, Jack decided it was good manners that he tell the Forresters of his plans as well.

Not that he was going to a hell, of course . . . just getting the hell out of here. And maybe, finally, having some fun.

Five

Two things happened, delaying Jackson Fletcher's departure from the Whitford banquet. One could easily be interpreted (at least by the newspaper coverage of it the next day) as a disaster of epic proportions. The other, a simple kindness propelling it.

As Jack looked around the party for a Forrester to inform of his departure, he was beset upon by Lord Forrester, who intended to make good on his promise to Jack and introduce him to any military men of his acquaintance. And so, instead of leaving, Jack was gratified to be introduced to Lord Fieldstone, the director of the War Department, a man easily as tall as he was wide, and Sir Marcus Worth, head of the security section within the War Department—who was actually an acquaintance of Sarah's.

"My wife Phillippa has taken very much to Sarah," Sir Marcus said by way of explanation. "She very much enjoys befriending young ladies in society . . . mostly because of the number of sons she has at home." He was an alarmingly tall man, who wore spectacles and a pleasant affable demeanor. Other than the gray coming in at his temples, and the lines of age at the corners of his eyes, one might mistake him for a man many years younger, and of less importance.

Jack instinctively liked him.

His wife . . . less so.

Oh, that wasn't fair. The truth was, Jack found himself terribly critical of everyone Sarah chose to keep company with.

From what he could tell, Lady Phillippa was a pleasant enough woman, if one measured up to her standards—and since he was a friend of the Forresters, he luckily met this criteria. But absolutely everyone else, the flatterers, the fawners . . . why, the Sarah of old would have been utterly bewildered by them, then laughed when she figured it out. But one flatterer in particular stood out, if only because he had his own retinue of fawners: the Comte de Le Bon.

Without meaning it, Jack's gaze roamed over the crowds and found Sarah, in her shining golden gown, amidst her crowd of admirers . . . which included the Comte.

"So, Lieutenant Fletcher, I understand the *Amorata* took some heavy pounding around the Cape," Lord Fieldstone was saying.

"Hmm?" Jack turned his attention back to the men in front of him. "Oh yes. Unfortunate. But I have every hope that the navy will decide to let her sail again."

"Yes, you should," Lord Fieldstone replied, laughing. "What with the state of the navy these days, you'd be hardpressed to find another ship to take on a sailor even with the most sterling of reputations, like yourself."

Jack's mouth pressed tight. It was a subconscious action, as of course he meant no disrespect toward the head of the War Department. But the wide man seemed to catch his own faux pas, as he reddened slightly and changed the subject. "Right . . . well, uh, Forrester, tell me about this Holbein you've acquired."

As Fieldstone and Forrester turned away, Sir Marcus stepped in and filled the void.

"You were off the coast of India before that, correct?" Sir Marcus asked, and at Jack's nod, he continued. "Then you must have heard a great deal about him."

Sir Marcus nodded in the direction of the mass of people surrounding Sarah—but Jack knew exactly which one he was talking about.

Jack had heard a great deal about the Comte de Le Bon in

the past few days. Because England had heard a great deal about the Comte de Le Bon in the last few months. For that was when he arrived in London, to bring out his stepsister.

While the sister, Miss Georgina Thompson, was shy and retiring, the Comte certainly was not. He cast himself the hero in one hell of a story . . . and brought a witness to it, to boot.

The Comte, a Frenchman by birth but having lived in British India since a lad, had apparently been a member of an expeditionary team of explorers, who wished to traverse the mountainous Bengal region of East India. As a longtime resident of India, the Comte was naturally versed in the local language and culture, and set about making himself useful.

"But then I became ill, and I'll spare the ladies in the room the gorier details of my tropical illness," he'd smiled at them when retelling the tale of his exploits (again) one day when he came to call on the Forresters. The sight of his white teeth and the way his eyes crinkled set off no small amount of titters and sighs from the preponderance of women making their calls. "So they went on without me, and when I moved to join them days later—I'm afraid I became a bit lost, and ended up just over the border in Burma!"

Apparently, Burma's expansionist ideals were rivaled only by Britain's, and this threw them often into contention with their British Indian neighbor. Seeing he was white, they took him captive. Learning that he was not British, but instead French, they took him to Rangoon.

"There I am, sitting in my little cell, so I do my best to make friends with the guards, with the neighbors, practicing my Burmese. And suddenly, I am called up to see King Bagyidaw himself," the Comte continued, and everyone oohed and aahed at this point in the story.

Conversely, right about now Jack usually got very bored and stopped listening. But if he were to continue paying attention, he would hear (again) about how the Comte talked his way into the King letting him live another day and, with the help of another prisoner, managed to escape. That other prisoner was now at his side constantly, a tall, silent, utterly enigmatic man who looked incongruous squeezed into Western dress. Whether he insisted on the grave and dark Mr. Ashin Pha attending him at every event because, like he claimed, the man insisted on staying by his side until his lifesaving debt was repaid, or if he was just an excellent visual reminder of the Comte's wildest exploit, was unknown. But no one seemed to care.

When this story was made known to parliament, and the papers, it turned the Comte into the instant toast of the town. Now, generally, when he and his dark friend were not speaking with various men of political importance and women of social status, he was at Almack's, or Tattersall's, or at any event one could name. And lately, he had been doing so with the Golden Lady, Sarah Forrester, on his arm.

Everyone took notice. Every pair of eyes was drawn to them like light. Only one was set to a scowl.

"I have made his acquaintance," Jack looked askance in the Comte de Le Bon's direction. Indeed, Sarah made certain to show the man off to her entire retinue when he (finally) came to call. "He seems to have recovered from his harrowing travels well enough."

His flat tone must have revealed his true feelings, because Sir Marcus's mouth turned up at the corner. "I take it you don't think him the hero the rest of London takes him for?"

"I think he's far more lucky than heroic," Jack replied. At Sir Marcus's upturned brow, he explained. "When he came to call on Miss Forrester the other day, I mentioned that I had spent some time off the coast of Burma, and saw the city of Rangoon from the sea. He said he wished he'd known, as he would have run a flag up so we could come rescue him." Sir Marcus remained silent, his brow perched high. "You can't see Rangoon from the sea. It's thirty miles up the Rangoon River." Jack explained. "Considering he had no knowledge of the geography of Burma, I doubt he should have been on that expedition in the first place. Now he goes around town as if he is the expert on that contentious region."

Then, without realizing it, Jack grumbled under his breath. "And that's who she chooses to spend her time with."

Sir Marcus's gaze followed Jack's to where the Comte was standing, his hand ever present on Sarah's elbow, his lips always precariously close to her ear. And she always giggled when he spoke.

It was galling.

"Well," Sir Marcus said blithely, "one man's luck is another man's heroism. Whether on the battlefield or the dance floor." When Jack looked up at him quizzically, Sir Marcus simply shrugged. "I think I shall leave you with that enigmatic statement to go fetch my wife a punch. She looks thirsty."

As Sir Marcus whistled and walked away, Jack let his eyes fall from Sarah to Lady Worth, who was seated on her other side. She looked no more or less thirsty than at any other time, but who was Jack to contradict? After all, Sir Marcus likely knew his wife better than Jack did.

Suddenly, standing alone, Jack realized he had let Lord Forrester walk off with Lord Fieldstone, likely still talking about that Holbein painting, or the Historical Society in general (Fieldstone was a member), without fulfilling his purpose. Surely Whigby had found his aunt by now, and Jack still had to find a Forrester to tell of his impending departure.

And there was Sarah. The epicenter of all activity.

One man's luck is another man's heroism—on the battlefield or the dance floor.

What had Sir Marcus meant by that? Did that mean that he . . . ? Did the man think like Whigby did, that since he was in the same house with her he had an advantage?

Jack's brow came down in its now perpetual scowl, and his feet, without taking any direction from him, started to cross the dance floor to where she was.

After all, he had to tell some Forrester that he was taking off, didn't he? And she was the one he saw.

And so, with Sir Marcus's words, and Whigby's assertions echoing in his brain, Jack made his way across the room. He only intended to put a quick word in her ear (and maybe give her neck a break from being breathed on by the ridiculous Comte de Le Bon) and make his escape. But as Jack was quickly learning, when it came to Sarah Forrester, he would always get more than he bargained for.

ॐ

It was, in Sarah's opinion, a very successful evening. She was fairly giddy with it. And thanks to Lady Phillippa, the scale by which she determined success had shifted dramatically.

As her hand was kissed good-bye by her most recent dance

partner, and she took her seat in the midst of her courtiers on a raised landing that lead to the Whitfords' balcony—affording her the best view in the room (and, as Phillippa pointed out, everyone in the room would have the best view of her)—a happy realization settled over Sarah: It had been weeks since anyone had dared called her the "Girl Who Lost a Duke."

Instead, tonight, at the Whitford banquet, she was the Incomparable Sarah Forrester. The most desired woman in London.

The Golden Lady.

It was part of the strategy. Between the two of them, she and Phillippa had decided that gold would become her signature color. After all, someone wearing gold could not be mistaken either for being in mourning (as heavy dark fabrics would) nor prone to fainting (as washed-out pastels would).

Her mother originally did not understand the need for an entire new wardrobe—especially when they had just had one made a few months before—but when Phillippa took Lady Forrester aside and whispered in her ear, Sarah suddenly had leave to purchase two dozen new frocks.

Tonight, her evening gown was an original Madame LeTrois, and she had paid extra to have the most famous seamstress in London burn the dress pattern after she was done with it. It was heavy off-white silk, shot with the pattern of golden palm trees, in a Portuguese style. The small puffed sleeves and high waist allowed for a marvelous train to come down the back, which swirled delightfully when she danced. In this gown, Sarah was undeniably, universally admired.

And she could not have loved it more.

Not just the gown, but the way people had taken to looking at her. The way they smiled, in awe, in respect, when she glanced their way or even deigned to speak to them. All because she had followed Phillippa's advice to the letter. Always someone who obeyed readily, and did everything right, it took no time at all to fall into that pattern with Lady Worth instead of her parents. When Phillippa told Sarah to smile and chatter, she did. When Phillippa told her to lose her hat while riding, so the beautiful, interesting Comte could fetch it for her, she did.

Success did not arrive immediately, of course. It took a few days for people to change from thinking pityingly of Sarah to admiringly, and to turn their notice from other delicious scandals. Phillippa and Sarah were rather afraid in that first week that a Miss Felicity Grove, wearing a silver Madame LeTrois creation, would become a sensation over Sarah—but luckily that child quit town shortly after wearing the gown. Apparently, Miss Grove's guardian was not pleased with her. But, as Phillippa said, such prudishness was Sarah's gain, as the field was then clear for her to sweep the hearts of the ton.

And as the weeks passed, as her popularity grew and grew, Sarah found herself feeling *almost* as happy as she pretended to be. And if her mind, in the dark of night, happened to turn to what might have been . . . or if she happened to see a shock of red hair or saw a smile that reminded her of Jason's . . . she kept it to herself. And Phillippa had again been proven right: The less she gave those thoughts reign, the less they came to her.

And the more she refused to give in to people's expectations of her, the easier it was. Until no one looked upon her with pity, or concern, or worry, ever again.

Except of course . . . for Jackson Fletcher.

It was difficult to pinpoint what, in the past week, had set Sarah's back up so much when it came to Jack. It wasn't when he scolded her over breakfast. No, it had begun before. From the moment of their first meeting, in the foyer, just beyond those same library doors.

She had been as cordial as one could expect to be, when surprised by an old friend. Indeed, when he first arrived, and she saw Amanda wrapped around him—practically in the way she had as a child, embracing his leg and sitting on his foot as he walked—and her mother's shocked and happy expression, as well as Bridget's . . . well, Sarah could not help but feel the warmth he brought with him.

It was also something of a shock to see him so tall, and . . . masculine. His hair streaked blond, a smattering of beard along his jaw. Whenever they had received a letter from Jack, all the Forresters gathered around Lady Forrester and listened raptly as she reported his adventures—but in Sarah's mind's eye, he was always as she last saw him: sixteen, thin, and just

becoming handsome in his ill-fitting uniform. In her mind, he
was still a boy.

Then, in the foyer, surrounded by her family, he'd looked
at her.

At first she thought he found something offensive in her
costume. But he couldn't—it was her Madame LeTrois lemon
walking costume with a gold thread pattern at the cuffs and
hem, after all. And then she thought, briefly, that he didn't
recognize her—it had been nine years since he had laid eyes
on her—and nine formative years, at that. Formative for him,
too, she could easily note, as he filled out his lieutenant's uniform now, with no small amount of dash.

But the look in his eyes was admonishing. Judging. It was
the same look he gave her over breakfast the next morning.

It was . . . expectation.

And if there was one thing she had learned from Phillippa,
it was to defy expectations.

From that moment on, there had been a frostiness between
them that had never been present in their youthful endeavors
of playing pirates and sneaking the paper to read stories of the
Blue Raven.

But no, she told herself, stopping her brows from coming
down before anyone would see the dark thoughts crossing her
face, she would not let the burr that had been living in her side
(and her house) for nearly a week take away from the fact that
the evening was going so very, very well.

But then again, everything always went very well these
days. But no, it was going particularly well, not only because
they were practically holding court at one of the foremost
events of the Season—the Whitford banquet was after all a
massive feast where the decorations were decidedly patriotic
and the food entirely exotic, and absolutely nobody who was
anybody would miss it—but because of whom they were holding court with.

Sarah felt a strong warm hand fall gently on her left arm. She
turned, smiling, her eyes being met by the dark depths of the
Comte de Le Bon. She gave him that smile that Phillippa told
her to reserve only for those men who had her whole attention.

"I do believe, Mademoiselle, that your eyes are greener
today than yesterday."

"Are they?" she returned coyly, making certain that her greener-than-yesterday eyes did not waver from his dark-as-pitch ones.

"Perhaps they are envious," the Comte mused.

"Envious? Why?" Sarah asked, her brow coming down in a scowl.

"Envious of the fact that yesterday, your eyes were seen in daylight, sparkling in the sun. Now their beauty is shrouded in mere candlelight. They darken, you see, with their jealousy."

Oh yes, the Comte had her attention.

She liked to think she was getting used to it when some poor young lad fresh out of school composed a sonnet to her green eyes. That she was becoming jaded by the attention, as it were. But truth be told, she was still so very new to this kind of flattery that when it was done well—and with the Comte's deep voice and interesting accent, it was done superbly—she could not help but be affected.

Especially with that accent.

When Sarah had described the Comte as "interesting" to Bridget, she was not being playful. He really was the most interesting man in the room, not simply because of his heroic travels in Burma, but because he was the only one here who wasn't a stuffy, proper Englishman.

The Comte de Le Bon *was* fashion, as much as she was. From the tips of his well-shod toes to his burgundy hair and white smile against his tan, the ton was enraptured. It certainly didn't hurt that while in Bombay he struck up a friendship with the Duke of Parford, who had graciously let the Comte and his sister stay at his empty town house on Grosvenor Square—the most fashionable address in the most fashionable area of the city.

His sister—or Sarah should have said stepsister—was English, and a few years older than Sarah, but since Miss Georgina Thompson had spent most of her life in India, her lack of a Season up until now was excusable.

What was not as excusable was her cripplingly shy nature. The poor girl was never going to get anywhere if she blended into a wall.

But while Miss Georgina clung to the side of her hired chaperone—Mrs. Hill, a staunchly proper English gentlewoman of limited means—her stepbrother lit up the room with his stories. His beautiful voice and accent. His willingness to jump into any fun, and pull Sarah along with him. And fun was interesting. Fun . . . helped her forget.

Therefore, no man in England, even if he could trace his family name back a thousand years, could claim to be as interesting as the Comte de Le Bon.

And no woman a match for his status in society like the Golden Lady.

It was when she was falling, falling deeply into that hypnotic voice, possibly never to climb out again, that a remarkably sharp elbow hit her discreetly in the ribs.

Luckily, she had Phillippa to keep her from being too affected.

"My dear," Phillippa was saying, "you simply must tell Mr. Coombe"—Sarah looked past Phillippa to the handsome young man on her right, who couldn't have been more than a year or two out of Oxford—"about meeting Signor Carpenini. Mr. Coombe has an abiding love of music, you see."

"You've met the Signor, Miss Forrester?" came the awed voice of Mr. Coombe.

"Briefly, Mr. Coombe. Have you had the pleasure?"

While Mr. Coombe shook his head, Phillippa interjected, "Briefly? My dear Sarah, don't be so modest. Signor Carpenini visited the Forresters to hear Sarah sing."

"You've sung for the Signor?" Mr. Coombe squawked, his voice breaking on the last beat. There were murmurs in their group. Men talking over each other, speculating.

"He must have offered to instruct you—how could he not, having heard an angel such as yourself." Mr. Coombe continued, once he found his voice again.

It was on the tip of Sarah's tongue to remind Mr. Coombe that he himself had never heard her sing, and likely never would, when the Comte interjected.

"Your voice is more lovely than the songbirds in the morning in Bombay." He turned back to where his Burmese friend, Mr. Ashin Pha, who stood guard over the Comte (he *had* saved his life after all), quickly nodded in agreement. "Surely he must have wanted to whisk you away," the Comte continued, "like I was whisked to Rangoon—"

"Of course he did, my dear Comte," Phillippa turned her charm to him. Indeed, whenever the Comte got on the subject of India, and his heroics there, Phillippa was very adept at steering conversation back around to the here and now. "But of course, Lord Forrester would not allow such a thing, and Signor Carpenini left for Italy brokenhearted."

"Phillippa, don't be so dramatic . . ." Sarah demurred, and while doing so, blushed prettily. A tactic that allowed others to draw their own conclusions, or so Phillippa said.

The truth of the matter was, Signor Carpenini had been invited to the Forresters, a few years ago, while waiting for his ship to leave for Italy from Portsmouth. And while Bridget—her nerves not failing her back then—played pianoforte, Sarah had sung a small, soft tune, the most that her gentle voice would allow. And Signor Carpenini did offer his instructive services—to Bridget, whose skill at the piano far exceeded Sarah's at singing. But he was leaving for Italy, and as such, Bridget could not take advantage of his services—at least, until he came back to England.

It was unkind to steal her sister's glory on this one small point. But it wasn't as if *she* were the one to stretch facts. One leading statement from Phillippa and the gentlemen around them started fabricating the story in their own minds. Apparently, when building a reputation, only just enough information was necessary, and then everyone could draw their own conclusions. It was how one built fascination, Phillippa said.

Yes, she truly had become their Golden Lady.

Sarah's eyes scanned the room for her sister and found her standing by a wall, with her mother. She had a plate of untouched food and a surprisingly wistful, sad expression. Sarah wished she would taste the food at least, and try to find a little joy in this outing. The problem was Bridget had made little impression so far in her first Season out. And while Sarah had tried to include Bridget in her newfound popularity, for some unfathomable reason, Bridget wanted nothing to do with it. Which was unfortunate, because Bridget was lovely and accomplished and funny—when she wanted to be.

Sarah was still staring at her sister, when Bridget turned her head and caught Sarah's eye. Sarah raised her glass of champagne in a gesture of acknowledgement, only to see her sister's face go from lost and unhappy to a hateful scowl.

Sarah sighed. The scowl was not unexpected.

But instead of dwelling on the unpleasant, Sarah decided to focus on the much more pleasant expression on the Comte de Le Bon's face, as well as how his hand had somehow stayed delightfully on her arm.

He was not the most handsome man Sarah had ever seen. He was likely only the second or third most handsome. But far be it from Sarah to think in such shallow terms. He was just *so* interesting, every vowel coming out of his mouth an accented seduction. And he did say some very delightful things.

When he wasn't talking about Burma, that is.

He had been in the Indies over the Little Season, away from the gossip of the Event. Which, silently, Sarah had to acknowledge was one of his best attributes. As silent as the world had been on the topic of the Event ever since Phillippa took Sarah under her wing, it was still nice to have an admirer who could not have that in the back of his mind.

So, while the Comte de Le Bon continued to amuse her, little did Sarah realize that her evening was about to become infinitely worse.

"Ah-ah-ahem," came the hoarse clearing from the throat of the gentleman who had come to stand directly in front of her. She looked up—not the easiest task—past the obviously corseted waist of Lord Seton.

"My Golden Lady," he said addressing Sarah. "I believe this is my dance?"

Sarah looked at him askance, then at her dance card.

"I do not believe it is, Lord Seton," Sarah demurred. Indeed, her card did not indicate Lord Seton, whom she was sure she would have remembered giving a dance (since she had sworn to never do so again, since that first disastrous party when he pitied her with a dance and a groping leer), but instead Sir Braithwaite. But Braithwaite was nowhere to be seen.

Phillippa glanced over her shoulder and read her card, her eyebrow going up at the name there.

"It is, I assure you—I have Braithwaite's marker for it." And Lord Seton produced from his terribly tight pocket a slip of paper and showed it to Sarah. It said, "One waltz with Miss Sarah Forrester," and was signed with Braithwaite's mark.

"This is his waltz, is it not?" Lord Seton said brusquely, his moustache twitching with his sound reasoning.

The Comte and several other men in the group stood, crying, "See here!" and other such defensive postures that made Sarah feel the need to shush them, and placate them back into comfort.

In truth, Sarah did not know what to do. She glanced to Phillippa, whose upturned eyebrow seemed equally stumped. The old Sarah, when presented with this problem, would have acquiesced, and danced with Lord Seton, passing a somewhat tedious period of time on the floor, just to keep everyone happy. But she couldn't help but feel somewhat used by the current arrangement—it was almost as bad as last Season, when her mother, in an attempt to inspire flirtation and make her appealing to two frankly unworthy gentleman, had begun gambling Sarah's dances as hands of whist.

It was as if she had been . . . purchased.

Apparently, Phillippa was thinking the same thing, because she turned her coldest gaze on an unprepared Lord Seton.

"Tell me, how much did Braithwaite owe you that you took this marker as comparable restitution?"

The number that came out of Seton's mouth was large enough that it caused the gentlemen in their presence to stop their blustering and look on Seton in disbelief.

"Well, I'm afraid you are mistaken, Lord Seton, because this is not Braithwaite's dance." Phillippa concluded with a sad little smile painted on her face.

Sarah felt the Comte's hand tighten on her shoulder. He had—very scandalously, one might think, if there wasn't something far more scandalous going on right now—moved it there upon standing and posturing.

Of course, Sarah thought with relief, the Comte would come to her rescue.

"But I was told—" Seton had turned red-faced, whether from embarrassment or frustration it was unclear, but Sarah was never to know, because at that moment, another figure joined the group.

"Ah, Lieutenant Fletcher!" Phillippa cried, and Sarah's head whipped up to Jack's tall form, imposing in his starched and pressed dress uniform. "You are here to collect your dance partner."

As Jack made his bows, Sarah . . . well, she couldn't help it, but under her breath she said, "I believe he may prefer Mr. Fletcher."

It was an easy, if indirect hit. Why should a man not on a ship be referred to by his rank, after all? Indeed, some navy men had begun leaving off their blues altogether for civilian clothes. But as Jack's eyebrow went up, Sarah immediately felt shamed. No, she would not be put down by his manner. Indeed, it was *his* doing, after all! There was undeniably something about him that set her back up.

Sarah connected her eyes with Phillippa, then glanced in the Comte's direction, hopefully giving her friend insight to what was in her head. But Phillippa—that contrarian!—shook her head imperceptibly, before turning her smile up at Jack.

And Sarah again found herself doing as she was told.

"You were almost too late, the waltz is about to begin." Then Phillippa turned her focus to the still red-faced (indeed, had he been holding his breath the entire time?) Lord Seton and petted his hand kindly. "I'm afraid you have been misinformed, Lord Seton. You see, it is Lieutenant Fletcher's turn. Braithwaite never had a dance to give."

One could not fight Phillippa—she was a force of nature equal to gravity. Therefore, with her unimpeachable pronouncement, Sarah had little choice but to rise and give her hand to Jack Fletcher, and let him lead her to the floor.

They took their places.

And waited.

The music came up.

They were still standing.

Suddenly a very unsettling thought settled over Sarah.

"You do know the waltz, don't you?" she asked worriedly.

With one easy step, Jack closed the gap between them and placed one hand at her waist. He raised his opposite hand and let her place her smaller one within its grasp.

"Of course I know the waltz, I was roped into being your partner by your dancing master more times than I could count."

As they began to move with the music and the flow of the other dancers, Sarah rationalized her hesitation. "Yes, well, I did not think that you had much opportunity to practice since then. Being on board a ship and all."

A small smile lifted the corner of his stern expression. "I do not forget things as readily as you, Miss Sarah."

Her brows came down, but she forced the expression to clear quickly. Nothing would incite gossip about her and Jack faster than seeing a scowl on her features. "And what is that supposed to mean? Have I forgotten something? Not your birthday, that's in the fall."

He shot her a look that made her crow inwardly with triumph. But instead of crowing outwardly, she simply rolled her shoulders and said, "For heaven's sake, you spent enough birthdays at Primrose. I don't forget things as easily as you insinuate I do."

He took her into a turn. She was right, he hadn't the grace of a well-practiced waltz partner—his moves were too blunt, too powerful. But one could not help but obey, and follow.

"If we both have such excellent memories, why is it that I suspect neither of us recall me asking you to dance?"

"Oh! Is that what you meant?" she asked, blushing with relief. Although why she was relieved she could not say. "You were roped into playing the savior, I fear," she began, and then recounted to him the story of what passed in the few minutes before he had arrived at their party's side. She told it in what she hoped was an amusing way, hoping to draw a smile out of him. Men who laughed with her, she knew what to do with. Men who were serious and unsmiling were different beasts all together.

But instead of laughing, his expression remained immobile, only quirking up a brow when she told him the sum that Seton had equated a dance with her to.

"A dance with you is worth fifty pounds?"

"No, a dance with me is priceless," she countered. And quite suddenly, she was very tired. Really, no matter how much Jackson Fletcher set her back up, and no matter how often she had to marvel at the unyielding changes in the man that danced with her from the boy she knew, the whole thing— her annoyance, his stiffness and looking at her as if she was somehow terribly wrong all the time—was vaguely tiring and completely ridiculous. "Now, would you please tell me what is it that has you in such a brown study? I am unable to countenance it."

And amazingly, Jack's rigid frame relaxed. He must have been as tired as she. And he sighed.

"Forgive me, Miss Sarah." He hesitated a moment, deciding what to say. "I recently had a rather unsettling conversation with my friend Mr. Whigby. I'm afraid I have let it carry over into my dealings with you. My apologies."

"Oh," Sarah replied, her relief genuine. At least his unsmiling countenance was not her doing, for once. "Perhaps it would be better if we simply started again?"

"Happily, Miss Forrester," he said on a smile. It was small, and reflected the absurdity of their conversation.

"I think that's the first smile I've seen on your face in days," she said.

"Really?" Jack replied. "I had no idea that you'd spent the last week looking."

And there it was—the supercilious tone that irked her so! A circumstance he must have become aware of, since his hand was situated so close to her back, and he immediately sighed again.

"I'm sorry. What I meant was that you have been very busy. I feel as if I've hardly seen you."

"I know what you meant," she said quietly. "The Season is a very busy . . . season."

"Especially for you." Jack resettled his frame, forcing her to move with him, jostling her. "Do you think we can start again. Er, again?"

Her eyebrow went up. "Last chance," she replied.

"And I'd be a fool not to take it." He smiled again, this time with his whole mouth, his whole face. And for the briefest of glimpses, Sarah saw the serious young man who first appeared on their doorstep at thirteen, living too much in his own head.

The one she taught to play pirates.

"Very good," she softened. "Tell me Mr. Fletcher, are you enjoying your time in London?"

"Some aspects of it," he replied cordially.

"Really? Which ones?"

"I am very happy to see your parents again."

"And us girls, of course."

"And you girls of course."

"Then tell me what on earth it was I did to earn your scowl this past week?"

It was a challenge, and he knew it, because the moment the words popped out of her mouth, his footing stumbled ever so slightly. Not enough that anyone would notice, but enough that she had to catch his hand to steady him.

Would he answer? She wondered as his face slowly went scarlet.

"Your conversation has become very . . . fearless, I see," he mumbled, but the pallor of his face took away from any sternness that he might have been attempting.

"I've learned there is very little to fear from conversation," she countered. "At least, not from conversation you control."

Jack was silent as they moved through a turn, as if he was concentrating more on the movement than on a potential reply. Which was perfectly fine, Sarah thought. If he had nothing to say, then she had no cause to feel shame and pity coming from his long looks from across the room. If he couldn't answer, he could no longer be irksome to her.

"You flirted with me," he said finally.

And then, she stumbled.

Not so anyone noticed of course, but she did trip ever so slightly over her own feet. But the strong arm at her waist steadied her before she could fall.

"I beg your pardon?" she replied coolly, when she recovered her footing. At least, she hoped it was coolly.

"You flirted with me," he said again.

"I did no such thing" she replied, trying to hold in a blush.

But by the look he gave her, he knew she was trying to politely cover the truth.

"I asked if you'd like to be introduced to my friends. How on earth was that flirting?" she asked defiantly, once she'd recovered herself.

He cocked his head to one side, and regarded her quietly. "I know flirting when I see it, Sarah."

As his eyes met hers, heat began to emanate from the place

where his hand connected to her side, as if the golden silk and embroidered palm trees that rested there had suddenly fallen away, leaving her bare to his touch.

Oh dear. She really had to retake control of this inquiry. Of this dance.

"Maybe I did," she conceded, putting her chin up, forcibly squelching that spreading feeling of nakedness. After all, if she didn't give him cause to stop looking at her like that, she would be naked and vulnerable before him in no time at all.

Er, metaphorically naked, that is.

"Maybe?"

"Yes, *maybe*," she reiterated. "But why on earth a little flirting would earn a week's worth of scowls is beyond me. I've found most men enjoy being flirted with."

"*Maybe* I did not wish to be lumped in with the masses. Especially when . . ."

She rolled her eyes, exasperated with his recalcitrance.

"When . . . ?" she prodded. Really, this entire dance was like talking to a wall. Although, he did move better than your average wall.

"Especially when I have seen you with your skirts over your head."

Sarah eyes went wide. Her mouth popped open to speak, but only a few nondescript vowel sounds emerged.

"You're the one that made me lose my balance in that tree," she said when she finally found her voice.

"I'm not the one who told you to hang upside down by your knees, though," he countered with a smile.

"But thankfully, you're the one who caught me when I fell. Besides, all you got was an eyeful of a twelve-year-old's pantaloons and petticoats," she admonished, blushing. But Jack was smiling, and all she could do was smile with him. "I'm afraid I've changed a bit since then."

A spark lit his eye. "In certain ways, yes," he conceded, and Sarah found herself blushing again, when her mind caught up to his meaning. "But you haven't changed enough so I can comprehend flirting coming from you."

"Fair enough," she repeated. "I shall endeavor to not flirt with you."

"Thank you." If they hadn't been in the middle of a waltz,

Sarah felt certain he would have clicked his heels together in a smart bow. "And I will try not to scowl at you."

"Heavens, we started on the wrong foot, didn't we?" And she was not referring to the waltz. "Are we friends again then?" she asked pertly, only to watch a cloud pass over his features.

"We're . . . getting there."

Sarah wanted to shake him in frustration. But alas, the hard planes of muscle under her hand, molded by life at sea, would likely react to her shaking as much as a stone would to a breeze. So she contented herself with a sigh and blasé manner. "And to think, I had finally been enjoying myself during this waltz."

"As was I, Miss Forrester," Jack replied ruefully. Then, with a quick glance over her shoulder, he added, "Although, best to not enjoy it too much I fear."

"Why?"

Again he was silent. Again, his face had gone impassive as stone! It was as if all the time they spent together as children had been for naught and he was once again a too proper, too stiff uniformed stick.

"Why?" she prodded.

"Because I wouldn't want to give the gossip mongers a show," he replied.

"Is that all?" Sarah said, letting her eyes roam the crowd. People were looking at them, as they danced, but that was something Sarah was, under Phillippa's tutelage, quickly becoming accustomed to. "I hardly notice them anymore. I've become used to it, I suppose," she shrugged.

"Well, I haven't, and according to Whigby, I'm as much the cause of stares as you."

At her raised eyebrow, he continued. "Apparently, my status as an unmarried naval lieutenant without funds, while living with your family, has become the subject of speculation."

"Oh dear," Sarah murmured sympathetically.

"Yes," Jack agreed. "Obviously, my being without funds must mean that I'm chasing after a bride, and my being in your house must mean I am chasing after you."

"That seems terribly unkind," Sarah replied.

"Indeed!" he exclaimed hotly.

"Although," she mused, "not the worst idea ever presented."

He looked at her so queerly then, Sarah felt certain he was about to have some sort of seizure or spasm. "Not chasing after me, of course," she added quickly. "But you could consider courting a nice young lady."

"Have you gone insane?" he ground out.

"Not recently," she replied sweetly.

"The *Amorata* will be sailing in a month's time—six weeks at the most. Courting *anyone* is the last thing I should be doing."

Sarah took a moment and regarded Jack. He was no longer smiling, his face so stern, yet his mood throughout the dance had been changeable enough to allow some of the ice between them to thaw. She would have to tread carefully.

"Yes . . . but, if it doesn't, Jack—if repairs take longer than anticipated, or heaven forbid, the *Amorata* no longer sails—"

"That won't happen."

"But if it does—" She swallowed. "If it does, you will have to find some means of supporting yourself . . . at least until your next ship assignment. And why not do so pleasantly?" His face was its unreadable self, but since he was no longer actively negating her, Sarah held hope that he might actually consider what she was saying, and thus took that as sign enough to continue. "Let me think . . . Juliana Devlin is very sweet—her father is in trade, so it's not as if she stands much change with a peer. And Cynthia Donovan has a neat little dowry; she might do for you—"

"*No*," he said firmly.

"Why ever not? Everyone does it." She waved her hand blithely, dismissively. "I'm not saying you should marry someone you dislike, after all, but if you do happen to find yourself liking someone, and it happens to be a young lady of means . . ."

"*No*," he repeated.

It was a misstep on her part, Sarah would reflect later, to start reeling off a list of names of young ladies for him to pursue. Indeed, while his body became stiff and cold, his eyes became so enflamed with anger and hate she thought he would set her alight. But her tactlessness was absolutely no excuse for what Jackson Fletcher did to her next.

He let go of her hand, let go of his hold at her waist.

And he walked away.

In the middle of the dance.

Truth be told, it was not the middle of the dance, they were near enough the end that one could feel the finis coming from the bold, slowing strains of the violins. But he released her with such force—practically shoving her away—that Sarah was left shocked and alone, and the subject of everyone's stares.

Her eyes, if not her feet, hotly followed Jack's retreating form, where he met up with another fellow in a lieutenant's uniform—taller and wider, one supposed this was Whigby—where she (and one supposed others) could hear him say, over the rising murmurs from the stunned crowd, "Let's go—this place is a viper's nest."

And as the blood drained from Sarah's face, the shocked crowd went silent, and turned to look at her; there was little she could do but stare at the hole Jack had left when he disappeared into the crowd.

And as she shook off her shock and gave into mortification, Sarah became very aware that the eyes of the partygoers had once again fallen on her.

And contrary to what she told Jack—she was very much aware of *these* looks.

They did not look at her with pride, nor with desire.

One dance, it seemed, was all it took to transform her back into the "Girl Who Lost a Duke."

Six

BY the time dawn was just barely beginning to lighten the sky, and Sarah had bundled herself into the carriage to go home, she was, in her own eyes at least, back to being the Golden Lady.

No longer the "Girl Who Lost a Duke."

But still utterly livid at the appalling way Jackson Fletcher had treated her.

The seconds of murmurs and mortification could have extended into full minutes, had not rescue come in the form of the Comte de Le Bon.

While Sarah had stood in the middle of the dance floor, the last strains of music being overtaken by the awful whispers of the crowd, she had resolved to straighten her spine and leave the dance floor with her head held high and a smile on her face.

But try as she might, the smile wouldn't come.

Because Jack—of all people, *Jack*—had shoved her away from him in disgust.

It was at that moment, when she thought she'd turn to ash, that a familiar hand grazed her elbow.

She looked up, and found the kind eyes of the Comte.

"You must dance with me now," the Comte said, his inflection more of a cajoling hope than a command.

And so, with the music starting up as quickly as it had faded away, the next dance began, and Sarah found herself led around the dance floor by the Comte's skillful steps for the quadrille.

But still, even without looking, Sarah knew the eyes of the ton were upon her. The Comte must have known it, too, because he did the most scandalous and outrageous thing that had happened to Sarah since . . . well, since a few minutes ago when Jackson Fletcher left her in the middle of the dance.

During a turn, where they clasped forearms, the Comte reached up and let his fingers graze the exposed inside of her elbow.

It tickled. And she couldn't help but laugh.

"There we are, I knew I could get you to smile," the Comte said, his expression reflecting hers. "My sister, Georgina, saw fury on that young man's face from all the way across the room. But your smiling makes them think his anger could not affect you. They will stop worrying about you now."

And indeed, the mythical *they* had stopped its worrying. Prying eyes turned back to their own conversations, fans fluttered to waist height, no one needing to conceal their lips any longer.

Sarah decided to try and like Georgina Thompson a little more.

"Tell me, Comte," Sarah asked, as they went through another turn, "how is it that you know so much about turning people's attention elsewhere?"

The Comte's mouth was set in a straight line, and he blushed, piquing Sarah's interest. In the few weeks that she had known the Comte, the one thing she knew securely about the man was that he was not the type to blush. "Actually, I know little of it, except that it is a happy side effect of hearing you laugh."

And at that Sarah laughed again, which allowed the Comte's steps to become lighter, easier.

"Now," he said, his voice becoming low and seductive, sending just the smallest of thrills up Sarah's back, "you must allow me to dance attendance on you, and fetch you cakes and feed them to you, and push your hair back behind your ear, so no one will even remember what came to pass . . . not even you."

And with those few words, she regained all of her confidence, all of her Golden Lady self. So she allowed it. Allowed him to fetch her punch after their dance. Allowed him to introduce her to his stepsister. And when they went on to the next event, she even insisted to Phillippa that he ride up in their carriage. And while he did not go so far as to tuck her hair behind her ear, she was certain that his closeness the entire evening saved her from utter scandal.

And so for the rest of the night, she did not allow herself to dwell on that devastating moment, or on the person that perpetrated it.

Jackson Fletcher.

That rat.

She would not think of him, or his probing questions and arrogant ways. Or of how he had caught her when she had stumbled, saved her from falling.

Or of how he then left her in the middle of the dance floor.

After all, if there was one thing Sarah had learned in the past month, it was how to put unpleasant thoughts out of her mind.

"My feet are numb," Phillippa said on a yawn, breaking into Sarah's thoughts. "I do hope I don't have any blisters. I intend to dance with my husband at least five times tomorrow night to make up for tonight's absence, and very well can't if my feet are bleeding."

She reached down and pulled off her dancing slippers, which would have been quite the shocking thing to do—if they hadn't been alone in Phillippa's well-appointed carriage.

"Sir Marcus left early this evening?"

"Oh, Lord Fieldstone had him run off and do something for the War Department," Phillippa waved her hand dismissively. "Likely involved filing a report, or something of equally insignificant consequence." She turned her gaze to Sarah's feet. "Any why are your feet not in pain? You danced every dance. Don't tell me it's the resilience of youth—I'll have to hate you."

Sarah shrugged, pulling back the curtain of the carriage slightly. The sky was turning to light already, but she was not too surprised. She had seen the dawn more often in the past month than she had in her entire life leading up to it.

"Yes, the Comte made sure of it," she met Phillippa's eyes.

"Indeed," Phillippa countered with a smile. "That man acted of his own volition. Indeed, tonight he showed himself to be very much under your spell."

Sarah blushed. While she was more than willing to latch onto the Comte as a source of fashion and fun, the simple fact was he had shown himself to be something more than a light flirtation that evening. "I find him a very interesting man," she confessed. "I like the way he speaks."

"His accent or what he says?" Phillippa asked shrewdly, but was met with a shrug and a laugh. "You are doing incredibly well—better than I ever hoped." Her feline smile slowly spread across her face. "Soon enough, you won't need me to guide you."

"What do you mean?" Sarah asked, suddenly concerned.

"Nothing to warrant such an expression, I promise you!" Phillippa replied on a laugh. "Simply that I have a husband and children, and in truth should not be spending every night out until dawn. But you are rapidly becoming established enough on your own to not need me by your side at every party."

"Oh." She was unable to contain a frown. This was unexpected. The idea that she would have to face the world alone . . . again . . . it was surprisingly unsettling.

But that was uncharitable to think—after all, Phillippa had done her a great service by befriending her, and giving her the tools she needed to thrive in society. But Phillippa could not be by her side forever.

"In fact," Phillippa said, as the carriage rumbled to a stop outside of number sixteen Upper Grosvenor Street, the house as quiet as the dawn itself, "Marcus and I are going to be leaving in a week or so for the country. Not a long stay," she assured Sarah when her eyes went wide with alarm. "But I'm afraid he needs to attend to some things, and I do not like to be without him for too long."

Sarah nodded dumbly, unable to find words to convey her feelings at that precise moment.

"But do not fret! You will be fine. Your mother will simply

have to learn how to stay out late enough to accommodate your dance card."

"She always goes home with Bridget," Sarah sighed. Lately Bridget had annoyingly taken to going home earlier and earlier, as she had tonight. It was as if she were trying to ruin Sarah's evening through passive means, when outright confrontation was not permitted.

"Well if not your mother, then perhaps Lieutenant Fletcher? An old family friend would not look too amiss as your escort."

"Lieutenant Fletcher?" Sarah looked up, suddenly alert. "Have you gone mad? I thought we were resolved to hate him! Not minutes before you called him an odious man!"

"No," Phillippa replied, then sighed. "I just want you to be happy, my dear. Lieutenant Fletcher is a guest of your father, hating him would only make life more difficult. Having turmoil in one's home will not allow you to have much peace, or to be at your best for society. You would do better to resolve your issues and befriend him again. Once society sees you as friends, the barest trace of tonight's unfortunate moment will be gone in a blink. And," she added, "perhaps I feel the poor lad could use a break. It cannot be easy, waiting to see if he'll sail again, living in such a state of . . . purgatory."

Sarah mulled this for a moment, knowing that Phillippa was right. Unfortunately, she doubted Jack would be willing to apologize for his behavior tonight. And there was no way any friendship could continue without it.

"I think I may resolve myself to a few weeks of early evenings." Sarah smiled quickly, allaying any fear. "Perhaps I shall decide to have a head cold for a week or so, and let all the ton go mad with wondering where I am. As you taught me, 'mystery' . . ."

"Is a thousand times better than explanation." Phillippa finished for her. And with that, she rapped on the ceiling of the carriage, indicating that her guest was ready to alight.

Sarah put her feet to the cobblestones and waved good night to her friend, as the shiny carriage took off down Upper Grosvenor Street. It was so deliciously quiet, in these few spare moments when the sky was moving from a dark gray to pinking up with warmth and energy to start the new day. In the next half hour, as she had learned from her previous nights, this block would slowly become populated with workers, char men, fruit and flower sellers, bakers, all starting the long tasks of their daily trade. But now, for these few minutes, the street was all hers.

The old of yesterday met the new of the coming dawn, and London felt wide-open to possibility.

It was the only time when she was alone that she was not lonely.

But the peace of the dawn would soon break, and if truth was told, Sarah was rather tired. Her feet may not ache like Phillippa's—but then again, vanity didn't have her ordering her shoes made too small—but they mutely protested the shuffling movement from the cobblestones, up the marble steps to her front door, where the butler's snores received her.

Or they did, usually.

But as she stepped through the door into the foyer, Dalton was not sleeping in his chair, as he normally was when she came home late. Always watching over her. Except now, she thought, her brow coming down, puzzled.

"I sent him to bed," came an easy drawl from the library doorway. "Told him I'd wait up for you."

Oh damn. And the dawn had put her in such a good mood, too.

Sarah turned. Leaning against the library doorjamb was Jackson Fletcher. The loose, easy movements he made toward her bespoke his inebriated state. That and the bottle in his hand.

"I doubt he would have trusted you in such a state," Sarah said, her straight back and clipped speech making her seem awfully prim, she knew. But when he came closer, all she could smell was whiskey. Whiskey, and something else . . .

She had noticed that same something else when they danced. Salt air. Even being off ship for more than a week, Jack still smelled like the sea.

But she would not let the way Jack smelled distract her from her distaste of his current condition. After all, the way he smiled at her was more than enough distraction.

Sarah shook herself. She was far too annoyed with Jack to be thinking such . . . *leading* thoughts. It must be her exhaustion. The pain in her feet.

The possibilities of the new day?

"He was asleep in his chair, Miss Forrester. I didn't have to wrestle him out of it, I promise you." Jack shrugged, taking a step backward into the library. "Maybe you should be more considerate of your household staff, and come home at an easier hour."

Sarah narrowed her eyes and followed.

"You are not one to lecture me on consideration, Jack."

"Oh, am I Jack now?" He plopped himself down on the sofa, letting his legs sprawl, dominating the close space. She ignored his jibe, and his sprawling, simply by standing in his way and staring him down until he gave in and sat up, allowing her to pass and occupy the opposite end of the couch.

If there was one thing that Phillippa had taught her, it was how to silently demand one's due respect.

But maybe Phillippa was right about something else. Maybe she should try. Maybe she should be the dutiful girl and beg his friendship back, just to make things easier. To relent her anger, however justified.

To give in to gravity's pull.

"A considerate man would not drink an entire bottle of my father's liquor," she chided, somewhat gently.

"Not your father's liquor," Jack countered. "I do have funds enough of my own to purchase a bottle of cheap whiskey. And I doubt Lord Forrester would begrudge me a night of indulgence. He's the one who told me to use my time in London as a holiday, after all."

"Well, a considerate man would not have left a lady in the middle of the dance floor," she couldn't help saying, "simply to go purchase a bottle of whiskey and drown himself."

"I did not leave you in the middle. We were somewhat to the side."

"Halfway through the dance!" she exaggerated, but was answered only with a shrug.

"Besides," he continued without care, "I did not go to specifically purchase a bottle of whiskey. But one happened to be there for the taking."

"And where was this place, where whiskey is so freely distributed?" Sarah asked, folding her arms over her chest.

"I believe one might call it a hell, what with the gaming

tables and women, but it was really quite pleasant. Nothing hellish about it." He smiled wide at his own wit. Sarah rolled her eyes.

"Not astonished? Not horrified?" Jack asked, his observational sense apparently unimpaired by the alcohol. Sarah was beginning to suspect that he was not as drunk as he seemed to be. Perhaps the cheap whiskey was watered down.

"Not at all," Sarah replied, her posture as straight as ever. "I'm afraid a hell is rather a predictable place for young men to spend their evenings. If you had told me you had gone and milked all the cows in Surrey, that would have been astonishing."

"I'm so sorry to have disappointed you, Miss Forrester. I shall endeavor to do better next time," Jack replied.

Silence descended. The light beyond the library windows was turning pinkish. The world was not yet fully awake, but it would be soon enough—and with it, the Forrester household. Maids lighting fires, the kitchen up and running, preparing breakfast and purchasing dinner from the merchants that came to their back door. But as tired as she was, Sarah didn't want to—nay, for some reason, could not—remove herself to her chamber just yet. She wasn't ready.

And so she turned her head ever so slightly, and said, "A considerate man would offer a lady a sip of his whiskey."

He cocked an eyebrow at her, but silently offered her his bottle. Sarah took a swig.

And immediately choked.

There is little more humiliating than being red-faced and laughed at, but at that moment, Sarah couldn't care. "Good God, how can you drink that stuff? It's awful!"

Jack's chuckles died down. "Of course it is. The experience of drinking does not come from the imbibing itself, rather its aftereffects."

Sarah shot him an unkind look. Oh, very well, she looked at him as if he were the devil. "I know that, Jack. But that doesn't mean it has to taste like licking a dead man's shoe."

"Ah. That has more to do with the bottle's price than anything else. To taste like licking a living man's shoe, one must pay extra."

Sarah could not hide a smile at that. It was moments like

this one, like when he asked if they could start again on the dance floor, that she was almost easy with him. That she felt the possibility of all the tension and silliness falling away, and that they might be able to be friends again.

This can be done, she thought. Surely, easiness can be achieved.

"So, how was your day today? I did not see you until the party this evening."

"Only because you sleep until the afternoon and spend the few hours in between paying calls and shopping."

Or perhaps, it wasn't so easy.

"That's what I did with my day, Jack. I asked what you did with yours."

"I went to the naval offices at Somerset House, to see if there was any word of the *Amorata*."

"And was there?"

"No."

"Oh."

Jack took another sip from his reclaimed bottle. "And how was the rest of your evening, Sarah?"

"It was lovely," Sarah replied. "After you left me on the floor, the Comte de Le Bon rescued me for the next dance. And I spent most of the rest of the evening on my feet."

"And so the world can rest easy knowing that your popularity was unaffected by my abandonment." He lounged in his chair, insouciant, and yet brittle and hard.

That was it. The final straw, Sarah thought, rising to her feet. No one could say she hadn't tried to be polite. But it seemed that politeness to Jackson Fletcher was undeserved.

"A few hours ago, I asked you what on earth I have done to earn such scowls from you. And I think you lied to me. I don't think my flirting with you set you against me. It began before." He remained silent, turning the bottle in his hand, examining its amber contents. "Ever since you came here, you have looked down your nose at me. What I want to know is, what on earth have I done to deserve that? And do us both a kindness and answer honestly this time."

Jack looked at her then, his eyebrows high into his forehead with surprise. She thought he might make his apologies, become contrite and beg forgiveness, as any gentleman might.

But then his eyes narrowed, focused on her. His legs sprawled out again, staking his territory. And Sarah remembered that Jack's ties to being a gentleman were tenuous. And possibly lost at sea.

"If I look down my nose at you, it is only because you look down your nose at everyone else." He replied calmly. But in his eyes lay the challenge.

"I do no such thing," she answered hotly.

"Oh really? The first thing I saw you do when I came to this house was put your sister down. The Sarah I knew would have never done that."

"Put Bridget down?" Sarah asked befuddled. "When?"

"You do it too often to remember a specific instance, do you?" He tried to smile, but it was too hard an expression, coming out a sneer. "Right there in that hallway. You said with a look and a line that any man that fell in love with Bridget would have fallen in love with you first. You told your sister in no uncertain terms that she was nothing to your incomparable light. The Golden Lady."

Sarah's fingers protectively grazed one of the glittering palm trees on her gown. Then she stopped herself, forced herself to not react self-consciously to his jibes. The way the old Sarah would.

"So this is about Bridget?" she said instead, her eyes flicking to the hallway, trying to remember what he was talking about. The day he arrived . . . well, she supposed she had said something nasty to Bridget, but it was likely only in response to something nasty Bridget had said to her. Indeed, her sister's unpleasantness had grown even sharper since then. "You've decided to hate me to take up her cause? I assure you, Bridget decided to hate me for some unknown reason long before you showed up to feel pity."

Jack stood on a sigh. "No, this is about you, Sarah. You just don't see it." He began to pace, to move, as if footwork would bring forth the words he couldn't find otherwise. "I look at you and I see somebody lost. It is as if you lost your light."

"My light?" she blinked. It had to be the whiskey that made him speak so—otherwise Sarah could not countenance a word he was saying.

"Yes!" he continued, his sense of disappointment giving

way to more passionate speech. "What happened to my friend Sarah? What happened to the smart, happy girl who liked to play pirates and looked forward to life and hated piano lessons, the one your mother described in all her letters? I know you were disappointed in love, but these airs you put on cannot—"

She held up her hand immediately. He stopped speaking, but also stopped pacing. Directly in front of her. She felt her feet inching backward. But he advanced with her in time.

"Th . . . The Event has nothing to do with this." She squeaked, then cleared her throat, and took a deep, considering breath. "It was his loss, not mine. I'm sorry I don't fit the preconceived notion you had of how I would be, or how my mother described me. You look at me and expect me to be a twelve-year-old girl, sheltered from the world and full of adoration for a boy in uniform. Well, she grew up. Changed."

He held her gaze, cocked his head to one side. "No one changes that much."

They were close, so close. Sarah could feel the library shelves at her back. She could smell the scent of the sea. His eyes were so sad, so terribly earnest that her gaze faltered, dipping—without her consent—to his lips.

She saw those lips part. Heard the sharp intake of breath. Immediately, her eyes shot back to his.

"Why not?" she blurted. "You certainly did." Ha! Take that, she thought, seeing confusion cross his features. Let us see how you enjoy being the one under the microscope.

"And what is that supposed to mean?" he asked, leaning back.

"Is the *Amorata* going back out to sea?" She narrowed her eyes and cocked her head to one side, a deliberate reflection of how he looked at her.

"It . . . it may or it may not." He backed away from her, beginning to pace again.

"What utter lies!" she crowed. "You know very well it will not, yet you can't give into the idea. You have to hold fast to it, because without it, what are you? Not the boy who loved the sea, who set off with such hope nine years ago, the one my parents adore like their own child." She took two steps forward. "No, you'll just be a washed-up lieutenant with no prospects. And at the one piece of practical advice given to you, you balk like a squeamish nun."

"Practical advice? You mean finding someone rich to marry? Well, I'm sorry I cannot sell myself as easily as you do yourself."

Sarah flinched as if struck. But Jack did not notice it . . . or if he did, he used it to fuel his ranting anger, because he did not stop. Did not look up at her, and did not see the stripe across her flesh that each word inflicted.

"How do you do it?" he mused, his voice little and angry. "How do you package yourself up to be sold? Buy new clothes, tilt your head, laugh coquettishly, flirt with every person who walks past? How do you make someone so intoxicated by you that they ignore the fact that they don't know you at all, and if they did, they wouldn't care to?"

His last words came down like a crash. A painful shattering that made the silence that reigned there after ring clear. Eventually, his eyes met hers, and she saw in his reaction that she was no longer able to hide the truth behind her mask: that the words he had just spoken had broken something fundamental between them. And as a single tear betrayed her will and slid down her cheek, she knew that this . . . this could not be solved with easy banter, or politeness across the dinner table.

"Wait," Jack cried, as she silently turned and moved to the door. "Wait, Sarah. I apologize."

He caught her arm and she stilled, just long enough to give him a look as cold as the dawn itself. "I did not mean you. I'm sorry. When I said that . . . when I asked why someone would get to know a person that they wouldn't care to, I was referring to myself."

She raised her eyes to his. His gaze stuttered, dropping to his hand on her arm, and then to his toes, as said hand quickly dropped to his side. "You're right, you see. What am I without the *Amorata*? Becoming a surgeon or a barrister would take time and money I can't afford, for work I'm not inclined to. The *Amorata* has to sail, because I'm a sailor, Sarah. Nothing more. Please believe I meant no offense toward you."

"I do believe you, Jack," Sarah began slowly, quietly. "And accept your repentance on that score." Her heart was beating as if she had just run up and down the stairs, but her feet would not let her move. "But that doesn't change the fact that you think I sell the world a bill of goods."

"Sarah, I . . ."

"No, Jack!" her voice finally broke, a jagged raw edge emerging out of pain and exhaustion. "You want me to be something I no longer am."

"It's a lie, Sarah," Jack finally said, pleading. "Maybe your family won't tell you because . . . they want your success. Hell, maybe I'm the only one who *can* see it. But . . . the men that wait on your doorstep, the flirting, the selling of your dances for fifty pounds . . . None of your new friends know the real you, because you do not let them. It's all a lie. It keeps you hidden."

"It is not a lie!" she said harshly. "It does not hide me, because it *is* me. It is Miss Sarah Forrester. The Golden Lady. And *everyone* loves her."

Sarah squared her shoulders, and without a backward glance she opened the door, gliding through it like the untouchable goddess she had transformed herself into. But before she was up the stairs and out of earshot, and could let her body breakdown with anger and collapse into bed, she heard his voice echo across the marble foyer, just coming awake with the morning light.

"No one changes that much," he said softly.

৵

Jack watched as she turned the corner at the top of the stairs, disappearing into the next day. His vision clear for the first time in a week.

"No one changes that much." He said again to himself. "And I'll prove it."

Seven

A FORTNIGHT later, as he was ducking into an unused cupboard in the London theatre that took up nearly an entire city block, placing a false moustache to his lip and tying a half mask over his eyes and hair, it occurred to Jack that he was in a most unusual situation, and could only marvel at how he arrived here.

"And I'll prove it."

Those are the words that had dropped from his lips, that vow. The idea that he could somehow break through the facade Sarah Forrester had built, and again let that light shine through. That was what drove him to this.

It was by no means his first attempt. In fact, some might say this drastic action was a last resort. Jack had spent more than a week trying to ingratiate himself with Sarah, trying to get her to, first of all, forgive him, and then secondly, act like the Sarah he knew of old.

She had built a bitter, hard shell around her real self, put it in a pleasant shape and decorated it in gold and glitter, to distract the world from its brittleness. But the true Sarah, the one that used to walk in light and hope, was sheltered within, like a baby animal, wounded and scared of trusting anyone enough to come out again.

It was a matter of bringing her out, is all.

Unfortunately, the only way he knew how to accomplish this was to do the things that would have enticed the old Sarah into smiling.

The old Sarah, whom he last saw at the ripe old age of twelve, loved organizing scavenger hunts for her sisters. And so, on the first day after their dawn-breaking fight, Jack woke up—much later than usual, and with a hangover the likes of which he hadn't experienced since he took his first drink of rum on deck of the *Amorata* at the equally ripe old age of sixteen, with a plan. And all he'd needed was an ally.

"Sarah, we're having a scavenger hunt!" Amanda cried, looking up from her spot at the escritoire, where she was dutifully writing out clues, with her governess Miss Pritchett keeping a watchful eye in the corner, while working on some embroidery.

"Are you?" Sarah replied, as she pulled on a pair of saffron-colored gloves. She ducked into the drawing room and went to look over her sister's shoulder.

"Yes," Amanda replied on a giggle. "We are supposed to find items of educational value, and leave clues in them for the next person to find." She then pitched her voice low, shooting Miss Pritchett a glance. "Although how educational they have to be, Jack did not specify. And I think cook's tarts could count as educational, don't you?"

"Jack?" Sarah echoed, her back straightening.

"Yes, well it was his idea," Amanda replied, her gaze falling to the sofa behind Sarah, where Jack had been sitting quietly, observing the entire exchange.

He watched as her posture stiffened. As her eyes, once filled with easy curiosity, became hard and unyielding.

"You should join us!" Amanda cried. "You used to make the best scavenger hunts. If you make clues for me and Jack, we'll make clues for you!"

Sarah's gaze was still riveted to Jack's. And he would hold it as long as humanly possible, no matter what pain was roiling around his head. (Indeed, cook's best hangover remedy had done very little, and it was possible that his face was as green as her eyes.) But steadily, and purposefully, he rose to his feet.

"Yes, do join us," Jack said, praying that his eyes held the apology he meant to convey. "You always did write the best clues."

Sarah glanced from Jack to Amanda, to the silent Miss Pritchett, whose bowed head did little to hide the obviousness of her listening.

"You'd do better to ask Bridget," Sarah replied. "She's been pounding away at the pianoforte all morning; she could likely use a distraction."

Indeed, a mournful sonata could be heard drifting down from the music room. It had followed a thunderous minor-keyed fugue. While Jack thought his head would like nothing better than to have Bridget stop playing piano for the barest of moments, he knew that her involvement would crush any hope of getting Sarah to play along.

"Come on, Sarah," Jack tried to cajole. "Surely you can spare an hour, for your sister."

Amanda, as if on cue, looked up at Sarah with the biggest eyes she could manage.

Sarah hesitated, deciding . . . then gave an apologetic smile to Amanda. "I'm riding Rotten Row today, with the Comte and his sister." She indicated her outfit, which Jack should have recognized as a riding habit much earlier. Not to mention that there was a habited groom waiting for her in the foyer.

"But we never see you!" Amanda pouted.

"But I'm going to the Burlington Arcade after and promise to buy you a new hair ribbon," Sarah cajoled.

Unfortunately, the promise of a hair ribbon was enough to satisfy Amanda, who treasonously shrugged and complied, happily returning her attention to writing her clues.

As Sarah turned to go, Jack took three long strides and met her at the drawing room's doors. His hand stilled hers on the doorknob.

"Oh, come now," he tried to sound casual and happy, but he was green to the gills and it must have shown. "You may be able to buy off Mandy, but I'm not so easy. You, of all people, are not above a good scavenger hunt." Then whispered, with more earnestness, "I merely hope to apologize for my behavior last night. I do wish you'd let me."

Jack thought for the briefest of moments that she would

acquiesce to his words, that she would soften, and forget about Rotten Row, and the Comte . . .

But then she removed her hand from under his, with no small amount of disdain. Her green eyes met his (probably) bloodshot ones. It was as if ice had overcome a forest.

"Last night, I resolved to no longer care about your opinion of me, Lieutenant Fletcher," she said coolly. "And the most remarkable part of that decision is that I no longer worry about trying to buy your favor. I, of all people, should be allowed to appreciate that."

His eyes narrowed as he stiffened. She continued, "Scavenger hunts are not quite the thing, anymore, are they? Nor is calling Amanda 'Mandy.' She declared herself Amanda months ago. We've all changed in some way."

Even you. It was the unspoken words that echoed through his brain, as she slipped free of him and out into the foyer. He had changed. Changed from a lieutenant of a ship to a landbound one, likely having to sign the affidavit and go on half pay. He had changed for the worse, and he knew, he *knew* in that moment that she thought she'd changed for the better.

It was at that moment, Jack decided to forgo soliciting forgiveness and concentrate on simply proving himself right.

That no one changed that much.

Although it was very difficult to prove to Sarah that she hadn't changed as much as she thought when she refused to speak to him. He thought to seek help from Lady Phillippa Worth, who seemed to have sway over Sarah's actions, but that lady had left town for a week in the country. And there was no way he was going to get past Sarah's watchdog of a Comte, who seemed to be everywhere.

Everywhere that Sarah was concerned, of course.

Jack tried finding things she might be interested in. He spent a shocking amount of money on a book about Blackbeard, only to find it riddled with inaccuracies. Sarah did not even glance at it.

He discovered there was a play at the theatre that was romantic in nature and silly in execution, and coincidentally, set in Portsmouth. He managed to convince every other member of the Forrester family to attend—as they had a box for the Season in any case—but Sarah had a previous engagement.

He thought that he was the only one who noticed a strain between Sarah and himself—seeing as Lord and Lady Forrester had not remarked upon it in the least—but apparently, he was less covert in his intentions than he tried to be.

"Maybe if you dunked her in the river, that would get her attention," Bridget said to him one evening at home, as they were playing cards. Sarah, again, was out, this time at an evening picnic at Kensington Gardens, which Lady Forrester had been eager to chaperone, as the Comte and his Burmese bodyguard, Mr. Ashin Pha, promised to be there, and Lady Forrester was not blind to the marked deference the Comte paid her daughter.

"I don't know what you mean," Jack replied, playing a trump.

Bridget examined her cards, her eyes never coming up. "Do you honestly think that I have not observed such similar determination in every other man in London?" She played a higher trump, taking the trick and winning the hand. It was the fourth hand she'd won in a row. "I'd hoped for better from you, that you'd see through it. But no, you're like everyone else."

It struck Jack that he might have an ally in Bridget— possibly the only other person in London not a little bit in love with Sarah Forrester's mellifluous laugh and cutting manners.

"I know there is tension between you and your sister, Bridget," Jack started to gather up the cards to play the next hand. "But I don't understand why. You used to muddle along well enough."

Bridget looked up then—her green eyes so like her sister's, but titled up at the corners, like a cat calmly observing from its corner of the world. "She took my turn," Bridget said quietly, taking her cards up into her hands and beginning to sort them.

Jack's brow went up. "But she used to be—"

Before he could even finish his thought, let alone sentence, Bridget put her cards down and rose from the table. "I'm bored by this. You can have stars in your eyes and think that Sarah is the same wonderful person who ran down the lane at Primrose to meet your carriage and was madly in love with the Blue Raven, but I'd rather not listen to it."

And with that, Bridget took to spending another evening at the pianoforte.

But Jack had been struck dumb by what Bridget had said. Not that he was like every other man in London, chasing after Sarah (because it was ridiculous), but her last little comment.

Because suddenly, Jack realized he had a leg up on all the other men in London who searched for ways to break through Sarah Forrester's golden exterior.

Because he knew the deepest secret that no one else knew. He knew her weakness.

⁊❧

"We're playing pirates!"

"I mastered my piano piece, let's go!"

"Dolls!"

The Forrester daughters exclaimed as they ran through the house, bearing picnic baskets in their arms. Sarah brought up the rear, carrying the heaviest load, as well as a thick blanket. But she still had a free hand to grab his arm as they went running past, dragging him with her.

It was terribly odd, being thrust into a new family, especially when one never expected to see much of their own family again. But that was exactly what was happening. He had been invited back, again and again to the Forresters, and it did not seem as if he was being treated as a sponsored student, who had to have the best possible grades and the humblest of demeanors. Instead, Jack was being treated as a long-lost member of the family, or at the very least, a treasured friend.

"And since you're in the navy, you will make the perfect Blackbeard!" Sarah's eyes sparked with mischief, as her declaration was met with fervent nods from her sisters. "Come on, Jack! It shall be an adventure!" She gave those words such power that Jack couldn't help but follow along.

Well, he'd tried to be the perfect Blackbeard. On the sloping hill next to the pond, he'd tried to assume the dastardly role, but it was blooming difficult when one did not know the rules, never having played pirates before. And didn't have a beard, black or otherwise.

"Jack, you have to capture Mandy. She's the Princess."

Apparently, he would have little choice.

"But . . . she cries every time she gets captured." Jack said squeamishly.

"That's her job," Bridget supplied, impatiently.

"Dolls," Mandy added, sitting on the ground, petulantly.

"No, Mandy, we are playing pirates, not dolls. Don't worry, Bridget and I will rescue you before you have to walk the plank," Sarah supplied.

Jack again went for Mandy, but when he reached her, she resumed screaming.

"That's it. This is far too silly. Besides I'm too old to play such games." He said, puffing out his chest.

"No!" all three girls cried.

"Jack, never fear, you are doing excellently." Sarah tried to cheer him up.

"But what's the point?" Jack asked, exasperated. "And aren't you supposed to be studying insects?"

That was the pretense under which the picnic was allowed, of course. That the girls' governess, Miss Pritchett, a long, thin, quiet woman would instruct them on various dragonflies and bugs that could be found down by the pond. But Miss Pritchett did not seem inclined for such instruction, as she was seated quietly under a tree, her head stuck in a novel.

"The point?" Sarah replied with a laugh. "The point is, when you go to sea, you will need to know what to do to elude capture from a pirate. And what better way to do that than to take the place of a pirate yourself?"

"Chase me!" Mandy supplied, attaching herself to his leg.

"And actually catch her this time, would you?" Bridget added.

And so, pressured by playful logic, little girl idolatry, and no-nonsense orders, this time when Jack chased Mandy, he actually caught her. She screamed and squirmed, but then gave the most impassioned, theatrical wail of "Help me! Oh, who will help me?!" which, apparently, was Sarah and Bridget's queue.

"I will save you, dear Princess!" Sarah cried. "Never fear, the Blue Raven is here!"

"Who's the Blue Raven?" Jack asked, committing the unforgivable and breaking character.

Although, he quickly learned that breaking character was

not the unforgivable act that he had committed. Rather, it was showing his ignorance.

All three girls looked up at him as if he had grown an extra head. Even Miss Pritchett had glanced up from her novel in something resembling shock.

"Who's the Blue Raven?" Sarah repeated, once she found herself capable of speech. "You cannot be serious!"

"It doesn't matter," Bridget said, rolling her eyes.

"Of course it matters!" Sarah declared, her voice alarmingly high, almost screechy in nature. And the soft-spoken lilt Sarah usually had did not take well to screeching.

After that, there was little point in playing pirates until he was properly educated about who the hero of the game would be. But as Bridget and Sarah talked over each other, and Mandy escaped her captor's grasp and went in search of one of her dolls in the picnic basket, Miss Pritchett decided it was a proper time to suspend the game and go and look at some dragonflies.

Thus the subject of pirates—and the Blue Raven—was suspended. Until after they had gotten back to the house that afternoon.

"Come here," Sarah whispered, grabbing his hand in the upstairs hallway. "Quickly! There's something I want to show you."

He was dragged into the nursery, and then beyond it—into the inner sanctum of girlhood, the Forrester sisters' bedroom.

Which was no place for a thirteen-year-old boy wanted to be.

But as he stood uncomfortably surrounded by lacy canopies and a staggering amount of dolls, keeping an eye out to make sure no one saw him in here, Sarah scrambled under her bed, her legs sticking out at awkward angles, as she struggled to reach something.

"There, I've got it!" she exhaled, wiggling her way out from under the bed. She pulled out a number of dust bunnies and a large, leather-bound album. "This," she declared, "is everything you will ever need to know about the Blue Raven."

He took the volume from her hands, opening the first page. Inside was pasted an article cut out from the London Times, which was titled, "The Blue Raven Saves Regiment from Ambush!"

"*You can't tell anyone about this,*" Sarah admonished. "*Mama doesn't like us girls to read the paper, so Papa sneaks it to us after he's done with it in the morning.*"

Jack nodded solemnly, knowing he was being bestowed with a great gift. "*But, who is he? The Blue Raven.*"

"*That's the mystery!*" Sarah replied, her eyes as bright as emeralds. "*He's a man who runs around Europe, helping General Wellington take down Napoleon, but no one knows who he is, because if anyone ever found out, they might tell the French, and then he would be captured and killed, and it would be horrible! He only leaves raven feathers to let people know he's been there!*"

She flipped a few pages in. "*This one is my favorite.*" She sighed, pointing to the article pasted there. The header was "*Blue Raven Lures Enemy to Capture, Lures Enemy's Wife to Ruin.*"

"*He's the most romantic hero in the world,*" Sarah sighed. "*And I'm mad about him.*" Then she turned to Jack, serious. "*And if anyone will be able to save you if you are captured by French pirates when you are fighting on a ship, it will be the Blue Raven, so you'd best study up.*"

And so he read. He learned about how the Blue Raven was working covertly in Europe, sending refugees to safe haven, and cutting down those that would harm them. He learned about how the Blue Raven would often pose as an enemy officer to intercept intelligence communiqués.

And he learned, more than anything, about Sarah Forrester.

❧

And that was that. From the moment he thought of it, Jack could not get the idea of the Blue Raven out of his head. Every single rational argument that could be made against this germ of an idea—and there were hundreds—fell prone against his conviction. Somehow this secret that Sarah had shared so long ago—the depth of her girlish adoration—would be the key to her undoing. If he could remind her . . . convince her to get swept up in her admiration for a childhood hero—a *real* hero, not some sod who didn't know Rangoon from Bombay—it would mean that *he* was right, and *she* was wrong.

That somewhere deep inside her, that light still existed. That she hadn't changed as much as she thought.

Of course, that would mean that she could be wrong about other things, too, couldn't it, Jack thought with relish. If she could be so deeply wrong about herself, then surely she could be wrong about him, couldn't she? About his future prospects, about the *Amorata*, about everything.

The *how* of getting Sarah to fall in love with the Blue Raven again would be the problem. He couldn't simply sit across from her at the breakfast table and say, "Oh, I found a number of old newspaper articles about the Blue Raven, how interesting. Sarah, would you like to see them?"

She'd likely bite his head off for even addressing her before noon, Jack thought grimly, before rolling her eyes at his idiocy.

One idea was to seed a story to the newspapers that the Blue Raven was back in action, but it was quickly dismissed. Even if he'd had the ability and connections to do so (which he decidedly did not), Jack was of the opinion that any newspaper story, new or old, would be dismissed by Sarah as folly. The young Sarah would have fallen for it, but skepticism was the brand of age, and the new Sarah—the Golden Lady—would be much tougher to convince. A few stories in the paper would be dismissed by her adult mind as folly. This Sarah would require convincing before she got caught up in youthful rapture. She would require . . . proof.

And that's when Jack realized Sarah Forrester would have to *meet* the Blue Raven.

This one moment of clarity was followed by a tumult of others—the chief among them, that as this was a private matter, and a . . . er, covert operation, he would have to limit the number of people involved to just himself. Not only would Sarah have to meet the Blue Raven, but Jack would have to pose as the man.

One might think that Jack would have had second thoughts about going this far, about playing such a strong trick on his once friend. But surprisingly, Jack had no qualms about the matter.

No, he was *relishing* the opportunity.

This way, *he* would be the one to see the light in her eyes the moment she turned back into the old Sarah, and she would be unable to deny that it had happened after. And *he* would be the one to make her see . . .

Make her see what, again?

Oh, it didn't matter. He shook any of the more ethical thoughts off. After all, he had far too many things to attend to, to fall prey to a fit of conscious.

The logistics of posing as the Blue Raven should have been easier. After all, no one knew what the man looked like. He could very easily be of Jack's height and physique, not to mention coloring. The difficulty was, to fool Sarah, the Blue Raven could look nothing like Jack.

Therefore, the meeting would have to be brief and somewhere dark. And in public. No darting into her bedchamber. No, a public forum would be just the place to discombobulate the senses.

Luckily, the Forresters' had taken a box at the theatre for the Season, and Sarah had promised to attend a staging of *The Marriage of Figaro* a week hence. And since her mother had invited a number of friends she deemed important, Sarah was forbidden to cry off.

Luckier still, Jack had already been to the theatre, to see that romantic play that Sarah had scoffed at him for (which she was apparently right to do, as it had turned out to be terrible), and as such, he knew the layout of the place, the nooks that existed behind curtains. And even once, he had stepped through a wrong door and ended up in an unused cupboard, with a window to the outside.

That unused cupboard was where he stood now, trying to paste on a false moustache in the dark.

Jack knew that timing was also going to be a factor. He was unfamiliar with the opera *The Marriage of Figaro* itself, but luckily, he knew someone who was far more versed.

"And then the Count seduces the Countess who he thinks is Susanna, and Susanna gets mad at Figaro for declaring his love to her while she's disguised as the Countess, but he knew it was Susanna all along, and in the end the Count falls back in love with the Countess and Susanna and Figaro *finally* get married," Bridget had waxed rhapsodic over supper, just the night before. Sarah of course, was dining elsewhere, with

Lady Forrester as chaperone. So it was just Jack and Lord Forrester and the two younger girls, which actually made for a pleasant, if somewhat muted evening.

Even when she was as cold as ice to him, Jack had discovered that there was nothing that made him more awake than the presence of Sarah Forrester.

An uncomfortable realization, that.

"For heaven's sake, that's a great deal to happen in one sitting. The audience doesn't get bored?" Jack asked nonchalantly, earning a grunt of admission from Lord Forrester.

"It's divided into acts, silly," Bridget giggled—*Bridget*. It seemed that if one gave the girl a topic of conversation that she was passionate about, any facade of glum cynicism fell away. Which was a nice change of pace, actually. "Four of them. With intermissions in between. They change the sets while everyone is talking and gossiping and in general not paying attention to the opera."

"Oh," Jack replied, his interest piqued. "And which set is the most spectacular?"

Bridget mulled the question. "The third act. The set is a great hall prepared for a wedding. I have to guess it would be the most spectacular."

The third act had the most spectacular set. Which means that the break between the second and third acts would be the longest. Which was when he would have to arrange for Sarah to meet the Blue Raven.

The first problem: He had to make sure Sarah would leave the box at the intermission.

The second problem: He had to make it known to Sarah that he was somewhere else at the time when she met the Blue Raven.

So, halfway through the second act, he accomplished both of these objectives with one simple sentence.

Sarah was seated in the front row, next to the Comte de Le Bon, who had somehow gotten himself invited to stay in their box between acts one and two. Mr. Ashin Pha stood behind them, stoic as ever. In fact, it was Mr. Pha they had to thank for the Comte's presence in the box. For when the Comte had explained to Lady Forrester, ever watchful of the foreign man in her box, that "Ashin" was not his friend's given name, but instead his title, any worries Lady Forrester seemed to have about the man dissipated with the Comte's ready smile.

"His title?" Lady Forrester had asked, bringing down her opera glasses, squinting at him.

"Indeed," the Comte replied, as Mr. Ashin Pha bent over Lady Forrester's hand. "It is the Burmese equivalent of 'Lord.' Little did I know I had rescued a Burmese aristocrat from certain death!"

"No wonder he is so indebted to you," Lady Forrester fluttered under the attention. "Isn't that interesting? Sarah, my love, don't you find that interesting? You must forgive my precaution, Comte, but one hears such things today about the uncivilized Burmese. Now, Mr. Pha, I mean, my lord, you must sit with me, and Comte, you take that seat next to Sarah . . ."

And just like that, Mr. Ashin Pha was seated next to Lady Forrester. She spoke no Burmese and he, not at all, but they seemed to communicate well enough through hand gestures— apparently they had somehow gotten onto the topic of Arabian horses, although how and what they were saying was anyone's guess . . . although Mr. Pha was enthusiastic about them— leaving the Comte free to lean far too close to Sarah during act two, and letting the world ogle them.

His own box now only contained his stepsister and Mrs. Hill, and was less advantageously placed for seeing and being seen, Jack noted cynically.

"Tell me, Miss Forrester," Jack leaned down from the row behind and whispered in her ear as Figaro was singing about someone named Marcellina, which was terribly confusing since he was supposed to be marrying Susanna, near the end of act two.

Sarah's face remained impassive as she kept her eyes on the opera's proceedings, but he could feel her attention pull to him as he continued. "Which young lady is Juliana Devlin? Or Cynthia Donovan?"

Her eyes flicked to him. "Why do you ask?" she replied, keeping her voice painfully neutral.

"I mean to take your advice." He replied, equally neutral.

"Do you?" Sarah asked archly. "I had thought my advice repulsive to you."

"Tough to swallow, more like," Jack countered. Then

watched, curiously, as Sarah herself swallowed, as if taking this new information in gulps.

"Miss Donovan is not in attendance tonight. But Miss Devlin's box is on the other side of the theatre."

Which Jack had already known, of course, and luckily, the path between their box and the Devlin's went directly past the small, unused cupboard, that he intended to put to good use. The cupboard that he had already visited once that evening before they settled into their seats, wherein he stored a cloak, a domino, and a false moustache, as well as a spare, dark pair of trousers (while his coat was dark and would be hidden under the cloak, nothing would give him away faster than his uniform's glaringly white pantaloons).

"Excellent, I shall introduce myself at the next intermission," Jack declared in a whisper.

"You will do no such thing," Sarah finally turned to look at him, shocked and surprised, anger in her voice. She smoothed her dress as she readjusted herself. "You must have a mutual acquaintance introduce you."

"Oh . . ." Jack said, hoping he sounded as if he was just learning this bit of etiquette. Then after a pause . . . "I don't suppose you are acquainted—"

"Yes, I am," she interrupted, sighing. "And yes, at intermission I will take you to her. Now can we go back to watching the opera?"

"Please," muttered Bridget, who was sitting next to Jack and apparently annoyed that they were not as enraptured by the storytelling as she herself was.

Thus, at intermission at the end of act two, Sarah and Jack excused themselves (thankfully leaving the Comte behind to assist Mr. Ashin Pha in his hand gestures to Lady Forrester) and walked the long distance from the Forresters' box to the Devlins. Sarah's pace was brisk, and her gaze forward, so she did not notice, when they passed the innocuous door of the unused cupboard, that he dropped something out of his pocket.

And, when Jack was introduced by the Golden Lady, Miss Sarah Forrester, to Miss Juliana Devlin (a pretty, if smallish sort of young lady, with pale hair and a smattering of freckles), he hardly had to bow over her hand before she began giggling from the, er, attention from the Golden Lady, likely not from him. But while they were in the Devlins' presence, Jack focused all of his attention on Juliana and her father, a factory owner from Lincolnshire.

"What a pleasant coincidence! I grew up in Lincolnshire. My father was a vicar in Stamford." Jack smiled, earning a happy guffaw from Mr. Devlin.

"Stamford!" that man cried, "I've been there, to view the running of the bull."

As Stamford was well known for its bull-running festival, Jack could easily reminisce about it, thus he and Mr. Devlin fell neatly into conversation, and soon enough Juliana was pulled in as well.

"I should head back and attend to my own guests," Sarah said after a few minutes of being ignored. "Oh no, Lieutenant Fletcher, do stay; it must have been so long since you've conversed with a neighbor. I shall see you back at our box," she said pointedly before making her escape, and leaving Jack with the Devlins.

This was when the clock began to tick, counting down. If he were going to pull off this little scheme, it would have to be done now. He was counting on two things: First, that the Golden Lady would be waylaid in conversation in the hall for some minutes. Second, that he would not be.

"Miss Juliana, may I have the honor of fetching you some refreshment?" Jack said, a full thirty seconds after Sarah had left.

"Oh yes!" the girl replied on a giggle. "I'll go with you."

"No— It was true madness out in the hall, making our way over here," he improvised. "I should hate for a delicate thing like you to be subject to such a crush."

Miss Juliana, with a ruddy complexion and freckles that bespoke of a love of the outdoors, could not have often been described as delicate, and she giggled and blushed accordingly.

As Jack ducked out into the hall, he kept hunched, keeping his frame low and his eyes downcast, less likely to catch someone's attention. There was one tense moment when he thought Lord Fieldstone might have seen him, but Jack sighed with relief when that man turned from his seemingly intended course toward the exit—opera not quite the thing for him, perhaps.

Jack did manage to spy Sarah locked in conversation with a more plain woman, whom he remembered was the Comte de Le Bon's stepsister, and that lady's companion. Sarah did not look to be enjoying herself, which made Jack smile, only slightly maliciously.

He quietly stepped into the door of the unused cupboard, and then madly set to work—the pair of dark trousers were an older pair of Lord Forrester's, and as such, they were large enough to fit over his uniform's pantaloons. Ruthlessly he tugged them on and got to work on the buttons. Then, he threw the dark, heavy cloak over his shoulders, tied from waist to throat, the mask—which was little more than a dark scarf with holes cut for eyes—was tied over his head and the hood pulled up, shrouding him in darkness.

The only thing that was taking any time at all was the damned false moustache!

It wouldn't stick to save his life. Even though the wig maker he had purchased it from had told him that the little vial of liquid would paste the dark strip of hair to his lip and chin, it was taking forever to do so. Finally, he settled on holding the hairpiece in place as he counted down precious seconds, waiting, willing the paste to dry.

It was during this time, holding a false moustache to his lips, dressed up as the Blue Raven, and hoping that somehow, someway, Sarah Forrester would see the items he dropped outside the door and follow them in here, that the folly of the situation finally struck him.

This was utter madness. Not to mention utter ridiculousness.

What in the hell was he doing?

His hand lowered from his face, the moustache sticking firmly for the first time.

He wasn't going to get away with this. He had no experience at subterfuge. He didn't know how to act like the performers on stage—dressing up in one another's clothes and fooling people they have known their whole lives into believing they are someone else. Even if (a ridiculously large "if," as well) Sarah found her way to this door, she would likely recognize him immediately and then laugh in his face.

Would she laugh in his face? Or would she spit in it?

The noises of the operagoers beyond the door, the wedge of moonlight coming in through the small window, and the anticipation and preparation for this moment could no longer distract him from the truth he had spent the last ten days avoiding.

That this was beyond a lighthearted prank.

This could make her hate you forever.

He had to call this off, he thought madly, suddenly. He had only been gone from the Devlins' box for . . . he checked his pocket watch . . . less than two minutes. He was not yet missed. He could put everything back, run out, grab a few drinks, and no one would be the wiser to his crazed scheme.

Yes. He could undo this, before anything was done. First thing first, he had to grab the items that were meant to act as a lure, just outside the door, before anyone saw them and thought to come in here.

A wave of relief rushed over him. Calling it off was the right thing to do. He creaked the door open slightly, kneeling on the floor and running his hand along the carpeting, trying to find the small black feather he had dropped in the hall, that lay just out of reach.

And why on earth had he thought this plan would work, anyway? He admonished himself. It relied on the idea that not only would Sarah Forrester be the only one to see the small black feathers along the path, but also that she would be curious enough to follow their short trail. Hell, he should be amazed that he even made it into the cupboard without being discovered. Indeed, there is no way the plan should have worked at all.

But as his hand brushed the feather, they brushed something else, too. His eyes peered out beyond the cupboard, beyond the curtain, into the brightness of the hall, where he saw Sarah Forrester, the Golden Lady, crouching down to pick up the feather that rested there, his fingers resting over hers. She met his eyes.

There was no reason it should have worked, he cursed himself as he grabbed her hand and pulled her into the darkness of the cupboard.

Except, it had.

Eight

WELL, this night was not going as expected, Sarah thought as she was roughly pulled from her innocuous spot along the wall in the theatre corridor, into the shabby close cupboard hidden behind a curtain there.

First, she had to attend the opera in the first place. As Phillippa was still annoyingly out of town, her mother was her only possible chaperone, and as Lady Forrester was hosting a number of her friends, it was either spend an evening at home or attend with the family.

And so, for the first time in several weeks, Sarah did as her family wished—not the other way around.

It was not as if it was a terrible thing, spending time with the family, of course. It was very quiet, very polite. Very correct.

And it was very tiresome being very correct. It took a great deal of concentration. Almost as much as it took to be popular.

And the reason she was so very certain she had to be very correct was sitting directly behind her for the first two acts.

She was not about to give Jackson Fletcher the satisfaction of doing something more for him to find fault within her. So her posture was very correct, her comments all very banal.

She even kept herself from remarking on Bridget's overt enthusiasm for the performance. Because even if she said something *nice*, such as it was pleasant to see Bridget enjoying herself for once, Sarah had no doubt that Jack (not to mention Bridget) would twist it into something cruel and unkind.

Luckily, the Comte came to call after the first act, and it would have been terribly rude to not let him stay, when they signaled the end to the intermission. (He wouldn't have had time to make it back to his own seat, surely, her mother had rationalized, Mr. Ashin Pha at her side.) The Comte made the evening somewhat interesting at least. His breath tickled her ear when he asked to see the libretto, when he whispered the baritone was going to sing at a dinner party next week, when he asked her to do something only one other man had ever asked of her, giving her just the slightest jolt of thrilling fear. He asked that she start calling him by his Christian name—John. (Or was is spelled Jean? She would have to be certain to ask.)

Ha! She could only hope Jack had overheard that!

But she would not come to know if he did or did not, as when Jack leaned down, his breath caressing her ear and sending a wave of shock down her spine, he didn't harass her about her lifestyle—instead, he'd decided to dip his toes in her advice and be introduced to an heiress!

She should have been pleased, she thought later, after she had deposited him at Juliana Devlin's side—having been thoroughly ignored once they arrived there, she couldn't help but be slightly miffed—and making her meandering way back to the opposite side of the theatre's boxes. She should have crowed with triumph. So, why did she feel so . . . muddled by it?

It was in this muddled state that she ran into the Comte's—John's (Jean's?)—stepsister, Miss Georgina Thompson. Georgina, whose mother married the Comte's father when both she and the Comte had been school-aged (as it had been explained to Sarah when they fell into conversation at the Whitford banquet), was positively aglow with pleasure at running into Sarah, so much so that one might, from a distance, call her somewhat clinging.

"Oh, Miss Forrester!" Georgina had cried, her huge wet

eyes filled with relief, taking Sarah's hand. For someone so small and fragile seeming, she had an impressive grip. "I was so deeply worried when the Comte left our seats after the first act, but then I looked up at your box and saw he was with you, and it filled me with such joy!"

Really, quite clinging.

It was then that Sarah noticed Mrs. Hill behind Georgina, gently pulling the lady back into social correctness.

"Would you be so kind as to tell the Comte we are leaving?" Mrs. Hill said, clearing her throat. "Miss Georgina has a headache, and I am quite weary myself."

"Oh, I am so sorry to hear it," Sarah replied. "Allow me to fetch him to you. You should not be on your own."

Indeed, while the Comte had been very attentive and interesting so far this evening, in her muddled state Sarah had no need to hear him tell tales about traversing the Bengali mountains. Again.

"Oh, I will not be alone. Mrs. Hill is with me. Besides," Georgina whispered conspiratorially, "I doubt even the King of Burma could pry him from your side." She winked—winked!—at her.

"Yes, but I hate to rob you of your escort. Not even Mr. Ashin Pha—?"

But Georgina, if possible, turned paler, shooting Mrs. Hill a glance. "That is unnecessary," Georgina replied kindly. "I was watching your box, and Mr. Ashin Pha seems so comfortable with your mother. I fear he is never nearly so comfortable with me."

Sarah could not help but notice the skittishness in Georgina's voice. One tilt of her head had Georgina divulging further.

"He makes me nervous is all, surely you understand. I will never understand a man who walks around barefoot and keeps all manner of swords in the house." She laughed a little, a nervous trill. "As Mrs. Braeburn said when I explained it to her"—Georgina indicated a tall woman with a huge floral configuration in her hair, standing by her former MP husband, bored out of his mind—"foreigners, no matter how civilized, still have some touch of barbarism to them."

"Yes, but Mr. Ashin Pha owes your brother—"

"You must forgive us, Miss Forrester," Mrs. Hill interrupted, steering this conversation back to the acceptable and decidedly less interesting, "but our carriage is waiting for us."

Thus Georgina and Sarah made their curtsies, and for the first time Sarah was actually sorry to see her go.

Sarah meandered through the crowd, in her still muddled state, nodding hellos and giving surface greetings to people she knew in the mad crush of people stretching their legs, as she headed back toward the Forrester box.

Or she would have, if something hadn't caught her eye. She was trying to get back to the exterior wall, which was the least blocked path back to the box—it was how they went out, after all, and the sooner she got back to the box, the sooner the opera would be over, and the sooner her mother would finish trying to shove her and the Comte together, she rationalized—when there was the slightest of movements. One of the wall hangings rustling. She shouldn't have taken notice of it—there were so many people in the hall that someone bumping up against a curtain was not at all noteworthy. But what piqued her curiosity was the fact that the curtain seemed to be moving from the *inside*.

She would have left it at that, shrugged, and moved past the spot on the wall where the drapery moved if she hadn't also noticed something else. Her eyes were down, she was trying to be sure of her footing, and there it was . . .

A black feather. Nay, a trail of them.

Large. Perfectly shaped. And black as midnight, so black in the candlelight it shone with blue. Had a bird gotten in and wreaked havoc? Had some well-dressed lady lost them from her coiffure? She bent down to pick one up.

And that's when the man's hand grazed hers.

Her eyes shot up. Searched the dark beyond the curtain (and the door that resided behind it) for the briefest of moments before they found his masked ones.

Eyes that seemed to make a decision, then and there.

And every nerve in her body was suddenly alert with shock. Awareness.

And before she knew it, before she could make a sound, she, and the feather, were pulled from their innocuous places in the hall, into the tight space of a dusty, empty cupboard.

Empty of course, except for him.

"Did anyone see you?" he whispered in a hurry, his voice gruff and low, his hand still on hers. In fact, the only bit of skin of his she could see was his hand. Everything else, his face, his body, was hidden by a massive cloak.

"What?" she asked, bewildered. She must have asked too sharply, because he put a gentle hand up over her mouth.

"Shh . . ." he admonished, leaning close. She could see then that he had a dark moustache that drooped at the edges, full lips, a strong jaw . . .

Her eyes quickly returned to his.

"Did anyone see you come in here? Think!"

"I . . . I don't think so." She stuttered, once his warm hand left her mouth. "Who—"

"Good. That just may save your life." He grunted, and fished in his cloak's pocket for a moment.

"But who—"

"I'm not the one you need to worry about, Miss Forrester," he replied.

Sarah's spine went rigid. "How do you know my name?"

She watched his lips curl into the slightest of smiles. "Everyone knows your name." Then he shoved a dirty little packet, wrapped up in oilcloth, in her hands. "Take this."

"What?" she cried. "No!"

"They cannot find it on me. Go back to your seat. I'll retrieve it from you later."

Sarah felt as if her brain was going in a thousand different directions at once. What was the packet? How would he get it back from her? Who were "they"?

But none of those sentences were what came out of her mouth. Instead, she was left saying something completely sensible.

"You're mad. I am going to call a guard."

A completely sensible sentiment that would prove to be her undoing.

Because as she turned away from him and opened her mouth to cry out, the cloaked figure ruthlessly pulled her back. He caught her against his body and held her there as she struggled. And then, when her eyes met his, she saw in that split second, the decision he made.

It was a ruthless kiss. It quelled any sound that was about to come from her throat, but still she struggled against him. But the more she wiggled, the more she pressed, and the deeper she fell into his embrace.

And suddenly, she was kissing him back.

This was unlike her ex-fiancé's kisses. Those had been teasing, light. This was power and desperation, his moustache raking against her upper lip, scoring her. His strength seemed to radiate out of the hard planes of his body and sap her of hers, so much so that by the time he pulled back, she was breathless from it.

If he was as shocked as she, he didn't show it. Instead, he took advantage of her dumb state, pressing the oilcloth packet into her now willing hand, before he gave a tiny salute, and promptly jumped out the small window.

A small squeak emerged from her lips as she scrambled to the window, hoisting herself up over the ledge and peering down. But she could see nothing in the swirling night fog below.

He . . . whoever he was . . . was gone.

Jackson Fletcher would be the first person to admit that his plan had not been flawlessly constructed. It was beyond a miracle that things had turned out the way they had. He had been on the verge of calling it off when Sarah had appeared—there was little he could do in that moment but go through with it. He had lured her into the cupboard, befuddled her, and then kissed her senseless.

Although he would have to ruminate on the kissing—and how oddly senseless it had made *him*—at a more fortuitous time. For, in this terribly flawed plan of his, the one thing that could easily be called the most flawed was his escape.

The window of the unused cupboard overlooked a narrow back alley. When Jack had scouted the little space earlier in the week, he had noticed a handy little ledge running about three feet below the window. It led around the northwest corner of the building, where Jack knew there was another window leading to another theatre cupboard, although this one less empty and more filled with mops and brooms. There he could divest himself of his costume, run to the refreshment table, and be back at the Devlins' box likely before Sarah was back at the Forresters'. The ledge should have been able to bear his weight.

Should have, being the operative words.

For when he swung himself out onto the ledge, thinking he could maneuver along it and around the corner of the building fast enough so Sarah would think he disappeared into thin air, he instead found his foot catching on a damaged, crumbling spot of the not-as-wide-as-he-thought ledge, and his footing gave way, plunging him (silently, thank God) into the fog below.

Luckily, he'd been only two (well, no more than three) stories up. Unluckily, it would have been enough to break his legs. That is, if he hadn't (luckily) landed on something that broke his fall.

That *thing* he landed on was a brute of a man, twice his size, who would have likely flicked him away like a crumb on his shirt, if he hadn't had the misfortune to be taken by surprise from above.

"Murphle Ooof!" Was the muffled exclamation that emerged from underneath Jack's thick cloak as he struggled to get to his feet. Feet that, miraculously, were not broken. Nor was anything else, as far as he could surmise—although his entire left side was going to be one extended bruise on the morrow. He put a hand to his ribs—intact, but sore. The brute might have broken his fall, but it still hadn't been a pleasant experience.

"Excuse me, my good man," Jack began, aiming for joviality, but the wind having been knocked out of him, his voice was harsh and graveled. He hunched down to check on the thankfully still breathing form he'd landed upon, but found him unconscious. Jack looked up, was about to call for help, when he saw just what kind of situation he had landed in.

Other than the man he had landed on, there were two other gentlemen—although by their shabby clothes and general lack of teeth, they bespoke themselves as anything but—both of whom were half the size of the man he had landed on, staring at Jack as if he was an avenging angel. In one of the men's hand was a short, ugly knife. At the other man's mercy, was a woman.

She was backed up against the theatre wall, her body pressing into the brick, trying as hard as she could to get away from the men. But she, too, had turned her head to look at the commotion going on at the mouth of the alley.

And suddenly Jack understood. He'd landed in the middle of a band of robbers (or worse) exercising their trade. And purely by accident, he'd taken out the biggest and baddest bandit amongst them.

The overgrown thug he'd landed on groaned unconsciously, his body still prostrate on the ground, but obviously alive. As Jack stood up tall, his cloak swirled about, kicking the dust and fog up in puffs at his feet, making him feel like he was floating in a cloud of the stuff.

Apparently, he wasn't the only one who thought he was floating, because one of the two smaller, more conscious thugs, dropped his knife from his shaking hand.

"It's a ghost!" Small Thug One cried, backing away and stumbling over his own feet, falling hard on his rear—but his eyes never leaving Jack's form.

"N-n-n-n-o!" Small Thug Two stuttered, as Jack took a step closer to them. "A ghost couldn't take out Big Ned—'tis the Devil hisself!" Then, being either the more superstitious or smarter of the two of them, Small Thug Two released his menacing hold on the woman and skittered over to the alley's opposite wall, and then ran as if the aforementioned Devil himself was chasing him, past Jack and out into the cold night.

"Hey—wait for me!" Small Thug One cried, pulling himself up off the ground and making similar tracks out into the foggy night.

Jack watched him go with something akin to stunned bemusement—after all, less than a minute ago, he had been in a tiny cupboard kissing Sarah Forrester, and now, he had foiled a robbery—when he turned and found himself wrapped in the embrace of one very thankful and colorful woman.

"Oh, kind sir! You're an angel, you are! They was coming to take my earnings, which they got no right to. They know I'm one of Billy's girls—" She was saying, pressing herself into his cloak, her hands going around his back, under that length of fabric.

He pulled her away from him, finding a younger face than

he expected, hidden under the weight of garish face paint. Her gown was equally garish, cheap and shiny in the moonlight that managed to penetrate the fog.

"You should go," Jack said roughly, as his masked (thank heavens he was still wearing the mask!) eyes found hers.

"But, sir . . . let me thank you for helping me. I'm awfully good at saying thanks." She batted her heavy eyes at him—eyes that if Jack was not mistaken, had the sheen of someone who nipped at cheap gin to make it through the night. With her line of work, he couldn't blame her.

"I'm sure you are"—he smiled kindly—"but you should go. Before Big Ned wakes up."

That set her to rights, as she gathered her skirts and dipped to a curtsy, and disappeared into the fog beyond the alley.

And now, Jack was merely faced with the conundrum of how to get back inside the theatre, without anyone noticing he had been outside of it.

He couldn't very well go around to the front of the theatre and use the main entrance. Too many people. Not only that, he needed to get back to the second floor. He couldn't go home—eventually Sarah's befuddlement would wear off, and he knew that she was smart enough to be suspicious of any man without an airtight alibi. Therefore, he needed to be exactly where Sarah expected him to be—the Devlins' box—and nowhere else.

Therefore, there was nowhere to go . . . but up.

Jack used precious seconds to examine the wall of the theatre. Ragged brick, but not ragged enough. Luckily (and luck was his savior this evening!) there was a drainpipe at the far end of the alley, running up the juncture of the theatre wall's connection to the building next door. And of course, that ledge at the second floor window.

But if there was one thing Jack could do, it was climb.

On board the *Amorata*, they'd had competitions on the long, boring days at sea, when there was no foul weather or foreign ships to contend with, to see which crew member could climb the rigging of the main sail the fastest. And much to everyone's surprise, Jack, at sixteen, a new midshipman with long limbs and a gawkily prominent Adam's Apple, moved faster than any bo'sun or ship's mate or deckhand in the history of the challenge. And so, he became the one—even though he was an officer—who would volunteer to climb up to the crow's nest to deliver the crewman on guard up there his ration of rum, or to unknot a particularly bad tangle of ropes.

Thus he was up on that ledge—the one that had failed him earlier—in a matter of seconds.

Jack was aware of a certain amount of luck helping him this evening. And so, as he maneuvered himself along the ledge around the corner, and into the window of the second, better used cupboard (simply because if he went back to the old one, he chanced Sarah still being there), he sent up a prayer of thanks. He realized that all of it—the cupboard, the befuddlement, the kissing, the falling, the landing, and the climbing back up, had taken somewhere in the vicinity of less than ten minutes.

And so, when he divested himself of his costume, stowing the pants, cloak, and mask in a bundle behind some brooms, and stepped back out into the hallway, it was just in time to hear the bells ring, indicating intermission was ending. He trotted over to the refreshment table, cutting the line of other gentlemen and stealing two glasses of weak Madeira, and briskly moved back toward the Devlin's box, handing over one of the glasses to Juliana Devlin mere seconds before the curtain went up.

"I'm so sorry it took so long," he said with a smile. "It seems the last act made everyone quite thirsty."

Juliana, her eyes on the play in front of them, whispered back. "No need to apologize. But it's far too late for you to go back to your own seat. You should watch the third act with us, shouldn't he, Father?"

As her father grunted in assent, Jack raised his own glass to his lips—and felt the liquid get caught in the hairy brush of his false moustache.

Oh, bloody hell! But—yes, luck held him—both Juliana and Mr. Devlin's eyes were on the play, they had not looked at him too closely when he returned. Quietly, he raised a hand to his lips and quickly, *painfully*, peeled back the moustache. He whimpered in pain.

"Did you say something, Lieutenant?" Juliana turned to look at him finally, a small smile on her lips.

"Just, er, that I would be honored to stay by your side for the next act, Miss Devlin."

As she blushed, Jack exhaled in blissful relief, his eyes felt at ease to search the other side of the theatre boxes. There, the Comte was escorting Sarah to her seat. But, in her right hand, clutched tightly, was a familiarly shaped packet, badly hidden by the folds of her golden skirt. Yes. He had gotten away with it. Gotten away with it all.

Luckily.

॰॰

For Jackson Fletcher, ignorance was bliss, for if he knew everything that had transpired that night, he would have been very worried for what was to come. Oh, he was aware enough of most of it, and he cannot be blame for missing two material points, as he had been so rushed and fevered in the jumble of happenings. But—back in the alleyway, as busy as he had been with the various thugs he was landing on and scaring into fleeing, he perhaps should have taken better notice of the woman.

For the first thing he missed was that when she embraced him, her hands went with a decidedly practiced ease, in search of his coat pockets. And finding one, she drew out its contents. But she did not know what to make of it.

After all, what kind of man went around with a pocket full of black feathers? Her Billy—when she told him the story—would think that part a particularly rum bit.

And the second thing Jack missed, in his haste to climb back up to the second floor, was that the woman was not nearly as fast a runner as he had surmised. That she had even turned back once, and could have sworn that she saw, through the fog—the man who saved her hide flying up into the night.

Billy would find that bit of the story funny, too.

Nine

I T was all Sarah could do to not tear into the packet that was burning a hole in her reticule the minute she walked back into her room that evening. As it was, she had decided to forgo the parties after the opera, managing to claim a headache and earn pouts of dismay from John—Jean . . . er, the Comte— and the silent Mr. Ashin Pha. And surprisingly, her mother. But as much as Sarah would have welcomed the distraction of society and entertainment, there was no possible way she was going to be able to go through an entire evening without finding out what was in that packet!

Indeed, it was amazing that she had made it through the second half of the opera.

After the mysterious man in an oversized cloak jumped out the window and disappeared, Sarah stood in shock for what felt like an eternity but was likely little more than a moment. There is no way he had . . . disappeared! Just out into the night!

Suddenly, the world rushed back to her, as Sarah remembered where she was. The muffled sounds of the people in the theatre filled the air from beyond the cupboard door. And she realized she had to get back to her seat.

But not before she did some investigating.

Sarah ducked her head out of the cupboard door and edged her way out from behind the curtain. The ranks of people were thinning, anticipation of the next act starting had them stopping conversation and returning to their seats. Neatly, she edged her way to the main stairs and lightly treaded down them, heading to the opera's main entrance. She really had no notion of where she was heading, or what she was looking for, but . . .

But nothing! She had been accosted in a cupboard by an unknown man, and something needed to be done about it! So when Sarah reached the front entrance, she found a house footman and took him aside.

"Do you know that there are men in cupboards accosting women?" she said indignantly, before the servant could speak.

"M—miss?" The usher replied looking somewhat surprised. He was younger than Sarah, and obviously not the man in charge.

"Men. Masked men. Accosting women in cupboards. Did you let a masked man into the theatre tonight? Dark cloak. Scratchy moustache?"

If possible, the footman looked even more surprised. "I don't believe so, miss. Are you perhaps speaking about an actor? On stage?"

"No! I'm speaking about a man in a cupboard! Who went out the window . . ." Sarah began, but then sighed. "And you must think I'm ridiculous."

"No, miss. Er . . . you saw this man go out a window?" The footman began, to which Sarah nodded vigorously. "So, you were in the cupboard with him?"

Her head shot up, a blush creeping up over her face, as her mind went back mere minutes, to the fact that yes, she was in a cupboard with the man, and to just what they had ended up doing in there.

It seemed as though her blush was enough of an answer for the young footman, because he barely hid his smirk before he continued. "Would you like me to ask the house steward, miss? To see if we should be searching for this masked man?"

And with sudden clarity, Sarah could see the headlines in tomorrow's gossip sheets: "The Girl Who Lost a Duke Loses

Masked Lover in Cupboard." Which is exactly how the story would go around, lover or no, and as such, Sarah decided it was time for a tactical retreat.

"Do you know, I think you are right. It must have been something on stage!" She trilled gaily. "I believe I've enjoyed too much Madeira tonight."

The bell rang, indicating that the next act was about to begin. And just in time, too, she thought.

"Very good miss," the footman said, his smirk in full show. "Would you like me to see you back to your seat, miss?"

"Oh no, I'm certain I can find it," she said, raising her hand in a little wave.

"Well, would you like me to take that refuse from you, miss?" the footman pressed, his eyes on her hand in the air.

Sarah looked down at the small packet, still clutched in her hand. In the candlelight of the main hall, she could see that the oilcloth was smudged and frayed, and the twine holding it together practically black with dirt. She almost dropped it, certain it was destroying her gloves. But of course, she didn't.

"No, thank you," she murmured, and hurried her way back up the stairs, slipping into her box just as the curtain began to rise.

"There you are," the Comte said, rising as she entered. "We had begun to despair of you."

"Not at all," Sarah replied. "I—ah—ran into your sister on the way back; she despairs of ever seeing *you* again." She smiled, focusing her fractured attention on the man in front of her.

The Comte laughed. "Unfortunately the next act has begun," he whispered as they took their seats. "Or should I say, fortunately, else I should have to abandon you and attend to my sister's calls."

"No need." She'd smiled shakily. "Your sister and Mrs. Hill have gone home with a headache."

Sarah had nestled herself into her seat as the Comte expressed the correct amount of worry over his sister, which gave her time enough to let her heartbeat slow down. She almost didn't notice when Bridget took her eyes off the performance long enough to whisper, "And did you lose Jack in your travels, as well as time?"

Sarah's mind snapped back to the present. Jack! She had completely forgotten about him! She scanned the Forrester box, and then, her eyes roamed the dark to the other side of the theatre boxes and landed on Jack's uniform.

"He's with the Devlins. Right where I left him," she replied nonchalantly. And then as her sister's gaze shot across the theatre, her eyebrows up in surprise, Sarah settled back into her seat and focused her eyes on the trials and tribulations of Figaro, surreptitiously sliding the oilcloth packet from her hand into her reticule. The mystery would have to wait.

Until now.

As soon as her bedroom door closed behind her, Sarah moved quickly to her white cherub covered dressing table and began tearing at the buttons of her gloves, the knot of her reticule.

"Would you like some help with that, Miss Sarah?"

Sarah's head came up so fast that she was surprised she didn't break her neck. Her maid, Molly, stood by the wardrobe, having been waiting for her mistress, ready to assist in the preparations for bed.

"What?" Sarah said sharply. Then, her tone and panic softening, "Oh, no thank you Molly, I can manage on my own."

Molly's eyebrow went up. "If you'll forgive me, Miss Sarah, you cannot reach the buttons on that dress by yourself."

Oh hell, Sarah thought, sighing. She would have to let Molly undress her, and then brush out her hair, and then send for tea, all delaying her ability to open this blooming packet!

But, Molly was right. She couldn't manage the buttons by herself.

Thus, she submitted herself to Molly's ministrations and chatter. Which before had always been soothingly pleasant, but now, it was interminable! But Sarah hummed at the right spots, and replied that the opera was very nice when asked about the evening—all in all giving Molly just enough information to keep her from suspecting anything was amiss.

Finally, finally, Sarah was in her nightdress, her hair pin free and combed through.

"Thank you Molly. I believe I'll read a little before bed. You may retire."

Molly curtsied before she left, and Sarah was at last alone with her reticule.

She tore it open, delicately sewn jet beads being loosed from their threads in the process and scattering across the floor. But it mattered little, as Sarah withdrew the packet and undid its string.

The contents of the packet were few, she laid them out on her dresser table one by one as she withdrew them.

A map, creased and yellowing along its folds, ink bleeding through the back. She could not decipher what area it was meant to depict, and there were no places named upon it.

What Sarah originally took for a timepiece turned out to be a compass—broken, with some mathematical markings scratched on the back.

And a black feather, similar to the one she had found in the hallway of the theatre.

A black feather, that led her to the man in the cupboard.

Could it be . . . ?

Sarah's mind flew back in time, to days spent playing pirates and secretly pouring over the newspapers that her father sneaked to her. To stories of glories won on the battlefields of Europe.

But, those stories, they were all myths, were they not?

Well, her mind reasoned, if they were myths, why were they in the newspaper?

But . . . if it was true, she thought, awe tingling along her spine, didn't he disappear? After the wars?

Maybe he's back. Her mind teased her.

She sat down at her dressing table with a thud.

A black feather. A masked man.

The Blue Raven.

But it was utterly ridiculous! If he was back, why on earth would he have pulled her into that cupboard . . . *why would he have kissed her like that* . . . why would he have entrusted this packet to her care?

"For heaven's sake, things like this simply do not happen to ordinary people!" she told herself in the cherubic mirror's reflection. "Do *not* get carried away."

Then again—she was hardly ordinary Sarah Forrester anymore.

"Everyone knows your name."

Sarah looked down at the items spread out across her dressing table. And suddenly she felt that most curious sensation of being pulled toward them, as if they held their own gravity, and held the promise of adventure.

Maybe she should let herself get involved.

Get carried away.

Because if he *was* the Blue Raven, and he did come back for his packet, she would see him again.

And this time, she thought, with a quickening heartbeat and a growing smile, she would be ready for him.

Ten

WHILE Sarah Forrester sat contemplating the packet on her dressing table, attempting to decipher its meaning and unaware of the game being played out around her, a spare few blocks from Upper Grosvenor Street, another game was afoot.

Namely, chess.

"Checkmate!" cried Lord Fieldstone's son, Reginald, who, at the age of seventeen, was nearly as tall as his father was wide, which was a goodly height indeed. Scheduled to start at Cambridge in the fall, he was a smart lad with a sweet tooth, which, when he was no longer the energetic teenager that sat across from his father, would lend him to the same general rotund shape as said parent.

Lord Fieldstone took a moment to study the board as his son popped a petit four (far too late in the day for such tea cakes, but Cook was indulgent to master Reggie and Lord Fieldstone alike) into his mouth.

"I'll be damned," Lord Fieldstone murmured to himself. He traced the movements on the board—Reggie had indeed bested him. At *chess*.

It had been a long time since anyone had bested him at chess. And never his son.

"I don't know whether to be livid or proud," he said, finally looking up, catching his son's grin.

"I'd go with the latter," Reggie said as he stood, stretching his frame. "After all, you taught me."

"True enough," Lord Fieldstone conceded, laying down his king and then extending his hand to his son. "Well played."

Reggie lit up like he did as a child confronted with a tray of sweets, and then, stifling any youthful enthusiasm, gravely shook his father's hand.

"Well, it's late, and I'm meeting the Burtons at the park tomorrow—we're to have a shooting match, and then Vincent wants to haunt Tattersall's. Again," Reggie said, popping one last cake into his mouth.

"Again?" Lord Fieldstone replied mildly. "Hasn't young Mr. Burton decided on a mount yet?"

"He has, but for Vincent, it's less a matter of deciding on a horse than it is convincing Mr. Burton of the expense."

"Ah," Lord Fieldstone grunted. "Well, have a good time. Just don't come home trying to convince me of the same."

"I know better than to try and convince you to purchase a new mount for me, Father—at least until I graduate university."

"With a First."

"With a First," Reggie repeated, with nary a roll of the eye. Then he bade his father a good night and whistled his way upstairs, where he would likely regale his younger siblings of the triumph of finally besting his father at chess.

He's growing up. The thought came unbidden, as Lord Fieldstone watched his son's form retreating from the doorway of the sitting room. It was amazing how quickly life passed— the son overtaking the parent, in less than the blink of Father Time's eye. And Reggie was quickly turning from happy child to a pleasant, upstanding young man. It was little more than the tick of a clock.

The thought drew his eyes to the mantle, and the clock that rested there. Good Lord, was that really the time? He still had a packet of information to get through before the briefing in the morning. While slumber sounded blissful, his soft, round wife's gentle snores pushing him like waves on the shore into restful oblivion, Fieldstone had no choice but to go up to his library and attend to business.

He headed up the stairs to the second floor, where he found a lone candlestick providing light for the hallway. Strange. Usually the wall sconces were lit until his valet had informed the household that he had gone to bed. It would have made Lord Fieldstone suspicious, but then he remembered that he had given his valet the evening off to attend the fireworks in Vauxhall, and the house must have acted accordingly, and thought nothing more of it. Picking up the candlestick, he made his way down the hall, to the large double doors with the sticky latch, and entered his library.

It was long since that Lady Fieldstone mandated Lord Fieldstone keep his hobbies confined to one room, and so, he picked the room with the most shelf space and the benefit of a double-height ceiling. After all, one never knew when they might acquire an Egyptian obelisk to round out their antiquities collection, did they?

He loved this room, with its jumble of cool marble statues—his favorite being the voluptuous Venuses, most of which didn't reach higher than his knee, in varying qualities. The paintings and bas-relief tiles that lined the walls and took up any available space made the room feel as close to a Grecian temple as one could get this side of the British Museum. Just a few more acquisitions, and he was sure to be made a fellow of the London Society of Antiquaries, he kept telling his wife, whenever she saw another crate being delivered to the house.

Sadly, he had yet to acquire an obelisk—his wife once deftly pointed out that it would be difficult to get one up the stairs and through the door, in any case—so his pièce de ré-sistance remained the sarcophagus, which sat in the center of the room. He would never part with it. He may well decide to be buried in it—if he would fit—as he had told Phillippa Worth when that lady offered to purchase it from him, shortly after her marriage to Marcus Worth.

At the thought of Sir Marcus Worth, Lord Fieldstone's brow came down, and he sought out the pile of papers his secretary had left for him on his desk. Worth had been in Calais far too long, waiting for his contact to emerge from the shadows and feed him a scrap of information. His wife, Phillippa, had given him an alibi, removing herself and the children for a country sojourn for a week or so, while he sneaked off to the French coast. But the Security Section of the War Department ground to a halt when Marcus took it upon himself to complete a mission. And if Lord Fieldstone was piecing together the information in front of him correctly, the head of the security section could not be jotting off to Calais, reliving his espionage-filled youth. He was going to be needed here, in London.

Added to that, he was worried about the boy, although it was difficult to call anyone who had gray coming in at his temples and two sons of his own a boy. But, over the past few years, Lord Fieldstone—in his capacity as head of the War Department, naturally—had come to think of Marcus as something of a son, someone he could teach, and mold.

Someone who would someday best him at chess, and take over his position.

That was a few years off, of course, but for that to happen, Marcus had to stay politically positioned, administratively inclined, and most importantly, alive.

If he wasn't back in a day or two, Lord Fieldstone would send his brother Byrne after him. Byrne Worth's ability to locate anything and anyone had served them all very well during the wars. Or worse yet, he would put a word in Phillippa's ear, and Marcus would be back in London in a heartbeat.

The man needed to be back in London. Lord Fieldstone was eager to hear what he had discovered, and whether or not the letter he was halfway through writing needed to be sent.

Instead of contemplating that letter, Fieldstone settled into his desk and picked up the packet of papers in front of him, bearing the official seal of the War Department. His brow furrowed as he leafed through the communiqués. This was not his expected correspondence. He almost rang for his secretary, before remembering that man had every other half Saturday off.

Fieldstone dug into the pages. They were reports of enemy troop movements in the Far East, counter to Bengali and British interests. There were other reports on the sharp rise in sales of gunpowder in that region. Skyrocketing prices of Indian silk—an indicator that it would soon be difficult to come by. Witness accounts of brutality against British forces.

A suspiciously sharp escalation of tensions in the region from the previous weeks.

These papers made it seem as if war was about to break out immediately.

But stranger still, that he had no note from the Governor of India about such matters.

Half Saturday be damned, Fieldstone thought. He wanted his secretary here *now*.

And Marcus Worth would get one more day in Calais, no more, Lord Fieldstone decided firmly.

When Marcus came back, he would use his keener-than-most insight and get to the bottom of this strange aberration in reports. They couldn't be right. And yet . . . hadn't there been odd rumors floating in the air of late, the word "Burma" constantly in the papers? It struck those off-key notes in his mind that sounded a warning.

Perhaps he should send Phillippa a note tonight, the sooner the better—together they would manage the latest intrigues that threatened their great Empire.

He laid down the papers and rubbed his eyes in the low candlelight and leaned back, letting himself have five spare seconds of contemplation before jumping into action.

Those five seconds would cost Lord Fieldstone dearly. For, as he felt a slight pinch, a sudden jolt of pain to his throat, he looked down, wildly finding a flash a metal, then a spill of darkness spreading down from his neck across his white shirt-front.

Blood. His blood.

His mind, rather than fighting to preserve rationality, fell into fear. Fear, because he could not cry out—just a desperate gurgle that no one would hear. Fear for his wife, sleeping upstairs. Fear for his children: Reggie, becoming a man but not there yet—not ready for this. Fear, because he had missed the signs—the lack of light in the second floor corridor, the shadows of his Grecian temple that so hid the person whose knife had slid into this flesh.

He held on long enough to turn in his seat. Just a little, just a hair. But enough to see his attacker.

It was a face he did not know.

That scared him most of all.

Eleven

THE morning after his adventure as the Blue Raven, Jackson Fletcher should have been crowing with delight. Had he been the crowing kind. And had he been delighted.

The night before had been as thrilling and terrifying as going to battle in his first year onboard the *Amorata*. He hadn't known what he was doing the entire time, but by God, he would bluff his way through it. And so, once he had reseated himself with the Devlins, and the curtain rose on act three, his heart was near to bursting out of his chest. His eyes would not focus on the story, nor would he let them stray to the box across the room, where he knew Sarah sat, her mind likely racing over and over the same events that his did (minus falling and landing on some local ruffians, of course).

The rest of the opera was interminable, although he was certain it was performed very well. But Jack's body and mind would not calm down. He had *so* much energy. From the exhilaration of pulling off his scheme? From foiling a robbery?

From the guilt?

If he spoke to Sarah at that moment, he would either burst out into nervous laughter, or he would tell her immediately and confess his sins. And sins they were.

That was the only calming gravity his body would allow to break through the rush of excitement he still felt, and it only lasted until the next wave of astonishment drove him back up to giddy heights.

The fact that he was able to remove himself from the Devlins after the last curtain finally fell without giving himself away in any measure was remarkable, but he knew he could not pull the same feat off twice. Therefore, he considered it lucky that the Forresters (lead, it seemed, by Sarah) decided to call it an early evening and head directly home.

He, on the other hand, needed to walk. Needed to burn off this feeling of elation mixed with strange dread. And so he did, pacing the streets of London briskly until he knew the Forrester house would be asleep.

Thus he had seen no one in the Forrester family until that morning at the breakfast table. Where, since he had been the last one to go to bed, he was also the last one to rise. And, therefore, was greeted by the entirety of the Forrester family upon entering the room.

"Jack, my boy," Lord Forrester said, "where did you get off to last night? I didn't see you after the second act."

"I was in the Devlins' box for the rest of the performance," he replied, trying very consciously to not stare at Sarah while he filled his plate with potatoes and ham. "And then after, I decided to meet up with Whigby and spent the rest of the evening with him." The lie he practiced all night rolled neatly off his tongue.

"Did you?" Bridget asked, her head coming up from her plate. She tilted her head to the side quizzically. "We ran into Mr. Whigby and his aunt on the way out of the theatre, he did not mention that he was meeting you."

Unready for this, Jack hemmed and hawed for a moment, certain that he would be unmasked by this one tiny lie and they would all be able to read it on his face. His fortune, however, was that Sarah was paying him only the smallest amount of attention.

"Mr. Whigby has yet to say even the barest of coherent sentences in my presence," Sarah said calmly, her eyes never even flicking to where Jack now seated himself. "Requiring him to impart important information to us might be a bridge too far."

With that, Bridget narrowed her eyes, shot her sister a look, and returned to her meal.

And with that, Jack decided that all his scheming and worry had been for naught. He shook himself imperceptibly, wanting to laugh. Why did he think that one encounter with the Blue Raven would return the Sarah Forrester of old into the welcoming arms of her family? Why did he think it would make her take interest in something other than herself? That she would fall into old patterns, forgoing the new ones?

He sighed, and glanced at Lord and Lady Forrester. Sarah's cool quip to her sister seemed to have set off another silent conversation between her parents. One that, with a sigh and a shrug, Lord Forrester again lost.

"Would you care for the paper, Jack?" Lord Forrester asked him, flustered and covering, when he saw that Jack was observing them.

"Thank you," he said, taking the proffered *Times* and promptly burying his head in it.

No, nothing would change. Bridget would continue to snipe, and Lord and Lady Forrester would continue to silently challenge each other on Sarah's behavior, because Sarah would continue to fly higher and higher, until she was so far above them all—far above who she used to be—that she couldn't see them anymore.

Even now, Bridget and Sarah were arguing over something, Jack mused, as he flipped through the pages, caught briefly on an article about reported skirmishes in the Far East, letting the noise filter over him like the meaningless squawk of seagulls.

"But theoretically, if you weren't doing anything . . ." Sarah asked, her voice peeved.

"But theoretically I am, so I am unable to assist you in . . . what is it you need help with?" Bridget replied, her tone moving from hostile to vaguely curious.

"It's just a . . . a puzzle of sorts. You have no plans for this afternoon correct?"

"You're asking me to 'help' with your puzzle because I did not receive an invitation to whatever tea or salon or boring thing you think is fun that you are attending this afternoon, correct?"

"No, I'm asking because you're better than I am at maths, and always have been," Sarah countered.

If Jack had been paying attention at that moment, he would have seen the room go still with the admission that Bridget was better at something than Sarah. He would have seen when Bridget blinked, nonplussed, and then awkwardly replied that she might be able to assist Sarah in her puzzle problem that afternoon. He might have also seen a surprised and highly approving look pass from husband to wife, and the wife's relieved expression. He might have seen those things, had his attention not been caught by a snippet of an article in front of him. The theatre review.

While acts of a sentimental nature played out on stage during The Marriage of Figaro, *perhaps the more interesting dramatics were being played out just beyond the theatre's walls. Upon leaving the theatre, more than one attendant reported seeing an unfortunate, while in her cups, recount to anyone and everyone who passed, how she had been saved from robbery by an unseen man. Although her assailants were not found, she described the man as wearing a mask and heavy cloak and being able to fly up the walls of buildings. Perhaps the most interesting bit of information was the aviary item purportedly pulled from his pocket. While the opera itself was a tepid affair, this reviewer would have appreciated the more exciting plot that this poor woman played out in her head.*

He was riveted by this scrap of information, reading it over and over again. So focused was his mind that he almost missed it when—even though he had been convinced otherwise—something *did* change.

Luckily, she brought it to his attention.

"Jack?" she asked, bringing his head up from the pages. "Can you hear me?"

"Hmm?" he replied, snapping into the present.

"I asked, when you are finished with the paper, may I have it?"

He met her eyes across the table. He was shocked, unblinking.

"Of course," he started. "Here, you can have it now."

He handed the paper to her and she took it with relish, her

eyes shining with anticipation as she began to flip through the pages, like a starving man presented with sustenance.

This time he saw the silent frown on Lady Forrester's face, cut off by an equally silent smile on her husband's. He saw Amanda read over Sarah's shoulder, and Sarah hand over those pages she did not desire to her youngest sibling. And he saw a sliver of the old Sarah Forrester peeking out from behind the Golden Lady's facade.

There was no reason his foolhardy plan should have worked.

Except that it had.

No, it was not a miraculous change, he thought, astonished. But it was a start.

Twelve

"OH, Phillippa! I'm so glad you're back!"

Sarah enthusiastically enveloped her friend in a hug, regardless of the other guests in attendance at Mrs. Braeburn's garden luncheon. Everyone knew Phillippa and Sarah Forrester to be great friends, of course. Besides, it was entirely possible that Sarah was freezing cold and merely sought the benefit of Phillippa's warm shawl.

Mrs. Braeburn, a fashionably tall woman, was well practiced in the art of being a society hostess, as her husband had been very active in the House of Commons for over two decades. However, upon her husband's decision to retire from public life a few years ago, which coincided with the marriage of her daughters, Mrs. Braeburn had found herself with nothing to display to the world, no reason to keep her hand in the game. And so, she turned to making her London town house's garden the most spectacular showcase ever.

It was, therefore, unfortunate that she chose to hold her massive welcoming party the day after a freak night of bitter frost.

Not only were the guests bundled up against the unnatural cold, but the flowers—the tulips and daffodils, the crocuses and the rose bushes that had only the tiniest of buds sprouting on them, all had their colors muted under a thin, protective layer of muslin.

But the weather be damned, it was June, and thus tea and cakes were being served alfresco.

"Yes, well, I wish it was under warmer circumstances that I am back," Phillippa replied. Then, a slight frown crossed her face. "And happier."

Sarah immediately sobered. "I'm so sorry, I didn't think. Did you know Lord Fieldstone well?"

Phillippa's eyes fell to her waist. She wore a modest gray silk underneath a dark woven Indian shawl. She was not kin to Lord Fieldstone, but Sarah knew Phillippa's penchant for happier, bolder shades and took this as her own kind of mourning.

"He worked very closely with Marcus, of course," Phillippa replied, her voice betraying a certain amount of emotion. "And I admit I was very fond of him, too."

"At least he went peacefully," Sarah consoled, laying her hand on her friend's arm. At Phillippa's sharp, quizzical look, Sarah explained. "It was his heart, was it not? That's what the newspapers said, in any case. That his heart gave out in his sleep."

"Yes, of course," Phillippa replied quickly. "But it is still a shock. Marcus is in such a state. He has so much work to do, I'm afraid he is going to disappear into the War Department all together. The only reason we are even here now is that he wanted a chance to converse with Mr. Braeburn."

Sarah's eyes flitted to where Marcus Worth had cornered a well-bundled Mr. Braeburn. Marcus seemed to be arguing a point, and Mr. Braeburn was nodding and shaking his head at turns. Then with a quick glance around, Braeburn turned and headed indoors, with Marcus following.

"What manner of things do they have to discuss?" Sarah asked, her imagination taken by the grim and determined expression on Marcus's face.

"Oh, just something to do with funding, I'm sure. Braeburn spent so much time in parliament Marcus naturally seeks out his advice. But never mind that," Phillippa said, shaking off the unwanted subject with a bright smile. "Tell me all about you! I can't believe I stayed away so long. But the boys love being in the country and I find it terribly difficult to deny them. What have you been up to?" Then with a sly look, "Or should I say, what *haven't* you been up to?"

"What do you mean?"

"For heaven's sake, child!" Phillippa said laughingly. "You told me you might take some early nights when I was unavailable to play escort, not disappear from society altogether! Upon my return to town, I was told by no less than five people, one of whom was my own housekeeper, that the Golden Lady had become housebound with illness. That I had to rush to your side to make certain you were not dying of some terrible wasting disease brought on by too much food at the Whitford banquet!"

Sarah threw back her head with laughter. "So *that's* why Lady Whitford keeps calling on me, with deeply concerned looks. How ridiculous—the banquet was weeks ago!"

"True," Phillippa's eyes were full of mirth, "but Lady Whitford is very conscious of scandal coming from her banquet." Phillippa replied cryptically before sobering from her own smiles. "Now tell me what has happened. Did your mother restrict your movements for some reason?"

Sarah pressed her lips together pensively. How much should she tell her friend? "No, nothing like that," she finally replied. "I think, perhaps, I started to find the whole thing a little . . . dull."

That, at least, was not a lie. And it had been dull. Ever since that night at the theatre a se'ennight hence, when a man in a mask had pressed a packet into her hands and then pressed his lips to hers, everything else had lost a little luster. Became grayer in the cold light of day.

But what Phillippa had said—that she had become a virtual shut-in—was patently false. She *had* been going out. But every time she went to a ball, or the park, or the opera (to which she had gone no less than three times, each time making certain to pass by a particular cupboard behind a curtain), the problem was she spent the evening looking for a man who she couldn't identify. Although, she was certain she would be able to identify him when they met again. After all, wasn't there something written about the fates, and how a soul could recognize it's mate instinctively? Well, she was convinced she would be able to do so.

Indeed, in the past week, Sarah had indulged—admittedly a little too much, but that was part of the fun, was it not?—in the fantasy of the Blue Raven.

If it was him—and it had to be him—she was well positioned to determine the truth. After all, she had scoured every word of him as a child, and still had that book of pasted-in articles . . . drat that it was still at Primrose! But she could recall with perfect clarity all those articles. She let her imagination run away with his deeds of heroism . . . his sneaking into ladies' bedrooms . . . then she let herself imagine that he might sneak into *her* bedroom . . .

And the best part was, she could indulge in these thoughts without worry. After all, it was not as if she was risking her heart in a daydream.

But suffice to say, those daydreams certainly spurred her desire to find him! She could only say he was of a certain height—maybe, he had been somewhat hunched when they met. Also, she could say he had a cultured accent . . . but that could be faked. She knew he was a single man. After all, what married man would kiss her like that? (Although . . . oh God, what if he was married?) Upon further depressing reflection, Sarah had to admit that she knew almost nothing about the Blue Raven. The single thing she knew for certain was that he wore a moustache; therefore, she spent far too much time courting the attention of gentlemen who wore moustaches. Heavens, she even considered Lord Seton and his moustache as a possibility, until the thought was too laughable to further contemplate. She may have known little about the Blue Raven, but she knew he did not wear stays. She invariably ended every conversation, or dance, utterly disappointed.

By the time she went through the card party, or ball, or theatre performance, her nerves were frayed from being on constant alert, not to mention she was entirely exhausted. Thus, she started going home earlier and earlier.

Then, she decided, why not stay home altogether? After all, the Blue Raven said he would retrieve the packet from her . . . well, how was he going to be able to do so without knowing where she would be? It was better to remain home . . . where he would know where to find her.

Besides, she and Bridget were still trying to work out the

mathematical equation on the back of the compass . . . her curiosity about the man's identity was almost as strong as her curiosity about what he was up to, and as such, she and Bridget had become embroiled in mathematical texts, atlases (they thought it might be a method by which to tell latitude and longitude), and anything else their less-than-scholarly minds lead them to. It was the first time in her life that Sarah had wished she'd gone further in her studies, past what was dictated proper for young ladies.

"Dull?" Phillippa repeated, pulling Sarah, blinking, out of her reverie.

"Well, y-yes," she stuttered. "I mean, none of it really matters, does it? The parties, the gowns, they can be fun. But if you know you are not to meet with someone of some worth, then it's all cake and no stew." She crinkled her nose. "Do you understand my meaning?"

"I do," Phillippa replied carefully. "Such notions are often why I enjoy country respites with my sons almost as much as they do. But I did not think you would suffer from exhaustion with your fame so quickly." Then Phillippa stepped closer and, dipping her head, lowered her voice, glancing aside for the potential of prying ears. "But you do know the importance of keeping up your current level of . . . er, social interaction, don't you?"

"Of course I do," Sarah was quick to say. "And do not think that I impugn all of your good advice, Phillippa. I doubt I would have survived a single week in society without your assistance. But I . . ."

"But nothing, my dear! You've had your respite. Now that you've had the entire town rabid for your appearance you have to capitalize on it. Return brighter and better than ever. I have even been told that you have refused *two* invitations to go riding with the Comte de Le Bon."

Sadly, as the Comte was without a moustache, Sarah thought it wiser to spend the time she would have been riding, working on deciphering the clues. She did not mean for him to think he had lost her favor, but what other option was there?

Besides, if she had to hear the story of how he walked out of a Burmese prison one more time . . .

"If the Golden Lady has thrown him over as one of her

favorites," Phillippa continued, "we should be finding you a new one . . ."

Phillippa would have continued on in that vein, blithely dictating Sarah's return to form (apparently the Braeburns' garden party was a good start, but not a spectacular enough one, and her dress was too yellow and not enough gold—this would have to be taken up with Madame LeTrois) if not for the look that inevitably crossed Sarah's face, caught by Phillippa's keen eye.

"Unless you have found a new favorite, all on your own," Phillippa said, her shrewdness making Sarah blush uncontrollably.

"I don't know what you mean," Sarah tried, futilely.

"You've met someone!" Phillippa cried, loud enough to draw the attention of people huddling for warmth nearby. Shocked into propriety, she took Sarah's arm and practically pulled her into the house.

"Come with me," she said in a rush. "This conversation requires privacy. And something warmer than this tea."

Once the privacy and warmer substances were located (the Braeburns' library and its sideboard provided both of these quite neatly), Phillippa sat Sarah down.

"Tell me everything."

Sarah knew she should demur, and say that there was nothing to tell. But the truth was . . .

"Oh, Phillippa, I've been absolutely bursting to tell someone since it happened!" She began, clutching her friend's hands tightly. "And I couldn't tell anyone—not my mother, not my sisters, not anyone. But I'm sure I can tell you. Can I tell you?"

"You haven't told anyone about him?" Phillippa replied, alarmed. Likely shocked by the strength of Sarah's grip. "For heaven's sake, what do you mean, 'since it happened'?"

"Since we met! I cannot even describe him," Sarah began dreamily.

"Well, why don't you give it a try," was the bemused reply. "Tell me where you met."

"At the theatre—*Figaro*—and it was only for a moment, but it was magical. Simply magical." She bit her lip, remembering for the thousandth time those few minutes in the cupboard of the opera house.

"He wears a moustache—" she began.

"Well, we will simply have to make him shave. Nothing more passé than a moustache."

But even Phillippa's comments could not stop Sarah's reminiscing. "He's tall—but not too tall—and well formed, or at least I think he is, I've only ever seen him in looser clothes."

"Then we shall have to get him to a tailor if he's to be seen with you on his arm."

"I don't know if he'll ever let himself be seen with me on his arm," she replied darkly. "Indeed, I don't even know if I'll ever see him again."

"See him?" Phillippa scoffed. "Of course you shall see him again. I shall arrange it."

"I don't think you can." Sarah covered her mouth and closed her eyes against the pain of it. "You see, Phillippa—I do not even know his name."

Phillippa cocked her head to one side. "Do you mean—you were not introduced? I'm afraid I am terribly confused. Sarah, have you even properly met the man?"

"I . . . I don't know." Sarah took a deep breath. And then . . . it all came out. "I need someone—I need *you* to tell me I have not gone mad, and that I'm not imagining things. Although I know I'm not imaging things, else how did I end up with the packet and the puzzle I cannot possible solve?"

"Sarah!" Phillippa exclaimed, steadying Sarah's arms at her sides. Apparently she had been gesticulating rather wildly. "I am half an inch from slapping some sense into you. Should I call for some wine?"

"Yes . . . no . . . I don't know anymore. All I know is that the Blue Raven handed me a packet of items in a cupboard at the theatre, then kissed me senseless, and I have not been able to think of anything since."

Phillippa's hands froze on her arms. "Did you say Blue Raven?"

Sarah nodded sadly. "Which is why I couldn't tell anyone. Not only must I protect him, no one would believe me." She looked up into Phillippa's wide, unblinking eyes. Shocked into silence. "And you do not believe me, either."

"No," Phillippa replied carefully. "I believe you. But I think you should start over. From the beginning. Tell me exactly how you met and what happened. Er, slowly."

And so she did. Sarah told her everything, from finding the feathers in the hall of the opera, to being pulled into the cupboard. To the little packet of clues, and how she had tried to solve the clues that were laid out before her. To staying in, because she knew that she would have to be in a place where she could be found. To . . . well, to be honest she stopped short from telling Phillippa how it felt to be kissed like that.

Really, truly kissed. Hard and panicked and thrilling all at once. She'd been kissed before, of course. She had been affianced to Jason, certain things had been permitted. A peck here, a sweet caress there. But he was always so careful with her.

The Blue Raven had not been careful. Why should he? After all, he was the Blue Raven; he had more important things to do that worry about bruising some poor girl's mouth.

It was incredible.

But the mottled blush across her cheek and the awkwardly high pitch her voice reached must have been all the further explanation needed, as Phillippa had begun to turn an alarming shade of white.

"It's completely unbelievable," Sarah finished miserably, seeing her friend's pallor.

"No!" Phillippa cried, quick to assure Sarah by clasping her hand. "Not unbelievable, just a little . . . curious. Yes, curious is the correct word, I should think."

"I just . . . I feel like there has to be a reason, something fated, that brought me to that cupboard that night. There has to be a reason he trusted me enough with his little bundle of secrets. But I don't know who he is or if he's married—good God, what if he's married?—and he said he was going to come and retrieve his items, but I haven't seen him in over a week, and now I despair that he'll never—"

"Dear, you're rambling again," Phillippa calmed her. Then, a serious, shrewd look overtook her features. "Over a week you say?"

"Yes, we went to *Figaro* on . . . Saturday last, I believe, and then he disappeared."

"Last Saturday," Phillippa murmured to herself. Then shaking her head free of any musings, refocused her gaze on Sarah. She looked for a moment as if she were about to say something of grave import, of absolute necessity, but such desperate words would never find their way from her lips, because at that moment, a cursory knock sounded on the door, and Sir Marcus Worth let himself in.

"There you are darling," he said, his eyes drawn naturally to his wife, like a lark to sunshine. But his face did not reflect any such light—in fact there was only grim determination. "I'm afraid we have to go, with what Braeburn just told me it's worse than I—" At his wife's conspicuous cough, Sir Worth came out of his own head, and seemed to realize he and his wife were not alone.

"Ah. Miss Forrester," he began, quickly turning into the charming and affable gentleman that Sarah knew him to be. "Lovely to see you again. I hope you've been well without my Phillippa to keep you company."

"Quite well, thank you," Sarah demurred.

"Indeed," Phillippa replied, with a sparkle to her eyes. "She's been quite well."

Sir Worth tilted his head, far more able to decipher his wife's tones than anyone else. "You've just been bringing my wife up to speed on all the London gossip, I hope, and that is why she looks like she is about to burst from a secret?"

Sarah looked desperately between her friend and her friend's husband. *Please*, she pleaded with her eyes, *please don't tell him what I've just told you. Please keep my secret.*

"Now, Marcus, you know we don't sully ourselves with gossip." Phillippa replied, nodding coolly at Sarah.

And with that, Sarah breathed a sigh of relief. Of course Phillippa wouldn't spread tales about the Blue Raven and the cupboard and the packet of clues. Her secrets were all safe.

And as Sarah was content, she bid adieu to the quickly departing Worths, and lent herself to the task of warming up enough before braving the rest of Mrs. Braeburn's garden party. And so, turned to the library fire, she missed the serious exchanged glances between husband and wife as they waved good-bye from the door; the looks that said in absolutely no words at all:

We need to talk. Now.

Thirteen

WELL, it could have been worse, Jack told himself as he stalked out of the Royal Navy offices at Somerset House, almost oversetting a gentleman hunched over his cane. But he couldn't be brought out of his head enough to notice—indeed, his body was somewhat numb. Yes, indeed, it could have been worse.

How could it have been worse, one might ask?

Well . . . it could have been worse if they had placed him on half pay immediately. Yes, that would have definitely been worse, seeing as his current five pounds a month was barely sustaining him, and he was living in London on the charity of the Forresters. But kindly, they had allowed his salary—and all the rest of the crew—to extend another month complete.

It could have been worse if they stripped him of his uniform then and there—especially as Jack had no desire to walk home naked.

It could have been worse if the *Amorata* had been blown to pieces in combat all those years ago, like her sisters, and Jack had never lived past the age of sixteen. The fact that she made it this far, and that he did with her, was a miracle.

Oh, who the hell was he kidding, he thought, his brow

coming down as he wrapped his cloak around his shoulders, shielding himself from the unseasonable cold that had settled over London in the last few days. Although, it could have been all warmth and sunshine out and Jack would have still felt like wrapping the cloak around himself, protecting his body against further slights and blows.

Because the worst had happened.

It was official. Word had come down from the Admiralty of the Navy.

The *Amorata*, his home for nine years, was to be fully decommissioned—her hull and flanks, her cannons and boards, broken up for scrap, anything worth keeping to be reused by the armory in outfitting newer, faster ships. Although the Royal Navy wasn't much in the business of building those these days.

His beautiful lady wasn't even to be kept in ordinary, held ready in case Britain required more support at sea. No, she was past salvation.

And all hope was gone.

What am I going to do now?

Interestingly, even as that question echoed through his head, Jack felt a strange sense of calm. Maybe his mind, even though he willed the opposite outcome, had been preparing him for this eventuality over the past few weeks. Maybe, he had made peace with it. Or maybe he had been too preoccupied with his Blue Raven farce of late to give his and the *Amorata*'s future much thought.

Indeed, while Sarah had spent the past week trying to solve an insolvable puzzle, Jack had been faced with a large puzzle—namely that of Sarah herself.

Jack's state of being rocketed wildly between amazement and guilt at his actions as the Blue Raven. So much so that he found it almost impossible to be around her.

Because he shouldn't have done it—the meanness of the prank outpaced the problem it was meant to solve.

Because it worked—for the past week, Sarah found herself far too preoccupied to spend much effort on being the Golden Lady.

Because of that kiss.

Bruising, rough, and thrilling, it was a kiss that sent light-

ning through his body. A kiss that came out of nowhere . . .
except when he did it, Jack's brain caught up to the rest of his
body, and he realized that it was not impromptu. That he had
been thinking about kissing Sarah since . . .

Well, suffice to say, he found it difficult to be around her.

The irony of which was that for the past week, Sarah had
never been so difficult to avoid!

She *stayed home*. She *refused invitations*. How the hell was
he supposed to avoid someone who was always underfoot?

Even though she had not forgiven him for their fight and,
when they were in the same room, their conversation was as
strained as ever, Jack knew his reasons for curtness were not
the same as hers.

So what else could a man do, but go out? He walked; he
wandered. Hell, he even paid a call or two on Juliana Devlin,
just to keep up appearances. He brought Whigby with him, as
Jack himself was not up to conversation, and Whigby always
was.

But mostly, he spent most of his days haunting the naval
offices at Somerset House, awaiting word of the *Amorata*. And
while he waited, chatting amiably with other officers, making
certain that all of the *Amorata*'s reports and logs were filled
properly, sometimes popping over to the Historical Society to
visit with Lord Forrester, his mind would drift. Drift into a
cape, a half mask, a false moustache . . . a close little room
held still in the moonlight, and a warm body, trembling beneath his touch, in fear, in fury, in wonder . . .

But today, word of the *Amorata*'s fate came.

And his own.

But for whatever reason—possibly the one his mind tended
to drift to—while the blow stung, it did not destroy him. All it
left him with was possibility.

What do I do now? He asked himself again, as he walked
along the banks of the Thames, walked without purpose but,
thanks to the river's lines, with direction. He was headed toward the shipyards.

He had nearly a decade of on-ship experience. He was a
gentleman. Perhaps he could find work upon a merchant vessel. He would have to give up his position in the navy to do
so—foregoing even the measly income of an officer on half

pay—but it would be a living. Of course, the purpose of transporting goods was hardly the same as protecting the Empire.

He let his feet carry him west, until his eyes began to burn from the sun moving from midday to setting. He ambled in pursuit of purpose until he came within view of the London docks.

Blearily, he blinked in the sun, realizing he'd walked all the way from Somerset House to Wapping.

The London docks were new additions to the Thames River—finished sometime in the last decade, they dug in canals, inlets, to allow ships to dock without the fear of being set upon by river thieves—not to mention that room had gotten a bit tight in recent years, with the onslaught of shipping from the many corners of the British Empire. He watched for some minutes as a clipper vessel was unloaded, barrels upon barrels of wine, as well as pallets and huge crates labeled Spices and Coffee moved from their place in the holds by an elaborate pulley system onto the docks by experience crewmen.

It was as if his feet knew where to take him. His own despair only extended to his conscious brain, not his body. Because his body, his feet, knew exactly what he should and would do.

He located the Custom Office, a neat box of a building with two stories, that housed all the comings and goings of some of England's most prominent merchants. Surely, if he applied within, he would find that some ship, going somewhere, would have need of an officer with his years of experience.

But he hesitated in taking those steps. Because while he argued with himself about the prejudice against men in business versus the more gentlemanly pursuit of defending his country on ship (honestly, he was the son of a vicar no longer living, his claim to the life of a gentleman was never that great), his great wonder was . . .

Would he find a purpose there? And would it be enough?

Somewhere in his core, he knew the answer to both questions.

And so, he hesitated. And because of that hesitation, Jackson Fletcher's life would become a great deal more complicated.

Since he hesitated, Jack's eyes strayed from the Custom

Office to the movements of the people that made their way around the docks. His gaze fell upon a familiar shape.

Falling out of an opera house window is a decidedly rare occurrence. Thus, one is bound to remember the face of the person they landed on.

The large gentleman who had kindly broken his fall—whom the other, smaller thugs had called Big Ned—leaned just outside the door of a nearby building. By the jubilant noise within, and the happy stagger of some of the gentlemen who exited, Jack guessed it was a pub. It was, after all, the docks at sunset, and the businesses that lined the docks tended to cater to the men that worked them.

As one such hopefully off-duty seaman tripped merrily out the door, he was accompanied by a comely looking young woman, the color of her dress and the prominent display of her breast marking her . . . well, something other than a gently bred lady. Jack watched as she launched the man on her arm out the door, waving him off as he shook his shoulders and tried to walk straightaway down the backstreets into the maze of London's East End.

She turned to go back into the pub, but seemed startled to find Big Ned waiting by the door. Words were exchanged. And up until this point, the goings-on at the door of the unnamed pub may have been none of his business, but then he saw as Big Ned roughly grabbed the young lady's arm and dragged her around the corner into an alley.

And suddenly, it very much became his business.

Jack moved quickly and lithely toward the pub, making sure to remain out of view from the alley. He sidled up alongside the building and edged himself to the mouth of the alley, peeking in.

"You have to pay for your protection, Alice," Big Ned growled, his hand at Alice's throat, her back up against a wall.

"I dunna need anything from you Ned, or any man—I'm a waitress, not a whore!"

As Big Ned's grip tightened on Alice's throat, and her spirited responses were reduced to gurgles, Jack decided it was time to intervene.

"I don't suppose you learned anything from the last time I found you threatening girls, Ned," Jack said, with a surprising amount of bravado. He let his voice echo through the alley before he stepped into view. The sun behind him cast a long shadow, almost touching the shadowy depths at the back of the alley. Ned turned to him and blinked, either surprised by the interruption or rendered temporarily blind by the sun behind Jack. But then, the larger man's brain clicked into function.

"What's that, then?" Ned called out.

He sported a bruise on one temple—the side of him that had hit the ground during their last encounter—faded to a yellow and green after more than a week. All it did was make him look more intimidating.

"The last time I found you threatening girls. Don't you remember? Although, I wouldn't be surprised if there is a hole in your memory. Being knocked unconscious will do that to a man."

Jack watched as comprehension dawned. Surprisingly, it took less time than expected. However, as Ned focused more on the figure at the entrance of the alley, his grip loosened on Alice, and she managed to wriggle free and run. She didn't move fast, but her scurrying must have caught Ned off guard, because she managed to make it past Jack and out of the alley and back into the safety of the pub before Ned had even moved.

"'Ere now. You just cost me a pigeon." Ned narrowed his eyes at Jack.

"According to her, she wasn't your bird to begin with," Jack countered, all the blood pumping to his extremities, his body about to jump out of its skin. Instead he took a single slow step forward, and braced himself for the brawling that was inevitable.

But not before one last surprise.

Because just then, not two, but three other men—different men than the superstitious pair that had scrambled from him outside of the opera house, bigger men—stepped out of the shadows at the back of the alley.

"I found some new associations." Big Ned grinned. "Smarter ones."

Well, it seemed Big Ned was not only the brawn, but the brains of the operation, Jack thought with a betraying gulp of fear.

It was not the first time in recent history that Jack questioned his own intelligence. But it was perhaps, the strongest example of his newfound ability to get in over his head.

Now in that moment, time did him the favor of freezing in its tracks, allowing Jack a split second to think.

He could run. He had about twenty feet separating them, and he certainly could lose them in the public mire of the docks.

And he did not have the element of surprise or advantage of position in this fight—and it was not as if their last encounter could be considered a fight to begin with. Not that he'd even been in that many fights, period. He was usually the voice of logic, talking an inebriated friend and fellow *Amorata* crew member out of something stupid. But those occasions when he'd had to become involved, the odds were generally more even—certainly not one to four.

But then, Alice's face shot into his memory. As did the face of the girl being harassed outside of the opera house. And suddenly, out of nowhere, his memory assaulted him with the look that Sarah Forrester had given him, after he had so thoroughly kissed her. All shock and hope all at once. Looking up to her hero. As if she had just realized in that moment that he might be a hero instead of a villain.

Yes, he could have run away.

But he was in no mood for running.

Instead, Jack ran toward them, at ramming speed, closing the gap between him and Big Ned. The alley was narrow, and he had them cornered there. That was his advantage. Another advantage was (he assumed) his greater agility. As he ran toward them, he put his foot up on the rough brick of the alley wall, launching him higher than Big Ned's head.

How's that for the element of surprise? Jack thought spitefully, before tackling Big Ned to the ground.

This is where any advantage Jack could lay claim to ended.

He pummeled at the larger man, his fists making contact with the remains of the bruise on the side of his head, his ribs, his jaw.

Now, unfortunately, when Jack landed on Ned this time, it wasn't with enough force to knock him out. So he had to deal with the fact that Ned was not an inert mass, and had the wherewithal (not to mention strength) to turn the tables and flip Jack onto his back.

It was Ned's turn to land the blows, his meaty fist taking the wind out of Jack when it connected with his solar plexus. He heard a crack when Ned's fist came down on his nose and Jack tasted blood.

He had to get unpinned; it was his only chance. So as the three other men held back, circling them and laughing like hyenas, Jack wriggled his arms free from under Ned's weight. When Ned reared back to deliver what was sure to be an almighty blow, Jack brought both of his hands up in a modified upper cut, catching Ned just under the chin and sending him reeling back. Ned's hold on his legs then loosened enough for Jack to bring up a knee in one swift motion, that single motion that strikes fear into the core of every man everywhere. Jack's knee connected with his target, and Ned crumpled into a ball and rolled off of Jack.

The hyenas circling them stopped laughing.

Jack scooted back in the alley to where there was a pile of debris from the pub—empty crates and broken chairs, and the like, evidence that this was a lively establishment, indeed.

"Kill . . . him . . ." Ned wheezed from his position on the ground.

Jack grabbed the first thing his hand found in the pile of debris—a chair leg—and set to the task of defending himself.

But to no avail. He swung wildly, the chair leg connecting with one of the men in the stomach, another on the back of his shoulder. But three to one were not odds that his inexperience could handle. Eventually one of them caught his modified club mid-swing, and he was forced to again resort to his fists. That but closed the distance between them. Six fists to two.

And three-to-one were not good enough odds.

They got his arms, two of them holding them out as the third man worked his ribs—ribs that had yet to fully recover from his fall out the opera house window. Then, the one who was assaulting his ribs must have gotten tired of all the work involved, because he took a blade from a sheath hidden beneath his coat.

"We softened up the meat enough, boys." He grinned, his mouth a pit of black teeth and grime. "Time to stick the pig."

The hyenas began their merciless cackle again, as Ned's voice came from behind them.

"No, boys. He's mine."

Ned lurched to his feet and stumbled over to them. He took the knife out of Black-tooth's hand, and ran it over the buttons of Jack's uniform jacket.

"This'll be fun." He leaned close, his breath sticky and warm at Jack's neck. "I ain't killed a man in uniform since the war."

"Neither have I," came a voice from behind Ned.

All five men blinked and turned their attention to the man who had come to stand behind Ned. He was dressed neatly, if plainly, his black hair gleaming with blue light in the setting sun. He carried a brass-handled cane.

A brass-handled cane that he brought down on Big Ned's temple.

"However, I have the ability to tell a friendly uniform from the enemy," he drawled, as Ned fell in a heap, face-first into the pile of broken crates, bottles and chair legs.

Then the stranger looked Jack dead in the eye, and quirked a winged eyebrow.

He didn't have to be told twice.

Using the surprise appearance to his advantage, Jack wrested his arms free from his captors and rammed his body against the thug to his right, slamming him into the wall of the alley. Two precise blows to that man's head and he was on the ground, unmoving.

Jack then turned his attention to the two men left.

Although, he didn't really need to.

The stranger was holding his own against them, as graceful with his cane as the most skilled fencer was with a sword. He threw one into the other, both of them hitting the wall hard. One went down, leaving him with one last, slightly deluded and terribly outpaced thug to fight.

But as the stranger traded blows with him, Jack watched as the second, downed thug—it was Black-tooth—staggered to his feet, and went to Big Ned's prostrate form . . . and retrieved his knife.

Jack didn't have time to think out his actions; he just did them. Using all the strength left in his body, he grabbed hold

of the rough bricks of the wall, his fingers and toes finding
grooves enough to hold his counter weight. He moved quickly,
up, and up again, and just as Black-tooth raised the knife
above his head, about to bring it down on the stranger's back,
Jack cried out.

"Oy!"

Black-tooth turned, and Jack launched himself off the wall,
tackling Black-tooth to the ground. And just as had happened
the last time he had landed on someone from above, Black-
tooth was rendered unconscious upon impact with the ground.
And the knife skittered across the alley, away from where it
would be of use to anyone.

The last thug, who was incidentally the youngest looking,
took stock of how the odds had shifted. And ran.

The stranger watched bemusedly as he disappeared out the
mouth of the alley.

"Finally, some intelligence." The stranger shrugged to
himself. Then he turned to Jack, and watched, equally bemused, as Jack came to his feet and shook the alley dirt from
his cloak and uniform—the former of which was likely beyond repair at this point.

"You should have shown the same intelligence before the
fight even began," the stranger said to him, as Jack approached.

"I'm inclined to agree," Jack wheezed. "I cannot thank you
enough for your intervention," he said gratefully, and extended
his hand. "Lieutenant Jackson Fletcher," he introduced himself. "A pleasure."

A sardonic smile stretched the stranger's features, his eyes
taking on the fire of the sunset, making him look like the devil
himself. He took Jack's hand and shook it. But he did not, as
expected, let go. Instead, he held it in a death grip, and his
voice as cold as ice, introduced himself.

"The Blue Raven. And really, the pleasure's all mine."

Shock coursing though his veins was the last thing Jack
would remember, before that brass-handled cane came down
swiftly upon his head, and blackness overtook him.

Fourteen

"That'll hurt like the son of a bitch it is."

The words came to him through the filter of haze and time, blackness giving way to a dim gray in his vision.

He was aware of a cold, hard surface, slammed up against his left cheek and shoulder. He could feel the rough drag of rope binding his hands and legs tight. He was strapped to some straight, rigid object—a chair, he imagined—but lying on his side.

He moaned as he came to, completely now, throbbing pain shooting up and down his left shoulder, compressed between his own weight and the floor.

"What?" Jack rasped, his eyes searching the darkness, finally falling on a bit of movement. A flash of gold, catching the faintest stream of light, from a tin lantern hung above him. It was the brass-handled cane, last seen heading swiftly for his left temple, being spun between a pair of hands.

"You fell over. In your chair." It was the stranger's voice. He leaned into the light, his expression lacking any humor. "I merely commented that it would hurt."

"But at least it had the benefit of waking you up," came another voice, similar, but less stark and forbidding than the first. And as the owner of that voice stepped into the light, Jack realized, it did not belong to a stranger.

"Sir Marcus Worth!" Jack's surprise was masked by his pained speech and decidedly uncomfortable position. He had not seen Sir Marcus since their short conversation at the Whitford banquet. "I'd not realized you had returned to town." Then, because manners were drilled into him as surely as latitude and longitude, he asked, "I take it Lady Worth is well?"

"I am pleased to see you again," Sir Marcus said, leaning down from his impossible height to find Jack's eye. "Although, the circumstances are rather unfortunate."

"Yes, well," Jack exhaled. "I might have difficulty rising to greet you. Unless you could convince your friend over there to untie me."

Sir Marcus shot a look to the stranger—whom Jack suddenly remembered with a flash had identified himself as the bloody Blue Raven. A myth made flesh, who quirked his brow in reply to the taller gentleman's silent inquiry.

One thing was for damn sure. Jackson Fletcher had just gotten himself in way over his head.

Using all the strength he had left, Jack rolled himself onto his front, then reared up onto his knees. As the two gentlemen looked on, decidedly bemused, Jack—still well attached to the chair—jumped from his knees to his feet, and then rocked back just enough to sit down in the chair. Properly this time.

"Agile," Sir Marcus drawled, taking off his spectacles and wiping them on his coat before replacing them on his nose.

"You should see him climb a wall," the Blue Raven replied.

"Explains a great deal," Sir Marcus agreed.

"Like how he managed to climb up the wall of the theatre."

"And how he managed to climb into Lord Fieldstone's library, and slit his throat."

"Which do you think he did first?" the Blue Raven asked, conversationally.

"Oh, the theatre of course. Lord Fieldstone himself had attended that evening, but left early. I suppose you missed your chance with him there," Marcus replied.

"And then had to sneak into his house later on," the other man finished. "Lucky his residence is only a few short blocks from the Forresters."

"Must have been surprising having been walked in on by Miss Forrester while changing costume. You seemed to have talked your way out of that one though. Well done."

"Thank you," Jack replied automatically. Then realizing what he said, not to mention being confused beyond all reckoning, he tried to backtrack. "Wait—I didn't mean that I—"

But both men were on him too quickly for any excuses.

"So it was your plan to attack Lord Fieldstone that night at the theatre?" Sir Marcus asked. "Missed him when he left early and had to revise your plan?"

"No!" Jack cried.

"But you said—"

"I've never attacked Lord Fieldstone! Or planned to! I thought the man died of a heart seizure."

The Blue Raven again looked at Sir Marcus. "Well, his heart likely seized when he realized his throat had a gaping hole slashed in it."

"What my brother means is," Marcus interrupted, "the story was . . . massaged. To keep public panic from erupting."

"He's your brother?" Jack asked dazedly.

"Did he not introduce himself properly? Tsk-tsk, Byrne." Marcus replied with a smile.

"He said he was . . ." Jack's voice trailed off.

"I'm retired," Byrne Worth shrugged, his cane rolling steadily between his hands.

As the brothers Worth each gave a small chuckle, enjoying their private joke, Jack thought it might be prudent to take stock of his surroundings.

They seemed to be in a basement of some kind, the moistness of the air and the stones of the wall told him they likely weren't too far from the docks. No windows, but there was a set of stairs. That was all he could see in the light of the single lantern. His shoulder, having broken his fall, felt like a dozen knives were being stabbed in and out of his wounded flesh.

So. He was in a basement. By the docks. Hurt but not incapacitated. And Sir Marcus Worth, head of the powerful Security Section and now likely de facto head of the War Department, had a brother, who during the Peninsular War acted as the anonymous agent of the Crown known as the Blue Raven.

And they were interrogating him.

"How did you know I was . . ." he began, unsure of how to phrase his query.

"How did we know that you have been the man running around dressed up as the Blue Raven, foiling rapes and robberies in dark alleys and seducing the Golden Lady in theatre cupboards?" Sir Marcus asked.

"It sounds strange when you put it like that," he grumbled back.

The corner of Sir Marcus's mouth turned up. "Miss Forrester told us." At Jack's shocked expression, he continued. "Well, she told my wife. And she didn't give us your name, as she doesn't know that it's you, after all. But she did tell us all about meeting the Blue Raven at the opera, the night Lord Fieldstone died. And about the moustache."

"Knowing a fair bit about assuming disguises, we checked with local theatres and wig shops, to see if anyone purchased a false moustache in the week or so previous to the opera." He looked at Jack pityingly. "A naval officer purchasing a false moustache tends to stand out in people's memory. After that, it really wasn't that difficult to track you down."

Jack blew out a breath, exasperated. It seemed the one bit of disguise he had invested in to hide himself from Sarah's discerning eye was the piece that gave him away.

"Of course, we didn't really know until today," Marcus continued. "Byrne was following you for days."

"He was?" Jack asked, surprised.

Byrne Worth cocked his head to one side. "You didn't notice, ever? Not even when you left Somerset House today? I could have sworn you found me out."

The man he had almost run into. Hunched, aged, with the cane. He had been still when everyone else was moving or talking. He was not looking at Jack, but his posture had been so tense, in hindsight Jack could see he had been . . . paying attention.

"I did," Jack began slowly. "But I didn't think . . ."

"Of course not. And that's what allowed me to follow you for hours." Byrne smiled. "That and your blessedly slow pace," he added, indicating his cane.

However, before Jack could say anything in his own defense, there was a knock at the door (or at least Jack assumed there was a door) at the top of the stairs.

The brothers looked at each other again—the conversations they were able to have without speech mystified him—and Marcus gave Jack a quick nod.

"Excuse me, would you? Won't be but a moment."

And with that, Sir Marcus took the stairs two at a time, due more to his long gait than any urgency.

Leaving Jack alone with the obviously more dangerous element.

Who was staring at him the way a snake in the grass watched its prey.

Just stare him down, Jack told himself, trying to will himself into leveling the playing field. *Just keep calm.*

"Don't do it," his captor advised calmly.

"Don't do what?"

"Scream for help," he replied.

"Well, there would be little point." Jack remarked. As Byrne raised a quizzical brow, Jack continued. "If Sir Marcus is comfortable enough moving about . . . wherever we are, the structure is likely under his control. Add to that, I can't hear a thing beyond this room; therefore, I doubt anyone could hear in."

Byrne blinked a moment. And then, in the most chillingly possible way, smiled at Jack.

"A very coolheaded assessment. You're doing better than expected, you realize. Most people, when locked in a basement with the Blue Raven, end up blubbering."

"Maybe we can save that for later," Jack quipped, his levity earning a half smile from Byrne, but no reprieve from his intense stare. "Mr. Worth, I apologize. I didn't mean to step on your toes. Dressing up as the . . ." Jack cleared his throat, and started again. "I didn't even think you were alive any longer."

"A common misconception. And it's *Sir* Byrne Worth." Byrne replied, his eyes never leaving Jack's. Then he cocked his head to one side. "Why did you do it?"

Jack took a deep breath, kept his gaze on his interrogator, who was in half shadow.

"For her."

"For Miss Forrester?" Byrne asked. "She's fashionable enough to warrant a little foolishness from some young idiots, but somehow I don't think such stupidity comes naturally to you."

"I can't explain it," Jack blew out a rush of air. "I thought it would be a way to . . . return her to herself."

And so he told the tale. Of how Sarah had undergone marked changes in manner, and how they had fought. He told him of how she used to delight in Blue Raven stories and how he had rationalized that if anything would bring her back to herself, it would be this.

As Byrne listened to Jack's tale, he crossed his arms over his chest and leaned back in his chair.

Finally, when Jack had let the tale trail off, Byrne sat forward again, bringing his face back into the light.

He was laughing.

"My boy, that is the biggest pile of bullshit I've ever heard."

"It's the truth—" Jack began, but was cut off with a sharp movement of Byrne's hand.

"No. The truth is, Sarah Forrester got under your skin. And you couldn't stand it. So you devised a way to get under hers."

As Jack tried to rationalize his intentions, he became increasingly aware of a series of random, pitiful sounds emanating from his mouth. "But . . . I . . . Wait, that's . . . No . . ." Until finally his brain came back to him and he managed to form a complete sentence.

"Perhaps we can revisit the issue of Lord Fieldstone? I didn't kill the man, I swear." Jack blurted. "I wouldn't even know how."

"It's not that difficult," Byrne replied, cool. "I think you could have figured it out."

"Er . . . Yes, but why?" Jack argued. "Why on earth would I have done such a thing? I met the man precisely once in my life, and had no notion of ever seeing him again."

"Yes, why?" Byrne drawled. "Perhaps we should enlighten the lieutenant on just what he's stumbled into."

"I'd be happy to," came Marcus's voice from the top of the stairs.

❧

"How much do you know about Burma?" Sir Marcus asked. His affect was casual, but his intentions far from it.

But Jack knew barely anything about Burma. And that is what he told them.

"I know fuck all about Burma," Jack replied sharply.

"I see your sailor is coming through," Byrne said laughing. But Marcus's face was impassive.

"I think you know more than that," Sir Marcus replied quietly as he took a chair out of the shadows and sat directly in front of Jack. "In fact, you're the one who alerted us to the Comte de Le Bon's seeming lack of knowledge of the area."

"This is about the Comte?" Jack asked, becoming increasingly bewildered.

"We'll come back to him. Again I ask, what do you know about Burma?"

"I know what I've studied in maps." Jack sighed. "We spent several years in the Indies, but never made port in Burma."

"Of course you didn't. British India and Burma aren't exactly on the best of terms." Sir Marcus said genially. "I know little more than you, of course, but it seems that England is about to learn a great deal."

And then, Sir Marcus continued with a story of such global proportions that Jack had to acknowledge that, yes, indeed, he was in way over his head.

Burma and British India were no friends, that was a well-documented fact. The reason for this was that Burma liked to acquire new territory as much as Britain did, but differed on one material point. In whatever territory the Burmese conquered, such as Assam and Manipur, they took the occupants as slaves. When said occupants fled across the border to the sanctuary of Bengal or any of the East Indian states, Burma invaded, to "recover their property." The governor of India was annoyed by this. But even as he offered truce after truce, Burma persisted in pushing the boundaries of their kingdom, especially in the direction of British India.

In other words, they were spoiling for a fight.

"But the governor-general of India, is not inclined to give it to them. So we keep negotiating for peace resolutions, and they keep defying them." Sir Marcus lectured. "The head of the War Department receives constant updates and missives about the state of affairs in all corners of the British Empire, including those corners adjacent to Burma."

"As one would assume," Jack replied slowly.

"On Fieldstone's desk, when he died, were reports of heightened conflicts in Burma . . . extremely heightened, more bombastic and alarming than we had previously seen until now." He paused in his speech. "Do you follow so far?"

Jack blinked once. "I still don't know what this has to do with Lord Fieldstone . . . or me."

"Lord Fieldstone is . . . er, was the head of the War Department." Marcus intoned.

"Yes, I'm aware."

Finally Byrne sat forward, his drawl cutting to the point. "The knife he was killed with was left behind. It was a *dha*."

"A *dha*." Jackson repeated, and suddenly, everything made sense. Why he was being lectured on Burmese history, and why *he* of all people was sitting here, tied to chair. A *dha* was a sword. But more specifically, it was a sword from the Indies. Jack had seen numerous *dha* in the shops whenever they docked in Bombay or the island of Shapuree. They varied by length and ornamentation depending on the region they hailed from, but if he had to guess, the sword found in Lord Fieldstone's office drenched in his blood was a Burmese *dha*.

"And you hid this from the public," Jackson concluded.

"For as long as we can," Marcus replied. "I do not think it can be forever. Servants in the Fieldstone house saw him, as well as his wife and son."

Silence fell as the words were absorbed. Then Marcus filled it. "There is more."

"I should bloody well hope so," Jack replied earning a small smile from Byrne.

"A week before Fieldstone died, he sent me on a mission. To France, to investigate the Comte de Le Bon." Marcus's face became hard with the memory. "Why, he would not say, only that he wanted to make certain the man's origins were as he said in his long-winded stories."

"And are they?"

"As far as I could learn about his early life in France, yes." Marcus shrugged. "But that was before he was grown and had become best friends with a Burmese aristocrat."

Realization dawned. "And you think they had something to do with this."

"It is too large a coincidence. My primary theory is that Lord Fieldstone's murder connects to the Comte and Mr. Ashin Pha somehow."

Jackson would have rubbed his chin in contemplation, if he was not still tied to a chair.

"And your secondary theory is . . . that I am an insane man who runs around dressed up as the Blue Raven, kissing girls in cupboards and murdering men in their homes, and since I've spent the last few years in the East Indies, I could very possibly have a *dha*."

Sir Marcus shot his brother another look, this one decidedly bemused.

"I do, by the bye, have a *dha*. Purchased it from a tourist shop in Bombay. But I'm fairly certain it is securely locked away in my room at the Forresters."

"And we'd very much like to see it," Sir Marcus said. "For purposes of ruling you out, of course."

"Happily, I'll take you to it right now if you'd untie me." Jackson bantered back, much to the amusement of Byrne. "But I can rule myself out right now, if you'd prefer."

"How?"

"First of all, I am neither insane, nor do I have a motive for killing the poor man."

"Don't you?" Byrne leaned in again, making himself known, as if they could have forgotten him. "If Lord Fieldstone's true manner of death were to become known, bloody *dha* and all, how quickly do you think Britain declares war on Burma?"

"Some might see benefits from it—arms manufacturers and the like," Jack rationalized, "but I have nothing to gain if war breaks out."

"Really? You don't suppose the navy will need a number of officers to outfit ships in ordinary if war breaks out in a region controlled by the East India Company?"

"I . . ." but Jackson had no reply to that. He hadn't thought he had a motive for provoking war, but then again . . .

"How can I prove it to you? I . . . I never entered Lord Fieldstone's house—I was walking around London all night."

"A terrible alibi." But then Marcus looked at him straight on. "But you can help prove your innocence."

"How?"

"By finding the proof against another." Marcus took a breath. "There was something taken from Fieldstone's desk."

"What?"

"A piece of paper—or papers. We can tell by the patterns in the blood drops. Whoever has it is our killer."

The room went still. Jack's head moved slowly back and forth between the two men who played his captors. "Do you suspect Mr. Ashin Pha? Or the Comte de Le Bon?"

Byrne answered. "We don't know. Luckily proof for both would reside in one place."

"Either they are in it together, or one is leading the other around by the nose." Marcus sighed. "We know so little of both of them. We only have the Comte's vouching for Mr. Pha. And while the Comte's sister comes from good English stock, the Comte himself is entirely a mystery, having grown up outside of the eyes of England. Even with my trip to France, I could only trace the Comte's life until he was ten. And, as you so deftly pointed out, Lieutenant, his lack of knowledge of the topography of Burma indicates a lack of respect for it. He may be a patsy. But it is also very possible that he could have brought Mr. Pha here under false pretenses, so there would be someone to point the finger at when the time came."

Jack tried to follow the circuitous logic of spy games and only found himself cross-eyed. "Wouldn't a man who has committed murder, expecting chaos to result from it . . . *act* differently?" Jack asked. "From what I know of either man they are both, er, normal."

"Unfortunately he has not given himself away." Marcus replied, with an eyebrow lifted. "You're right, one would expect the killer to act strangely, to close up shop, to flee the area. Mr. Pha remains a silent guard, and the Comte is just as public, just as gregarious as ever."

"And just as annoying," Jack said under his breath, but in a room this still, it could have been heard a mile away. And it was—as both Byrne and Marcus gave a small, identical grunt of laughter.

"Er, yes. Except . . . no one has been inside the house the Comte has borrowed for the Season."

"What . . . at all?" Jack replied, astonished.

"No. They've never allowed it. Blamed it on some Burmese custom that no one has ever heard of, but also that no one would question."

"All right," Jack rationalized slowly. "I don't know what you would have me do about it, however. Break in . . ."

"There are too many guards." Marcus shook his head. Then he took a deep breath before venturing forth. "Indeed, our reports tell us that the only person who holds any sway over the Comte is Miss Sarah Forrester."

Jack felt the world pull at the edges of his body, pulling him down, down, into sharp focus, and landing with a thud into reality. "Are you mad?" But it was not a question. It was a threat.

But Sir Marcus's gaze did not falter. "Unfortunately not. I would rather not involve Miss Forrester, but we are running out of time and options. If the Fieldstone murder is made public—or it is not, and God forbid they feel they need to strike again to make their point known . . ."

Sir Marcus didn't need to say the rest. If such a thing occurred, parliament would follow the clues to Burma, then that rage would carry over into a swift and merciless call for war. It was entirely possible that war would break out on its own, Jack mused, given the contentiousness between Burma and British India, but someone was trying to provoke the fight ahead of schedule.

But to involve Miss Forrester . . .

"You never thought I had anything to do with Lord Fieldstone's death, did you?" Jack blurted, suddenly realizing the truth of it. Neither man made a reply, but Jack continued. "You just need to find a way to get to Miss Forrester."

"You may have been a less likely candidate than most," Sir Marcus conceded. "But your innocence is still under question."

Jack sighed, long since too tired for this conversation. His body slumped with weariness, but could only slump so far.

"Well, since I'm a less likely candidate, could you at least untie me from this chair? I think I've lost feeling in my fingers."

A nod from Byrne to Marcus had the taller gentleman loosening the knots behind Jack. When Jack stood, his joints cried out in relief. He nodded his thanks to Sir Marcus.

And then he hit him with the full force of his right hook.

Marcus hit the packed earth of the floor, his spectacles going askew.

Shortly thereafter, Jack found himself viciously pinned to the ground, staring up into the black eyes of Byrne Worth, a hard cane pressed against his throat.

"I won't let you endanger her in this way."

"Then we'll have you tried for the murder of Lord Fieldstone. Imagine it: having to publicly explain that you dressed up as the Blue Raven to play a trick on the Golden Lady. Think she'll appreciate the press?"

Byrne menaced, but was cut off by a warning, "Byrne . . ." from his brother.

Marcus stood, his steps wobbly, as he dabbed at the blood coming from his lip. "You think I want to do this? You think I want to involve innocents like Miss Forrester? If my wife ever found out, she would kill me. *But I have no choice.* My friend is dead and there is a killer at large! One who is trying to provoke war! And who will protect Miss Forrester if it *is* the Comte? His fascination with her is surely more dangerous than my request."

"The joke's on you then," Jack ground out, his throat burning against the pressure. "Sarah Forrester despises me. She would never do anything I ask of her."

Byrne smiled, then. That frightening, cold smile. "She would do anything the Blue Raven asked of her."

Jack's eyes widened. Byrne simply smiled wider.

"And you know it."

Fifteen

I T was not while Jack was donning the half mask again and gluing on the moustache that he realized the gravity of the situation he was about to walk into.

It was not when Sir Marcus came to the door of number sixteen, under the pretext of taking Jack to the War Department to discuss possible employment—thereby providing a suitable alibi, should anyone being to wonder why, whenever the Blue Raven appears, Lieutenant Jackson Fletcher is never in the room.

No, it was while he was crouched in shadow, in an alley two blocks away from number sixteen, being lectured on espionage etiquette by the Blue Raven himself, that Jack understood that he was about to enter a war zone.

"I would feel far more comfortable doing this in a public place," he muttered, as his eyes scanned the rough brick walls of the fancy pastry shop on one side of the narrow space, and the milliner's on the other.

"Too easily seen."

"Yet, without the distractions of other people, or the possibility of being found out, she's far more likely to recognize me."

But Byrne just shrugged. "It will be dark in her room. You're certain she's gone to bed?"

"It's past two in the morning. And they returned from their evening out before midnight." As well he should know, Jack thought glumly. On Byrne's instructions, he had been waiting in this alley all night, almost since Marcus had picked him up. He had seen the carriage with the Forrester family crest (a tree and a primrose, naturally) drive by ages ago.

"Yes, well then, at most, she will light one candle. Keep your hood up and she'll have no idea. Especially now that you have the right disguise."

Byrne, of course, had only come by in the last half hour to deliver instructions. And clothes.

"I cannot believe you had been wearing those oversized trousers and your *naval uniform jacket*. You're the luckiest bastard in the world that she did not recognize you before."

He would have grumbled and protested about necessity being the mother of invention, but he had to admit, the black linen shirt and close fitting trousers, as well as a lighter wool cape and light, flexible leather boots made movement a hell of a lot easier. Plus, it looked more Blue Raven–esque. Add to that a firmly affixed moustache—having had a chance to adhere properly this time—well, if he had a mirror, Jack doubted he would recognize himself.

"She could still very well knock me over the head and cry for help," Jack countered.

But Byrne just smiled. "Doubtful. In my experience, catching a woman unawares in her bedchamber tends to make her more . . . receptive to whatever you have to say."

Jack shot him a look. "Aren't you married?"

A black winged brow rose in reply. "How do you think I learned that particular information? Now, remember," he said, returning to the more important business at hand, "we need to get Miss Forrester to get the Comte to invite us into his home." Then, with a twinkle in his eye, he said "Use any means necessary."

The idea of seducing Sarah Forrester made Jack freeze with dread, with anticipation. Because that's what Byrne expected him to do, of course. And once he showed himself to Sarah . . . well, judging by her wistfulness for the past week, he wouldn't be surprised if that's what *she* expected, too. And the idea of kissing Sarah Forrester again made his fingertips tingle with hope, and his mind dizzy with nausea.

Because more than anything, he wanted to kiss her again.

"You should be the one doing this," Jack rationalized quickly. "After all, you *are* the Blue Raven."

"Not anymore," Byrne said, indicating his cane. "I haven't been in a long time. Besides, I won't even be in London that much longer."

Byrne grew silent, losing himself in his own thoughts. When he shook himself back to the present, his expression became serious.

"Listen, when you are in there . . ." he turned Jack to him, made him meet his eye. "*You* must be the one in control. You must have her under your spell, not the other way around. Until she agrees to what you ask."

"And then?"

"And then you get the hell out of there as quickly as possible."

Jack gave Byrne a look that he hoped expressed the murderous tendencies he was feeling right now, before setting himself to the task of sneaking over, and then breaking in, to the Forrester home.

With one eye on Byrne, Jack moved to the drainpipe that ran along the joint between the pastry shop and the milliner's back wall extension. Using all of his upper-body strength, he hoisted himself up along the not-meant-to-bear-his-weight pipe, until he could latch his hands onto a narrow window ledge. Then he used that ledge to lever himself up to the next one a story above, and then the next, and then finally the roof.

When he cleared the roof, he turned to look back down in the alley. And found Byrne looking up at him, decidedly impressed. Giving a small salute, Jack turned around and began moving lightly across the rooftops, toward the direction of number sixteen Upper Grosvenor Street.

It went smoothly—he didn't run into any curious chimney sweeps, and the eyes of the lazily patrolling night watch did not go above street level. Jack decided he now knew how the unknown killer managed to get into Lord Fieldstone's town house. The rooftops of London were easy to traverse, and free of scrutiny.

The only hitch in his travels was when he came to a break in the rooftops, caused by the presence of a street below. But it was a fairly narrow street, only leading back to the mews behind the houses. He stepped back and made a running jump for it, clearing the gap with only inches to spare. Unfortunately, he landed rather harder than expected, and the resounding thud echoed through the night air.

A sleepy night watchman below, who had been walking at an easy pace, twirling his stick in time to his slow pace, suddenly froze, alert.

Jack hit the deck, pressing his body against the hard tin of the roof. Luckily, he did not hear any noises from the house beneath him, and after a good thirty seconds, he felt safe enough to continue on to number sixteen.

When he swung down the backside of the house, the side facing the small garden lot behind the Forrester's home, Jack was grateful for two things. First, that the Forresters had given Sarah the room with the balcony—it made entry so much simpler than having to hang onto a ledge. And second, the unnatural cold of the previous few days had broken, and it was warm enough to warrant leaving the balcony door open.

But when he stepped onto the balcony, and carefully pushed the door open wider, he realized his one mistake this evening—other than the massive one of dressing up as the Blue Raven in the first place.

Because, Sarah Forrester was not, as he had insisted, asleep in her bed. She was instead sitting at her dressing table, lit by the light of a candelabrum. Wearing nothing but a simple, gauzy nightdress that fell off her shoulder, revealing inches of tantalizing skin.

And when her eyes met his, he knew, he just knew . . . that he was not going to be the one in control of their conversation.

Not one bit.

ॐ

Sarah hadn't been able to sleep that night. Indeed, it had been almost a week since she had slept a full night through. For all of her recent conversion to keeping less extreme hours, those hours that she would have spent enjoying slumber were instead spent here, at her dressing table, trying to think through the recent twists and turns in her life. The usual aspects of femininity had been swept aside—instead her dressing table had become more of a desk: spread out before her, again, as they had been every single night since those fateful few minutes in a theatre cupboard, were the contents of the little packet that had been thrust into her hand.

A tin compass, with an equation scratched on the back.

A map, the shoreline she thought she had figured out by now.

A black feather.

It was as she was contemplating these objects—these tiny things that had disrupted her sleep—that the larger object that had constantly disrupted her sleep appeared at her balcony doors.

At first she thought it was the wind, he moved so silently, the only thing she had heard was the creak of the door hinge. When she turned, and her eyes finally found his in the dark, she couldn't help jumping a bit, and giving a small sound of exclamation.

Oh, all right. She yelped.

"Shh!" came the desperate whisper from the man—the Blue Raven!—at her balcony door.

"I . . . I'm sorry," she whispered back, shock coursing through her veins. "But you surprised me."

"Did I?" he replied, his voice gruff, as he kept to the shadows. "I had thought you might be expecting me."

Sarah blushed, and felt her entire body go up in heat. She *had* been expecting him. For the last week, she had been on the lookout for him. She thought she saw him in the face and jawline of every man she danced with, hoped for him every time she stepped out onto her balcony at night, wondering just where in the world he was, and when he would find her—as he said he would—to collect the articles he had entrusted to her care.

She had even kept her balcony door unlocked, just in case he . . .

She blushed even harder at that thought.

While she had been contemplating her unlocked door, she

hadn't noticed that he moved silently from his spot near said door, and over to . . .

The bed.

Oh my goodness.

He moved with grace and elegance—she could see just how well muscled he was by the cut of his trousers. Indeed, he seemed much more comfortable this time. More at his leisure. Like a great black cat.

She watched, silently, as his hand ran over the surface of the bed, the soft linens of her sheets, the feather-down pillows, and finally coming to rest on the silky robe she had left there.

And then he tossed it at her.

She caught it, surprised out of her stupor from his presence. "What are you—"

"You should put that on," he said, before she could finish. His voice was gruff, a deep scratch scoring the potent air between them. "You'll be . . . warmer."

The way her body was heating up at the thought of his hand on her bed, she had absolutely no need to be *warmer*, she thought grimly. Indeed, how would he know if she were too warm or too cold? He wasn't even looking at her.

Her eyes naturally flicked down to her over-warm body. And saw what he saw. The drop of her shoulder. The thin material of her nightdress.

Her face went up in flames as she hastily wrapped the robe around herself.

But underneath the embarrassment, the mortification, was a spark of realization. She affected him. She must, else she would have been able to stand stark naked in front of him without him batting an eye.

Is it possible I affect him the way he affects me?

The thought was dangerous . . . powerful. Out of all the men in London that she had brought to states of dizzying adoration, she could not imagine a single one that she wanted to have that dominion over. Except him.

When the robe was around her shoulders, the belt tightly knotted, she stood from her place at her dressing table, and tiptoed across to him.

"I'm warmer now," she whispered in his ear, and was gratified by seeing him jump. Almost imperceptibly, but jump, he did.

"Good," he said when his voice finally came back to him. A little higher this time, she noticed. But then it was back to its normal, gruff depth. "I . . . trust you've been well."

Sarah almost laughed, but knew that it was not the time. There was too much energy in the air, like the minutes before a lightning storm over the ocean. "I have. Although I had begun to wonder if I would ever see you again," she whispered.

He nodded, and leaned in a little bit. It was then that Sarah noticed that when she had sneaked up on him, he had not backed away as she had expected him to. He stood his ground, tantalizingly close. Giving her no quarter.

And then he looked down at her—his eyes black, shining pools, peering out from beneath a mask and a hood.

She sucked in her breath. For the first time since . . . since the Event, since she transformed herself into the Golden Lady, Sarah feared she might be outmatched. He didn't cower before her.

And she didn't want him to.

"It's been a mere few days, Miss Forrester," his head tilted to the side, regarding her, making her skin go warm . . . everywhere.

"It has been well over a week, nearly two! I'm used to men being far more . . ."

"Eager?" the masked man supplied.

"Punctual." She retorted. Where she found the wherewithal to be playful with him, she did not know. Last time she had been shocked into a tongue-tied state. One would assume that when a man burst in through your bedroom window, such loquaciousness would be beyond one's abilities!

"I'm sorry to have kept you waiting. I've been busy."

"So I've read," she replied.

"Have you?" he looked at her queerly.

"According to the papers—there was a masked man who foiled a robbery the night of the opera, and ever since then, a masked man has popped up in the newspaper stories almost daily."

He crossed his arms over his chest and harrumphed in

amusement. "I'll be damned," he whispered to himself. When her brow rose in reply, he answered the unspoken question. "I always thought the papers fabricated some of the B—er, *my* adventures. Now I know it's true."

"Or you have someone out there who's pretending to be you," she replied smartly, dancing away from him. "In which case, how do I know you are the same man who I met before?"

He took two steps toward her, closing the gap between them. She felt the blood rush to her heart, her core, as he took her hand, and brought it to his lips. "You know."

Oh my goodness.

"I . . . ah, I kept your packet safe for you," she blurted. Then she turned to her dressing table and felt her face flame up anew.

Her dressing table. Her silly, childish dressing table, covered in ridiculous carvings and cherubs. How mortifying! The Blue Raven was known to have sneaked into palaces and the bedchambers of the most elegant women in Europe, and here she was, the Golden Lady, with this utterly ridiculous piece of furniture.

But she tamped down her humiliation, and trotted over to the table, retrieving the objects, as well as the oilskin they had been wrapped in.

"You went through them," he stated.

"Yes," she replied baldly. "I'm not about to keep anything for anyone and not know what it is. For heaven's sake it could have been a murder weapon or stolen gems."

She tried to offer the items to him, but curiously, he crossed his arms over his chest again.

"I . . . ah, I have to admit to a certain curiosity, and you cannot blame me for wanting to know just what manner of objects I secreted away for you," she finally managed to say. "The map is obviously the northern Spanish shoreline—"

"It is?" he asked abruptly.

"Yes—or at least, I thought so . . ." She gently unfolded the map. "Isn't this the inlet for the Ria de Villaviciosa?"

He took the map from her and scrutinized it. "I suppose it is . . ." he mumbled under his breath.

"It took me a long time with my father's atlas to figure that out," she preened. "But we had no idea what the mathematical equation was meant to decipher. We thought perhaps it was meant to give latitude and longitude, to be used in correspondence with the compass, but—"

"We?" he interrupted her—again. She looked up from the compass in her hand, only to see him looming above her. Close. So very, very close.

"My sister," she blurted. "She helped me. Bridget's always been better at maths than anyone."

"You involved your sister?" he asked quietly.

"I . . . I didn't tell her about you, of course." Her eyes shot to his face, desperately trying to reassure him. "I wouldn't do that to you . . . but she's actually quite brilliant . . . when she's not mad at me . . . and it was actually quite useful to have someone to talk to about this."

It *had* been good to have someone to talk to—to have had Bridget. Especially since Phillippa had been out of town for so long. It was as if she and Bridget, while working toward a common goal, had called a détente. Of course, they spoke nothing about anything having to do with the Season—no matter how much Sarah wished she could council her sister on how to turn her failures into successes. But instead, they would discuss, of all things, maths. Music. Proportion. The balance of numbers and harmonies that Bridget understood in a way that Sarah never would.

It was a relief to have, at the very least, this part of her sister back.

But even as Sarah looked up, searching the darkness for those eyes that held her captive, to reassure him of her carefulness with his secrets, she decided she would not let him cow her into regretting her actions. No, she would not—

But then he brought his hand to her chin, delicately nudging her face up, aligning it with his.

"And you didn't think it was better for your sister to be kept in the dark, to be kept safe?"

Her resolve faltered. "I . . . I did not think . . ." He moved forward and she stepped back with him, until the back of her legs hit the dressing table.

"If I had a family . . ."

"You have no family?" she asked, as he leaned forward, plucking the black feather and the oilcloth from the dressing table, taking the map and compass from her and methodically wrapping them, his packet becoming intact once again.

"Not anymore." He took two steps away from her.

"Friends?" She stood up, and closed the distance between them.

"Some," he replied. And then, thoughtfully, "But as close as friends can be, it is no replacement for the real thing."

Quiet enveloped them, and Sarah wished she had the bravery to reach out and take his hand. But for once, her bravery failed her. Instead, she whispered into the darkness. "I used to read about you, as a child. I followed your exploits in the war with bloodthirsty adoration." He chuckled lightly at that.

"I used to think you the most dashing, daring, wonderful man on earth," she continued. "But now I must think you the loneliest, too."

He turned to her then, his hands found the way to her face, holding her, framing her. She knew that he would kiss her then . . . she *knew* it . . .

"Do not worry, sweet," he breathed, and the last word made her glow with warmth at her very core. But instead of wrapping her in his arms, like every fiber of her being was *begging* him to do, he instead backed away, and pressed the packet into her hand. "These items do not matter any longer. I apologize for having to involve you in this way."

"Oh," was the only reply she could manage. She bit her lip. These things she had agonized over . . . no longer held any weight. It made her feel sad for these discarded scraps that she had spent so long trying to decipher. They were no longer useful. And because of that, her life would go from this exciting anticipation . . . back to normal.

"Can I keep them?" she asked suddenly.

Even though she could not see underneath the hood of his cloak, not to mention the half mask, she knew an eyebrow had risen in amusement.

"Why? They are worthless."

"They are not worthless to me." She glanced down at her toes. "I'd like something to remember . . . this . . . by," she breathed, placing her free hand on his chest. She didn't have to glance up to meet his eyes—the heavy rise and fall of his chest told her everything he was feeling.

But then her head came up.

"Wait," she said sharply, all intimacy gone from her expression, replaced only by a puzzle to be solved. "If you don't need the packet, then why are you here?"

He held still for a moment. Then, not moving a muscle, not advancing on her backing away, he stated plainly his purpose. "I must request a . . . favor."

A slight thrill went through her. "From me?" she squeaked. She couldn't believe it—she got to continue this adventure? Her life didn't have to return to the normal that now had dulled edges.

"I need you . . . to exert your influence with the Comte de Le Bon."

"The Comte?" Her brows came down. "Why?"

"He . . . he may have some information I require. But I need to get into his house. Which no one—at all—has been into."

"How am I supposed to get you into his house?" Sarah asked. "As a single woman, I am not permitted in his residence—"

"You can if you convince him to throw a dinner party," the Blue Raven replied. His voice had gone gruff again, but not in that seductive manner that cast a spell over the room. This was more severe, businesslike.

"You would attend a dinner party?" Hope ran through her.

"Not attend, no—but if the house is open to guests, it is much simpler for me to make an unseen entry," he clarified.

"Oh." She replied dumbly. The thought of the Blue Raven attending a dinner party was slightly laughable, but then again, thrilling. Simply because she would get to know . . . him. Who he was. Where he came from.

"Sarah," he whispered. "It is well known that the Comte is under your sway . . ."

"I would not think so. At least not anymore," she rushed to explain. "I have not been as attentive to the Comte, ever since . . ." The opera, she thought silently. Well, it was his own fault for not having a moustache, really.

"If you don't think you can do it, tell me and I'll find another way," he declared in a rush, his hands coming to grasp her arms. Was it a challenge or a plea?

"I can do it," she rushed to assure. Then feeling bolder than she had any right to, Sarah took a deep breath and held her ground. Close, so close to him.

And suddenly, Sarah felt a rush of *something*. Something that made her—who had always done everything right, everything she had ever been told to do, whether it be by her mother, her father, or Phillippa—want to do something she knew was *wrong*.

To give in to gravity's pull.

She looked up into his eyes, defiant.

"I'll do this for you—if you grant me a boon in return."

He cocked his head to one side. "What?"

She hesitated just the barest of moments before she managed her voice.

"Tell me your name."

Sixteen

TELL me your name.

The words echoed in Jack's ears, hollow, like a distant yearning. Tell her his name? He almost laughed aloud. He would love to. It would end this farce. It would free him from having to entangle her in this mess with the Comte de Le Bon and the Worth brothers. It would free him to tell her . . .

It would free him.

But he couldn't do it.

He couldn't give up the lie.

How he had managed for this long to pull the proverbial wool over Sarah's eyes was a complete mystery to him. Maybe it was the clothes, the false moustache, or the whispers in candlelight, but something had overcome him and he . . . transformed.

He transformed himself into the man that he knew Sarah wished him to be. The Blue Raven. The one from old newspaper articles—roguish and rakish, from a time when she did not know what roguish or rakish *really* meant. He acted as the Blue Raven would act, said what the Blue Raven would say. (Admittedly, he might have thrown in a dash of Byrne Worth to the mix—he was, after all, the original.)

And she was pert and flirtatious and in awe.

She looked at him like he was a god.

Tell me your name.

He paused in his movements when those words came out of her mouth, just a breath, floating past like a prayer. He was a fraction away from her then, leaning over her, against the edge of the girlish dressing table. He had been expecting—hoping, dreading—that she would ask him for a kiss. But instead what she wanted from him was so much more frightening.

"You know I cannot tell you that," he whispered, hopefully keeping the panicked laughter out of his voice.

She quirked up an eyebrow. "Haven't I proven that I am worthy of your trust? That I can keep your secret?"

Well, given that she had not only involved her sister in trying to solve the gibberish equation he had written to befuddle her, *and* she had blurted out to Phillippa Worth the details of their encounter, which landed him in this current mess, Jack would have to say that no, Sarah had not proven that she could keep his secret. But he wasn't about to say so out loud. Instead, he just shook his head.

To which she responded with a coy tilt of her own. "Well then, I suppose you don't want me to get the Comte to throw a dinner party. My, my, you are terribly ambivalent about your quest."

"Ask me anything else. But you must know—for your own safety"—brilliant line, that!—"that I cannot let you know my name."

Her face fell, becoming broken with vulnerability. "I just want to know something true about you. Something that the newspapers and . . . and any other women do not know." Her hand came to rest gently on his.

"I hate salted pork," he answered automatically.

She looked askance at him. "I'm being quite serious."

"As am I. Salted pork is disgusting." He smiled at her. But her expression remained still.

"Please," was all she said. All she really had to say.

He let out his breath slowly. Leaned back and regarded her, the plea in her eyes. The resolution.

"All right," he conceded. "But you have to close your eyes."

"Why?" she replied, distrustful.

"Because it's easier," he countered. "Please."

She relented, her lids coming down, making her as vulnerable to him as he was about to become to her.

It was truth she asked for, and truth he intended to say.

"I was a little boy once," he began, and was gratified by the corners of her mouth pressing into a smile.

"That's hard to imagine."

"But true—everyone was young at one time or another. But when I was a lad . . . I lived near a little girl. And she had a way about her that made the stars seem dim in comparison. I used to count down the days in between getting to visit her. Because no matter how terrible things would seem, or how unhappy I was, she would always find a way to make it better.

"We both grew up, and our lives led us in separate directions. But I think that, in a way, I've spent my life looking for the spark that she had. The light that made the stars dim."

"Oh," Sarah breathed. Her eyes remaining tightly shut. Then, after a moment's hesitation . . . "Have . . . have you ever found it? That spark?"

"I might just have," Jack replied, his voice barely louder than the slight breeze from the window. And then, because the moment called for it, he leaned forward to lay the lightest of kisses upon her cheek.

He would have let that be the end of their moment. He would have let the breeze from the window carry him away from her, so that when her eyelids finally fluttered open, he would be gone—the only trace of him the packet that still rested in her hand, and the remembrance of a *chaste* caress.

That's what he would have done.

But that, unfortunately, is not what happened. Because Sarah did not open her eyes *after* he kissed her. She opened them before. And in doing so, read his intent . . . and adjusted accordingly.

She turned her head in the split second before his lips met her cheek, and instead captured his mouth with hers.

And that was it. He was gone.

Because that thing that he had been hoping for, that thing he had been dreading since Marcus and Byrne told him of their plan for Sarah, it was happening now, and all he wanted was *more*.

He caught her head with his hand, held her steady as he took her deeper. She steadied herself against the dressing table, but it wasn't enough. She let her hands, shaking as they were, wind around his neck and found her balance by pulling him closer. All the while, never relenting in that sweet pressure against his mouth.

Who had taught her to kiss? The thought went wildly through his brain. He wanted to kill whomever it was, because she was doing just splendidly. But what if . . . what if he took it just a step further?

He pressed his free hand to the small of her back, forcing her body in alignment with his. He knew the moment she felt his full, rigid length straining against the skintight trousers, because she opened her mouth in a gasp of surprise. Which was exactly what he wanted.

He plundered, he stole. He took what lay just beyond his reach and did so gleefully. She hesitated, but then, something inside of her must have shifted, because she chucked aside caution, and began to dance those ancient steps with him.

Somehow, Sarah ended up sitting on the dressing table. Somehow, his hand had found a way to the tie of her robe, and quickly worked the knot open. Somehow, her naked legs began to open, and snake their way up to his flanks. Somehow, his reaction to that feeling was extreme enough to send the candelabrum flying from its position atop the dressing table, crashing to the floor in a bloody racket, and plunging them into total darkness.

The crash did not deter them. The dark only spurred them further, falling deeper into the abyss. It allowed their hands to roam without the constraints of propriety. And roam they did. He felt the soft skin of her calf, her thigh, pulling her legs all the tighter around him. She apparently decided that he must be much too warm, and needed freedom from his shirt, as she began to work at the buttons.

Her hand pressed against his bare chest, her fingers intertwining with the light sprinkling of curls that lived there. His hand came up in reply, his moves a mirror to hers, as he let the backs of his hands dance across the pointed tips of her breasts.

"Oh," she said, sucking in her breath. Then, her voice a

quaver of flirt mired in vulnerability: "You do know how to persuade a lady, don't you?"

He froze.

God damn it, Jack chastised himself immediately. He had let himself—hell, been eager to, even—get carried away.

"What is it?" she asked, all flirtatiousness gone. Now she was raw, exposed. And so very young.

He backed away violently, crossed the length of the room, using the distance to gather himself.

"Did I do something wrong?" Her voice was small, but oddly, wonderfully defiant.

He felt like laughing. Wrong? Didn't she have any idea of just how completely, thoroughly she had picked the locks of his resolve?

"No," he rasped. "You did nothing wrong."

"Then, what has happened?"

He turned then, but kept the length of the room between them. Lit only by moonlight, she looked like a goddess—an oddly prim one. She had straightened herself, her robe, and was sitting on the dressing table with perfect posture and her ankles crossed. As if ten seconds ago she hadn't been in the most wanton, provocative position imaginable. And he could imagine. He could imagine quite a bit.

For instance, he could imagine her reaction when she found out . . .

"One day, very soon, you are going to be made to hate me." His felt the truth of it down to his toes, rooting him to the floor. "But when that happens, I want you to remember that at least I am not the worst kind of thief."

She came lightly to her feet, and took two steps toward him, but he waved her back before she could get any closer.

"I won't ever hate you," she promised. "Please, just . . . I'll do what you've asked. Just don't—"

But her pleas were interrupted by a knock at the door.

"Sarah?" It was Bridget. Of course it was—her rooms were just next door—on the other side of the wall from the dressing table. "Are you all right? I heard a crash and . . . something like a moan."

Sarah moved quickly to him, and held a finger to his lips. "Please don't leave. I'll get rid of her, just don't leave." She commanded with her eyes, and he nodded in acquiescence. She trotted over to the door.

"I'm fine, Bridge," she said, on a yawn. "I, ah . . . I fell asleep at my table and knocked the candlestick over."

"The candlestick!" Bridget cried, alarmed. "Are you singed? Is there a fire? Let me in!" She began banging heavily on the door.

"Bridge, I'm fine! And there is no fire!" Sarah cried at the door. She turned to give an exasperated look to him—but found that he was already gone.

With nothing more than a breeze and the remembrance of a caress to indicate he had ever been there.

§

"You were gone awhile." Byrne worth smiled at him as soon as he landed roughly in the alley, a few blocks away.

Jack shot him a dirty look.

"Longer than expected." Byrne Worth was apparently impervious to dirty looks. "Did Miss Forrester require persuasion?"

Jack decided that the most articulate answer was a short one, two words, seven letters, and as one would say, with his sailor showing through.

But Byrne's smile just grew wider. "Not me, surely." Then with a seriousness that belied any mirth . . . "I bet you managed to get under her skin this time."

Jack would wager that he did, as well.

And it scared the hell out of him.

Seventeen

SARAH was humming to herself when Jack walked into the breakfast room the next day, neither of them apparently the worse for wear from the previous night's activities. Jack's first instinct was to avoid Sarah, to grab some food and turn tail and run, lest she see on his face the memory of their shared evening. But truth be told, he was too tired. He was too tired of meddling in her life, and then trying to remove himself from it. He was too tired to worry about whether or not she maintained her cross stance with him. And he was too tired from his utter lack of sleep.

Because once he had returned to number sixteen as himself, there was no possible way for him to sleep.

"Good morning," Jack said, gathering a plate of food from the sideboard.

"Good afternoon is more like it," Sarah replied with a smile, but her expression remained somber. "You're getting to be worse than me."

Jack looked dazedly at the mantle clock. "Is that why we're all alone?"

Sarah nodded. "Father is already at the Historical Society, Bridget is at her piano lessons—although what else she has to learn is anyone's guess—and mother took Amanda to the modiste. She outgrew her last day dress. Again." Then she tilted her head, in the exact same manner that she had the previous evening when she was being pert. His mind flashed back to that moment so vividly that he missed what she was saying.

"What was that?"

"I asked if you had a late night?"

"Oh. Yes." He looked dumbly at his plate of food. He was supposed to have been out with Marcus Worth. He must get his head out of this stupor, and remember his lies and alibis.

"Yes, well, if anyone deserved to, it's you. Indeed, your last two days of staying out all hours were well earned."

His brows came down. "Why is that?"

She looked at him quizzically. "Because of the *Amorata*."

It was then that he noticed the newspaper at her elbow. The *Amorata*. Of course. Had he only received that news two days ago? Had he only gone through the madness of meeting the Blue Raven in an alley and the Worth brothers in a dark cellar just the day before yesterday?

He reached forward and she handed the paper to him. But no, the date at the top bore the truth out.

And there, inside the section reserved for military dealings, the fate he knew had fallen in three lines:

Decommissioned: The HMS *Amorata*, a sixth-class Banterer ship. Fought admirably in sea battles of the past wars. Due to age and wear the Admiralty of the Navy have deemed it not seaworthy. The *Amorata* will be broken up and pieces put to use in ordinary.

"I'm so sorry, Jack," Sarah said, her voice breaking through his haze. He shook his head to clear it.

"It's not as if we didn't know that this was coming. You're the one who called me out on my denial, if you recall," he said gruffly.

"Yes," she conceded, "but that doesn't make it any easier."

"Doesn't make what any easier?"

She shrugged lightly, bringing a cup of strong morning tea to her lips. "Giving up the life that you had planned on."

Jack stared at her. And it was as if he saw her for the first time in her truest form.

"I'm sorry," he said simply. Because for the first time, he truly understood. What she had been through. And how she had survived it. Turning herself into another person.

After all, hadn't he done the same thing?

"It's not your fault the *Amorata* is gone, Jack," she tried kindly.

"No, I'm sorry for everything," he said, his kippers and biscuit suddenly taking on new interest, as apparently he couldn't take his eyes off of them. "Everything that happened since I came back. For judging you harshly. For embarrassing you on the dance floor. For . . . everything else. I had no right."

He chanced a look up, and could see by the blush on her cheek and the stillness of her frame that his words had hit home.

"You've apologized a dozen times over for those things," she replied, her eyes not moving from her own plate of food.

"I've tried. But you never accepted because . . . probably because I never understood before."

"Understood what, Jack?" She laughed just a little, betraying herself.

"What it's like. Giving up the life you had planned on."

"Oh," she breathed. The sound of the clock ticking was the only movement in the room. "Well, I am accepting now."

"Thank you, Miss Forrester."

"You're quite welcome, Lieutenant." Then, after a pause, she turned her smile to him. "And I apologize for . . . my bluntness, I suppose. And making you uncomfortable."

"Apology accepted." Then he quirked his head to one side. "What are your plans for the day, Sarah?"

Her gaze locked onto his eyes, and then quickly back down to her plate. "Nothing exciting," she replied although the blush of her cheek told otherwise. "I thought I might go shopping, or on a ride in the park, settle my nerves before the Gold Ball tonight."

The Gold Ball. Jack vaguely recalled being told it was a premiere event, thrown in honor of the King, and in promotion of his Regent's Park. Or some such thing. As it was with all functions Sarah attended, everyone who was anyone would be there.

"And as the Golden Lady, you must attend." Jack surmised. "But why are you nervous?"

"I—ah—I haven't seen my friends in a while, is all," she hastily added.

"Such as Lady Phillippa, and the Comte de Le Bon?" he ventured, and watched as her blush went utterly crimson.

"Now, don't start judging my friends again, in that voice . . ." she warned, but her warning was weak—her mind was elsewhere. On other "friends" she expected to see.

"I didn't intend to." He held his hands up, in a gesture of surrender. Then, impromptu, he stood from his seat, and came around the table to sit next to her.

"Might I propose something?" he said, leaning forward, which beckoned her to do the same. "How about—for the sake of your nerves—we take a short trip today. Just you and I. You leave the Golden Lady at home and I'll leave the angry lieutenant, and we'll have some fun."

"I . . . I don't . . ." She hesitated, looking back and forth between the clock and his face.

"I'll make sure you're back in time. Besides," he said, taking her hand, "it will allow me to truly apologize for my transgressions."

Her hand in his sent waves of electricity through his body, a pulse of pure memory. Whether or not she felt the same, he could not know. But she stopped looking at the door . . . and held fast with his eyes. He smiled, giving her the most mischievous grin he could conjure. "Please?"

He saw the moment she made her decision. And thanked God it was in his favor.

"Very well," she said with a smile that matched his own. "What shall we do?"

❧

"Do you mean to tell me that playing bowls is your way of apologizing?" Sarah asked, yelling against the warm breeze.

"No, letting you win at bowls is my way of apologizing," Jack called back, as he unloaded the old set of bowls from the back of the carriage.

"Jackson Fletcher, you've never *let* me win at anything—I

always beat you soundly," she retorted, her eyes flaring, gratified to see his wide smile in return.

They were west of the city—an hour's ride by carriage, almost to Greenwich, where the green fields sloped down into the Thames, affording a view of the ships gliding past, their billowing sails blending with the puffed clouds of the glorious June day. It was the perfect day to do this, Sarah thought, enjoying the view almost as much as she was enjoying the breeze. It was the perfect day for a respite from her life— because if she had to be in Grosvenor right now, paying calls or shopping, having to play the part of the Golden Lady, by the time tonight came, her mission in front of her, she would work herself into a ball of nerves.

Although, that she wasn't currently a ball of nerves was something of a miracle, in and of itself.

Last night had been just the most shocking, exciting, wonderful experience of her life. If she had been obsessed with the Blue Raven for the past week, last night had shifted all of that focus, all of that obsession into place, like the tumbles of a lock, and she was completely and utterly in love with the man.

Which is exactly what she wanted to be.

Why else would she have let him touch her in that way? Why else would she have let his hand snake up over her legs, her breasts? Why else would she have dared a lifetime of doing everything right for a spare moment of doing something wrong?

Why else would she have promised to help him with the Comte?

Because she was completely in love with him.

And with that realization, for the first time in weeks, Sarah Forrester slept like a stone.

But with the morning, came the blush of understanding. (And the need to send Molly to purchase some face powder, because absolutely everyone would see the love bite on her neck otherwise.) She sat at her dressing table, unable to reconcile its silly scroll work and the glee of the little girl who had picked it out with what she had been doing on top of it just the night before.

With a man who made no mention as to if or when she would see him again! Her mind rollicked wildly between *what have I done?* and *no, he felt something for me, too—I'm certain!* with no means to make it stop. Until she remembered: She did have one thing that would ensure his continued presence in her life.

She had promised to help the Blue Raven, a master spy, on one of his quests. He had asked her on an adventure. The thought at once calmed her down.

But then . . . she realized what she had promised.

It was at breakfast, while she enjoyed the solitude (and being very mindful of the placement of her collar) that the nerves began to creep into her belly. The queasy fear of what the night held. What if she couldn't persuade the Comte? Why did the Blue Raven want in his home anyway? Was he a villain? What if the Comte became suspicious by her asking and began to question *her*?

Sarah looked over the expanse of lawn, the happy removal to nature at such a close distance to home.

"Thank goodness for Jack," she breathed.

"What about me?" Jack asked, surprising her from behind. She jumped. Jack always made her jump.

"Nothing," she replied quickly. "I just said, thank goodness it's Jack I'm playing, because Amanda has become absolutely wicked at bowls."

"It's her reach, one would expect," Jack shrugged. "Too bad for you I'm still taller than her."

Jack took the bag of bowls—green and black ceramic balls that were hefty enough to have momentum when thrown—and dropped them at her feet. Then he rifled through, finding the kitty—the smaller, white ball that would be their target. At some point in the past decades one of the Forrester sisters had painted a crude kitty's face on the ball. He wound up, and pitched the poor kitty down the field.

Far down the field.

"Height has absolutely nothing to do with bowls," Sarah countered haughtily.

"And how would you know?" he came back, teasingly holding his hand over her head, as if to indicate her stature left something to be desired. She retorted by taking a green bowl from the pile and, after a good windup, sending it down the field.

It rolled to a stop mere inches from the kitty.

"I believe it was I who taught you to play this game, correct?" she returned.

Jack quirked up a brow, and got his own ball—a black one—and sent it down field.

Sarah couldn't help but laugh when she saw where it landed.

"This isn't a flat, manicured green," Jack grumbled.

Sarah laughed even harder at that. She picked up another green bowl and sent it flying.

"I can't believe you wanted to play bowls today," she sighed, shaking her head. "And thought to let me win as apology."

"It was rather short notice." Jack said with a smile. "It was either this or playing pirates—which I always let you win, too."

"You were always the pirate, Jack, you had to lose." Sarah smiled at him. "It's the only way for justice to prevail. Now stop complaining and take your turn."

And so they played. They played a childhood game like the children they had once been. Bickering as they would have over whether or not a bowl had touched the kitty. Laughing when one of Sarah's bowls rolled away under a tree where it surprised a poor man whose leisurely lunch in the park had turned into a leisurely nap. Applauding as Jack took to running a victory lap around their makeshift green when he finally won one of their seven games.

Yes, thank goodness for Jack, she thought again.

Who would have thought even twenty-four hours ago that she would be thanking anyone for Jackson Fletcher?

Whatever wrought this change in him—whatever wrought this change in her—she was glad of it.

Which is exactly what she told him when they settled down on the grass to eat the cold sandwiches that cook had hastily packed for them.

"To think we could have been getting along this whole time," she said in between bites.

"To think," he agreed, on a mouthful of cheese.

"Makes me feel rather foolish for sticking my nose up in the air at you."

"As well you should," he replied with mocking laughter. "Why did you do such a thing, anyway?" He stretched out his long legs and lay on the grass, propping himself up on his side with one elbow.

"I believe it had something to do with you calling me a fraud, and saying that my entire life was a lie," she replied kindly.

"Oh yes," he recalled. "Well, that was rather silly of me." Then with a ponderous expression, "Do you have any idea why I was so rude as to snub you on the dance floor?"

"I believe it was my suggestion that you court a young lady of fortune," she glanced at him out of the corner of her eye. "How is Miss Devlin, by the bye?"

Jack swallowed audibly. Then bought time by wiping his mouth with a napkin. "Fine," he finally said. "But I'm not as close with the family as you might think."

"Really?" An eyebrow went up. "You didn't call on her at home twice last week?"

He and Whigby had, of course, but he was surprised to learn Sarah had taken note of it.

"How did you . . ."

"Everyone tells me everything, Jack." She smirked at him. "It's one of the more interesting aspects of being the Golden Lady." Everyone did tell her everything, that was true. But it didn't mean that she did not keep her ear out for particular information. And somehow, even while she was focused so keenly on solving the Blue Raven's mysteries, she had been attuned to any news about Jack and Miss Devlin. Likely to see if he was taking her loathed advice, she told herself, and for no other reason.

But while her quip had meant to disarm and be amusing, Jack instead looked serious. Intent upon working something out. "Do you miss him?"

"Who?" she asked, blinking.

"The Duke."

"You mean Jason?" she asked, as he nodded.

"You became her to forget him," he intoned.

"No—I became her to survive," Sarah replied quietly. Then after a moment's thought, "Maybe the Golden Lady did . . . help me put him aside for a little while, so I wouldn't feel the worst of the pain. But the truth is I don't miss him. At least not since . . ." She blushed, her mind flashing to a man in a dark cloak. "At least not anymore."

She looked down at her half-eaten sandwich, having lost the taste for it. She had more to say, and blessedly, he held silent and waited for her.

"I miss what could have been," she said finally. "I miss having the security of knowing that I've done it. I've found the man I will spend the rest of my life with, and therefore it can begin. No more waiting. No more balls, no more inspections from bachelors and probing questions from their families, wanting to see if I measure up."

"But you're so good at it," he replied. "Er, the balls and things."

She laughed, a little sadly. "Yes, but that doesn't mean that I wanted to start the whole thing over again."

"I don't know if I want to start the whole thing over again, either. Er, with the navy I mean, on a new ship," he clarified when he caught her look. "If we were to look at the *Amorata* the way you looked at your Duke—"

"Yes, let's do, because that makes perfect sense," she couldn't help but quip sarcastically.

Gratefully he ignored her. "When I was a boy, I was in love with the life. But I was on board the same ship for nine years. I knew its ins and outs, I knew the crew. I knew how to take her over shoals and get her to fly fast. I remember when I was seventeen—in the waning days of the war, we came across a French flyer off the coast of Spain, doing something nefarious no doubt, because she engaged immediately. We were caught off guard, but the captain led the men and turned the wheel over to me. And I stayed there, following his yelled-out commands the whole time. Twelve hours, that action, and not a single loss of life." He looked to the horizon, where the ships moved easily on the Thames. "The *Amorata* and I have been through a lot together. And now everyone is scattered to the four winds. Back to their families. To other ships."

Except me. They were the words that she knew he could not say. "I never thought of you as lonely, Jack. You were always . . . such a self-sufficient lad."

He kept his eyes on the horizon, but she saw by the clench of his cheek, the ball of his throat, that he had indeed heard her.

"Even if I was so lucky as to get a new commission—which is unlikely in these times—I would have to question whether

I want to spend the next nine years building another home that is impermanent. I may be a good sailor, a good officer. But I don't know if I would miss the life . . . what could have been. I always wanted a life of service to the Crown, but one of adventure, too. For all the *Amorata's* comfort, it can be too comfortable as well. I've been thinking . . . very much of late . . . that I need something more."

She wanted to ask him what he would do, then, without the sea. She wanted to ask him if he intended to make a strong suit to Miss Devlin. She wanted to ask . . . so many things. But instead, she just laid her hand over his, stilled him from plucking at the grass, and stared out onto the horizon with him.

And as pink began to tinge the sky, the sun calling an end to their day, they sat further still. Until Sarah finally spoke.

"I missed this."

He looked up at her, and then down at their joined hands.

"I did, too."

❧

They stepped through the front door of number sixteen Upper Grosvenor Street just as dusk gave up its hold, and night took over.

"Thank goodness," Sarah sighed as she glided through the door in front of Jack. "I was afraid we were going to be too late."

"I told you I'd get you back in time." Jack replied, as he handed his hat to Dalton. Dalton dutifully brushed the grass off of it. "Besides, you said you weren't going to arrive at the Gold Ball until, what, three hours from now?"

"Yes, but I have to get ready," Sarah replied, shaking her head at him. "I can't very well arrive at the Gold Ball in Regent's Park with dirt under my fingernails and twigs in my hair. Nor can you." She glanced down at his clothes, which had, after sitting on the ground and running about playing bowls, taken on a decidedly earthy smell.

"I like you with twigs in your hair," Jack said, his eyes going automatically to her unkempt hair arrangement, where slick, heavy locks threatened to slip free of their knot and spill over her shoulders. He abruptly shook off the image, and retook the role of friend. "Perhaps you can start a new trend."

They'd had such a wonderful day. The day of playing on the green and leaving their troubles behind them, if only for a few hours, had made Jack more relaxed and happy than he had been in weeks—hell, months.

He let go of the sadness that encompassed the fate of the *Amorata*. He left behind his guilt over playing a cruel trick on Sarah . . . he said good-bye for a few short hours to the weight of the Blue Raven, that mission the Worth Brothers had placed on his shoulders.

Until they stepped through the door again.

As Dalton moved off, with mention of how the rest of the family was deep in preparations for the Gold Ball tonight, they were left alone in the foyer.

He could tell her now, he mused, as she brushed down her skirts. He could tell her, and hold her back from possible danger. She would hate him—but perhaps, a fraction less so than if they hadn't just played *apology bowls* all afternoon.

He could tell her now, he decided. And he would.

If only she didn't say what she said next.

"All I can say is thank goodness you forwent wearing your uniform today—I asked Dalton to have it pressed for tonight."

His eyebrow quirked up. "I did not think I was included on the invitation to the Gold Ball."

"Of course you were—and we need you especially. Lady Fieldstone asked Phillippa to take over the table she had purchased, and Phillippa refuses to let there be an empty seat at Lord Fieldstone's table."

His brow went up. "What do you mean, purchased a table?"

Sarah took his arm and they began to make their way up the stairs.

"The Gold Ball was founded by the King while he was still Prince Regent, to benefit the construction of his park." Sarah explained. "It's grown quite a bit in its charitable function since then, and this Season, it was asked that attendees purchase a table for the supper courses. Apparently Lady Fieldstone purchased a table before . . ." Sarah let the sentence trail off without unnecessary explanation. "It's a point of pride for Phillippa that Lady Fieldstone's table not sit empty. Thus, we need you."

But the truth was, he could never tell her.

Lord Fieldstone's death. A Burmese *dha*. A missing letter with Fieldstone's blood on it. Someone trying to start a war. As unkind as his actions had been to Sarah, it was now bigger than his foolish pride, and his guilt.

But he could still try to keep her safe. Uninvolved. For just one more day.

"What if . . . what if we don't go to the ball tonight?" Jack asked, and Sarah came to a halt.

"Don't go to the ball?" she asked, appalled.

Don't go to the ball. Don't charm the Comte back in love with you. Don't let yourself get mixed up in this any further.

"What if we continued our good day, and just left the outside world to their own devices. Just for a night." Jack took her hand in his, and hoped that she heard his plea.

He watched as hesitation overcame her, then she made a decision—and he cursed God that it was not in his favor.

She smiled a little sadly and patted his arm. "Jack, I'm so glad we patched up our differences today. But those things we left behind to do so? We have to pick them up again."

She leaned forward and with a glance down the hall to make sure no one was watching, kissed him lightly on the cheek. Not with any intention other than friendship, he knew, but it burned him, burned his skin. And saddened him to the core.

And as she let go of his arm, and retreated down the hall, Jack thought vaguely he should call after her. He would say . . .

But he couldn't.

So he determined he would do the only thing he could. Watch over her.

No matter what.

ॐ

That night, amongst the glitter and glamour of the Gold Ball, Jack watched when, as expected, the Golden Lady made her triumphant return to form. Sarah was universally feted and admired, charming the crowd with her smiles and flirtations. He watched as the Comte fell under her spell again.

And he watched as she asked him about the prospect of visiting his home.

"My dear Comte, how was I to let you know of my comings

and goings for the past few weeks?" Sarah pouted prettily, as they sat at the table in between dances. She had favored him with the last two in a row—one more and they might end up engaged. "A woman is not permitted to send notes to a gentleman, nor is she allowed to pay calls."

"You are quite right," he said, kissing her hand. "I am merely sorry that you were out when I paid *my* calls."

Jack cocked a brow, knowing full well that Sarah had not been out, but that was neither here nor there.

"Besides, if I were to pay a call, I wouldn't even know where to go," Sarah said leadingly.

"Miss Forrester, you know where I live." The Comte looked befuddled. "The Duke of Parford has graciously lent us his home for the Season. He was so admiring of Mr. Pha and myself when we met in Bombay—"

Sarah put on an expression of wonder, and interrupted him before he could go any further. "Do you mean that lovely large house on the corner of the square?" As he nodded, she exclaimed. "But no one's been in there for years! They say he has some of the most beautiful paintings in his gallery."

The Comte tilted his head to one side. Jack shook with suppressed laughter, seeing the man—this possible villain—so easily befuddled.

"Yes, there are some nice paintings, but—"

"Oh, my dear Comte—Jean—I must see them. Is it possible? That I could come to call?"

"I don't really think—"

"Oh, of course, you're right, it wouldn't do. You should throw a dinner party! That way everyone could see the Duke's collection." Sarah's eyes lit up as she leaned forward, letting her breasts, confined by scraps of embroidered gold silk, just barely brush the Comte's arm.

Jack's expression darkened as the Comte's grew warmer. "Well, I don't know about that—" the Comte was saying, but his eye line indicated his attention was elsewhere.

"Miss Georgina"—Sarah turned to the Comte's stepsister, who was sitting next to them, meek in her burnished gown— "would it not be fun to host a dinner party? Why I would be gratified to help you with the arrangements."

The Comte went still as he turned to his sister. "I don't

think it would work at all, Georgie . . ." he began, but Georgina, normally so small and wide-eyed, brightened immediately at the prospect.

"But of course we should, Jean! What fun. I would relish the opportunity to get to know Miss Forrester better"—she shot her stepbrother a pleading look—"and can only hope with the Golden Lady's help, we shall have the best dinner party imaginable!"

Thus, Jack watched as Sarah committed herself deeper than her promise to the Blue Raven commanded that she go, committed herself to spending several days in the presence of the Comte, the Burmese gentleman that was their guest, and possibly a murderer.

And he only had himself to blame for not stopping it.

Eighteen

"SARAH, what do you mean there will be no music at the dinner party?" Bridget practically screeched, when she stormed into Sarah's room without knocking.

"Do come in, Bridget," Sarah said, as Molly pinned the last of the flowers into her hair. Her hair never had and never would curl, so therefore the only whimsy that she could inject into the coiffure was flowers. Which pricked at her skull.

But it was worth it she told herself. Tonight would be perfect. It had to be.

The planning for the dinner party at the Comte de Le Bon's home had taken place in a whirlwind of activity over the course of the last week—and oddly, only at the Forrester residence.

When word leaked of the party, everyone who was anyone clamored for an invitation, not only because the Comte and his Burmese guest managed to hold the public's fascination, but also since the Duke of Parford's London home had been closed for years, and its opening and the subsequent viewing of the paintings was highly anticipated.

Apparently, the attention and madness so overset their entirely Indian staff that Miss Georgina and the Comte had to plan the whole affair from Sarah's drawing room.

While the Comte and his stepsister, hovered over by Mr. Ashin Pha, of course, conferred about how to place the tables, Sarah grew more anticipatory by the day. She kept her fractiousness under wraps, even as the Comte tried to charm her by mispronouncing certain words, or slurring them in his French/British Indian accent—which was so terribly odious! How did she ever find his accent the most interesting part of him?

And if she had found his accent to be the most interesting part of him—well, the rest simply did not qualify for so much as an afterthought. But as annoyed as she was by his voice (and by the fawning ever presence of her mother, who insisted on "helping"), she was more annoyed that even when planning a dinner party with them, she was still not admitted to the Comte's house.

How was she to help the Blue Raven break in if she could not point out the best entrance? Or where he would need to search? Or places to avoid? How would she be able to help him?

And then, he told her.

Halfway through the week, a note came. There was no signature, beyond a small flourish, that looked like it might be a drawing of a feather. The wax that sealed the paper was a dark blue—dark enough to be black. And the content of the note was a list of names.

The people the Blue Raven wanted her to invite.

It was steadying to have that note in her hand—to know that he was aware of her actions on his behalf and anticipating the event, the same as she was. But the list—aside from Phillippa and Marcus Worth, who were of course, already invited—was of the silliest, most blindly glamorous people the ton had to offer. People of little to no substance, who only wanted to have fun and make merry. And Sarah would know—she was friends with most of them! They were a terribly distracting lot.

And then she realized. The Blue Raven needed as much distraction as he could muster.

The only hiccup was getting the hosts to accept them.

"I don't know . . ." Georgina said tentatively, as she eyed the list. "I think we were hoping for more men of . . ."

"Influence?" Sarah provided.

"Eligibility," Georgina replied with a blush. "At least that's what Mrs. Hill would like."

Sarah reached out and took Georgina's hand. In all the goings-on, it was easy to forget that the Comte was in London to bring his sister out—or at the very least he was there under that pretense. "Of course if there is someone who has captured your attention, we will invite him. What does the Comte think?"

Georgina slid a glance to where the Comte was making small, clipped conversation with the ever-present Jack.

"I'm not certain. But Mr. Ashin Pha is not happy about the party."

"Has he said so?"

Georgina nodded. "Or at least, that's what he said to Jean. I don't understand Burmese, unfortunately. It is such a terse, angry language. When he speaks to Jean, sometimes it looks like he's yelling at my brother."

A cool trickle of dread went down Sarah's spine, as she eyed Mr. Ashin Pha's cool, dignified but stern countenance. But she was in too deep now. She could only push ahead.

"I assure you, all of the people on the list are well-known to your brother and are such fun, they will make the party an utter delight, one even Mr. Ashin Pha could not disapprove of." She smiled with enthusiasm, and was gratified to see Georgina smile relievedly back.

Thus, the guest list was altered accordingly, and the rest of the week moved at once too fast and too slow for Sarah's liking, until that moment, where, in the act of getting ready, her sister had one more thing to add to the preparations.

"There has to be a piano, or something—how will people dance? I've been practicing a new waltz all week," Bridget pouted.

"You were intending to play?" Sarah's eyebrow went up. Not because she questioned her sister's talent, but Bridget very rarely played in public. Her nerves got the better of her, she would say. Which was truly unfortunate, because Bridget had a rare ability.

"I was going to try," Bridget grumbled. "I thought, perhaps I would be able to make an impression. But if there is to be no music—"

"There will be music—the Comte has persuaded Mr. Pha to play a sitar, a native instrument, for us. Besides, the Comte apparently does not have an instrument for you to play." Sarah shrugged.

"Why would an aristocratic man from India—"

"Burma."

"Whatever you say, play his own instrument?" Before Sarah could answer that she didn't know, but point out that Bridget was a member of the upper class and played her own instrument, her sister continued her whine. "And how does the Comte not have an instrument—or the Duke of Parford, for that matter?"

"I don't know, Bridge, perhaps they don't appreciate music the way you do. But I'm certain that if you are set on playing, we can have one brought in."

"No. My nerves would likely me fail me again. Especially if a pianoforte is brought in special for me. Too much expectation." Bridget slumped onto Sarah's bed. "It was my only chance to shine. My only chance to get him to notice me."

Sarah perked up in her seat. She sent Molly a look, which the maid interpreted correctly as "best to leave and I'll fill you in later," and she curtsied her exit.

"Get who to notice you?" Sarah asked, turning in her seat.

"No one," Bridget said sullenly. "But it will never happen now."

"Bridge—why don't you try smiling, and being . . . pleasant? You'll have plenty of men notice you if you do that."

"Smiling and being insipid is your area of expertise. I have music," Bridget snapped.

Oh dear, Sarah couldn't help but think. She's back to being angry at me.

And she was finally just too tired of it.

"All right, Bridget, what did I do now?" Sarah sighed. "I thought we had been getting along better, but for the past week you've grown more and more snippy with me."

"You didn't do anything," Bridget grumbled, "and there's the trouble. You didn't do anything, and people flock to your side. The Golden Lady."

"It's better than my acting like I'm in mourning, isn't it?" Sarah countered, standing angrily.

Bridget's face went pale with shock and then bright red with shame. Oh yes, Sarah thought, she remembered saying those words to their parents all those months ago. But Bridget stood as well, and rallied her anger, and joined in the confrontation.

"You were walking around like someone had died, and suddenly all everyone can talk about is you. Then you stopped walking around like someone had died, and everything was *still* all about you! How is anyone supposed to see me with the Golden Lady as my sister?"

"Well," Sarah exhaled. "You finally said it." What she had long suspected, long known. "Brava."

"And I can do nothing about it!" Bridget continued. "I can't outshine you. I can't get anyone to see me without seeing you, except those rare occasions that I play in public without my hands shaking."

"Or when you do maths better than me," Sarah replied quietly. "But why are you so angry now?"

"Because before Jack was just as unhappy with you as I was, and now he's half in love with you again!" Bridget covered her mouth, shocked by her own honesty.

Sarah stilled. "This is about Jack?"

Bridget wouldn't look at Sarah. But the mortification burned on her cheeks.

In reflection, Sarah could see that the date of her sister's swing back into unhappiness with her could be dated to her and Jack's apology picnic. But she had been so wrapped up in her own high dramas that she did not see Bridget, or anyone else.

And suddenly, it was as if lightning struck.

So wrapped up in her dramas . . . that she didn't see anyone else.

Sarah had been wrapped up in herself for six months now. Well, it was high time she came out of it.

"Sit down," Sarah told Bridget, kindly but firmly. Bridget sat on the edge of the bed, again. This time, Sarah joined her.

"I'm sorry," she began. "I'm sorry for many things I have said to you in the past few months. And I'm sorry that you have felt short changed this Season. Truth be told, so have I." Bridget's eyes came up, disbelieving. "I didn't want this Season, you know. But you wanted yours. And the fault for not enjoying it lies on your shoulders, not mine." Sarah went so far as to touch her sister's shoulder. "The world would love you, Bridge, if only you would let them."

"I don't want to be feted, like you," Bridget shook her head.

"You think I wanted to be? But when the choice is feted or pitied . . ." She let the thought trail off. "But the worst of it is, I had to spend the past few months without my sister."

Bridget seemed to soften at that, but the spiny shell that held her apart from Sarah was still in place. She shook off Sarah's hand.

"But you have all of London instead," she replied, not a little sadly. "The Comte, and now Jack . . ."

"Jackson Fletcher is not in love with me," Sarah cut in, adamant. "He and I managed to mend fences, that is all." As she let Bridget take that in, she continued. "And I have to say, you're not in love with him, either."

Bridget's spine went rigid at that, and she began to stand. "Excuse me, you know nothing of my—"

Sarah grabbed the back of her skirt and pulled her back down to her seat. "Yes, I do know something of your feelings, Bridge. You just want his attention like you did when we were younger. Once you had it, you would become bored and be playing music and forget that you had it."

"You're just saying that because you want to keep his attention," Bridget tried.

Sarah rolled her eyes, sighing. "Bridget, what's your favorite piece of music? That allegro thing?"

"*Adagio*," Bridget corrected.

"How does it make you feel, when you play it?"

Bridget frowned for a moment, and then straightened, and closed her eyes. "It's hard to play," she mused. Her fingers began twitching, moving over invisible ivory keys. "My hands are not large enough, so I have to stretch. But it is worth it. It's so worth it because those few times that I get it right . . . it's like I'm flying. The notes . . . they play in time to my heart, against my ribs, and I'm . . . I'm completely at ease."

Bridget's eyes came open. She seemed slightly embarrassed by how she had just spoken, but held silent.

Sarah nodded, and then asked. "Does Jack make you feel the same way?"

"Well, of course not," Bridget replied. "Why do you ask?"

"Because that's what love feels like," Sarah surmised, and watched as Bridget opened her mouth to argue, but then closed it, silent. "Love is hard. It's difficult. You worry all the time over the other person. Whether they are safe and happy, and when you might see them again. But it's worth it. Because when you are together it feels like flying. And being completely at ease."

Bridget's eyes softened. "You're in love. Right now?"

Sarah felt herself blush as she nodded.

"With whom?" Bridget asked. "With Jack? After all, you are completely at ease with him now, like you said—"

"No, not with Jack," Sarah rolled her eyes.

"Well, with whom then!" Bridget grabbed at Sarah's arm. It was too wonderful having this moment, when her sister dropped all notions of being upset and turned . . . well, turned into her sister again, that Sarah could not help but want it to continue.

"I can tell you that he's wonderful . . . And terribly handsome. And heroic. And just so wonderful . . ."

"You already said wonderful."

"Well, he is!" Sarah said laughing.

"Oh, for heaven's sake! Is that all you're going to tell me?" Bridget joined in on the laughing. "You think he's heroic and marvelous—you might as well be twelve years old again and talking about the Blue Raven!"

Sarah froze in her mirth. Just for a moment . . . just a spare second. But Bridget, whose eye had always been keener than Sarah liked, noticed. Her laughter died with a raise of a quizzical brow.

"Sarah . . ." Bridget began, but was cut off by a laugh—too forced, damn it all!—from her sister.

"That's completely mad, of course," Sarah trilled. "Ah . . . what are you going to wear this evening? What about the ivory silk with the Indian embroidery?"

But Bridget did not respond. At least not immediately. She instead had taken on a look of calculation—her brow furrowed, her gaze intense but unfocused, as if she were trying to follow the clues to a mathematics solution, or work out the next sequence in a minuet. And suddenly, her expression became one of awe. Of alarm.

"Sarah, when did you meet—I mean, you can't describe what he looks like, can you?" Bridget asked. "He hid his face?"

"Bridget, don't be ridiculous," she tried to protest. "It's not the Blue Raven. Now, about your gown . . ."

"No." Bridget stood up abruptly. "I have to go. I'll be . . ."

But she didn't finish the sentence. Instead, she moved with twitching determination to the door and let herself out.

Leaving Sarah feeling wretched, certain she had just stumbled, and could only hope that her sister was discreet with any information she thought she knew.

§

"Are you coming or going?" Jack asked as he rounded the corner in the hallway, and found Bridget at the door to his bedchamber, with her hand on the knob. By the little jump she gave, and the way she blushed thereafter, Jack knew he had surprised her. What he didn't expect was the way she turned on him, with accusation in her eyes.

"Neither," she said coldly, coming right up to him, stuffing something into her pocket as she did so. But his curiosity about the content of her pockets would have to wait, judging by the way she assessed him coldly.

"You look lovely tonight, Bridget." Jack decided to try with a charming smile. After all, he knew that she responded to his compliments in a girlish way—he wasn't blind to her crush. "Are you ready for the dinner party?"

"I've decided not to go," she answered directly. No hint of girlishness. She assessed his clothing, his very casual attire. "Are you?"

Jack looked down at himself and felt the blush spread on his cheeks. "I'm not going. I have previous plans with Mr. Whigby."

"Do you now?" Bridget drawled. She crossed her arms over her chest.

"Bridget," Jack began, slightly wary, "what is it? Have you been fighting with Sarah again?"

"No, quite the opposite."

"Oh. Good."

"What are you doing to Sarah?" she asked, her head cocked to one side.

"I?" he asked bewildered. "Nothing. I'm doing nothing to her."

Bridget leaned forward. "I think it best if you keep it that way. Forresters don't take well to being played for fools."

Jack's mind ratcheted around, looking for some kind of explanation. And landed on Bridget's feelings for him, and her sister, respectively. "Bridget," he sighed gently, "you know that I am just friends with your sister. As I am friends with you."

But the girl simply held his gaze, as if she could see straight through him, to his every last secret. And stalked past him, her head held as high as a queen's.

It would be much later that Jack realized what Bridget was saying. After the family had left for the Comte's dinner party. After he gathered up his disguise, but could not locate his false moustache, and was forced to go without it. Yes, it was right around the time when everything was going to hell, that Jack decided he would have done better to heed Bridget's warning.

Indeed, it was proved, Forresters don't take well to being played for fools.

Nineteen

"WHERE is your moustache?" Marcus Worth whispered to him as he unlocked the music room window for Jack.

"Missing," Jack shrugged. "Laundress might have mistaken it for lint."

"Or a rat's hide," Marcus grinned. Which only made Jack wrinkle his nose in disgust. "You're late."

"I had to wait for the carriages to thin out, and the guards to loop around again," Jack replied. "Too many eyes." Indeed, Jack had been waiting on the rooftop of the mansion across from the Duke of Parford's stately classical home in the heart of Mayfair for over an hour. The arrivals of the glittering ton who had garnered an invitation to what had turned out to be the dinner party of the Season had taken ages, with people making their entrances as if they were attending a royal wedding—moving with that stately grace reserved for being seen. Of course, this meant they moved abominably slow, and Jack found it difficult to leap from the next-door roof across the high wall to the Duke of Parford's roof without causing a stir.

"A little performance anxiety?" Marcus grinned at him.

Jack shot him a droll look. "If I wanted cheap shots at this time, I would have made your brother come along."

"He couldn't, you know that." Marcus replied.

It was true. Over the past week, Jack had spent the daylight hours playing watchdog over Sarah—because he would be damned if he was going to leave her alone with the Comte, knowing what was suspected of him. A courtesy she seemed to appreciate, if not for the same reasons. The number of times she sent him an amused glance over her shoulder or an eye roll when the Comte was pontificating again on his Burmese adventure had made Jack's heart sing. Meanwhile, his nights had been spent working with Marcus and Byrne on their plan of attack for the Comte's dinner party.

One that Jack would be infiltrating alone.

After making sure Jack pulled off the first part of the adventure, Byrne had left the city for his home in the Lake District. When Jack asked why the Blue Raven would possibly leave halfway through an operation, Marcus replied carefully.

"My brother . . . he has certain weaknesses the city caters to. He can keep this part of himself in check if his family is with him, but falling into the Blue Raven business . . ." Marcus looked down at his desk, contemplating, then returned his eyes to Jack. There was bleakness there. "Suffice to say I do not begrudge him the decision to go home. Nor will you," he commanded. And that was all Marcus would say on the subject.

Marcus had managed to obtain the original sketches of the floor plans for the Duke of Parford's home from the days of its construction. How Marcus was able to obtain these papers, Jack did not question—but they turned out to be a gold mine of information on how they would enter and search the residence. It wasn't a terribly old manse, Georgian in style and built within the last century and, therefore, easy to navigate—not Byzantine like some medieval structures, nor involving some of the more elaborate "romantic" architecture that was now popular, with turrets and passageways that lead nowhere.

Even though Jack could have been invited, if he so desired, he knew it was best if he not attend as a guest—he could too easily be noticed as missing from the dinner table. Therefore, they decided that Jack would enter through the garden, when everyone was still arriving—all of the attention would be at the front of the house, not the back. But to get there, he would have to jump from the roof of the property next door, over a high wall and into some fortunately thick shrubbery—without arousing the suspicion of any guards that happened to be posted nearby.

Of which, it turned out, there were several.

From there, Marcus, who they had made certain was invited to the party, along with his wife, Phillippa, would make sure the path was clear for him to enter through the back gardens, where he would quickly slip in a downstairs window, to the music room. Since Jack had somehow managed to persuade Sarah to exclude traditional music from that evening's entertainments, that room would be dark and unused.

And apparently, quite dusty.

"I don't think anyone's been in this room in years," Marcus whispered, as he ushered Jack in through the window. "Be careful not to disturb the drop cloths, or any of the surfaces. You want to leave no trace of having been here."

"What kind of French aristocrat doesn't have his home—even a borrowed one—dusted regularly?"

"The kind who either doesn't appreciate music, or is harder up for money than we thought," Marcus replied.

"Well, it will make searching the rooms the Comte and Mr. Ashin Pha occupy simpler." Jack mused in a whisper. At Marcus's quizzical look, he continued. "If the dust in a room is thick and undisturbed, then no one has entered for a number of years—therefore, no hidden secrets from short-term residents in those rooms."

Marcus nodded in agreement. "Good point. Now I must hurry back, before anyone notices I'm missing. We're still all in the sitting room, but will be going into dinner shortly. You'll be most free to move about the house then. You know what to look for?"

Jack looked heavenward. This had been drilled into him. "Just a guess . . . letters stained with blood?"

"Not only will they prove either the Comte's or Mr. Pha's involvement, but hopefully they can give us a clue as to who is pulling the strings. Best get to it, then." Marcus said, slapping him on the shoulder before he tiptoed to the door.

"Marcus," Jack called, and he turned. Jack's voice became

a grumble as serious as thunder. "Don't leave Sarah's side to-night."

Marcus nodded gravely, right before slipping out the door and back into the brightness of the hallway beyond.

Leaving Jack to carry out his mission. Careful not to disturb the dust of the stale room, he immediately went to where he knew the hidden door to the servant's staircase to be, and slipped inside.

This particular corridor he knew, thanks to memorizing the house's schematics, lead to the servants' bedrooms—and since all of the maids and footmen would be dealing with the party, it was predictably unoccupied. A quick rifling of all the servants' rooms turned up nothing. Except for the fact that *none* of the servants appeared to be English. Jack wondered briefly what had happened to the housekeeper and skeleton staff most aristocratic houses retained even when they were not in use. But since he located no letters, let alone blood-stained ones, he put his questions into a spare corner of his brain and moved on.

Since the main floors of the house were occupied by the party, Jack moved silently up the servants' staircase to the top of the house, where the storage rooms and nursery were. The nursery was predictably dusty and unused (no call for someone without young family to open up those rooms), but the attics were clean as a whistle . . . and unaccountably empty. Jack searched every corner, but came up with nothing. It was deeply suspicious, because the Duke of Parford was said to have been a collector, with every one of his homes full of beautiful things. Even if he had lent this house for the Season, why would he have bothered to clean out the attic?

There was, indeed, something very strange going on in this house.

But since there was nothing in the way of communiqués, Jack had no reason to stay, and as such, he began working his way down the house, room by room. And coming up with nothing. Even the Comte's bedroom—which was a mess, and spoke to his valet's lack of discipline—contained nothing of note that Jack could find. Nor did Mr. Ashin Pha's—and he seemed to be living in a state of dissolute grandeur to rival his friend's.

There was a hairy moment or two when Jack knew he had

to move from the family rooms to the public rooms below, the sounds of laughter, warmth, and clinking silverware drifting up the main staircase. Apparently the dinner party was a great success. But Jack would have to ruminate on Sarah's party-planning abilities later, as he was confronted by the unexpected—a footman, stationed at the top of the staircase.

Judging by the dark man's size and the ill-fitting uniform, he had not been "just" a footman in India. And he was to make sure that no guest moved up the stairs to the family rooms.

Lucky for Jack, he was not expecting anyone to be moving in the opposite direction.

It was dark enough at the top of the stairs that dragging the heavy man's inert form into a linen closet went unnoticed—but Jack knew his absence would be noted soon, and therefore, his search of the most important rooms would have to be as quick as it was thorough.

He slipped down the staircase, holding in a shadowed alcove, as a number of servants moved past with empty trays and decanters. The doors up the hall from him were the dining room and drawing room, respectively. From the sounds and light, Jack guessed dinner was in its last throes.

He would have to hurry, then.

There was only one door at the end of the hall—the Duke of Parford's library. And if Jack was going to wager money, he would bet that what they looked for was in there.

When the last servant passed with the last tray of empty plates, Jack slipped out and made his way to the library door. Of course it was locked, which only heightened Jack's expectations.

Now he just needed to pick the lock. Luckily, the Blue Raven spent the better part of a week teaching him how. Less luckily, that had always been with much better light.

"Come on," Jack breathed to himself, as he maneuvered the mangled hairpin in the latch. Byrne could do this with a breath and wrist flick, he thought ruefully. Female noise from down the hall were getting louder . . . The ladies were retiring to the drawing room . . . They would be in the hallway at any moment.

Blessedly, the latch gave way with one last flick of the

wrist, and Jack slipped inside the library door, just as the dining room doors were opening.

Immediately, Jack knew that had he been a betting man, his pockets would be fuller right now. The Duke of Parford's library absolutely tingled with discovery.

This room was used, and used often. Even in the dark, Jack could see the piles of papers, maps, and objects from foreign lands scattered seemingly at random about the room.

He moved swiftly to the desk, and the stack of papers that was haphazardly strewn there. Nothing but bills—massive ones, but just bills all the same. No bloodstains. He rifled the books, to the same result. The cushions of the lounge chairs, the uncomfortably high desk chair . . . and found nothing.

The only thing he found out of place was the excessive amount of ash in the fireplace—it had been too warm for the past week for any need of a fire. Was someone burning bloody letters?

He had just ducked and begun gingerly sifting through the ash when he heard a sound at the door. Someone was turning the knob.

Swiftly he pulled his hood firmly over his head, seeking darkness, obscurity. He moved to hide himself beside the doorjamb . . . quickly pulling out the seaman's dagger he had concealed in his boot. He waited, as the door handle clicked . . . and the massive carved plank of solid oak was pushed in . . .

And Sarah Forrester ducked her head around the corner.

"*God damn it,*" he breathed.

When she turned, and saw only a dark figure in the dark with the shine of a blade in hand, she did what any sane person would. She opened her mouth to scream.

Which he could not allow.

Thus he did the only thing he could think of at that moment. Roughly, he pulled her to his body and kissed her.

❧

Up until that moment, Sarah could rightly say that the evening had been inauspicious.

Aside from the excitement of Bridget's strange exit from Sarah's room and their conversation, and then Bridget's subsequent announcement that she would not be attending that evening's festivities, Sarah had begun to think the night would turn out to be terribly dull.

So far, everything about the dinner party was going according to plan. The people invited were glittering in their diamonds and feathers, the majority of the ladies donning Indies-inspired fashions. Sarah had to admit that the golden embroidery along her hem was the scrolling leaves and decorative flowers associated with Indian textiles. But there was absolutely no reason for the Marchioness of Broughton to be wearing peacock feathers in her outlandishly styled turban, making her almost twice the height of her usually diminutive form.

Sarah had arrived early with her mother in tow, and helped the Comte and Georgina, whose natural timidity had returned in force, her eyes shining with presumed nerves as she shook hands with everyone who entered. But by the time the last person had made their way down the row of the Comte, Georgina, and Mr. Ashin Pha (who looked regal in an elaborate headdress, the feathers of which tickled the nose of more than one guest, he bowed so deeply), Georgina had relaxed a bit, and they took them all into dinner.

Sarah was not seated next to the Comte as planned. Instead, she found herself next to Marcus Worth, although she had been certain she had arranged the seating differently. But it mattered little—the Comte's voice carried, and his stories were ones Sarah had heard far too many times at this point. The gaiety of the guests, as well as the unexpected delight of the traditional Indian courses that were served, kept the spirits of the room up, but Sarah's mind could not help but flicker to the man who at that moment must have been sneaking about the house, and where he could possibly be.

It made appreciating the dinner and the conversation very difficult.

Finally, after half a dozen courses of exotic meats and spices had been massacred on the table, Georgina, prompted into her role of hostess by Mrs. Hill, stood up and led the ladies into the drawing room.

And that was when she saw him.

Or at the very least she saw something, thanks to Georgina forgetting to follow protocol and have the higher ranking ladies walk with her, instead grabbing Sarah's arm and pulling her along. When her hand touched Sarah's skin, she could tell why. Her hands were shaking.

"I'm more nervous about sitting with the ladies than I was about dinner. At least at dinner Jean was able to carry the conversation." Georgina whispered to Sarah in her little voice. Georgina's sweetness and timidity snapped Sarah out of her worrying about the Blue Raven's whereabouts, and instead back to the difficulties of the dinner party itself.

"They are all so much more . . . glamorous than I." Georgina's eyes darted to the far-too-fashionable plumes and turbans of the other women there, and then down at her lovely, if somewhat plainly designed gown, which maintained a sole note of interest due to the red Indian silk it was made of.

"You're doing fine," Sarah replied, patting her hand. "Now, you should make sure the servants are ready with the special tea you brought back from India with you—"

It was at that moment that the burly footmen opened the doors to the main hall, ushering the ladies out—and Sarah, at the front of the women, caught a glimpse of movement.

It was just a flash, a sliver of light as a brass door handle moved a fraction of an inch—but it was enough to start Sarah's heart beating faster. It was all she could do not to run to the door just then and fly into the unknown room. Instead, she was careful not to spare the door a second glance, while memorizing which one it was. She knew he was in there. She felt it in her bones.

And a mere ten minutes later, she was proven right.

Because no one else kissed like the Blue Raven, she thought on a sigh, as she leaned into his arms.

Although, there was something different this time.

"Where—where is your moustache?" she said in a whisper, when he finally broke off the kiss.

"Ah—I shaved it," he replied quickly, after returning his knife to its place in his boot. Then he looked up at her from the depths of his cloak. "You shouldn't be here."

"I know," she replied, chastised. "I know it's stupid. I should have stayed with the ladies."

"You'll be missed, and soon," he warned, as he stalked over to the fireplace, and began inspecting the ashes.

"I know," she repeated.

"Then why are you here?" he asked, frustrated.

Why was she here? She narrowed her eyes furiously. "Maybe I'm here trying to find the necessary, which is the excuse I gave the ladies when I stepped out of the room. Maybe I'm here because I've spent a week planning a party that you asked me to create and I wanted to make certain that you were finding what you needed, and I find myself invested in the outcome of this adventure. Or maybe I'm here because I haven't seen you in over that amount of time and with all I'm doing for you, don't I have a right to a little consideration?"

He straightened, having apparently not found anything in the fireplace. "It's too dangerous for you to be here. You have to go," he claimed, taking her by the arm, and pulling her toward the door.

"If I go back to the room now, it would be even more suspicious." Sarah rationalized. "Women know how long it takes for us to . . . arrange ourselves." He paused right before the door. "Besides, you look like you could use some help."

He seemed to be indecisive. His thumb on her arm began to move gently back in forth, making his mind up. Finally he breathed, "Damn it."

"Have you found what you're looking for?" she asked quietly.

"No," he admitted. "And this is the last room to check."

He released her arm, and stalked back to the desk, which was littered with papers.

"Let me help. What are we looking for?" she asked.

"A letter. There will likely be . . . droplets of blood on it," he answered as she paled. "But these are all just bills—from reputable companies."

"High ones," Sarah said drily, returning to regular color as she perused the papers. She placed the paper back down where she found it. "Well, let's get to work, then."

Over the next few minutes, they scoured every surface, explored every piece of paper in the room, every book, every crevice that could hold a note, every tiny little scrap, straining their eyes to read in the moonlight.

And coming up with nothing.

"I don't understand," she whispered after some minutes.

"If I know the Comte, he's the type of man who would hide his secrets in plain sight, thinking he's being clever and out-witting everyone."

"Which makes this lack of anything suspicious all the more confounding. Unless, of course, he's not guilty of trea-sonous activities as suspected."

"You suspect him of treason," Sarah repeated, feeling a line of coldness trickle down her spine. "You never told me that."

"I didn't want you to know," he grumbled, as he began feel-ing around the seams of the desk—hoping for a secret pocket, or a button to depress, most likely. "For your safety."

"And yet you left me alone with him all week," she replied quietly.

Without changing from his course, he answered easily, "You were never alone with him."

"How do you know that?" she asked, suspicious.

He froze in his movements, his head coming up ever so slightly. Even in the dark, she could tell that he was regretting his words. Words that gave him away.

"How do you know that?" she asked again, taking a step closer to him. "Were you . . . were you keeping an eye on me from afar?"

"Something like that," he replied, his voice strangled. Then, he turned to her, his voice intense. "Sarah, I should tell you—"

"How did you do it? Did you pay off the servants, or—"

"Jesus, Sarah, I can't keep lying—"

"Truth be told I don't care how you did it—I'm just glad you did." She smiled at him, her eyes a little watery. "I'm glad you trusted me enough to help with your mission, and glad that you cared enough to make sure I was safe."

She rose on tiptoe and kissed him on the cheek. This was not an expression of passion, of heat—but of gratitude. She was just happy to know that he cared.

But that kiss seemed to break something in him. Because he pulled her to him, holding her steady, as he braced her against the desk.

"Of course I care," he rasped, as he leaned over her. "I've always cared. You may not think so, but I have."

Sarah felt her heart going fast, so fast she thought she

might faint. But being here, in this moment with this man of all men staring down at her, was far too important to succumb to such weakness. Far too important to give any attention to the soft click of a lock, or the silent creak of a door. The way he stared at her—only the shine of his eyes from beneath his cloak visible—she knew he was on the verge of telling her something imperative. Something real.

Something that would have to wait.

"You really think this is the best time for that?" came a whispered voice from the door. Sarah whipped her head around, and was astonished to see Sir Marcus, Phillippa's husband, peeking his head around the door. He slid into the room and quickly crossed to them.

Curiously, he didn't seemed shocked at all to see a cloaked man embracing her.

"You have been missed," Sir Marcus addressed her. "And you have been too long in this room," he said, turning his attention to the Blue Raven.

"I know, but this is the only room to have any potential. Everything else is neat and spare, to the point of bareness," the Blue Raven whispered back.

"Sir Marcus, you . . . know each other," Sarah stated the fact, her brain catching up to the situation. "Of course you do—you're the head of the War Department now. I keep forgetting."

"Many people do," Marcus replied jovially. "A truth that works to my advantage on occasion." Then, more pointedly, "I take it that information was withheld from you does not bother you?"

"Not as much as one might suppose," Sarah replied. "On the contrary, I am happy to learn that he has not been alone in this." She touched the Blue Raven's arm. He remained still, impassive, not responding to her touch. Embarrassed, she withdrew her hand.

"Yes, well, your part has been played admirably, Miss Forrester, and it's time to get back to it. People are questioning your absence and I volunteered to fetch you."

"But we've been searching—"

"No more. You've risked enough," the Blue Raven said tersely.

"So I must risk my patience instead?" she replied, frustrated. "Playing along with people I find as false as that painting?"

All eyes flicked to the wall she indicated. "This painting?" Marcus asked, as he took two steps toward the painting. It was a huge portrait, from the time of the Tudor court. A woman, who must have been very, very wealthy, or perhaps a mistress of the King, stood proud and tall in her court dress. "How can you tell it's false?"

"I cannot," Sarah replied. "But my father—he's head of the Historical Society, you know—he's been talking about this painting for weeks now. The Holbein. Apparently the society just purchased it in a private auction. So if the society has the original, this one must be a fake." She looked between the two men. "Am I wrong?"

"No, you're not wrong," the Blue Raven mused. "There is a Holbein at the Historical Society, which looks remarkably like this one."

"And while you may not be able to ascertain its falsity, Miss Forrester, I can," Sir Marcus piped up, leaning close to the painting and touching a section of blue dress that held his fingerprint. "It's only been done in the past few weeks. It's still a bit wet—and I can practically smell the linseed oil."

Sir Marcus leaned in closer, looking around the edges of the painting this time, circling out to the wall behind it. "There's a seam here. In the wall."

"There's one over here, too," the Blue Raven replied. "It's a door," he breathed. "But there was no door on the architect's drawings."

"Must have been added later," Marcus replied. "The painting is attached to the wall most securely—perhaps if we pull on it, it will open . . ."

The Blue Raven nodded from within his cloak, taking his meaning. Together, they began to pull on the painting from the gilt frame. Neither the wall nor the painting budged an inch.

"There has to be a latch somewhere," Sarah added, and moved in between the two of them, and began inspecting the seams. "Here, let me—"

Unfortunately, she decided to do this as Marcus and the Blue Raven decided to give pulling at the painting one last try, and . . . the results were predictable.

But, for Sarah, inconceivable.

She and the Blue Raven fell back at the same time, he threw his arm out to catch her. Their tumbling over set a number of books on the edge of the large desk in the center of the room, gravity having them crash to the floor in a muffled racket.

Sarah cringed at the noise. Then she turned to the man who held her, her first instinct to ask if he was unharmed, but before she could, she saw his face.

She saw his face.

In all the movement, the hood of his cloak that he kept up so protectively had fallen back, revealing his profile. The half mask still covered the top half of his features, of course . . . but she could see his jaw and, without a moustache, his lips perfectly. Lips that she had seen set into a hard line of condemnation or, lately, twist in wry amusement, hundreds of times.

His eyes met hers, and he must have recognized her shock. But he did not move. Possibly because she was lying on his arm, but his stillness allowed her to silently reach up, and pull the half mask off, revealing his face in full.

Revealing *Jackson Fletcher's* face in full.

"I don't understand," she said, her voice shaking. Her gaze darted quickly between Marcus Worth and Jack. Jack! How the hell—it couldn't be . . . "I don't understand," she repeated again.

It was as if all the sound fell away, dampened by a heavy curtain, enveloping her and Jack and blocking out everything else. And then the curtain lifted, and all the sound came roaring back.

"Sarah, I can explain—" the Blue Raven—Jack!—began, his voice returning from its grumble to his normal tenor. But he wouldn't be given the chance to explain, because their falling to the floor had caused enough noise to bring footsteps to the study's door.

"You have to go," Marcus ordered Jack. Jack was stone-faced, pale as a ghost. "I know. I'll take care of it." He said to Jack's unasked question. "But you have to go *now*."

Jack's eyes flicked to window. He stood, moving with a grace and fluidity that Sarah could not believe came from the frame of the gawky boy she had known, and swiftly, silently, swung himself out the window.

And he was gone.

Sarah was still frozen in her position on the floor, when Marcus grabbed her by the shoulders and lifted her to her feet. "I will tell you everything. But right now, you've had more to drink with dinner than you thought. Understood?"

Marcus's usually kind eyes bore into her with an intensity she did not know the mild-mannered man had possessed. She nodded quickly, just as the door to the study opened, revealing their host himself.

"My word—" the Comte exclaimed as he surveyed the room. His intense expression momentarily frightened Sarah, unused as she was to such fury coming from the man. But it was gone in a moment, once his eyes fell on Sarah. "Miss Forrester! How on earth did you get in here?" Then they narrowed again when he saw Sir Marcus's hand upon her arm.

As confused as she was, as raw and exposed as she had been mere seconds before, she did not need to look at Sir Marcus again to know the part she was meant to play. The Golden Lady.

A tipsy Golden Lady, that is.

"There you are!" She smiled wide, and let herself stumble toward the Comte. "Oops!" she laughed, when the train of her skirt snagged on her foot. She finally reached the Comte, and leaned heavily enough on his arm that he was taken aback—but not displeased. "I got lost."

"Indeed," Marcus replied. "I was sent to look for Miss Forrester by my wife, and found her here."

"It's very nice in here," she said, sillily, going so far as to place her head on his shoulder. "The chairs are so cozy. And it's cool in here."

The Comte's brow went up. His gaze locked in on the heavy brocade curtains, pushing out in the breeze. "Who opened that window?"

"Er, I did." Marcus supplied. Then, pointedly, "I thought Miss Forrester might benefit from some air."

The Comte's entire body relaxed. "Well, we shall get you some tea, and hopefully that will make you feel better, eh, my sweet?"

Her head was still on his shoulder, so he couldn't see her face. Or how much it burned with embarrassment at having to

play this part. But she schooled herself into her role, and nodded, and as they exited the room, Sarah shot one quick, mean-
ingful glance back at Sir Marcus.

He nodded, acknowledging what went unsaid.

She deserved answers. And she meant to have them.

Twenty

SHE sat alone in her room. Molly had long since left her to her own devices. She had been silent as the maid pulled her out of her gown, as she pulled the brush through her long hair, making it shine like a river of gold in the candlelight. She sat alone, at her silly little dressing table, staring at her reflection in the mirror. And could only wonder who it was that stared back at her.

Was she the gullible child? The hard-hearted crone? The one-and-twenty-year-old Golden Lady?

What age was she now?

That answer, she knew, would be determined by what he had to say.

So she sat, waiting for her answers. Because she knew he would come, and offer them.

What she didn't know was just how he would arrive.

"I expected you to come through the window." She hadn't moved from her seat. But then again, he hadn't knocked on her door. He just let himself in, slipping in as quietly as death. If she hadn't been expecting him, she would have thought Jack simply materialized behind her in the mirror.

"It's easier this way," he replied, his voice calm but clear.

"Yes, it must be pleasant to allow the pretense to fall away."

He had not been home when they returned from the dinner party. She had been worried that he had been captured by one of the overgrown guards that lurked around the Duke of Parford's mansion, but no, he arrived back at the Forrester residence, an hour or so after they did, singing a silly song, acting as if he'd been imbibing all evening with Whigby.

Her tipsy act had been much more convincing, Sarah thought, slightly miffed.

When she, the Comte, and Marcus had stepped back into the drawing room, the entire party was assembled. She toned down her affected silliness a touch, blending in perfectly with the rest of the more social partygoers. She took a cup of tea in hand and waited, patiently, with a smile painted on her face and a happy laugh for anyone that turned her way.

Waited for her answers.

But when his eyes met hers in the mirror, he seemed reluctant to speak.

"All right, then," she said, more to herself than anyone, "I'll start. When did Sir Marcus approach you?"

She waited, her back to him, but holding his gaze. He hesitated, his mouth opening to speak, but no sound emerging.

"It's a very important question. Really, the only one that matters," Sarah stated baldly. "Shall I tell you why?" When he didn't make any sound, again standing as still as a statue, she finally felt fire in her veins, and turned around to look him directly in the face. "From what I've managed to get out of Sir Marcus in the few seconds between leaving the party and being thrown into my carriage, he recruited you into his scheme, because he needed to be able to get to me, as apparently I'm the only one who could convince the Comte to open the Duke of Parford's doors to the world. Now, I wonder, when were you recruited? Was it before or after you decided to disguise yourself as someone heroic?"

Her words had bite, she knew, and by the way he flinched back when she said them, that her hit had landed. But she was owed these words. They belonged to her, and his feelings about them be damned.

"You see, if it was *before,* and you decided to become the Blue Raven as a means to Sir Marcus's end"—she stood from her chair, and began to walk around him, in a slow, wide circle, her hands behind her back—"it means you used what you knew about my childhood adorations for your own purposes, uncaring that your actions thrust me headlong into dangerous situations. But, if it was *after*," she continued, her voice becoming harder, colder. "Then you dressed up as the Blue Raven simply to make a fool out of me, and Sir Marcus somehow found out—likely through Phillippa, come to think of it—and he used it against you.

"Neither option reflects particularly well, but I would like the truth, if you don't mind," she concluded, coming to a stop directly in front of him, her gaze a challenge.

A challenge that he met, and held. "After," he replied simply.

"So . . . when I met . . . *him* . . . in the theatre cupboard, it had absolutely nothing to do with helping catch a murderer?"

"Correct," he affirmed. "That bit came later."

"I see," she said nodding, her voice halfway to breaking. There really seemed nothing else to say.

If only Jack felt the same way. "May I have a chance to explain?" he asked, taking a half step closer to her.

"There's no need," she replied, holding up a hand, to stop him in his movements. Then, "Actually, yes, there is something I would like to know. What did I do?"

He cocked up a brow.

"What did I do to deserve such a trick?" her voice cracked, but she forced it down. "I was snobbier than you liked? I was invited to too many parties? I said something pert? I fought with my sister? What on earth did I do that made you so crazed that nothing less than tricking me into falling in love with a phantom would make you feel better?"

"Nothing!" he cried, some fire finally breaking through that stern demeanor. "Damn it, Sarah, you didn't do anything that deserved it. I discovered that almost immediately, but I was too stuck in my own willful idea, in my own stupidity to see it." This time, his voice broke, not in pain, but in desperate laughter. "And then when I finally did, it was too late! After the cupboard . . . I was never going to see you again as the Blue Raven. But somehow Marcus knew, and blackmailed me . . . and I could hardly be in the same room with you without jumping out of my skin at the time—"

"Why? Afraid you wouldn't be able to help crowing with triumph?"

"No, I was afraid I would take you into my arms and make love to you on the breakfast room floor!"

That made her stop in her tracks. She stood stock-still, her breath coming in odd jerks, her eyes unable to stray from his face. He seemed to have the same reaction to his unexpected words.

Her cheeks burned with remembrance. The press of his lips against hers, unexpected, in a theatre cupboard. The way he had held her—just over there, on her dressing table!—pressing against her in the most intimate manner . . . Heat wrapped her body, and it was all she could do to stop from melting in embarrassment . . . in *want* . . .

He must have felt the heat coming from her, because he came to her as a moth does to a flame, seeking that warmth, wanting to be nearer. He stopped inches from her, tentatively raising a hand to her face, gently letting his fingers dance over her jaw.

"Damn it, Sarah, you got under my skin," he exhaled slowly, his breath as ragged as hers. "From the very beginning. I don't know how. It was a look, or a word, but something that convinced me that the cutting Golden Lady that stood so beautiful and stylish only hid the Sarah Forrester I knew. You got under my skin. And I wanted—needed—to get under yours."

Her eyes caught his then. Jack's eyes. It was Jack's arm that was coming around her back, and holding her steady. It was Jack's mouth that descended toward hers.

Not *his.*

Not the man that she had been dreaming about. Not the man who populated her fantasies, allowing her to escape from the silly intrigues of a society existence. Not the man who had made her think about life beyond the ton, beyond the Golden Lady. Beyond all this.

A simple hand to his chest stopped him, a fraction of a second before his lips touched hers. She broke the spell.

She pushed him back.

"You *needed* to get under my skin? You needed to humiliate me, you mean. You needed to make me look foolish, for your own secret glee."

She pushed him again, this time forcing him to step back.

"Not only to you, but to my friends, you needed me to reject them and go back to paying attention only to you—as if you were still the godlike boy in his cadet uniform who lit up Portsmouth." *Push*—another step back. He didn't fight her, instead looked astonished at her vehemence. "You keep saying I changed, but you've changed more. That boy would have never set out to play me for a fool. That boy would have *never* used me for his own amusement. He was so much better than that." *Push*—another step. "You, on the other hand, are nothing but a bitter, washed-up lieutenant with too much time on his hands." *Push*—another step. "One who decided to teach me a lesson, but not before he had his fun with me—and with my body." *Push*—but this time he caught her hand, and held steady.

"No, I didn't," he rasped. "I told you, you would hate me someday, but I wouldn't be the worst kind of thief." She was too angry to blush this time, instead just held his gaze defiantly. "If I recall correctly, you were the one very eager to have fun, and offered up your body to me for the occasion."

She wrestled her hands free of where he had them pinned to his chest.

"Not to you," she said darkly. "I didn't offer it up to *you*."

This time using all of her strength, she shoved, one last time. His feet passed the open balcony doors and he was out on her small terrace.

"Well, you can consider your lesson well taught, Lieutenant." She said very calmly. "In fact, I will be very suspect of whom I associate with in the future. Now, if you don't mind, I think it best if you show yourself out the way you came in."

And with that, she pushed him over the railing.

As he flailed his arms and eventually lost his balance, the only regret she had was that she wished the shrubbery that lined the house below her window hadn't been quite so voluminous and cushioning.

One last glimpse over the railing to make certain he had landed properly (he had, and was struggling to remove himself from the roses, allaying the more well-bred guilt that could not be quashed) and she turned and shut her balcony doors behind her with decided finality.

The hateful man deserved every bump and bruise that he got.

Twenty-one

"**H**AVE you lost your mind?!" Phillippa Worth's voice carried as she screamed at her husband from behind closed doors. Jack shared a look with the seemingly unflappable butler of Worth House, who looked, likely for the first time in his life, rather flapped.

"My love, I had to involve Jack, you know that—" Marcus argued with his wife.

"But you did NOT have to involve my friend Miss Forrester! You did not have to throw her very much in harm's way, without giving her any idea of the consequences!"

Jack found himself rather agreeing with Lady Worth. Of course, she had the ability to stand up to the very powerful head of the War Department. Unfortunately, she was doing so a little bit too late.

"They'll be just another moment, sir," the butler said, the tips of his ears red with embarrassment. "Are you certain you do not wish for some refreshment?"

Jack stood by the mantle in a fantastically pink sitting room— the heavy double doors from behind which the argument came Jack knew concealed Marcus's study, having spent many an hour there in the past week. In the past week, Phillippa Worth had been nothing but kind and accommodating to him. Of course, in the past week, apparently Phillippa Worth had been kept very much in the dark from certain things.

From what he could gather in the past ten minutes of the back and forth exchange, Phillippa had been informed of the extent of the mission last night, on the presumption that Sarah was going to confide in her in any case.

"When time is of the essence—"

"That is nonsense and you know it! You could have *found another way*." Phillippa's voice shook with her anger.

Jack would not have wanted to be Marcus Worth last night.

Then again, as he massaged his shoulder, he hadn't very much enjoyed being Jackson Fletcher last night, either.

While he had been picking thorns out of his flesh, Jack had time to think over his actions—not only of last night, but of his entire time in London. And while firstly, he was grateful that Sarah had peeked out over the railing, to make certain he landed safely, he knew, wholly and completely, that he had deserved every bit of her spite last night. Every shove. Every fall. Every thorn.

Goddamn, but Sarah was right. He had changed. He'd become strangely cynical, and lost. He'd just been too wrapped up in how much *she* had changed to see it.

He hated that. He wanted to be that boy again—the one with hope for a marvelous, adventure-filled future. The one who caught Sarah Forrester when she was hanging upside-down from a tree. He'd wanted to protect her from all the hurt in the world, then. He'd wanted to be there for her in that way . . . and somehow he got sidetracked, and failed miserably.

It was as he was contemplating these failures, and listening to Marcus be taken apart by his wife, that the object of his thoughts was let into the room.

Jack straightened immediately upon seeing Sarah. He may have had the night from hell, and looked like death warmed over to prove it, but Sarah looked as glossy and calm as ever. Indeed, she looked particularly lovely, wearing a blue day dress—possibly the first time that he'd seen her in a shade other than gold. It made her look fresh, and young. Even if the expression on her face did not agree with that assessment.

"Oh," she said, upon seeing him in the room. But she only

paused for a moment, before she raised her head high and walked into the room, taking a seat on the farthest possible end of the sofa.

"Miss Forrester," Jack said, nodding his head. "Come to call on Lady Phillippa?"

"Sir Marcus, actually," Sarah replied. They let the silence descend, as saying words took more effort than either of them could seem to manage at that moment. Speaking, explaining, apologizing again . . . it was all too much. And so, they existed in silence.

Well, a sort of silence.

"If you think for one moment that I am going to allow you to do *anything* more involving that poor girl—" came Phillippa's voice from beyond the door.

"Philly, I already said I wouldn't—I promise, we'll find another way back in . . ."

"Don't you dare call me Philly right now!"

Jack caught Sarah's expression as she listened to her friend give her husband hell. At first it was astonishment, then the corner of her mouth went up, just a fraction. But when her eyes fell on his, her expression was quickly smoothed back into nothingness, her gaze averted, and distant.

"Do you think they'll be long?" she asked, her voice slightly strained.

"I can't imagine it would be much longer," Jack exhaled. "They've circled back on the same argument twice already."

"I see."

And thus, silence descended again. But this time, Jack decided that perhaps he was too tired to *not* talk. Too tired to remain reserved.

"You can look at me, you know," he sighed. "My visage won't turn you to stone."

An eyebrow went up, but still her attention remained forward, like the best-trained soldiers in formation. "And who will I see?" she asked quietly.

"You'll see me, Sarah. The same as always," he replied, unable to keep the sadness out of his voice. "Besides, you won't see me for that much longer in any case."

Those green eyes shot to him in alarm.

"I spoke with Whigby this morning. His uncle has invited

me to travel with them as far as Lincolnshire when they leave town in a week or so. Whigby will be aboard the *Dresden* by then, so they shall have room in the carriage."

"You're just going to go?" she blurted, surprising even herself with her vehemence. "With . . . with barely a word to Father, or Mother, or Bridget and Mandy?"

He nodded slowly. "It is for the best. As soon as this business is over, I'll be leaving."

"This business?"

He indicated the room beyond, where the expostulations of argument had calmed to a buzzing murmur. "We didn't finish searching the last room. Sir Marcus needs to know as definitively as possible what is in there before he can act."

A look of concern crossed Sarah's face, then she began pulling at her pelisse's cuffs, thoughtful.

"Do you think there is anything behind that painting?" she asked.

"Yes," Jack replied definitively.

"Why? Because you don't trust the Comte?"

"Because there is something very strange in that house," he answered. The spotless, empty attic. The Holbein reproduction. The all-foreign staff. The closed-up music room. Yes, there was something very strange going on in that house.

But if Sarah was going to comment on it further, he was not to know. Because at that moment, the door to the study burst open, admitting a charging Phillippa, with a clearly defeated Marcus quick on her heels.

"Sarah!" Phillippa exclaimed. "I am so, so sorry. Had I known that by telling Marcus of your encounter with the Blue Raven that you would end up in such an untenable position—"

"It's all right, Phillippa. But thank you for being so concerned." She took her friend's hand.

"There is so much I need to explain to you," Phillippa began, her eyes beginning to shine with tears. "My darling Marcus—he's trying to protect the country, you see, and saw an opportunity when he discovered *that one*"—she shot a spare glance over to Jack— "decided to dress up like—"

"I said it's all right, Phillippa." Sarah interrupted, soothing her friend's arm. "I've managed to piece most of it together, I think."

"And you!" Phillippa suddenly turned on Jack, her watery eyes drying at an alarming rate. "What on earth possessed you to dress up as the Blue Raven? I've never heard of such a hare-brained scheme to get a lady's attention." Behind them Marcus conspicuously cleared his throat, but this went unanswered by his wife. Instead she kept her anger focused on Jack. "And who in their right mind goes along with such a dangerous scheme concocted by my husband and brother-in-law? Have you no grace, sir? No sense of decency?"

"It was either that or face murder charges, ma'am," Jack said on a bow. But Phillippa waved this away with an easy hand.

"Oh, don't be ridiculous, Marcus would have never brought an obviously innocent man up on charges. You need to play cards a bit more often, I think—and learn to spot a bluff when you see one."

"My dear," Marcus interrupted finally, "before you go on giving away all the family secrets, perhaps it would be best if Lieutenant Fletcher and I spoke in private."

"Not on your life!" Phillippa replied. "You do not get to scheme and plan anything else on your own, especially if it is going to involve my friends and society at large! You'll just make a muddle of it."

"Be that as it may, madam," Jack replied, seeing that Marcus might be too worn down by a night and day of having been reprimanded, "we do need to plan our next move. Somehow we need to get back into the Comte's—er, the Duke of Parford's home."

"Exactly," Sarah piped up. All eyes turned to her. "What do you need me to do?"

Jack felt all the blood drain from his face. "You will stay as far away from this as humanly possible. This is not your affair."

"Neither is it yours," Sarah replied. "And yet, you find yourself mired in its center, intent upon solving the mystery. Well, so am I. I want to help."

Jack turned to Marcus. "Tell her she can't . . ."

"Last time you asked for my help, I did not know all the circumstances. This time I do, and I'm offering up my services." Sarah stepped forward, her head held regally high, daring anyone to challenge her.

"Now, for the last time, what do you need me to do?"

ॐ

"Georgina!" Sarah cried as she was met at the door of the
Duke of Parford's home the next morning. She was out of
breath, in her riding habit, as if she had just rode over from
Upper Grosvenor Street in a mad dash. Which is, of course,
exactly what she had done. "Is the Comte at home?"

"No," Georgina replied tentatively, somewhat taken aback
by Sarah's appearance, which of course was the plan. "He
went to Tattersall's with Mr. Ashin Pha. Apparently, there is
an Arabian he's thinking to purchase."

Sarah squelched the impulse to raise an eyebrow, knowing
what she did now of the Comte's spending habits. But instead,
she grabbed Georgina's hand and pulled.

"Excellent! Then you shall have to come with me. Oh, Mrs.
Hill! You must come, too!" Sarah cried, noticing Georgina's
stocky companion over Georgina's slight shoulder. "You will
not believe it!"

"Good gracious, what is the matter?" Georgina cried,
slightly taken aback.

"It's a miracle!" Sarah cried. "You know how you mentioned that you did not feel you were up to snuff in terms of
fashion? Well. I mentioned this to Lady Worth, just thinking
that she would brush it off like I did, because of course your
clothes are lovely, for foreign styles. Well, Phillippa gener-
ously offered up her next appointment with Madame LeTrois.
But it is in twenty minutes; you must come now!"

"Oh . . . Sarah, I do not know . . ." Georgina demurred,
looking aside to Mrs. Hill. But Sarah was insistent. "Oh,
Georgina, you cannot say no. Madame LeTrois books her clients seasons in advance. Only a recommendation from one of
her other clients will get you in. And it may be possible that
Phillippa mentioned this in front of Lady Whitfield, and some
others . . . so if you say no, it will be just impossible for you to
go out without anyone and everyone commenting on your
dress." Sarah made sure to look as crestfallen and shocked as
possible.

The normally staunch and leading Mrs. Hill, when looked
to for help, could only shrug her shoulders and say, "Tis your
decision, Miss Georgina. But we have a full evening planned."

"And she should have a new gown for it!" Sarah cried.

And it seemed the ruse worked, because Georgina looked momentarily conflicted, which Sarah pounced on. "It will be such fun—Madame LeTrois will create something in your very own style. There will be only one Miss Georgina Thompson."

With a shrug of her small shoulders, Georgina relented, and Sarah clapped her hands. "Oh, wonderful! Mrs. Hill, call for a carriage, we must go at once. Phillippa will be meeting us there. I'll have my horse stalled in your mews, shall I?"

"And I should write a note to my brother. Let him know we have left. He does not like me to leave the house without him," Georgina supplied by way of explanation.

Sarah froze. If the Comte was aware the house was empty, he might return post haste. Therefore, thinking quickly, she altered the plan slightly. "Excellent idea! Why not have him meet us at Madame LeTrois?"

"Why would my stepbrother meet at a ladies' modiste?" Georgina asked, as she pulled on a straw hat, better suited to foreign climes.

"Why, because he will want to show you off immediately thereafter, I am sure!"

And with that, Sarah managed to get Georgina, Mrs. Hill, their Indian driver and footman riding along with them, away from the house for hours in the sunny afternoon, leaving only burly foreign servants to guard the house.

It was as empty as the place was going to get.

੨੦

Jack watched as the carriage filled with the harried and excited women, led by an ebullient Sarah, rumbled away from the Duke of Parford's home. He had been on that corner since dawn, and planning for this since yesterday, when they had all met up together.

"We have to make the house as empty as possible," Marcus had mused, as they sat in Lady Phillippa's overly pink drawing room discussing strategy. "Now, I have a friend that can make sure a certain Arabian horse is up for sale at Tattersall's tomorrow morning, which will get the Comte and his friend out of the house—they seem to have taken a liking to horseflesh.

But Miss Georgina rarely leaves unless it is to accompany her brother somewhere. She does not pay calls often, nor does she do the household shopping."

"She is very shy," Sarah agreed. "Even when she was the hostess of the party, she was terribly nervous, and felt not up to her guests' sparkle."

"Well, do we have to worry about her?" Phillippa asked. "If she is so shy and retiring, what are the chances that she will notice someone skulking about the study?"

"The chances are good," Jack replied. "I sat in the desk chair of the study last night. It was a very high, somewhat delicate seat. Not built for a man. *She* sits at the desk, worrying over her brother's spending habits."

Marcus took in this information with a raise of the brow. "In any case, if we remove her, she takes a servant or two with her, and the house will be slightly emptier."

"That only leaves the rather oversized servant staff." Sarah asked. "How do we remove them?"

"Some will attend the Comte. But the rest . . . it's far too tricky. The best I can do is buy a window of time with distraction. But if the Comte comes home and puts together that the entire house was out, he will become highly suspicious," Marcus said, turning his attention to Jack. "So you will have to be very, very quiet."

And so he was. Since he was breaking in during daylight, Jack could not use the shadows as effectively as he did at night. But he could still use the rooftops. And since it was a breezy day, his footsteps did not echo across the slate tiles like they had at night.

He also forwent the dark costume he was becoming accustomed to, with the cloak and half mask. Nothing more suspicious than a man in a mask in the day. Instead, he wore the dusty, raggedy clothes of a chimney sweep. His hair darkened and dusty with charcoal powder. His face blackened into unrecognizability with coal—actually greasepaint, but it gave the same effect.

Luckily the wind was such that it carried the entire conversation Sarah had with Georgina up to his ears. The women were removed. The Comte and Mr. Pha would be occupied at Tattersall's and then, if Sarah had her way, at the dressmaker's for many an hour. Still, he would prefer to get in and out as quickly as possible.

It meant that, even in daylight, he needed no eyes to fall on him.

Which is where Marcus's distraction came in.

Jack waited until he saw the signal from the suspiciously tall and spectacle-wearing fruit-cart driver. A quick tip of his hat before he set out to take the turn around the square, driving a mite too fast for safety.

"Never fear," Marcus had said, with a decided twinkle in his eye. "I'm adept enough at causing trouble when I have to." To which his wife was enthusiastic in her agreement.

There was a swerve, a yell, a screech from a startled horse, and then the street was paved in orange. Er, that is, oranges. They spilled out from the back of the suspiciously poorly latched cart, rolling this way and that all over the street, causing no small amount of turmoil as the cart somehow managed to lose a wheel—directly in front of the Duke of Parford's home.

Everyone pulled back their curtains, some people spilled out of their houses to view the catastrophe that would likely be the talk of London for a few days. A number of Indian servants, incongruous in their neat British clothes, came flying out of the front door, picking up oranges and yelling curses at the poor, inept, and yet somehow missing orange cart driver.

This was his only chance. No one would notice a chimney sweep moving between houses at that moment.

The guards that patrolled the house on the night of the dinner party were gone—or at the very least, severely reduced. Strange, considering at some point that night the guard Jack had rendered unconscious would have been discovered. Jack had expected a heavier patrol, not a smaller one. Perhaps the Comte was careless. Perhaps he did not have the funds for the extra wages. Either way, Jack counted it as luck that he could count the guards on one hand this time. And for the moment, they were distracted by fruit.

He again prepared to jump from the roof of the home next door—but this time, instead of jumping *into* the safety of the back gardens, he had to land *on* the high wall.

Barely a foot wide, solid brick. And he had to land perfectly.

"Nothing to do but leap, Mr. Fletcher," he breathed to himself. And so he did.

His feet hit brick, one sliding off the side for the barest moment, before he circled his arms and managed to recover.

He couldn't take the time to marvel—it was only a matter of time before the oranges at the front of the house lost their appeal. He ran nimbly across the top of the wall until he came up against the house itself. Then he leveraged himself up via the decorative masonry that ran along the rear corner of the building. Climbing higher and higher, as fast as he could, until he was safely on the roof. From there, it was a hop, skip, and a few small jumps to the attic window.

"The attic." He had told the pink room definitively, pointing to a spot on the architectural drawings of the Duke of Parford's home. "The attics are empty, and the windows face the back of the house. It could be days before someone notices one has been broken."

And so, Jack—feeling blessed by the noise of the wind—used the handle of a chimney sweep, and shattered a small pane of glass. Then, with his hand as shrouded as possible, he reached in and unlatched the window.

He stepped into the too familiar empty space, leaving his chimney sweep in a corner of the room.

Now for the difficult bit.

"But if you use the attic window, you'll have to walk past almost the entire house to get to the study," Marcus had mused.

"I'll just have to do so very, very quietly," Jack replied.

Over the past few weeks of playing this part, Jack had learned definitively the necessity for grace in movement. And so, he tiptoed like a ballet dancer—all strength and control—through every hallway, every room of the house, along the route he had memorized, always keeping in mind his alternates, if they proved necessary. Coming to the door of the study without any complications (as during the dinner party, it was locked, but much simpler to open this time, considering the practice he'd had two nights ago). Jack relaxed ever so slightly for the first time since yesterday.

But when he slipped inside, his stomach dropped to his knees.

The room was spotless. No bills lying about. No papers sticking out between pages of books.

Whoever had gone through the room, they had been thorough. Which made the hairs on the back of Jack's neck stand up.

Had a maid simply been doing her job, cleaning up a mess? Or had someone itemized everything—making sure nothing was amiss? Had they raised suspicions?

Had that someone removed whatever was behind the painting?

He turned his attention to the wall with the Holbein on it—or the fake Holbein, as Sarah had claimed it to be, and as Jack had confirmed, having taken a tour of the Historical Society with Lord Forrester yesterday afternoon. The Holbein painting of this woman, with her noble dress and haughty demeanor, had been hanging in the middle of the Historical Society's great rooms, for all to see.

In the daylight, it was much easier to see the seams in the wall behind the painting, and see that it was, indeed, a hidden panel. Getting behind it, however, still remained a challenge.

"Look for a latch, or a hinge," Phillippa had said. When she received strange stares from her husband, she simply shrugged. "There's always a latch or a hinge."

And, of course, Phillippa Worth was correct.

Jack made sure to move with caution, as he ran his fingers along the seam near the left side of the painting, where there was a divot, a sinking into the wall. The hinges were on the other side, meaning the wall would swing *in*, not *out*. The other night they had spent so much time pulling, perhaps all it needed was an easy push.

After some minutes of trying, he had to admit that was not the case. Well, his logical mind told him, if hinges were on the left side, that meant the latch was likely on the right. Jack took a step back, to get a better look at the wall he was trying to penetrate, and the painting that adorned it.

It was identical to the one in the Historical Society. Identical in size, shape, expression. Jack was not educated enough in the world of art to tell if the blue of the dress was the exact same hue as the other one. In fact, the only thing he could tell was different at all was the frame.

The frame.

Jack wanted to smack his palm to his forehead. The frame of the painting in the Historical Society had been plain, "a temporary replacement," Lord Forrester had mentioned. But the frame on this painting was gilded, ornate. And stuck so well to the wall it was almost as if it was a permanent part of it.

Access to whatever was behind the wall would be found on the frame. Quickly, he ran his fingers over every rise, every bump and divot of the swirling rococo frame, looking for the spot that would respond to pressure.

Finally, he found it.

The latch released with a rush of air, a heavy click of relief. And the painting on the wall swung in. Jack held his breath.

The inside was quite dusty. Nothing like the newly cleaned exterior of the study. In fact it was a very small space behind the painting, perhaps enough room for one small person to fit. And Jack was not small. However, the hidden cupboard was only occupied by a small wooden box on the floor.

He lifted it out, gingerly. Covered in dust, too, it was obviously old, and had long since gone untouched. However, he rationalized to himself, it was so dusty in that space, a box placed there in the past few weeks could have easily taken on the same ghosts as had lived there.

He gently placed the box on the desk, careful to displace as little dust as possible. Opening it, his heart soared when he saw what was inside.

Letters.

Three, no four letters. "Let one of these be what Marcus needs," Jack whispered the prayer into the still room.

He picked up the first. It's wax seal was too broken and brittle to decipher. Opening it, however, he knew in the first few lines exactly who it was to, and from.

My Dearest Willy, it began . . .

I hav aked for yur touch these many months, but me mum wilna here of my coming to you. She says you are too hi above me, and to dreme of you is to dreme of the moon. But I dreme of your hand on myne, your lips on myne. It canna be helped. Twas the last tyme I was a live.

He opened up the second letter, and the third. All written in this same feminine, untrained hand. All badly spelled. All addressed to a young Willy, who had, by the look of it, fallen madly for a young woman of lesser means, and she for him. And, he knew, the Duke of Parford's given name was William.

These were not evidence of treachery. They were instead, evidence that a man was once a boy and capable of a defiant love. Even if that man was now in his sixties, and living in the East Indies, he had held on to these letters and kept them safe, and hidden.

This was the Duke of Parford's greatest secret. Not the Comte de Le Bon's.

Jack gently placed the letters in his pocket—Marcus wanted to see what was behind the wall, he would want to make sure that they were not some encoded communiqué. But Jack was human enough to recognize the emotion on the pages, and their honesty, and he vowed to return them to their place as soon as possible. And the least he could do, he thought, was make certain the box he had found them in remained undisturbed.

Which turned out to be a bit of a mistake.

For, as he was bending to place the box exactly where he found it, and coming to the realization that they had broken into this house—twice—for nothing, the proof that he had been looking for came up and opened the study door.

He had to be quicker. He had to listen better. Because when Mr. Ashin Pha poked his head around the corner of the study door and yelled a terrific, "Oy!" Jack was more than taken by surprise.

Mr. Pha did not allow him time to think about how to get himself out of this situation. Nor did he allow Jack time to get out of his low position and face him man-to-man. Instead, Mr. Pha set on him with a fury that promised to break all the bones in his body, if not all the furniture in the room.

Maybe it was the way they fought. Maybe it was the exclamation "Oy!" that had announced his entry to the room. But suddenly, Jack realized why no one had ever heard Mr. Ashin Pha speak in public, and if they did, it was whispered in the ear of the Comte who spoke for him. Why his bedchamber looked like that of a drunken lout on a gambling binge.

This man was not an aristocrat from the Far East.

By the way he fought, he was a thug.

It was these spare thoughts that ran through his head as he fought back, his punches landing with precision. Across the jaw, to the gut. He knew the faster he got out of there, the better. Besides, he thought, as he picked up a spindly chair. The racket they were making was going to have people come running.

"Sorry, Mr. Pha, can't stay long," Jack said, as he broke the spindly chair across the back of the non-aristocrat. His only luck was that Mr. Pha was not an outsized thug, like the guards that paroled the house in the guise of servants. Of course, he certainly had the ability to *call* for the guards . . .

Which he did. In English. With a decided cockney accent.

"You're not even Burmese, are you?" Jack stated in wonder, unable to stop himself. His opponent paled in shock—Jack knew it was now or never. He seized the split second that he had caught Mr. Pha unaware, enough time to pick up a second straight-backed chair.

Mr. Pha ducked as he made to hurl it at him. Instead, Jack released on the backswing, and it flew through the window behind him.

If *that* noise didn't bring the household running, nothing would.

But while the not-Burmese Mr. Pha ducked, startled by the flying glass, Jack braved the cuts and scrapes and dove through the window.

Searing pain lanced through his arm as he landed and rolled. It was only a half story off the ground of the back gardens, but the glass had landed before him, and now, he was fairly certain a large chunk of it was embedded in his side. But it didn't matter—he had to run. He had to get out of there.

He glanced quickly behind him—Mr. Pha was gingerly climbing through the broken window after him, while two newly arrived guards shouted and gestured wildly.

It was only a moment before Jack realized what they were gesturing at.

A door, at the back wall of the garden, which was guarded by a young dark-skinned man in livery. The men wanted him to stop Jack. But at that point, nothing was going to stop Jack.

He put his head down and barreled through not only the young man, but the door beyond, out into the mews.

Any number of startled stable hands and carriage drivers—not only of the Comte's but of everyone on the street who shared these same mews. Jack took advantage of their shock, and ran blindly toward his goal: Sarah Forrester's mare.

The horse luckily saw past his haste and recognized him, and took him up on his back. Then, kicking away the one or two stable boys who tried to stop him, Jack with a mighty "Hah!" put the horse into a gallop, and they flew out of there.

Jack gave one last glance over his shoulder and saw Mr. Ashin Pha come around the corner of the garden gate. His face was scuffed and scarred, blood dripping down from his crown. And that man's murderous glare burned into Jack's memory as he rounded the corner, and escaped into the chaos of London in broad daylight.

Twenty-two

SARAH paced her bedroom anxiously, unable to think on anything beyond the past few hours. Namely, those hours that Jack had been missing.

The sun was dipping below the horizon. She was supposed to be dressing for dinner. Instead, she had cried off, told her mother she had a headache, and retired for the evening with a tray of cold meats from the kitchen. The only instruction she gave was to her maid Molly, which stated that if a note came from Worth House, or if Lieutenant Fletcher came back from his outing with Mr. Whigby, she was to be notified immediately, no matter the time.

There was so little for her to do now, and every nerve of her body was awake and fidgeting. She had spent the day in a dress shop, being as frivolous as she could manage, dragging the entire ordeal out, dressing Georgina in this silk and that ruffle. But she had never, never forgotten the purpose of her being there. But then, she had Phillippa sitting by her side, keeping her company, keeping her surprisingly placid.

In fact, everything seemed to be going well, until the Comte showed up.

"My dear Miss Forrester!" the Comte had cried, and took her hands in his. "I was so pleasantly surprised by your note." Then, sotto voce, "If you only knew how often I tried to convince my sister to make an appointment with the madame. You have truly worked a miracle."

"I think you will find it is madame who has worked a miracle," Sarah had said kindly. As she did every time she had been in the Comte's presence since being asked to arrange the dinner party, she looked at him with a more observant eye, trying to find any signs of the traitor Sir Marcus and Jack thought him to be. Again, she found nothing but someone jovial, if a little too self-important. And someone who very clearly admired her.

"I was made to understand that Mr. Ashin Pha was with you," Sarah had said, glancing over his shoulder. "Pray tell me you did not leave him outside?"

"No, I dropped him off at the house," the Comte replied easily. "He is more baffled than intrigued by English women's fashions."

As Sarah felt her stomach drop to her knees, she struggled to keep a smile plastered on her face. A quick look to Phillippa fortified her. Her calm was borne of experience. After all, as she had reminded Sarah right before they set the entire plan in action, "It can be frightening. But I simply tell myself over and over that Marcus has always returned to me."

Never mind the shock of such an intimate thought, that Jack was as dear to her as Marcus was to Phillippa, now the recollection of that conversation only brought her comfort— small though it was.

Instead, they had to take the information in stride, and ooh and aah over every single dress plate that Madame LeTrois brought out for their approval.

Discreetly, a few minutes after they settled down, Phillippa called over one of her footmen, who was already loaded down with a few dozen packages.

"Smith," she said, while Sarah and the Comte had their heads bowed over the dress plates—the Comte bowing closer to her than Sarah was comfortable with, but she gamely played her part, "Take this note to my husband, if you would. He's going to try and get out of going to the Felton's dinner this evening and I cannot allow that," she explained, turning her smile to the Comte and Sarah.

"And how do you intend to force him into keeping the engagement, Lady Worth?" the Comte asked playfully.

"Oh, I have a feeling a wife knows how to coerce a husband," Sarah replied, letting the innuendo hang in the air. Playing her part. The Comte threw his head back in laughter, and then met Sarah's eyes.

Now, after a long afternoon of dresses and fittings, of keeping the Comte and his sister occupied throughout the day, Sarah was able to sit still, her mind going back again and again to that moment.

Even in her fear and panic for Jack, some part of Sarah was able to look at the Comte objectively, when he had smiled at her, only the slightest amount of well-practiced lasciviousness slipping through. It had been long since that she no longer felt swayed by his looks and interesting accent, but this time, she noticed that he did not blush at the innuendo, the way Jack would have done. Oh, the Comte looked at her adoringly, but it was controlled.

And Sarah could see that he was playing a part as much as she was.

Now, if it had been Jack . . . Jack would have gone red to the ears, and then his eyes . . . his eyes would have borne into her from beneath the hood of his heavy cloak with all the intensity of a starving beast.

Not Jack—that was the Blue Raven. Jack.

Keeping them separate in her head was becoming a trial. Having the two halves of the man she thought she had known since a child, and the man that she had fantasized about without seeing his face, was enough to drive a woman insane. But Sarah was not about to allow herself to fall into such panics. Therefore she had tried to keep the two separate in her memory. Jack was the man who resembled the boy she'd taught to play pirates, a sailor with no ship. The Blue Raven was a ghost, the object of all things alluring and powerful in her mind.

Jack was the one who played apology bowls. The Blue Raven would never apologize for what he had to do to keep his country safe.

Jack was the one who had tricked her. So was the Blue Raven.

And Jack was the one who had disappeared for the last five hours, God knows where, running around London with her horse and whatever he pulled out of the Duke of Parford's house!

Strangely, as she paced a hole in her carpet, her mind decided to pluck the memory of the last time she had been this worried about Jack from its stores, one both soothing and startling, as if it had been resting just below the surface the whole time.

꙾

That night, Sarah had sought out her tree. The long summer days in England had the sun setting well past supper. Even now, the hazy oranges and pinks that made up twilight danced against the few clouds in the sky.

Sarah was melancholy. No, that wasn't the word for it. Muddled. Muddled was a better term. And when she was muddled, Sarah tended to seek out her tree, climb, and think. She had been muddled for the better part of a week, or so their governess Miss Pritchett had said. Because this was the week Jack was going away.

He'd graduated from the Royal Naval College with all the fanfare that implied, and would be going on board the HMS Amorata *in a mere few days' time. His parents had even come down from Lincolnshire, for the first time since he'd become a part of their lives. Even now, the vicar and her father were discussing something large and global and considered too big for the young ladies present. Although, Sarah could follow their conversation with perfect ease. However, she and her sisters were sent out of the room, and Sarah was left feeling muddled.*

"Red sky at night, sailor's delight," a voice came from below her. She didn't need to glance down to know who it was. His voice had changed in the three years they had known each other, deepening to the tenor of a serious sixteen-year-old that she had to prod into adventure. But he always proved willing to play along, even when he was too old for the games of little girls.

She wasn't so little anymore herself. She was growing up and out in ways her mother called blossoming, although it only made her want to hide her figure from the eyes of boys like Jack. Because they—boys and Jack alike—were starting to take notice. She could tell. Looks lingered, and sometimes, he stood just a hair too close. It was too strange, too . . . real to deal with at present.

"Hopefully no red sky tomorrow morning," she ventured, as he climbed up beside her, faster than she could have ever managed. Jack always was a marvelous climber. As he seated himself beside her on the long branch, she straightened as best she could, becoming as proper as she had always been taught.

"I shan't worry, Captain Healy says the weather will be fine, and I believe him," Jack said with all the adoration a young man could have for a new hero. "Now what has you so down?" Jack asked, at her look, he shrugged. "You always end up in a tree when you're down."

"I don't know," she replied. She could always talk to Jack. He brought her head back round to right more often than anyone else, but today . . . today she just felt strange all around. "Everything is changing. Don't you find that odd?"

"A little. But everyone changes, you know."

"I don't want things to change," she replied. "I want you to keep visiting on school holidays and Father to keep sneaking me the papers, and—"

"I'll still come to visit," Jack was quick to say.

Sarah shook her head. "Every few years when your ship makes port nearby? You'll hardly recognize us by then, and we you."

"Maybe, but I have a feeling we'll still be fast friends." Jack bumped her shoulder. It was times like this that Sarah couldn't guess what was in his head. Was he just placating her? Was he making fun at her expense? He was about to go off into the world, to sail the seven seas! He was practically already a man. What did he care for the muddles of one young girl?

"Are you scared?" she asked suddenly.

Jack shook his head. "Excited. Done with books, done with waiting. I'm finally going to have that adventure you're always prodding me into."

"Maybe you'll even meet Blackbeard," she mused.

"He's been dead for ages, but I'll be certain to keep an eye out." Jack laughed and threw his arm over her shoulder.

Sarah froze. It was not as if she had never been touched by Jack before. They had been friends for ages, and he had been the girls' dancing partner on more than one occasion, for goodness sakes. But this . . . as casual as the gesture was, it set every nerve in her body tingling. What did he mean by it? Did it mean anything at all? He was sixteen, and she only twelve, surely he did not mean anything more than the brotherly affection he had always expressed.

One thing was for sure. Sarah had spent far too much time of late trying to figure out what things meant.

Dangerously, deliciously, she thought she could test a theory. To see if the little touches—the arm over her shoulder, the bumping into her—meant what her blossoming brain thought it did.

She leaned into him and kissed him. Just a peck on the cheek. If a person watching blinked they would have missed it. She straightened immediately, and hoped that the sunset did not illuminate her burning face. But she couldn't help sliding a glance to Jack.

He looked stunned, staring at her with wonder, his hand on his cheek where her lips had just barely touched it. Then he leaned in, and kissed her back. On the cheek as well, a return of her childish kiss with one worth more than riches.

"Oh my goodness," she said.

And then, it sent her reeling.

Quite literally. Suddenly she lost her balance and wobbled back, finally falling and ending up hanging by her knees around the tree branch.

"Aaaaa!!" she screamed, her arms flailing above her head. But what was worse, her skirts were flailing around her ears.

"Sarah! Hold on!" Jack cried, scrambling out of the tree with more speed than grace. She threw her arms up, trying with all her might to pull her skirts back into place, but gravity was having none of it.

"Give me your hands," Jack said from below her on the ground. Reaching up, his fingertips barely grazed the top of her head.

"No!" she cried, struggling with her skirts and her mortification.

"Sarah"—he was unable to hold in a laugh— *"I don't care about your skirts, I swear. Just lower your arms and I will catch you."*

"Promise?"

"I won't let you fall," he intoned seriously.

"I meant about the skirts!"

Another laugh escaped him. "Yes, I promise. Now give me your hands."

She did, throwing her hands down and her skirts going above her head in one fell swoop. He caught her arms, but she let go over her legs too early, and they landed in a heap on the ground, all skirts and limbs. With him breaking her fall.

"Oh, Sarah." He chuckled as he sat up, setting her to rights. "Promise me you won't change too much."

❧

How had she forgotten all of that? Not the actions, per say, but the feelings? What it felt like to be worried about him. What it felt like to hold someone so close to yourself, in spirit if not in body, that their plights became yours?

They were so different now, but it was exactly the same.

Oh my goodness . . . her mind became alight with wonder.

But before she could ponder on that further, a voice came from the window.

"You're going to pace a hole in the carpet."

"Jack!" she cried, running to his side. "Where have you been!" She tried to maintain a whisper, but knew she did so terribly. But by the time she reached him, she was ready to yell at him at full voice.

"You're bleeding," she stated dully, fear knocking out her immediate anger, and causing her eyes to fly to his.

"I fell on some glass," he reassured. "I'm all right. It must be dry by now."

"But not clean," she replied. "Stay here, give me just a moment."

She left him out on the balcony, shrouded by darkness. She crossed the room quickly and pulled a cord. Within a minute, Molly was at her door.

"Molly, could you bring me a hot water bottle and some cloths?" At her maid's silent upticked eyebrow, she offered the only explanation a woman can give. "I feel my courses coming on. Please, Molly."

"Yes miss," Molly replied. "Would you care for a powder as well?"

"Certainly," Sarah agreed. Not knowing exactly what Jack would need, surely a powder couldn't hurt, could it?

When the maid left, Sarah trotted back quickly to the balcony.

"For heaven's sake, you're shaking," she cried, her eyes popping wide. She bent down and helped lift him. He winced slightly when she touched his arm, but he bore through it, allowing her to help him into the room.

"I've been running all day. Your horse—"

"I don't care about the horse," she replied quickly. "Get on the bed."

Jack gave a short, silent laugh at her insistent pulling. But he let her lead the way. "I've dreamed of you telling me that," he said, blearily. She held off on blushing by focusing on the task at hand, namely, getting Jack to sit down and take off his shredded coat. "Your horse is fine, by the bye. She's back in the mews."

"Thank you," she said quietly. The task of removing his jacket done, Sarah tossed it on a nearby chair. Then she tilted her head to the side, examining the wounds on his arm and side through the rough twill of his workman's shirt. "Although, that will be terribly difficult to explain to the Comte and Georgina."

"Why?" his head came up.

"While you were out running all over God knows where . . ."

"Mostly Whitechapel," he supplied.

"Excellent, you are very likely even filthier than you appear," Sarah surmised flatly, at his mention of that seedy, labyrinthine section of London.

"Kept me away from more watchful eyes," he remarked.

"And Worth House couldn't have done that?" she argued. That had been where he had agreed to meet with Marcus after the mission. Worth House, thanks to Marcus's connections and Phillippa's exactitude, was a fortress.

"They followed me. I didn't want to lead anyone back to you," he replied quietly.

Sarah, unable to respond to that properly, stilled briefly in her probing. "Ah . . . like I was saying, while you spent the afternoon running around, I spent it in a dress shop with Georgina and the Comte, and then when we came back to the house it was in total uproar. Because apparently a man had broken in, stole a few thousand pounds worth of personal items, broke a window, and stole my horse to make his escape." At his stunned expression, she continued. "The Comte offered to buy me a new one, but I settled for reporting it to the police, as a neighbor had seen the uproar and sent for them."

"I didn't steal anything," Jack said, puzzled.

"I didn't think so. But the mystery gets deeper. Apparently, Mr. Ashin Pha has gone missing, too." A soft knock at the door stilled Sarah's hands. Then she leveraged him up fully onto the bed, and drew the bed curtains closed. "Not a sound," she admonished, before closing him in.

It was, as expected, Molly at the door. "Here is your hot water, and your cloths," she said. "I've also brought some thin broth—always a help to me in my time," she blathered as she tried to enter the room. Sarah stopped her with a hand.

"Thank you Molly," she said firmly. "I'll take that from you. If you don't mind, I'd like to be alone just now."

As Sarah turned and put the tray of cloths, hot water, powders, and broth on the surface of her dressing table, her eyes fell to the chair by her bed, where she had tossed Jack's lacerated jacket. She turned back, and stared Molly dead in the eye, holding her gaze, willing her not to notice the jacket.

"Thank you, Molly. I'm sure I'll feel much better in the morning."

Her nonplussed maid took that as a firm dismissal, and if she noticed the jacket, or the closed bed curtains, she was far too professional to mention it. When the door clicked shut, Sarah returned to her charge.

Who, somehow, had silently managed to remove his shirt.

Oh my goodness.

She froze, her arm in midair, holding back the bed curtain, as light from her bedside lamp spilled over his well-formed chest. She had been crushed up against that chest, his arms and cloak wrapping around her, so she could have guessed what had been underneath the heavy cloak. But she had no idea he was hiding *this*. All those years of life on a ship had honed his muscles into bulging ropes of strength, his belly flat and his chest broad. And at the moment, crisscrossed with red, angry cuts of varying lengths and depths.

She got so lost in staring at his torso—and perhaps, the line of muscle on his side that slipped beneath the line of his trousers, down to . . . *elsewhere*, that it took her a moment to realize he was speaking to her.

"I'm sorry?" she asked, forcing her eyes up to his.

"I said that Mr. Pha must have taken some treasures as he absconded out of there," Jack said, as he pulled his arm out of the cuff of his shirt, thereby freeing himself from it completely. This arm was far worse than his torso—especially the angry red gash that ran for five inches down his shoulder.

Sarah nodded in agreement, even as she kept a grim eye on that gash. "That's what Marcus decided as well. He came when Phillippa called for him. In fact he was remarkably nearby, likely having been inspecting the entire incident at the Duke of Parford's home since Phillippa had sent that note out. But why would Mr. Pha run away in the first place?"

"Because his lie had been discovered." Jack surmised. Then, with a look to her, "He is not Burmese. And there are ramifications of that discovery."

"But how do you know?" she asked, as she remembered her purpose and fetched the hot water and cloths to the bedside. And so, as she sat gingerly next to him, he told her. Told her of the fight, and how men of aristocratic birth would never fight like that—no matter where they are from. Then he told her why the man never spoke in public.

"He likely doesn't know a word of Burmese," he said in conclusion, as she dabbed hot water on the smaller cuts on his arm, wiping away dried blood, dirt that had congealed into a paste with sweat. He'd gritted his teeth, but talked his way through the worst of her ministrations.

"Does Sir Marcus know?" she lifted her eyes to his. "When he arrived on the scene, the Comte was very upset, so he took

him to his club for a drink to calm down," she explained. "But
I don't think he really took him for a drink, if you take my
meaning."

In fact, while Miss Georgina and Mrs. Hill had acted with
the practicality borne of women, going through each room,
trying to decipher what had been taken, questioning the staff,
and speaking to the police about increasing foot patrols of this
supposedly good neighborhood, the Comte had simply started
going red and blathering that it wasn't his fault, and who knew
where his friend—the missing Mr. Pha—was now. When
Marcus offered to take him up in his carriage "for a drink at
the club," the Comte agreed readily.

Miss Georgina at first seemed worried—she was rightfully
nervous about she and Mrs. Hill being left alone in the house
without any male protection. But the Comte simply looked her
dead in the eye and said, "Georgie, never fear. I'll be fine."

She seemed to swallow that, and sent her stepbrother away
with a whispered word and kiss on his cheek. Little did she
know she was sending her brother—alone for the first time—
into the arms of those who suspected him of treason.

"Yes, Sir Marcus knows," Jack said. "I managed to get
word to him."

"How?"

Apparently, getting word to him involved a hastily scrawled
note to be delivered into either Sir or Lady Worth's hands, and
paying a young street lad to hand deliver the note to the door
of the Worth's house while he watched from around the corner. Given the commotion that occurred in the following minutes after the note was successfully delivered—horses being
ordered, and missives being sent—Jack could rightfully conclude that the message had reached Sir Marcus's ears.

"So the Comte is now in the War Department's custody,"
Jack surmised. "Finally. At best the Comte was duped by Mr.
Pha like the rest of us, at worst he orchestrated the entire affair." He looked down at her then, his eyes following the line
of her arms to where her hand hesitated, at the large gash on
his shoulder.

"I managed to get all the glass out, I think," he said, in a
way that was likely meant to reassure.

"This may hurt a little bit," she warned, as she sucked in a deep breath, and finally applied her attentions to the large gash on his shoulder.

He swore briefly, silently.

"I'm sorry," she said, her entire body tensing with his exclamation. "I'm rather new to this nursemaid business. The last time I had to tend to a scraped knee I was ten, and we were a mile and a half out in the woods—"

"And Bridget tripped over that rock," Jack finished for her.

"It was Mandy, not Bridget. If Bridget scraped her knees, she would have been too proud to let anyone tend to them."

"That's right." He laughed, just slightly, but enough to make Sarah relax back into cleaning the wound. Carefully, tenderly, she dragged the wet cloth over his flesh, wiping away anything that hid him from her. When her job was done, she took the dry bit of cloth and wound it tight around the gash. Then she inspected her work.

"Well, it's far from professional—"

"I'd prefer to avoid a professional right now, and their questions. If Marcus can arrange it, I'll see someone he trusts tomorrow."

"Good. Good. Your arm should stay on until then." She nodded, like a ninny. *Stop being an idiot*, she admonished herself. *It's only Jack.*

But she knew she was fooling herself. Jack had long since stopped being only Jack.

"But what was behind the painting?" she said suddenly. "Surely you must go to Marcus tonight, and let him know what you discovered."

"I already have. That was the second bit of information in the note."

"You did find something," Sarah's eyes went wide. Was it the proof they sought? Was the Comte as duplicitous as they suspected? But Jack simply nodded over to where his shredded coat rested on the chair.

"In the front pocket," he said. Curious, she took the jacket and rummaged in the pockets, pulling out an old piece of paper. At his nod she opened it.

"It's . . . a love letter." Some poor young woman pouring her misspelled heart out onto paper.

"To the Duke of Parford—likely when he was a lad." Jack

leaned forward. "It's Parford's most precious possession, judging by the way he kept it safe." And then with finality, "And nothing to do with the Comte."

Sarah couldn't help reading the letter. As terribly written and plaintive as it was, she couldn't help but feel that she was being terribly rude stepping into these people's lives, into their pasts, wherever they happened to be now. Also, another part of her, a smaller but stronger piece of her soul, recognized the bravery it took to confess one's feelings. And in contrast, her own cowardice.

"So . . . if there was nothing behind the wall," she began, folding the letter back carefully, "and the Comte has been taken in for questioning—whether he knows it or not—" She finally turned her body, and met his gaze. "What do we do next?"

Jack shrugged, his eyes never leaving hers. "Nothing." Then a great sigh left his body. "I think our part in this farce of heavy consequences is over."

"Over," she repeated dully. "So no more . . . spying? No more of . . . this?"

"No more Blue Raven," Jack said evenly, his tone betraying no feeling one way or the other on the matter.

"Oh," she said, her voice decidedly uneven. It was a shock to the system—more than finding out exactly who the Blue Raven was—that he would now disappear altogether. But how she felt about it was harder to pin down.

"Sarah," Jack said, hesitation in his voice, "why did you believe me? Why did you fall under the Blue Raven's spell so completely? I was convinced you would see through me at any moment, but you never did."

Sarah looked down to her feet, the bedspread, finally her eyes falling onto her silly scrolled dressing table.

"I think . . .because I wanted to believe in it. In him." She answered quietly. "It was safe."

Jack glanced quickly at his arm and torso. "I can't imagine anything less safe than chasing after the Blue Raven."

"But it was." Her eyes met his. "It was safe for me to fall a little bit in love with him. So I ignored rationality and let myself. Because it was a fantasy, you see. And a fantasy can never hurt, because it's never real." She looked to her toes again. "Jackson Fletcher is far too real for my peace of mind."

Jack, it seemed, was curious about the same thing she was trying to decipher within herself. "Sarah—I know you liked him a great deal more than me . . ."

"Not true," Sarah refuted quickly, vehemently. "To be honest, part of me is relieved that he'll never be back. I would not like to spend my life pacing the floors, wondering if you are living or dying. But part of me will miss . . . it."

"It?"

"That feeling of being part of something bigger than myself." She looked up at him shyly. "And it's silly . . . but I sort of wish I had the chance to say good-bye."

He met and held her gaze, leaning back against the headboard of her bed, his torso exposed, his legs languid. His entire body a beck and call. But it was his voice, unconsciously deepening, taking on the rasp she knew in another form, cloaked and tantalizingly forbidden, that drew her in.

"What would you tell him?" he asked.

"I would say . . . thank you. For reminding me—somewhat aggressively—that there's more to life than my own little dramas, my own tragedies. Bigger things, more important things. That I can move on from this constant barrage of parties and intrigues and silliness that I've been mired in. That I lost myself in." She wet her lips. "I'm ready now, for what comes next."

He leaned forward, slowly, likely being careful of his wounds—but the effect was beyond seductive. The light played over his body, finding the planes and hollows of muscle. His eyes, already dark, were nearly black in the light from the single lamp by her bedside.

"You know I never meant to hurt you," he breathed, his hand reaching out to touch her cheek.

She jumped at that. It was what her skin cried out for, but somehow the tension in the air made her as skittish as a colt. But he withdrew his hand, and let the cold air touch where his hand had been, and she knew she could not have that. She needed the contact. She had to touch him.

"You know you're still wearing your mask?" she said, reaching for a cloth, dipping it in the still warm water.

His hand went to his face, and he drew back dark fingers. "The greasepaint. It was supposed to look like soot, as a chimney sweep."

"It does. So much so that I worry about what your grease-paint will do to my sheets." She put her fingers under his chin, reveling in the electric shock, the comfort of that touch, and gently began to wipe away the grime, revealing Jack underneath.

Jack.

As she concentrated on her work, she could feel that his eyes never left her face. Drinking her in. She kept her face from burning through a will that she didn't know she had. The closeness of him made her brave, she supposed. But how brave?

"You told me a story once," she said, her voice as nonchalant as she could make it in a whisper, continuing to wipe his face clean. "About a girl you grew up with, and how you've searched for a light like hers ever since."

He nodded, once, gently, careful not to disturb her work. She hesitated a moment. Somehow, she knew her entire existence hinged on this question, this spare breath. "You never said who she was."

He stilled her hand. Took it into his own, and looked her dead in the face. She dropped the cloth. The greasepaint had been wiped away, leaving only the man in front of her. Only Jack.

Slowly, he brought her hand to his lips, pressing them against her palm, reverently, with all the feeling in his body.

What was happening to her? Her entire being was a bolt of electricity, her mind reeling with the possibilities of what came next. He was a man, in her room, half-naked.

More than that, he was Jack.

He was the friend from childhood. The gangly boy in a too-small cadet uniform. The pirate Bluebeard. The misguided idiot who had played her for a fool. The man who had kissed her senseless right over there, on her silly little dressing table. The man who refused to leave her alone with the Comte when he learned he was a danger. The man who played apology bowls. The one and only thing that had occupied her senses for longer than she realized.

The one and only thing she had wanted. Since the Event. Since before.

She had been doing everything right, for so long. She had

done as she was told, by people who knew better than her, and failed and succeeded in equal measure. Maybe, maybe now it was time for her to decide what was the right thing to do.

"Jack," she said softly, pulling her hand back from his lips. He looked up at her then, seeming to come out of a haze. Gently, sadly, he put her hand back down in her lap.

"Right. Right," he repeated to himself, his breath coming in small shifts. "I should go . . . to my own rooms, I suppose."

"No, Jack," she said smoothly, even though her heart beat in her throat. "That would definitely not be right."

Then she took his face in her hands, and kissed him.

Twenty-three

IT took Jack a moment to figure out that what was happening was real. And when he did, he fell into Sarah like a man starving. In all of the different ways this adventure played out in his head, he never imagined *this*.

That wasn't exactly true. Of course he had imagined this. He had imagined her in his arms a thousand times, making sleep fevered and waking painful. He'd imagined those inches of skin she'd kept hidden from everyone but him, imagined her breasts, her eyes turned emerald with passion. He'd imagined every minute, every second. But he'd never let himself hope for it.

He held her face with his hands, keeping her in the here and now, making certain she would not disappear into the ether, like the smoky Sarah in his dreams did.

Slowly, he pulled her toward him, leaning back against the headboard of Sarah's bed, the solid thunk of skull on wood reminding him that he was, indeed, in the present. And Sarah was with him.

He grimaced in pain. She pulled back immediately. "I'm sorry. Did I hurt you? I'll stop." Her questions came in such a rush of worry that Jack almost laughed.

"Do not worry. Harder things than the headboard have tried to get through my head." He grinned at her. "And don't stop. Stopping would hurt infinitely more."

She relaxed her worry, giving him a relieved, yet still nervous smile. The smile of the inexperienced. Of the wanting.

If her inexperience gave him pause, then her wanting banished it from his mind. She wanted *him*. Jack. Not the ghost of childhood adoration, but Jack. And he was not about to begrudge her.

Slowly he slipped his arm around her waist, pulling her to him, pressing her against his length. She was not shocked by the hardness she found there. Instead she nestled against it, seeking, urgent.

All of his blood surged to the bottom half of his anatomy.

"Hold on," he rasped, his voice a desperate grumble. At her confused look, he explained. "If we don't slow down, this will be over before it's begun."

She nodded slowly, then laid a small, shy kiss at the joint of his neck and shoulder.

"That wouldn't be good," she agreed, her lips making their way to his ear. "I feel like I've wanted this forever. I feel this should last forever, then. Don't you?"

He breathed out slowly, his mind reeling from the way she pecked at his neck, his shoulder, his ear. "I'll do my best," he exclaimed on a breath.

The trick, he decided, was to think about anything other than what he was doing. Think about . . . tactical ship maneuvers, instead of how her flesh felt beneath his fingertips. Think about climbing the rigging of the main yard, instead of how easily the buttons of her dress came undone, how his hand was moving up her leg, finding its way to the temptation of her garters. Think about cannons firing, again and again, instead of . . . actually no, don't think about cannons firing. Ever.

While Jack tried to tame his brain into falling under his control, Sarah had decided that her skin was far too warm, and that the dress that was half off of her already should really be removed in its entirety. She pulled back from him, for the barest of moments, leaving him bewildered and forlorn.

Bewildered and forlorn that is, until she whipped the heavy silk up over her head, and let it fall away to the side of the bed.

He drank her in, drank his fill. She blushed under his scrutiny. "They're white," he mused aloud.

"What are?" she said looking down, inspecting herself.

"Your under things. I would have assumed the golden lady wore only a chemise of spun precious metals."

She cocked her head to one side, playfully. "And I would have thought the Blue Raven had feathers all over his skin. But no, no feathers here." She came forward on her knees, leaning into his chest, touching him ever so lightly there, where springy, rough curls had been flattened to his chest with the exertions of the day.

She was kneeling on the bed in front of him, doing her best to be seductive, to lure him into her—and having no idea if she was doing it properly. But she figured she had to be doing something right, because she could feel the rapid movement of his blood, his heart, just under her fingertips. She could be this bold, she thought, this *carnal*—as long as she relied on some of the sophistication she had earned in the past few months. Since she had decided on this course of action, that this was *her* right, then she simply had to do it right, as well.

And her plan seemed to be working—until she lost her balance, and ended up crushed against him. He fell back sideways, catching her against him so they lay together crosswise on the bed. And then, he laughed.

She was mortified.

She ducked her head against his arm. Hid herself from his view. Even as his hands came around her, soothing, she still stayed down.

"What is it, love?" His eyes came down and found her where she hid.

"Nothing . . ." she replied. "I ah, I slipped."

"I noticed. I caught you."

"You laughed," she said, in a mock accusation.

"Because it was funny." Jack slipped his hand up her leg, finding that spot where here garters still hung on, proud and steadfast. Gently he slipped his fingers beneath it. "And because it is you."

She shot an eyebrow up at that.

"Don't you see, Sarah? All this time—you don't have to be

perfect with me." The knot of her garter came free with surprising ease. "In fact, I would much prefer it otherwise."

"How did you do that?" she asked, her skin burning beneath his touch.

"I'm very good with knots. Now where was I?" he mused playfully, as his hand worked its way to the other garter. "Oh yes. I much prefer the Sarah who falls out of trees. And the Sarah who kisses strange men in theatre cupboards—"

"As long as that strange man is you," she returned saucily, as her second garter found itself untied and her stockings were dragged down to her ankles.

"Yes, I much prefer that as well. I prefer the Sarah who isn't trying so hard to be in control of her life that she forgets to live it."

She raised an eyebrow, and her knee, to better accommodate his removal of her stockings. "I much prefer the Jack who isn't angry." He shot her a glance. "The one who's found that maybe the path he's taken has ended but there are new ones available."

His brow came down. But she continued. "And I prefer the Jack who listens to me, even when I'm trying to control everything, much to my detriment. The very serious Jack who could stop a girl's heart in his cadet uniform—"

"You liked me in my cadet uniform?" his smile came up, wicked and inviting.

"You have no idea what that uniform did to the Forrester girls, did you? My goodness, it stilled my ten-year-old heart more than once, I assure you." She giggled—whether it be from the expression on his face or the way his hands had moved up her thigh underneath her chemise, she could not be sure. But either way, it felt so wonderful to laugh. To be free to laugh with him. With Jack.

Which he must have surmised, because he began to laugh, too. Softly, a chuckle that was born of mirth but still in awe of his luck. Of his life. He brought his free hand up to her face, brushing a tendril of hair behind her ear.

"How did we get here?" he murmured, laying a kiss on her temple.

"Crookedly," she replied. "But here we are, all the same."

Her voice became a breath, a caress against his ear. "There is nowhere else I would rather be, Jack."

His gaze came to hers then, intent, serious.

And there were no more words to be said. All that had happened before and all that would happen hence, hinged on this moment, and there was nowhere else they wanted to be.

He dipped his head and kissed her, with reverence, but soon lost all caution. Lost himself in the sensation of her skin, even the silk of her chemise feeling rough by comparison. Clearly, it had to go. As did his boots—how the hell had they stayed on his feet so long? Clearly Sarah had the same idea, because in a rush of movement, she leveraged herself up and began to pull at his boots. Jack could only watch as she struggled, her full body exposed to the light, finally freeing the boots from his feet, thudding to the floor on the other side of the bed without care for the attention the sound could draw.

Her eyes met his with a smile, and Jack stared. She was naked. Gloriously, wonderfully naked, her hair still pinned up in a ridiculously sleek arrangement that had his hands itching to let it down, let it drape across her shoulders in a golden curtain, reaching the tips of those high, upturned peaks . . .

"I lied," he breathed. Her smile faded into a question. "You *are* perfect," he answered.

The look she gave him convinced Jack that his trousers were as extraneous as his boots had been.

He lurched up to meet her on the bed, grabbing her about the waist and pulling her to him. They fell back together, Sarah under him protected from the air, from the world. His trouser buttons were undone, by him, by her—it didn't matter, it was lost in a frenzy of movement and feeling that burned their minds into one single being, both intent upon the same purpose. And when he finally sprang free of his trousers, it was as if Jack himself came free of his moorings, and he gave up on trying to distract his mind with thoughts of yardarms, daily bells, and the undulations of the sea (which did not work), and for the first time, let himself sink slowly into bliss.

She opened for him naturally, her body knowing things her lady's education had left out. This was what she wanted; she knew it to her core. Her nerves were raw, on fire. Her body slick with need. His fingers danced in places she barely al-

lowed *her* fingers, bringing her past thought, only to action.
She wanted it—wanted him—so much, she held herself back
from stopping him when he nudged himself inside of her, and
the pain she knew would come.

She froze beneath him, which brought him out of his
passion-fueled haze.

"I'm sorry," he said, raining light kisses down on her face.
"I should have been gentler."

"It's . . . it's all right," she breathed, her voice slightly
strained. "When . . . when I was engaged, my mother told me
about it. I knew it was supposed to hurt."

"I bungled it," he cursed.

"No! It's just . . . well, rather obviously, it's my first time."
She thanked the gods above that relatively little light from the
candelabra penetrated their cocoon of bedclothes and draper-
ies, else he would see that she was blushing *everywhere*. But
instead, he looked off to the side, and said something that
shocked her to her core.

"Mine, too," his voice was barely more than a grumble.

"Truly?" she said, once she finally found her voice. "But,
no, that can't be."

"Why can't it?" He shrugged—well, as much as one could
shrug when on top of another person. "I've been on a ship for
nine years. There were no women on deck. Trust me, I looked."

She smiled slightly at that. "But you're . . ." She wanted to
tell him that he was too handsome, too well formed to be without female company, but somehow it seemed wasted. He was
too beautiful, too resplendent in his uniform. He should have
had a woman under each arm every day. And she would've
believed it if he told her as much. There was no reason to
lie . . . therefore, he had to be telling the truth.

Bewildering.

"Surely you had opportunities . . ." she ventured. "You
came ashore occasionally."

"I did," he agreed. He thought for a moment about the
dusky, sloe-eyed beauties of the Indies, whose colorful garb
wrapped tight around feminine forms, giving Jack plenty to
dream about on long nights at sea. And he thought about the
doxies of the London ports, tied and pushed and painted into
what men were supposed to want, their skirts always itching

to come up. A drink or two and any man could lose themselves in a raised hemline, Jack included. But . . . "But none of them," he ventured, trying to explain to her, to himself, "none of them had any light."

"Oh," she breathed. It was as if that light that he spoke about began to emanate from her being, making her feel warm and safe . . . and loved.

"Well," she said, moving her body, nestling against him, "how will we know what to do?"

"What do you want to do?" he asked, his head dipping down so he could better lavish attention on her neck, her shoulder, her breasts. When he took the tip of her breast into his mouth, she arched up to meet him, her insides aching for him.

"This," she whispered, shifting her body so he came into her deeper.

He sucked in his breath; she could see the strains of muscle in his neck as he fought to hold himself still, keep himself in the moment.

"In that case, I think we will muddle through."

She laughed at that, and brought his face back to hers, holding him there, kissing him with more power and longing than could be expressed in words.

Slowly he began to move within her, her body fitting with his, spreading for him, taking him in, all the way to the hilt. Her hips demanded what her brain could not articulate, moving with him in a rhythm they did not need to learn.

Giving in to gravity's pull.

His lack of experience was not a detriment—indeed, the number of times he had imagined himself in this situation, the dance of it, the feel of skin on skin, only made him more aware of the steps he had to take to bring her as much joy as she was bringing him. And while feeling built in her, growing with the force of a tidal storm, he held fast, touching here, touching there, until he felt her break beneath him, riding wave upon wave of pleasure into oblivion.

Then and only then, did he allow himself to join her.

And in that moment, Jack knew that Sarah had been right about it all.

They found their way there crookedly, but there they were

all the same. And as he kissed her deeply, truly, he knew one thing with complete certainty.

There was no one else. No other time or place he could inhabit. This was it for him.

There was nowhere else he would rather be.

Twenty-four

THE next day, when the carriage bumped along in the rain toward Whitehall, Jack could only think that there was very much somewhere else he would rather be. And that place was back in bed, with the woman who sat primly next to him—a full two feet away.

"Why are you so far away?" He smiled at her.

"Because . . . we're in public," she replied, her voice staying low. "And I don't want the world to know that we spent all night . . . doing that."

If possible, his grin grew wider. "Do you think people can tell?"

If possible, she blushed deeper. "I could barely look at you over breakfast this morning. Bridget kept asking me if I was feeling well."

"Strange, I could barely stop looking at you," he teased. "Now, we are in a carriage, not in public. And we will be for some minutes," he reminded her, as she peeked at him out of the corner of her eye. His hand reached over and pulled hers out of her lap. Slowly he pulled at the kid that covered her fingers, freeing her hand from its trappings. And then trapped it securely in his.

Somehow, the distance between them had closed. She had leaned into him while he gently stripped her hand, seducing her more effectively with that removal than he could have if he'd stripped her naked.

"Would you stop grinning at me like that?" she asked, likely unaware that she was grinning foolishly, too.

"Sorry. Shan't. Happy." He laid a light kiss on her temple.

"How many minutes do you think we have?" she asked, her whisper a breath, her eyes emerald with anticipation.

"Enough to . . . muddle through," his voice was a grumble, his hand coming up to pull that last inch to him. And as Jack knew, Sarah rather enjoyed muddling through.

Last night, they had managed to muddle through, quite marvelously. In fact after they had exhausted themselves, and reveled in each other the first time, they went back for seconds. And thirds.

The second time he was more careful of her, and she of him, each exploring, finding their way to what they liked, what they wanted. They giggled, laughed, sighed into one another. The third had been a blind grope in the hours just before dawn, their minds hazy with sleep, but their bodies, having slept for hours next to each other, recognizing the heat, the desire in each other. Jack woke up fully as she clung to him, panting in passion. It was beyond erotic. It was ecstatic.

When the morning came, he was reluctant to leave her side—and she to let him go—but in their whispered conversations in between kisses and caresses it was decided that perhaps Lord and Lady Forrester would not take well to having placed their trust in him, if it was discovered he had deflowered their daughter. Therefore, he sneaked out of her room before the servants were up and back to his own room, with nothing to do but spend hours trying to figure out how to get Sarah alone again.

God bless Sir Marcus, Jack thought, as his hand found its way to the sensitive spot on the backside of Sarah's knee, *for summoning us to Whitehall.*

And goddamn the Forresters' carriage driver, he groaned inwardly as they pulled to a stop in front of the Horse Guards, the official offices of the War Department, *for being so bloody good at his job.*

☙

"Well, this was a muck up of extreme proportions," Marcus said, from behind his desk. They had been escorted through the labyrinthine halls of the Horse Guards to the security section of the War Department by Sir Marcus's secretary. While in the wake of Lord Fieldstone's death, Sir Marcus had been asked to take on his responsibilities, the efficient man with an armful of papers explained as they walked briskly, but he still hadn't taken that as far as moving out of his old office.

"Er, it was?" Jack asked, with a quizzical look to Sarah.

"Oh, not you two. You actually did as well as could be expected under the circumstances," Marcus replied, waving away their perceived concerns. "One of the most important aspects of this line of work is the ability to cover your feelings and improvise when necessary. Which both of you did quite adequately." Then his face turned into a glower. "Even though I still cannot be happy with the way things turned out."

Sarah scooted forward to the edge of her seat. "Can you tell us what happened when you escorted the Comte away? If there is still some danger—I have to imagine that his sister, Georgina, must be sick with worry."

"The Comte is still in our custody, and has not as of yet mentioned his connection to Lord Fieldstone's death, and in fact has admitted to nothing more scandalous than having danced twice with Miss Forrester. However, he did let it slip that his friend Mr. Ashin Pha would not be found—apparently they planned for this eventuality. According to the Comte, Mr. Pha is safely at sea, halfway back to India by now." Marcus summarized, taking off his spectacles and rubbing his temple. "That information alone warrants another few days stay with us. If only there had been some proof found in the Duke of Parford's . . ."

"But Mr. Ashin Pha—I told you, he is not truly Burmese. Surely that is proof of the Comte perpetrating a fraud," Jack argued.

"Mr. Pha fled before we could confirm that. And the Comte de Le Bon is a crafty fellow."

"How do you mean?" Sarah asked.

"We needed to bring him in having the upper hand. Unfortunately, we didn't and he knows it. The minute we pulled up to the Horse Guards he knew he was in trouble. He denies any involvement in Fieldstone's death, but keeps dropping hints of information about the perpetrator—the person giving him orders, he says." Marcus smiled ruefully. "He's trading these bits of information for material comforts. He's already traded himself up from the holding cells downstairs to his own more spacious accommodations in the attic tower. But I doubt anything short of amnesty will get him to reveal his master's name."

Marcus stopped rubbing his temple, dropping his hand to his side. Jack was struck by how very tired Marcus looked, and he suddenly felt very guilty for it. While he and Sarah had been celebrating the end of their mission and the beginnings of their love, Marcus had been dealing with problems larger than either of them could conceive.

"Don't worry about Miss Georgina," Marcus said to Sarah. "I've had a protective guard placed around her house, and had her informed that her brother is helping me with some issues of international importance. Unfortunately, there is little I can do to combat the rumors that are going to emerge from yesterday's fracas."

"Oh, poor Georgina," Sarah murmured, sitting back in her chair. Her hand lay limp on the armrest, and instinctively, Jack reached for it, and squeezed.

This did not go unnoticed by Sir Marcus. His eyebrows went up, but he did not comment.

"I asked you here to get a full accounting of yesterday's mission," he said, clearing his throat. "Just to make sure that nothing was missed."

And so they told him. Sarah began, stating how she lured Georgina and Mrs. Hill away. Then Jack, going over the details of searching the house, the trouble getting behind the wall, and his fight with Mr. Ashin Pha. He then turned over the letters the Duke of Parford had hidden away behind the wall, which Marcus read, a frown crossing his face at first, as he realized the letter was worthless, but then the slightest of smiles as he recognized the sentiments.

They brought up every detail they could think of, from Mrs. Hill and Georgina's eagerness for the Comte to join them at the shop to the lower-class accent Mr. Pha spoke English with.

"What will happen now?" Sarah asked finally, as Marcus took this all in.

"I would rather not incite a panic, so Phillippa is trying to minimize the rumors that will be flying—but this may be beyond even her abilities. We've been holding this in too long," Marcus surmised. "Meanwhile, the Comte will stay with us as we research his connections, and search far and wide for Mr. Pha. But I have little hope he'll ever been found."

Jack thought of the men at the London docks, workers and mates on merchant vessels. Half were English, half dark-skinned. Mr. Pha, who apparently had experience in subterfuge, would have no trouble blending in there, and sneaking aboard a ship.

"I can go down to the docks," Jack offered. "Ask around and see if anyone has seen Mr. Pha."

"And I can talk to Georgina," Sarah piped up. "Ask her about her brother's friends in India."

"And there is still something strange about the house, and the painting—according to Lord Forrester, the Duke of Parford would never agree to sell the Holbein." Jack mused rapidly. "I think the Comte sold it, to fund his activities."

"Which if we can prove," Sarah jumped in, "would be proof enough to—"

"No," Marcus said. "Thank you both, but no. We are looking into the sale of the Duke of Parford's belongings, but you have both done your part. And as long as the whereabouts of those men are unknown, I would like to distance anyone not employed by this agency as much as possible." He looked at Jack's eyes as he spoke. "The men that work for me take an oath to protect their country with their lives. And my wife—well, she just inserts herself without my asking anymore. But I never should have demanded such from you through blackmail. For that I apologize."

"But—"

"You have already gone above and beyond the call of duty" Marcus interrupted, pulling a sealed envelope out of a desk drawer. "And you should be rewarded for it."

He held it out to Jack, who took the paper with a certain

amount of trepidation. His heart began to beat faster as he recognized the seal of the Lord of the Admiralty.

"These are orders," Jack said astonished as he read. "To report as first lieutenant on the *Dresden* on Monday."

Sarah's eyebrows went up. "I . . . I thought it was impossible to get a position on a ship now," she stuttered.

"It is. In fact, this is the post my friend Whigby is to fill," he looked from Sarah to Marcus.

"It's the position he *was* to fill. I have it on good authority—via my wife—that your friend Whigby proposed to and was accepted by Miss Juliana Devlin, and has decided to forgo his naval career to learn her father's business."

Jack blinked twice in astonishment. Although, why should he be astonished? Those weeks that he had spent avoiding Sarah for fear of his secret coming out, he had dragged Whigby with him to pay cursory calls on Miss Juliana. It seemed, however, those calls were more than cursory for Whigby.

"When I discovered the post had been abandoned, I called in a favor," Marcus finished. "Unless, of course, you would rather not take it."

"No!" Jack cried. "Of course I will take it. Thank you very much, sir."

He held out his hand to Sir Marcus who shook it readily. As he stood, he turned to Sarah, expecting to see a happy smile on her face for the successful resolution of all their worries.

Her lips were white, a shocked tear rolling down her cheek. Suffice to say, it was not what he was expecting.

❧

"Sarah, wait!" Jack called after her as she trotted with increasing fury down the corridors of the Horse Guards. But she would not stop. Her hands resolutely clutching her reticule, moving with the prim determination of someone who simply had to get out of there.

Which way should she go? Left? No right—right was the way out. If only she had paid attention when being led in instead of ruminating on what they had been doing in the carriage. It was all going to be her undoing. All over again.

Her mind was stuck on the same refrain. The same ache that had occupied the pit of her stomach all winter.

Twelve hours ago, this was not the turn she pictured their lives taking. In the halcyon bliss that they discovered comes after lovemaking, she pictured they would have an intimate wedding in a few months, and then settle on an estate purchased with her dowry, and . . . and life would start.

Not this.

"Sarah, hold on one minute," Jack said, finally catching up to her, gently taking hold of her arm, turning her toward him. "You have to tell me what is amiss."

"Nothing is amiss. You've gotten a commission. Congratulations." Her voice shook as she said it.

"That doesn't mean I'm leaving you," he said softly, stepping closer to her.

"No, just the hemisphere," she retorted. "I thought you were tired of life on a ship. I thought you said . . . it would be the *Amorata* that you missed, not the life at sea."

"It is," he admitted. Then he looked to the side. "You're right, I can only hope to find a home so well suited to me."

You can find it with me, she wanted to say. *You can have that here.*

"But it's the only thing I know how to do, Sarah," he argued. "It's the only living I can earn."

"But you do not need to earn a living," she countered. "I'm sure my father will settle enough on me—"

"Oh, hell yes I do!" the words came from him savagely, shocking her more than his hand tightening on her arm. "You think that after all your father has done for me I can come to him and say, by the bye, I'm marrying your daughter without ability or means to support her? I cannot be any more of a charity case to your family, Sarah."

"You never have been," she replied quietly.

"If you ever stood on my side of the equation you would not say that," he intoned grimly.

He dropped his hand from her arm, letting it slide down, trying to take her hand. But she wouldn't allow it. She pulled away.

"I have a dowry, Jack."

He shook his head. "I won't come to you with nothing, Sarah."

You did last night, her callous heart whispered treacherously.

"But with some luck," he gently persuaded. "I'll have saved enough to support you in a few short years, and—"

"A few *years*?" she practically screeched. "A few years."

"Yes—maybe less if I get promoted to captain, or if combat occurs—"

"A few years before we can get married. A few years that you'll be out to sea, coming home rarely, and if there's combat, maybe never. And a few more years that I am left wondering when my life is to start. Left waiting. Again." Her response was fevered, but quickly her voice broke and the tears began to fall.

Jack stood there, simply watching her, his mouth agape. Unable to answer, or even begin to try. Instead he wrapped her in his arms, and held her steady while she cried.

But this couldn't be. As much as her heart craved his arms around her, her head knew better. They were in the middle of a public hallway, making a spectacle. There were men in uniform, passing with their eyes straight ahead, but she knew they were listening.

This time tomorrow, she knew, she would not only be the "Girl Who Lost a Duke." She would be the Girl Who Lost a Lieutenant. The girl who lost control of her own life.

And she had to get it back.

She took a deep, resolute breath. Dried her eyes. And stepped back from him.

"Do you even want to stay with me?" she asked quietly, calmly.

"Of course I want to stay with you," Jack replied, his voice filled with emotion—but to Sarah it sounded placating. "It's only in these past few weeks that I've discovered that my home, my true home, has always been with you. But I have to earn a living. I would detest myself if I became idle on my wife's money; you must see that."

"So last night—that meant nothing to you. You can go on a ship in a week's time and forget it." Her voice was a whisper.

"Last night will be burned in my brain forever. Because I was making love to my *wife*. To you."

"No," she countered, her voice steely. "You were not. You were making love to a foolish girl who . . . fueled by the excitement of the day and the intrigue, let romantic curiosity get the best of her. And that's all."

"Sarah," Jack pleaded, his face white, his eyes lost, "this is lunacy. I love you and we will get married. I promise."

"And in the meantime . . . I wait," she replied coldly, her voice as hard as crystal.

৵

When they informed the Forresters of the news, the entire family enveloped Jack in a celebratory mass of excitement.

"Oh, my dear boy, I could not be happier," Lady Forrester was saying, in between tears.

"Marvelous! Simply marvelous!" Lord Forrester cried, pumping Jack's hand. "I knew there was something suspicious going on this morning between you two." His keen eye fell on Sarah, who was blushing in the corner.

"Indeed, Father," Sarah replied. "I can take no credit for it. Sir Marcus felt Jack was the best man for the job and told the Admiralty of the Navy so."

"Yes, but you are the one who introduced them, I know it," Lord Forrester leaned over and kissed her cheek. "Therefore, Jack must acknowledge that some of his good fortune is to your credit."

"But that means that you are leaving!" Amanda complained, tugging on Jack's arm. "Much too soon!"

"Oh heavens!" Lady Forrester exclaimed, her face going from joyous to bleak at an almost comic speed. "I hadn't even considered that! Dear boy, whatever will we do without you?"

As the raptures over hearing of Jack's new position aboard a ship as illustrious and mighty as the *Dresden* continued, swinging wildly from congratulatory to mournful to celebratory again, Jack found himself at a loss to explain how his life had altered so radically in the space of a morning.

He had intended to ask Sir Marcus if he could come to work for him. That was what he was going to do this morning. Not as the Blue Raven of course, but as a clerk, or a scout—a job where he could learn, and could grow. He was willing to start at the bottom, and work his way up. The truth of the matter was, something had become clear in those hours of climbing and running around rooftops—he found the work interesting. In the same way he had expected to find life on a ship interesting, when he was young and there was important work to be done, defending a country, not defending merchant vessels from piracy.

It was raw, honest, and important. And he could do it.

But then . . . then Marcus had spoken of the mission they had just finished as a complete and utter disaster. If only he had captured Mr. Pha! If only he had prevented his escape! Jack cursed himself. He knew, in that moment, he had blown any chance he might have had at working in the War Department.

Even though the last thing he wished to do was leave, his body screaming in protest against it, he cowardly took the consolation prize. The one that would still save his pride, his status as a gentleman, and give him income enough to eventually carve out a life with Sarah.

Until Sarah rejected that notion, too.

So here he was, being feted by the family that loved him most for this perceived triumph, and all he could think was . . . he was going to lose everything.

As Amanda and Lady Forrester demanded Dalton bring out a few glasses of champagne—in either celebration or mourning—Jack could only stand by and watch as Sarah slipped quietly out of the room. For the first time in months, she went unnoticed.

"Jack." It was Bridget. She slid up to him, her voice low. Not that it would have mattered. Lady Forrester had apparently decided to plan a farewell dinner for him, and was busy ordering the staff and Lord Forrester around accordingly. Amanda seemed happy enough following after her mother, and being allowed to take part in this very grown-up activity instead of her lessons for the day.

"I . . . I don't know if you'll need this aboard your ship, but I thought you might like to have it back anyway." Bridget said as she reached into her pocket, pulled out something, and pressed it into his hand.

He knew what it was simply by the feel. Her fingers drew back from his hand and revealed his false moustache, looking rather small and pathetic in full daylight. He almost laughed. To think, that such a tiny thing had acted for so long as his safeguard against discovery.

As he turned it over in his hand, Bridget ventured carefully into the fray. "I must say, news of your commission was not the announcement I expected you to make today."

He let Bridget's soft-spoken, clear words sink into him, as he stuffed the moustache into the safety of his breast pocket.

"Neither did I," he finally confessed, his eyes falling painfully on the spot where Sarah had been, just moments before.

"I have to admit to a certain amount of personal reflection over the past few days," Bridget mused idly, when he did not continue. "And I can only see this Season as populated by people who are all too often afraid to say what they feel. For example, I never had the gumption to tell you how I felt about you."

Jack's head came up, startled.

"I know, I know," she replied, waving off his astonishment. "However, since admitting this aloud, I have become convinced that my feelings for you were relatively shallow, and will easily be surmounted. You and my sister, however, are another matter."

She looked up to him then, sincerity in her eye.

"I cannot pretend to know the precise depths of your feelings for Sarah," Bridget spoke softly, seriously. "I can only tell you, knowing my sister, that her feelings mirror yours."

"If that were true, then how could she walk away?" Jack asked, more to himself than Bridget. But it was Bridget who had the answer.

"Did she walk away?"

"Definitively," Jack replied. "She doesn't want a sailor." Then, harsher than he intended, "And at this rate, it is all I'll ever be. Damn it, Bridget, I have my pride."

"Women have pride, too, just as much as men." Then she shook her head, smiling. "I should know. It's not that you're a sailor. It's self-preservation. She's frightened. The simple truth is losing the Duke nearly broke Sarah, but what she doesn't realize is losing you most certainly will. Give her time."

Just then, Dalton came into the room, bearing the tray of far-too-early-in-the-day champagne, but even he had given up his disapproving scowl in the happy atmosphere. A glass was put into Jack's hand, one in Bridget's.

With no small irony, he clinked his glass with Bridget's.

"Time, I'm afraid, is the one thing I do not have."

Twenty-five

FOR Sarah's part, her sympathies were firmly in Georgina's corner.

It had been two days since the announcement had been made in the Forresters' sitting room. Two and a half days since Sarah had been blissfully happy. Two days since she had spoken even the most cursory words to Lieutenant Jackson Fletcher. And in that time, Sarah brooded enough for two lifetimes.

She knew she shouldn't be as angry, as hurt, as she was. But the only thing she could think was . . . he was going to leave her. His promises meant little . . . Jason, the Duke, had made overtures, and then left on a trip across Europe and promptly forgotten about her. And really why should Jackson Fletcher be any different? After all, he left once before as well. And they . . . had forgotten each other.

Sarah was going to be left. And she had to prepare herself for it. She was going to have to go through the whole process all over again. Pick herself up and smile in public and act for all the world like she was the heartbreaker . . . not the heartbroken.

At least this time, it wouldn't be nearly as public. Just those closest to her—Phillippa, Marcus, and from the looks her sister was giving her, Bridget—instead of the whole of society. Every prying eye, every pained expression . . .

But why, oh why, did it feel like it was going to be so much worse this time?

Because you fell, the voice whispered in her head, like a breeze that made one shiver.

With the Duke she hadn't fallen—she had floated, happily on a notion that everything would be as right as rain forever. But with Jack—the stumbles and gravity and history had made her fall hard. She had fallen as irreparably in love as one person can . . . and instead of it bringing her peace and hope, instead of making her feel protected and beautiful, she felt bereft.

He told you that he loves you, the voice came back, in the dark of the night, as she lay tangled in her sheets, restless, unsleeping. Knowing that down the hall was a similar figure, likely twisting and turning in the same way. The man she wanted to keep . . .

She could go to him. She could whisper the same words back to him and give him her body once again, in the hopes that it tied her to him forever. He would marry her, then. She could after all be pregnant—a possibility that was too frightening and powerful to give a voice to at that moment (and to Sarah's mind, one that Jack had likely not considered . . . in her estimation, men rarely did.) If she brought up that possibility to him, he would marry her in a heartbeat.

But he would still leave in a week's time. And she would still be waiting. Waiting for him to come home. And a wedding ring did little to secure affections, especially when faced with a two-year separation.

After all, Jason the Duke's affections had fled after a few weeks. She didn't want someone who didn't want to stay with her . . . if she did, she would have married Jason all those months ago, and lived in comfortable misery.

But Jack is not Jason.

This refrain she played over and over in her mind. Jack was not Jason, true. Jason had never known her the way Jack did. Never touched her heart, or her body, in ways that bound the two together—heart and body—into the most graceful bliss

Sarah had ever thought to experience. And she knew that she had touched him in the same way.

So if he was going to leave . . . why didn't he hurry up and do so?

It would be easier once he left, she thought, somewhat irrationally. Once he was no longer sleeping just down the hall. Once he was no longer across from her at the breakfast table, making Amanda laugh and her mother smile with his presence. But it would be so *quiet* once he was gone, her brain pointed out. He lit up everyone in the Forrester house, not just her. It would go back to being round after round of endless balls, fetes . . . events that meant nothing beyond putting a good face on things.

So, yes, Sarah was firmly in Georgina's corner. Because over the past forty-eight hours, it became apparent that Georgina was about to go through the same thing, too.

Yes, Georgina's heart was being broken into tiny pieces. But not by a lover . . . instead by circumstances beyond her control. And society was about to eat her alive for it.

Yes, Georgina, the skittish girl who had no social allure, the one whose constant eagerness to be liked and correct and accepted by the ton had been used to great advantage by not only her stepbrother the Comte and Mr. Pha, but by Sarah herself. And perhaps, that is why, with all the rumors about the Comte de Le Bon and his nefarious man at arms, Sarah had decided to throw whatever weight she had left within society into the girl's camp.

It had begun yesterday. There was absolutely no reason to sit at home, and if she did she might go insane. Therefore when Phillippa Worth sent a note over asking if she would like to go riding on Rotten Row, Sarah immediately sent a positive reply and quickly changed into her saffron-colored riding habit.

"Air," Phillippa was saying, "air is always required after such a heart-stopping few days."

They rode side by side, at a pace barely above a walk, as they were stopped every few feet to converse with one dandy or another. After all, she was still the Golden Lady. The past few weeks her mind may have been occupied with other things, but those things had been so covert, they had no impact on how society perceived her. She was still beautiful. She still had the backing of Phillippa Worth. She still had a coterie of gentlemen on her front stoop, waiting to see if she would be taking calls that day.

"I doubt the air of London has any recuperative effects," Sarah smiled at her friend, hoping to keep cover as much with her as with anyone.

"True. Normally, I would insist on taking the boys to the country, but I've already had a furlough once this Season."

Sarah's eyebrow went up. " 'Normally'? These kind of situations have a normal?"

Phillippa reflected silently for a moment. Then carefully, "No, I doubt Marcus's and my life looks normal from the outside. But you have come closer to knowing what it is like than anyone in quite some time. I cannot tell you how enjoyable it is to have a friend that I can talk to about these things." Then she hesitated. "But I trust in your friendship to keep the world from knowing . . . just how abnormal we are."

"Phillippa," Sarah said, as she pulled up on her mare, bringing them both to a stop. "I would never reveal any of your secrets. The stakes are too high—and even if they weren't, you have trusted me with them. I know the world to be too cruel to understand."

"Yes, it is," Phillippa surmised grimly. "Which is the other reason I stayed in town."

Sarah blinked twice, not knowing of what Phillippa spoke, but was soon to learn, as they approached Lady Whitford's phaeton, and her breathlessly urgent news.

"Have you heard? It's tragic, absolutely tragic!" Lady Whitford bemoaned, as she waved a silk fan printed with a union jack on it in front of her flushed face. "I've just had it from Lady Belvedere, and if true, it must be the most un-British act one could possibly imagine. Of course, he *is* a Frenchman."

While Sarah's eyebrows had disappeared skyward, Phillippa had answered coolly. "Indeed, what news is this?"

"The Comte de Le Bon of course!" Lady Whitford cried. "Lady Belvedere has it from Lady Grantham that two days ago the Duke of Parford's home was broken into. But now that man has gone up and missing, along with his strange Burmese friend, leaving his poor sister in the lurch!"

"In the lurch?"

"Yes! Because you see, they say the person who broke in was a creditor looking to reclaim his goods, after having been denied so long! Now his sister must go to Fleet Street."

"I sincerely doubt that," Sarah replied drily. Only to be leveled with a glare from Lady Whitford.

"You only leap to his defense because he has been one of your favorites, and it does you no credit, Miss Forrester. Why, if he is not in debt, would Lady Grantham say that her husband, who is a member of the Historical Society, told her that they recently acquired a painting that was rumored to belong to the Duke of Parford's private collection? That bold Frenchman must have been selling off his host's property to pay for his pleasures this Season!" Lady Whitford concluded with a harrumph.

"Lady Whitford," Phillippa began, but apparently, that was not a harrumph of conclusion, instead a breath to allow for what was to come.

"It makes one wonder about the sister—is she simple, to have not seen her brother's nefarious intentions? And what of that Mr. Ashin Pha? He was always a tricky one. Never trusted him. Why, he's Burmese—and they are on the brink of war with us! One hears such things these days about those heathens, in the papers. I even heard a rumor that Mr. Pha was seen ordering the Comte around—if the Comte was under his sway, who is to say what kind of people we admitted to our social circles? Never trusted the man—either of them. And they infiltrated *our* dining rooms! Why, think of all the dinners they attended with men of state—they could have been planning a coup d'etat!"

For a woman as patriotic as Lady Whitford to speak in French phrasing meant the sin was grave indeed. This was exactly the kind of hysteria Sir Marcus had hoped to avoid, too. But with women like Lady Whitford at the helm of the gossip, it would balloon quickly. And then, someone who was in the know, but shouldn't speak, would mentioned Lord Fieldstone's death was not natural, and all hell would break loose.

But it was none of this that had Sarah's brow coming down, her emerald eyes turning to frost. It was, instead, what the lady had said about Georgina. But Phillippa had better control, not to mention more experience, with these things.

"Lady Whitford, that is indeed a frightful prospect. If only the Comte *had* disappeared." Lady Whitford's ears perked up. Phillippa leaned in, conspiratorially. "I shouldn't be telling you this, I learned it in the strictest confidence, but . . ."

"Oh no, do tell. I won't tell a soul," Lady Whitford promised.

"Well, I *would* say your fears are truly founded. If only my husband, Marcus, hadn't asked the Comte to help him with a certain matter . . . of national security." Phillippa shrugged as Lady Whitford's eyes grew wide. "That is why he has disappeared. Certain to return, of course, but I don't know if it will be before the end of the Season."

It was a silly story, and a simple one, but it was what Marcus and Phillippa had come up with, hoping to combat the worst of the gossip and keep mass panic in check. And apparently it worked, as Lady Whitford nodded gravely, as if she fully understood the importance of the Comte's mission.

"I must go," Lady Whitford said, continuing to nod like an idiotic jaybird. "I must tell Lady Grantham . . . er, something else. Lovely to see you both!"

And with that, she turned around and headed back from whence she came, eager to spread the gossip that Phillippa had told her under the strictest confidence.

"Well done," Sarah said to her friend, as they watched Lady Whitford's retreating form. "I would not have had your composure."

"Few do," Phillippa replied with a smile. But that smile quickly faltered, as her sharp eyes fell on something across the expanse of Rotten Row. "But I fear it was not well done enough."

Sarah followed Phillippa's gaze, to the other end of the lane. There, she could see the small form of Georgina, recognizable by her new Madame LeTrois riding habit, and Mrs. Hill, riding staunchly next to her.

And they were snubbed by every person they approached.

Sarah shuddered as she remembered it, her carriage pulling up to the Duke of Parford's home the next morning. It had been worse the evening after Rotten Row. Everywhere they went, the Comte was decried as a schemer, and his companion a dangerous infidel, brought into their midst. And while Sarah, knowing what she did, secretly supported these character assessments (even though because of them she was given more than one askance look, as she and the Comte had maintained a flirtation), she pretended to think them foolish, and laugh gaily upon hearing them. However, it was the assessment of Georgina as guilty by association that had her truly incensed.

Interestingly, it was the rumor of the Comte's thievery of the Holbein that had most people agape. Unfortunately, the appearance of the new riding habit on Georgina seemed to indict her more than anything else.

Madame LeTrois's gowns were notorious for being the most talked-of ensembles—but usually, it was a bit different.

And so, unable to solve her own life, Sarah decided to do what she could to help Georgina, and decided to call on her that morning.

She had told her mother she was going with Phillippa. And her mother was so busy planning a going-away dinner for Jack (Sarah's heart constricted every time she heard that phrase!) that she gave it little mind. As well, Jack was out of the house—he'd gone to the naval offices at Somerset House to officially accept his commission. Therefore, he wouldn't rightly point out the danger of her entering the Duke of Parford's home. After all, while Mr. Ashin Pha was likely halfway back to India by now, it was not a known fact.

But Sarah was determined. She wanted to see Georgina alone. She would give her the same speech that Phillippa had given her, tell her that she had done nothing wrong, and therefore she should stop acting like it. To find a way to change the story, and make society envy her instead of pitying her. And to survive it.

She trotted up to the Duke of Parford's door, practicing her speech in her mind, and raised her hand to lift the heavy knocker.

And instead found the door unlocked. Not to mention unlatched. It creaked open, setting the hairs on the back of Sarah's neck in little spikes.

"Hello?" she ventured. The mansion's foyer was as quiet as death, her voice echoing across the expanse in chilling fashion. None of the curtains were open, so not only was the space quiet, but Sarah could hardly see.

"Hello? She tried again, stepping in all the way. She kept one toe in the light from the doorway, every instinct in her body telling her to flee. Until she heard it.

". . . 'ello?" It was the barest whisper. A female voice, so quiet, Sarah might have mistaken it for the last echo of her own tentative greeting, except for the words that followed. "Who's there?"

Sarah stepped in further to the great hallway.

"Georgina?" she asked the air.

"Sarah?" the voice came. Then a relieved cry. "We're in here! We're in here!"

Blindly, Sarah followed the voice to a door on the side of the foyer that she knew to be the door to the study. Her heart raced, her palms became slick. Her body prepared for flight. She knew, *knew*, that something was wrong. But she was not prepared for what she saw.

A heavy curtain billowed open from a breeze. The broken window—through which Jack had made his grand escape three days ago—was boarded up with cheap planks of wood. So cheap, in fact, that somehow it had been broken open again, and glass and splinters littered the floor of the study. And there, amongst the splinters, lay the lifeless body of one Mr. Ashin Pha, a red line stretching across his throat, spilling his blood out onto the carpet.

Sarah screamed. Screamed madly, screamed without any idea that she was going to be heard. But before her brain could command her feet to move, to get the hell out of there, another voice penetrated her brain.

"Sarah!" Georgina's voice came from seemingly nowhere. "Sarah is that you? Are you alright?"

"G—Georgina!" Sarah cried, unable to tear her gaze from the body—his glassy eyes told her he was dead, and his pallor suggested it had been quite a while. "Where are you?"

"We . . . we're stuck in here. Behind the wall."

Sarah turned wildly, her eyes finally landing on the false Holbein. Georgina rapped on the wall, confirming that her voice came from there.

"Georgina, you're behind the painting?" Sarah asked

wildly, running over to the painting . . . which was coincidentally the very furthest point from the form of Mr. Ashin Pha.

"Yes, Mrs. Hill and I," Georgina explained. Now that
someone had arrived, her voice began to give into the hyster-
ics she had obviously been holding onto this entire time. "It's
very cramped in here, and dark, and I . . . we locked ourselves
in here when we heard the men break in, and I don't know
what happened, you have to get us out, you just have to,
Sarah!"

Georgina's cries became further muffled. Sarah guessed
she was now pressed into Mrs. Hill's shoulder, as that woman's voice came through the wall now. "There, there," it
soothed. "Help is here now; we are saved." Then a little louder.
"Quickly if you please, Miss Forrester?"

"Right . . . how did Jack open this lock?" she asked herself,
panic making her mind sharp. The frame, he had said. It was
attached to the wall. She quickly began running her fingers
over its edges, looking for the scroll that Jack said decom-
pressed and . . .

With a snick and a catch, the hidden door released. Sarah
gently pushed it inward, revealing two very pale and dusty
female figures standing in the small space available, clutching
each other in hope and terror.

"Thank heavens!" Georgina cried, removing herself from
Mrs. Hill's embrace and throwing herself into Sarah's. "We've
been in there for hours. I didn't know if we'd ever get out!"

"Georgina, what happened? Where are all the servants?"
Sarah asked. Indeed, the house had the feel of one abandoned,
only wanting for dust cloths over furniture to make it feel truly
empty.

"They . . . they left," Georgina replied, in between gulps of
air and tears. "Yesterday! I went out to the park and came
home and the entire house was empty!"

Sarah shot a glance to the steadier, but no less dusty and
shaken Mrs. Hill. That usually stoic lady was pale with shock.
"We don't know what happened, but it seems the abandonment by Mr. Ashin Pha and the Comte—as well as some rumors about Miss Georgina's solvency—convinced them to
leave." Mrs. Hill grimaced. "With all the silver."

As shocked as Sarah was by such rash treatment by a

household staff—albeit a foreign one—she was still a little bit
more concerned by the dead body of Mr. Ashin Pha on the
floor, a mere dozen feet away.

"But what happened with Mr. Pha?" Sarah asked, her heart
beating like a hummingbird's wing.

It was Georgina who answered, her face as pale as a ghost.
"He . . . they. . . . We were in here, trying to find my brother's
bills and things, to see if we really were out of money. And
someone started clawing at the boarded up window. I knew
about the little room behind the painting—I was exploring in
here one day and found it—and so we hid in there." She took
a breath, steadied herself, held herself upright through sheer
will and the support of Mrs. Hill's shoulder. "I knew it was
Mr. Pha by his voice, but there was another one. They were
looking for something, but I have no idea what. And the other
man—he was speaking in Burmese as well—he kept yelling
at Mr. Pha. And then . . ." Georgina's face crumpled as her
eyes flicked to where Mr. Pha had fallen. She sobbed into Mrs.
Hill's shoulder.

"I think it best if we remove ourselves from this room,
don't you?" Mrs. Hill said pointedly.

"Yes, of course," Sarah replied, her reeling mind snapping
back to the present. But the same refrain was going on over
and over in her head: *There was another man. She had to tell
Marcus. She had to tell Jack.*

"Who is Jack?" Georgina asked, once they were in the
great foyer.

"Beg pardon?"

"You . . . when you were opening the door, you said Jack
had told you how to do it." Georgina replied vaguely, as if
talking of such a small oddity was somehow soothing, different from the horror of her last few hours.

"Jack! Of course." Sarah cried. "He should know about
this. Marcus, too. We need to tell them."

"Sarah—please," Georgina grabbed her hand, with a
shocking force, pressing Sarah's flesh white. "I have to talk to
my brother. Do you know where he is? I have to find him . . .
tell him . . . I don't know a lot of the language, but I do know
they mentioned my brother's name, and I'm afraid that the
man will go find him next."

"Yes, of course," Sarah replied. "We need to get Jack, too. He'll need to know this. We shall pick him up on the way."

"No," Mrs. Hill interjected sternly. "I doubt there is time for that. I will fetch your Jack to you, but please, take Miss Georgina to the Comte. I too fear the consequences if we do not reach him in time."

"You've been through so much," Sarah began to protest, but was cut off by a hand from Mrs. Hill.

"I am made of stronger stuff than that."

"She is," Georgina added, with a meek smile.

"All right," Sarah conceded. "Go to the naval offices at Somerset House, ask for Lieutenant Jackson Fletcher. And then meet us at Sir Marcus Worth's offices at the Horse Guards."

A quick look was shared between Georgina and Mrs. Hill, ended by a curt nod from Georgina. Mrs. Hill rose quickly and headed out of the house, hailing a hack as she went.

"Come," Sarah said finally, half lifting Georgina from her seat. "Hopefully the Comte can shed some light on this."

Twenty-six

"MARCUS, we need to see the Comte immediately!" Sarah cried, unable to hold it in any longer. They had driven across town in silence, Georgina pale and wild-eyed, Sarah holding onto her arm, trying to be soothing, fearing that she was instead gripping her friend's arm into numbness. Finally they had arrived at the Horse Guards, and then had to wait whole minutes while the guards contacted Sir Marcus to see if he was available to meet with them. Apparently, the word "emergency" meant very little to their ears.

Finally a guard took them back to the security section, where Sarah blurted out their intentions before the door to his office barely had time to close.

"Miss Forrester, good God, what is wrong? What has happened to the two of you?" Marcus exclaimed, offering them both seats, but neither took them. The need to move was too urgent, too desperate.

"What happened is Mr. Ashin Pha has been killed, and we were locked in a room, and if you don't let me see my brother right now, I'm going to scream!" Georgina piped up, her voice shaking.

Marcus could only blink at the two of them. "Perhaps it is better if you start at the beginning."

And so they told him, in alternating sentences, about what had happened just this morning. They were not halfway through their speech when Marcus jumped up from his spot on the edge of the desk, grabbed a set of keys, and ran to the door. The girls followed him.

"Guard," he called to a guard posted at a doorway down the hall. "I'm taking these ladies up to see the prisoner. Let no one in or out after us, understand?"

"Yes, sir," the guard saluted. And with that, they entered the door the man guarded.

It was a rickety, narrow staircase, circling the walls. Seemingly going up into a belfry. A wide mouth in the center made Sarah dizzy as they approached the top. The stairs were too steep and narrow to position a guard on, which is why they remained outside of the hallway doors. Sir Marcus flipped through the keys on the ring in his hand while he talked.

"Your stepbrother, Miss Thompson, I am sorry to say, is not the best of men. He has become involved in a conspiracy with international implications."

"A conspiracy?" Georgina asked, bewildered, as they climbed.

"Yes," Marcus replied. "At first he would admit to nothing. But slowly he has been confessing to small amounts of con artistry. As of this very morning, he mentioned a third person in on the gambit, and I think it is this man who murdered your Mr. Pha. We have to get him to tell us who is he and where to find him."

They reached a door, four stories up. It was heavy, built of iron, with massive locks and only the smallest slit where food could be passed through. Marcus unlocked the door with an oversized key, swinging the door open, to reveal the Comte de Le Bon, a shackle around one ankle, connecting to the thick stone walls. But the Comte himself was sitting quietly on an overstuffed chair, reading a lurid novel, for all the world comfortable and content.

"Sir Worth, this novel," the Comte said without looking up, "I do not know if the plot is worthy of any information I might have. You should talk to the people who see to my comfort—it requires better literature."

"Jean," Georgina cried, rushing to his side. He looked up startled, then happily taking her into his arms. Behind them, Marcus securely closed and locked the door.

"Georgie!" the Comte said, flustered. He caught her when she rushed into his arms. "How did you find me?"

"Miss Thompson, please step away from him," Marcus commanded. But Georgina, in all her flushed worry, paid him no heed.

"Jean, the worst has happened, Mr. Pha is dead!"

"What? No! Pha was supposed to flee via ship?" the Comte looked wildly from Marcus to Sarah, as if searching for confirmation from them.

"Someone killed him in our house, Jean!" Georgina said, harshly, drawing the Comte's attention back to her. Sarah watched as he focused on his sister's face, his expression inscrutable. "Sir Marcus said you mentioned a third conspirator." Then, harsher, "Did you mention a third conspirator, Jean?"

The Comte's inscrutable expression quickly paled. Sarah was surprised to recognize the fear on his features.

"Georgina, no, I didn't tell them anything, I swear."

"Not yet, at least," Georgina's normally fluttery, soft countenance was gone, replaced by a voice as hard as the steel blade that appeared in her hand from its hiding place up her sleeve.

Steel that slid into the Comte's belly with practiced ease.

Sarah wanted to scream, but she stood rooted to the spot, watching as Georgina Thompson sliced open her stepbrother's belly, then neck, and let him fall to the floor.

It had happened in less than a second.

"Sarah, run!" Marcus whispered in her ear.

They were at the door in a heartbeat, but as Marcus fumbled with the keys, Georgina's clear voice cut through their panic.

"I wouldn't do that if I were you," she said simply. They turned to see that she was holding a pocket pistol. Pointed easily, coolly, directly at them.

❧

Jack exited the naval offices at Somerset House, in much the same mood he was in the last time he found himself standing on these steps. That is, he was in a mood to walk. To brood. To feel the length and width of London under his feet, and to come to terms with what he had just done.

But he didn't have the time.

As he stepped out into the courtyard, much like the last time, Jack couldn't shake the feeling that something was amiss. His eyes scanned the other men, talking in small clusters or standing near the central fountain, most without a heavy overcoat on that warm day. He saw nothing amiss, no Byrne Worth lurking in disguise, nothing that justified the strange feeling in his gut.

Come now, his mind rationalized. *You know the cause of this queer feeling.*

What he had just done, of course, in the naval offices. Marched right up to the officer on duty, signed the paperwork, and set his life on its new course. Nerve-wracking, in its finality. Heart-stopping, in that he still had not squared his life away here, with Sarah.

Bridget's cool rationalization helped, of course, as he held out hope that Sarah would come to her senses and realize through her fears that his naval career was no impediment to how he felt about her. But as one day and then another ticked by, both of which she spent studiously ignoring him, he couldn't help but wonder if giving her time was exactly the wrong thing to do. It certainly wasn't doing him any good at present. He should have gone to her rooms at night, and claimed her in a way his body and soul ached to. Lying awake, tangled in his bed sheets, too restless to sleep. Because now he knew. He knew what Sarah's Forrester's skin felt like resting next to his. He knew what her snores (light snores, but snores nonetheless) sounded like. Half a dozen times he almost went to her door. Another half dozen he almost went to her window.

There it was again! That frisson of feeling, running up his spine. Jack glanced to his left and his right, careful not to give himself away by moving his head too much. He was out of the courtyard now, moving down to the Strand. Stopping at the side of the road to let a carriage pass before he crossed, Jack casually glanced over his shoulder.

There was no one behind him, except for a stout woman who bent down to pick up a dropped reticule. Jack turned back.

Every instinct in his body told him he was being hunted. And if a few weeks of playing the Blue Raven had taught Jack anything, it was to never ignore his instincts.

When the street was clear, Jack crossed it, but then, instead of following the route that would take him back to Upper Grosvenor Street, he made a sharp, unexpected turn.

He could hear footsteps behind him making the same sharp turn. His eyes narrowed; his shoulders tensed. There was no doubt now, and his body readied for what was to come.

He cut through the streets of London, zigging and zagging his way through traffic, certain his unseen friend was keeping up with him. Suddenly, he found what he was looking for: an alleyway, with enough debris and juts—and privacy—to suit his purposes.

He only had seconds, at most. He turned sharply into the alley and then ran for its back wall, where empty flour sacks, boxes, and crates—used to hold chickens, likely long since cooked in the pub's kitchen next door—assisted him in gaining the upper ground. Then he swung himself onto a ledge that ran along the second-story back windows of the pub. Then, he waited.

He didn't have to wait long. Barely a moment after he positioned himself on the ledge, he watched as the woman, who he recognized as the one who had been bent over at the road crossing, entered the alley, assessing, assured. Her right hand tucked behind her back.

When she looked up, and the spare bit of light that the alley afforded hit her face, Jack was taken by surprise.

"Mrs. Hill?" he whispered. It was her. The stout, proper companion of Miss Georgina carefully surveyed the terrain of the alleyway, looking for him.

Hunting him.

But why . . .

His hesitation cost him. He should have leaped down immediately upon her entry to the alley. But instead she had enough time to survey the scene, and look up above, and find him, looming there.

"Oh thank goodness. Lieutenant Fletcher," she said, her voice eerily calm. "I've been sent to fetch you. There's been a terrible accident."

"An accident?" he replied, still not moving from his place. The entire situation felt wrong. Everything about her being there seemed to click a truth into place for him, but he couldn't pinpoint what it was. The only thing he could decipher—as someone who had recently been living a double life—was that she was not all that she seemed, either.

"Yes. It's terrible. Miss Forrester. You must come at once," she tilted her head to one side. "What are you doing up there, Lieutenant?"

Sarah's name sent fire through his blood, and almost had him scurrying down to Mrs. Hill's side. But he held himself still.

"What do you have behind your back, Mrs. Hill?" he asked instead. The question hung in the air, as Mrs. Hill slowly dropped her proper demeanor, and smiled, like the devil herself had taken hold of her.

"Oh, I do enjoy a lack of pretense," she replied coolly, as she brought her hand out from behind her back. "Almost as much as I enjoy target practice."

She fired the little silver pistol at him, the sound echoing through the alley. Jack scrambled. But the ledge held little in the way of room to maneuver, and so, he ended up tumbling to the chicken crates below, crashing through the hay and wood and feathers.

"Oh my," came Mrs. Hill's voice. Her methodical footsteps approached. "Did I hit you? I do hope so." She tossed her pistol aside, its one shot used. Then she withdrew a second pistol from her pocket.

She thought she had hit him. The thought ran blindly through his head. Falling had cost him any advantage—but this might get a slice of it back.

He let the wreckage cover him. Above him, she began to pull back pieces of wood. He wrapped his hand around the most solid plank he could find.

"Lieutenant?" Mrs. Hill sing-songed, as if they were playing hide-and-seek. Well, he'd been taught to play hide-and-seek by the best of them.

When she pulled back the last bit of canvas that covered him, he swung as hard as he could, catching her completely by surprise, knocking the pistol out of her hand. Her face went from shock at his not being dead, to livid at losing her gun, to complete rage as she set upon him. All in a fraction of a second.

She was stronger than he suspected. Stronger than he ever thought a woman could be. Her stoutness was apparently all muscle, and quickly he lost any reserve at battling with a woman—since she was, after all, intent on killing him.

He managed to pin her. He took fists to her face, hoping to knock her into unconsciousness. But either the rage or her training kept her from passing into black oblivion. In fact, after a punch went wild, his balance went off center slightly. And Mrs. Hill, perhaps trained in fighting better than he could ever hope to be, took advantage of that.

She reared up, and rolled, pinning him beneath her. Her meaty hands closed around his neck, squeezing, pressing the life out of him.

She was killing him. Jack couldn't think. All he could do was act. Blindly reaching into the chaos of debris that was spilled beneath him, his fingers landed on something metal, and cool to the touch, just beyond his reach.

The second pistol.

Loaded, and ready to fire.

As the edged of his vision began to go dark . . . as his eyes felt like they were going to pop out of his skull . . . as Mrs. Hill foamed at the mouth in concentration and mad triumph . . . Jack managed that extra inch and grabbed the pistol, brought it against her gut, and fired.

The hands on his throat froze, then loosened and fell away. Surprise registered across Mrs. Hill's face, just as she collapsed on top of him.

His vision returned with every gulp of air. He struggled out from under her, flipping her onto her back as he went. While his breathing was deep, restoring, every ragged breath she took was panicked and shallow, blood spreading across the front of her dark dress rapidly, making the dark material sticky and black.

"Where are they, Mrs. Hill?" Jack asked, roughly, his voice gravel.

"You're too late," she gurgled. He must have nicked a lung. "They'll all be dead by now."

"*Where!*" Jack yelled, menacing over her. Which only made her cackle.

"My mistress, she's smarter than all of them. Sir Worth, the Comte. All of them. And Miss Forrester . . ."

"What about Sarah?" His blood pumped raw and angry. But his urgency only made her laugh.

"She'll be dead by now, too. They all will." And with a spasm of coughing, Mrs. Hill fell back against the broken crates, and joined the Comte in death.

Jack stood, stunned, for the time it took to process her words. *Sarah. The Comte. My mistress.* If Georgina was going after the Comte and Sir Worth, there was only one place to find them.

Jack turned to the mouth of the alley. A few people had begun to gather, stick their heads in. It had been little more than a minute since the first pistol shot rang out. The timid crowds were now just beginning to see what the commotion was all about. Jack had no time to answer to them. He lit out of there like he was on fire.

"You, sir!" he called out to a gentleman sitting atop a fine mare. "I need your horse. An emergency!"

He must have looked mad. Covered in dirt, flour, feathers, and blood, and wild-eyed to boot. Not that looking normal would have made any difference.

"I say—how dare you accost me sir!" the gentleman cried. "You can't simply take a man's horse."

Jack held up the pistol that was still in his hand, still warm from firing, and pointed it at the gentleman. "I beg to differ, sir."

The gentleman—who thankfully didn't realize that the gun in Jack's hand was one that had just been fired—quickly alit from his horse.

"You can collect it from the Horse Guards later," Jack yelled behind him, as he kicked the horse into a gallop, weaving in and out of the London crowds as he rode hell-bent for leather, right into the mouth of madness.

Twenty-seven

"WELL, Miss Georgina," Sir Marcus drawled, his hands held up but relaxed, "what do you intend to do now?"

Georgina leveled him with a look, the gun remaining steady in her hand. "First of all, I would like you to toss me those keys in your hand. Thank you," she said graciously, as he complied. "As for the rest, you'll have to forgive me, but as you can likely tell, I am now improvising. I did not expect Jean to be held at the Horse Guards, you understand. I had expected somewhere much more secluded."

Sarah found herself rooted to the spot, her eyes flitting from the body on the floor to Sir Marcus's easy nonchalance, to the woman who, just that morning, Sarah had been feeling so sorry for that she headed out to bravely offer her support. Slowly, sharply, pieces started putting themselves together in Sarah's head.

Georgina mentioned more than once Mr. Pha speaking Burmese—but Jack said he spoke English like an Englishman. *Georgina* headed home early from the theatre, right after Lord Fieldstone left. And *Georgina* insisted on writing the Comte that they were at Madame LeTrois, foiling Jack's search of the house.

It was so odd, so maddening, Sarah found herself laughing.

It was just a giggle at first, something that she tried to stifle. But smothering it only brought it out in greater force. And soon, tears of laughter were streaming down her cheeks.

"Oh dear, do you think you can make her stop?" Georgina sighed as if Sarah were a toddler to be rounded up. Marcus, with infinite care, took Sarah by the shoulders and whispered in her ear.

"You must keep your head," he told her, too low for Georgina to hear properly. "We will get through this."

"How?" Sarah asked loudly between laughs that died with each breath. "How do we get through this? Georgina—I never guessed you were as nefarious as your brother. We walked right into this; how do we get out of it?"

"Because Miss Georgina knows she will be able to walk out of here much easier with a living hostage or two," Marcus replied, thinking faster on his feet than Sarah could manage, and she was grateful for it.

"Oh, I don't think I'll need two," Georgina replied. "It's only a matter of deciding which of you is more controllable, and more desirable as a shield should someone try to stop me."

Sarah felt like she had stepped from her world—where life was solid, and her biggest problem was that the man she would marry had a career that would take him away from her for two years at a time—and fallen into a place that was as fluid as water, constantly shifting, and one had to work with the current to stay afloat.

She would marry Jack. She knew that now. A two-year separation would hurt, but it seemed so little when staring down the barrel of a gun. It brought her silliness into startling clarity.

"I'm glad things have ceased to be funny for you, Sarah," Georgina said, and Sarah realized her laughs had died away completely. "Think of how much better your chances are of becoming my hostage if you can keep calm under the circumstances."

"No," Sarah replied quietly. "I was simply thinking of how silly I had been of late." Georgina shot her a hard look, but Sarah refused to elaborate. Let her think what she will of that, she thought with a teaspoon of triumph.

But instead of acting on the annoyance that flashed across her face, Georgina, keeping the gun trained on them from the other side of the room, took the chair that her stepbrother had been sitting on moments ago and dragged it to the high window. Standing on it, she peered out of the window, which Sarah guessed looked down on the Horse Guards' courtyard.

"Sir Worth, what time is the guard change?"

"Noon," Marcus answered readily.

"Really, I could have sworn it was at eleven," Georgina replied, peevishly. Hopping down from the chair, she crossed the room, stepping over her brother's lifeless body as she came up to Marcus and grabbed Sarah by the arm and pressed the barrel of the gun into her temple. "I do not appreciate being lied to. Are you certain it is at noon?"

As the cold metal bored into her temple, Marcus hesitated a moment, seeming to try and figure out his options. But there were none, as he gave a short bow. "I was mistaken. It is at eleven."

Georgina released Sarah, who stumbled back, her body stiff with fear.

"Well," Georgina replied, "it's about quarter to eleven now. I suppose in fifteen minutes we will see if you are correct."

"Why . . . why do you need to know about the guard change?" Sarah asked carefully.

"Because it's the time of day that the most people are outside and the least amount inside the Horse Guards," Georgina replied. And then, when Sarah only blinked in answer, explained. "It's when I'm going to make my escape, Sarah."

"Escape to where?" Sarah asked. "You don't think people will be looking for you, with the carnage left in your wake?"

Georgina shrugged. "They can look all they like; they won't find anything. My bags are all packed, the servants taken care of. As well as Mr. Ashin Pha. All I had to do was wrap up this one loose end"— she indicated the body on the floor—"and I will disappear."

"But people know you," Sarah countered. "The Duke of Parford . . ." But Georgina just smiled pityingly at her.

"The Duke of Parford has no idea who I am, or that we have been occupying his house for the past months. All I had to do was get his secretary in India to write a letter to the household staff, which the Duke signed—the old man is apparently so blind with age he'll sign anything these days. And it was a tragic fact that the secretary died a few days later, robbed by ruffians in Bombay . . . a true pity. Especially for such a . . . *vigorous* young man."

Georgina began pacing slightly, back and forth, but the gun remained trained upon them. "I will not be easy to find. I don't think I'm spilling any true secrets when I say Georgina Thompson is not my real name. Nor is the Comte de Le Bon my real stepbrother. Our relationship was more . . . vigorous than that." She shot the corpse a look of disgust. "Next time I'll choose my scapegoats with greater scrutiny."

"The Comte . . ." Marcus interjected. "He was not a part of your schemes?"

"Only as someone to give me cover enough to move within society without notice." Georgina shrugged. Then her eyes narrowed. "If only he hadn't gotten so greedy with the damned Holbein."

"I'm afraid you've lost me," Marcus said. He shot a look to Sarah. *Keep her talking*, the look said. *It will keep us alive.* "So this had absolutely nothing to do with the rumors of a Burmese war?"

"Oh no, Sir Worth, it had everything to do with those rumors." Georgina stopped pacing, her eyes wide with astonishment. "After all, I started them."

Marcus and Sarah exchanged a look. While Marcus seemed politely curious, Sarah was totally baffled. Which must have read on her face, because Georgina interjected in their silent conversation.

"Why don't I start at the beginning?" she offered, with a quick glance to the watch pinned at her waist. "After all, we have the time."

❧

Jack leaped off the horse at the ivory mouth of the Horse Guards' main entrance, heedless of the commotion he was causing.

"Whoa there! Halt!" two guardsmen called out to him. But Jack would not stop. He had to get inside. He knew, he *knew* that Sarah was in there, and who knows what Georgina had done. But those two guardsmen caught up to him, as three others blocked his path.

"You can't go in there, sir!" one guardsman said sternly, taking in Jack's crazed appearance, his dirt and blood covered uniform.

"I have to see Sir Marcus Worth," Jack said in a rush. "I'm Lieutenant Jackson Fletcher, and he's in grave danger!"

"I don't care if you're the King hisself," the guardsman replied, "no one sees Sir Worth without an appointment."

Jack turned to him, wild-eyed. "Does that mean that no one has come to see him this morning? Two ladies didn't come here?"

The guard opened his mouth, then closed it. "How did you know that?"

"She's going to kill him! She's going to kill all of them," Jack replied in a rush, sounding mad, he knew, but unable to stop it. "You have to let me in, please."

The guardsman hesitated—long, too long. Every second counted. Finally Jack couldn't stand still any longer. "Oh, to hell with it," he said, lowered his head, and pushed through the line of men blocking his path.

Not the best idea, it turned out.

All five of the well-trained guardsmen set upon him, tackling him to the ground, stopping him from getting any closer.

"Hold him," the one guardsman said, then addressed one of Jack's captors. "Go tell the officer on duty we have a vagrant overcome with madness. We'll lock him in the lower holds."

If he was locked in the lower holds, he would never get out and find Marcus and Sarah in time. Or the Comte for that matter—Marcus said he'd negotiated a stay in their luxurious attic, away from the riffraff . . .

The Comte was in the attic tower . . .

Jack suddenly forced himself to his feet, the three men trying to hold him scrambled to take him back down. But Jack held up his hands in surrender.

"No need gentlemen, it's a complete misunderstanding . . . I'll be leaving," Jack said, docile as a kitten. Then, before they could regroup, Jack fled from the main courtyard and into the crowds of people and carriages that moved along Whitehall.

When he felt he was at a safe enough distance, Jack looked over at the grand structure that was the Horse Guards.

There. The highest window, small and cramped against the roof of the furthest wing of Horse Guards. Was it his imagination, or did he see a flash of movement within?

That's where they were. All he had to do was get there.

&

"What is it you have against the Burmese?" Marcus asked, as if he were at tea and doing nothing more than eliciting conversation.

"Absolutely nothing." Georgina replied. "I've never even met a Burmese. I'm sure they are very nice when they conquer their neighbors and enslave the natives."

"Your employers, then," Marcus countered, to which Georgina smiled.

"My employers have no problem with Burma, either. Their problem is with the governor of India, and how he simply refuses to rise to the challenge the Burmese continually set forth. Since they were having so much trouble with the men put in charge of India, they decided to try and wage a war of opinion here in London." Georgina shook her head. "Do you have any idea how difficult it is to wage a campaign of opinion?"

Marcus shook his head, but Sarah answered, "Actually, yes, I do."

"I suppose you do," Georgina conceded. "Making people think one way when they were previously thinking another— or worse yet, ignoring the issue—is exceedingly difficult. In between going to parties and whispering just how nervous my brother's Burmese friend made me into the ears of people with influence, I've had to plant articles in the papers about Burmese atrocities, about how gruesomely they treat their slaves and prisoners, and how encroaching they have become on British settlements."

"But how does the Comte—and Mr. Pha—come into play?" Marcus asked

"The Comte and I met in India," Georgina offered. "He was the best confidence man I had ever seen. Had everyone eating out of the palm of his hand simply because he had a title—that no one could source, of course—and spoke with authority. You would be amazed at how easily you can pass yourself off as something you're not, as long as you say it with authority."

"True," Sarah acknowledged.

"Anyway, since he was running out of people in Bombay to take advantage of, I came up with a scheme that we would travel to England and live high here. I would be his stepsister, coming to London for her first Season, he my guardian. He, of course, knew nothing of why I really wished to come, or my employers. I'm the one that came up with that absurd story about Mr. Pha and Jean meeting in a Burmese prison. Which worked like a charm. It—along with being known friends of the Duke of Parford—gave us entrée in to all the fancy places he wished to go, and to all the people I needed to whisper to."

"And it was convenient that you claimed Mr. Pha was Burmese—it gave you a dark-skinned man to place the blame on, should someone point in your direction for the murder of Lord Fieldstone."

"That as well." Georgina agreed. "Although, it wasn't supposed to be Lord Fieldstone who died. Any man high up in parliament would have done well enough."

"The death of a high-ranking member of society by a Burmese *dha* would have been enough to spur Britain into action against Burma itself," Marcus filled in.

"I threw a few forged reports on his desk of Burmese atrocities, and waited for London to call on the governor of India to declare war. It was to be my coup de grace," Georgina replied wistfully. "It was exceedingly distressing to have his death covered up—by you, I presume."

"So why choose Fieldstone? Was he getting too close to discovering your Burmese schemes?"

"No, he was getting too close to discovering that the Comte was not what he seemed." Georgina took the reticule that hung from her wrist and tossed it to Sarah. "Open it."

She did. Inside were only a few coins and a letter. Opening it, she looked past the droplets of blood, gone brown with time, and read.

"It is a letter from Lord Fieldstone to the Duke of Parford," Sarah told Marcus. "Not yet finished. Asking if he was aware that his Holbein painting had been sold, and ended up with the Historical Society."

It was the letter they had been searching the house for, over the course of two days, Sarah thought, scanning the contents. But it did not indicate any nefariousness on behalf of a Burmese interest—instead, it was about the theft of a painting.

"It goes on to ask if he has confidence in the Comte de Le Bon, who he had let stay in his home."

"Jean is—was—a greedy child," Georgina explained. "While everyone in town was smiling at him and fawning over him"—she gave a pointed look to Sarah—"he and Pha were making money hand over fist, emptying out the contents of the Duke of Parford's home. It made him happy." She shrugged. "I told him that he could make a few coins off the lesser works in the house, and the contents of the attics and what not, but paintings like that would draw notice. But he wouldn't listen, and one day I returned home to a false Holbein on the study's wall. He tried to hide it from me, can you believe it?"

She laughed, coolly, placatingly. Which only made her seem all the more insane. "Really, Lord Fieldstone chose which gentleman I would kill for me. If he looked any closer at the Comte, he would begin to see me, and I could not have that."

"Interestingly," Marcus drawled, "if you had chosen any other man to kill, I would not have covered it up, nor would anyone have looked further into the Comte. Fieldstone had sent me to France the week before to look into the Comte's background—although he would not tell me why. Those papers you threw on his desk misled me in the exact direction you wished me to avoid. And without that letter about the painting"—Marcus indicated the letter in Sarah's hands—"I had to assume Fieldstone's death was related to the Burmese issue, and the Comte connected to it."

"It is very possible I miscalculated some things," Georgina replied grudgingly. "You chief among them. And your friend, Lieutenant Fletcher. But never fear, Mrs. Hill will have tidied up that loose end by now." She checked her pocket watch. "And it is just about time for me to finish up here. You'll find, I do prefer things to close off neatly."

Sarah's heart began to pound at the mention of Jack's name. "Mrs. Hill?" she asked, her voice coming out wobbly.

"Yes, she's my protégée," Georgina answered. "And very dedicated, too."

They had sent Mrs. Hill after Jack. All this time, she had been standing here, stalling with some surprisingly candid conversation, waiting for Jack to arrive and save the day. And Mrs. Hill . . . Jack . . . oh God, the very thought brought palpitations to her chest.

Marcus, not noticing Sarah's distress—or perhaps because of it—turned the conversation back to the unfolding mystery. "But why keep the letter? If found, it would have unraveled everything," he said.

"I know why," Sarah said, the voice coming from deep within her. "It gave her control."

"Control?" Marcus asked.

"Over the Comte. You see, the letter did not incriminate *her*. In fact, none of us, even though she resided in the same house as the Comte, ever even suspected her. We thought she was the excuse he and Mr. Pha used to come to London, a poor victim of his influence. But this letter . . . if he ever got out of line again, and tried to sell another Holbein or talked of turning . . . well, she could say she had found it in his belongings, and suddenly he'd find himself hanging for the murder of Lord Fieldstone." Sarah stared Georgina down, hate in her eyes. "It gave her back control of the Comte. And control . . . is everything."

"Very good, Sarah," Georgina replied, admirably. "I knew you would have made an excellent protégée." Sarah couldn't help but register some surprise—and the rest of her was decidedly appalled. "I thought about trying to recruit you once or twice," Georgina continued. "After all, you were so very, very good at pretending to be someone else. But then you seemed to lose interest in make-believe."

She meant that Sarah had lost some of her hard, angry edges when the Blue Raven—when Jack—had come into her life.

"Anyway, after I showed the letter to the Comte," Georgina continued, "he was much more cooperative with my goals. He acquiesced when I agreed to your idea for a dinner party—I wanted to see who exactly was going to come after me, you see—but he slipped away from me when you took him into your custody, Sir Marcus. And he was eager to do it. I knew Jean wouldn't talk without some assurances and, therefore, had a little time to close up shop. But not much."

"You wreak so much havoc . . ." Sarah said, shaking her head. "And yet you call it closing up shop."

"I only do what I have to, Sarah, to survive. Much like you. Much like everyone else," Georgina replied. Just then a certain amount of commotion began from outside the window, in the courtyard below. "And that must be the guard change. Well, I suppose it's time. This has been fun, but I really must be going."

As Georgina smiled at them, waving her gun back and forth between them like the pendulum of a grandfather clock, Sarah glanced at Marcus. Their time was up, it seemed. Sarah felt her body go numb, her knees weak. But Marcus—God bless Marcus—held her gaze, his kind eyes becoming steel.

Stay strong, they seemed to say. *This is the moment.*

"Which of you shall come with me?" Georgina asked.

That was when Marcus leaped at her.

That was when the gun went off.

And that was when all hell broke loose.

Twenty-eight

J ACK was halfway up the wall when he heard the gunshot.

He had managed to sneak back to the building along the side, where the horses were kept. He moved along the back of the building, careful to avoid any of the guards who had tried to hold him earlier, careful to look as if he belonged as much as possible. As dirty as he was, he was still in his naval uniform. It was almost eleven o'clock, time for the ceremonial changing of the guards outside of the building. He would have to be quick, and quiet.

Luckily, the Horse Guards, built in the last century, had the ornateness of the Baroque style and the bulbous outcroppings on ledges, cornerstones, and cornices that made excellent footholds. He scrambled faster than he ever had in his life. Moved with speed and assurance that he didn't know he possessed. But it was there. As certain as he was that Georgina Thompson was in the little room and, therefore, Sarah Forrester, thus was the certainty of his movements.

And when the gunshot rang out from that room—it confirmed all his suspicions and fears immediately.

Unfortunately, it also managed to draw the attention of the guards he had previously eluded below.

"Oy there! Stop!" came cries, and clattering of men—men who, Jack recalled as he heard the click and snick of readying weapons, were well armed.

He moved like the wind, gripping the walls like he was born to it, like ivy, scaling the building in record time. He levered himself up onto the roof just as the first ball was fired at him. The second and third came at his heels, but he was already running—running across slanted slate, running past the railings that lined the roof, to where he estimated the small, high window was on the other side of the building. Shots were coming from the other side now, but he was too high above them for their shots to bear fruit. Then, he reached the corner where he needed to be, got on his belly, and hung himself over the roof's cornice, and caught a glimpse of what was going on in the window below him.

He spied the Comte, dead on the floor in a pool of his own blood. The drumming in his ears surged when he saw Marcus, seemingly lifeless, crumpled in a ball in the corner of the room. And Sarah, half naked, shakily stripping off her dress, while Georgina Thompson held a knife under her chin.

❧

Sarah didn't know what had happened. One minute, they had been standing there, and in a blink, Marcus had leaped for Georgina, knocking her gun hand skyward as he did so.

Georgina was shocked—shocked enough to pull the trigger, raining down upon them ceiling plaster and dust. But not shocked enough to not counterattack. While Marcus had her in strength and most especially in height, he did not immediately take the fight. Perhaps his natural chivalry made him hesitant to hurt a woman, maybe he thought to take her alive, either way, he was suddenly at a disadvantage. Using strength and balance that could only have been taught in the Far East, Georgina managed to flip him beneath her, and roll him across the floor.

The gun, having been fired and thus now worthless, skittered across the floor. And somehow in the ensuing tumult the keys skittered as well.

The keys.

The sight of those silver and black keys on the floor brought fire back to Sarah's brain, and movement back to her feet.

She dashed across the room to where the keys lay innocently on the wooden floor. Scooping them up, she dashed
back to the door.

"Gold!" Marcus said, his voice squeezed by the fight.
"Gold . . . key!"

Sarah flipped through the ring to the gold key, and fitted it
into the lock. Just in time to hear a deep gasp from the fight in
the corner. Sarah turned, unable to stop herself.

There, she saw Marcus and Georgina, both on their knees.
Georgina held him steady by the knife she held in his gut.
Slowly, he fell over on his side in a thud, clutching his wounded
side. Georgina slid the knife out of him, and held it to his
throat . . .

Sarah didn't need to see anything more. Swiftly she turned
back, turning the key in the lock with an audible click.

"Oh no, you don't!" Georgina cried, stopping before deliv-
ering the coup de grace to Marcus's throat, and instead leaping
across the room and slamming her hand against the door, shutting it before Sarah could open it. With her other hand, she
held the knife that dripped Marcus's—and the Comte's—
blood, right underneath Sarah's chin.

"You stop right there," Georgina said, all politeness gone
from her voice. Her face . . . she had not yet had enough blood
spilled. She wanted more. Sarah could tell.

And then, Sarah heard it. A commotion from outside, a
number of shots being fired from the back of the building.
Strangely, Georgina didn't seem to register it. She was too
bloodthirsty, her breaths still coming in gulps from her exertions with Marcus. And then . . . Sarah heard footsteps. Across
the roof.

Jack.

It had to be. No one else climbed like that. It had to be Jack.
Her heart soared, but her mind, blessedly, stayed in the present.

"D-Don't," Sarah managed, flinching back from the knife.
"You . . . you'll get blood on my dress."

"I'm about to get a lot more," Georgina replied, her eyes
feral. "I've decided I can do without a hostage."

"But you can't do without a clean dress!" Sarah said in a
rush. Georgina blinked once, and drew back, ever so slightly.

"You . . . you can't walk through Whitehall in your gown. You'll be caught."

Georgina's eyes flicked down. Her gown, once a soft blue-gray shade, with velvet spencer (a particularly nice creation of Madam LeTrois', Sarah noted), was torn, and covered in blood. The majority of which came from when Georgina slit the Comte's throat. But the tears of her sleeve and the blood matting her hair at the temple, that was all Marcus. While Georgina examined herself, Sarah chanced a glance to where Marcus lay unmoving.

Unmoving, that is, except for his eye. Which winked at her.

"You're right," Georgina replied, having taken stock of her ensemble and found it wanting. "I knew you would have made a good protégée." Then, extending her arm so the blade of her knife nudged Sarah's chin up, "Take it off."

Sarah immediately, but slowly, methodically, began working the buttons of her spencer. When she removed it, she took a gentle step backward, ostensibly to give her arms room to maneuver. She dropped the spencer on the floor beside Georgina, clear of the bodies that littered the space.

Then she began to work on the buttons on the side of her dress. Just as she brought the dress up over her head, she saw a flash of movement at the window. A familiar head of sun-streaked hair.

The percussion of her heartbeat threatened to break through the walls of her chest, as she drew the dress over her head and tossed it next to the spencer.

"Go stand over there," Georgina indicated the far corner of the room, away from the door and escape. Which was fine, the further from the deadly blade, the better in Sarah's mind. All she had to do was lower that knife, just for a moment, just a spare second . . .

BAM!!!

Glass flew into the room just as Georgina lowered herself to pick up the dress and spencer. Jack swung himself through the window, feet first, sending shards flying, one or two nicking Sarah as she protected herself with her arms.

Georgina was up in an instant, her knife at the ready. But it was Jack, *Jack!* who stood in front of Sarah, protectively.

"Miss Thompson," Jack said, surprisingly cordial, given the growl of his voice.

"Lieutenant Fletcher," Georgina replied. "Fancy seeing you alive. I take it you tied up a loose end for me?"

"Give it up, Georgina," Jack said, as they circled slowly. Sarah moved with Jack. "His Majesty's entire army saw me break through that window. They will be mounting those stairs at any moment. In fact, Sarah," Jack addressed her without turning, "why don't you open that door for them?"

Sarah started for a moment, and then realized that Jack had walked them a complete one hundred and eighty degrees, and the door was right behind her, with the key still in the lock. She turned it, then levered the heavy iron door open.

"Sarah go right on down, I'll be with you in a moment," Jack said.

"Aren't . . . aren't you coming with me?" she asked.

"No, he's not," Georgina replied for him, as she lunged forward.

Jack threw Sarah to the side, as he ducked the swinging of the knife and caught the ferocity that was Georgina Thompson.

And the world became a blaze of light.

Sarah dazedly came to her feet. Something . . . something was wrong with her head. She must have hit it on the wall when Jack pushed her out of the way. Her vision was fuzzy; she could only see two figures joined in combat. Sarah staggered against a floor that moved of its own volition.

"Jack," she said weakly, moving toward him.

She could see the red and silver of the knife pressed against Jack's throat, and how hard he worked to keep it from slicing into his skin.

She could see when Marcus, having not been as incapacitated as she thought, mustered up the strength to reach out and pull Georgina by the leg, pulling her away from Jack's neck, saving his life, before collapsing back down into a heap.

She could see, as she staggered along the wall, her vision double, her legs like pudding, that Jack and Georgina were standing now. But who had the advantage?

She . . . she had to get help. Jack needed her help. *Jack told her to leave.*

Down the stairs. There would be a soldier to help down the stairs.

She lurched for the door, but somehow miscalculated. She found herself grabbed by the arm. And the blade, the ever-present blade, stuck against her chin.

"Hurt her and I'll kill you," she heard Jack growl. She was being pulled, pulled toward the gaping maw of the door. Good, that's where she wanted to go. But then, then she was there, and peering out through it, and she shook her head, trying to clear it. The stairs. The rickety, narrow wooden stairs, that ran up the lonely tower in a spiral.

"I won't hurt her," Georgina purred at her ear. "But the ground will."

And suddenly, Sarah was being thrown. Whipped across the narrow landing, breaking through the thin handrail and hanging over the hard floor, four stories below. But when Georgina grabbed her, took her in her strong grip, she did not realize that Sarah had gripped back.

It was a miscalculation. When Georgina whipped Sarah down into the pit, Sarah's grip stayed, and gravity brought Georgina down with her. Now Georgina was holding onto Sarah, and Sarah was holding onto . . .

Jack.

He had her hand. His body laying flat on the landing, straining to hold their combined weight.

"Don't let go!" she managed to say, her vision still fuzzy, but she focused on him. Focused on him, and only him, and suddenly, things began to be clear again.

Jack had her. And Jack, more than anyone, would never let her fall.

"Never, sweetheart. I got you."

"Let me go!" came Georgina's voice, as she struggled against the death grip Sarah had on her forearm.

"If . . . if I let you go, you'll die," Sarah replied, her voice coming back to her.

"I'll take my chances!" Georgina screamed, her eyes as red as her face, the madness no longer in check. But when Sarah's grip didn't lessen, Georgina began to thrash. To move like a fish on the end of a hook, doing anything to get free, screaming, as her joints twisted and pulled against Sarah's grip.

And it was working.

Because her thrashing made the landing, already stressed

under the weight of three people hanging off the side, begin to creak, and shudder. And then . . .

One of the supports gave way.

As the landing angled down, Jack slid down with it, stopping only when his feet caught on the mouth of the iron door, and Sarah held onto his arm with more strength than she knew she had.

But it wasn't enough.

Sarah couldn't help it. She was slipping. Slipping. And to save herself, she had to give Jack both hands. Her body made the decision for her. Her hand let go of Georgina before her mind could protest.

Georgina didn't scream on the way down. She just went, landing with a thud on the bottom, some four stories below.

Sarah met Jack's eyes. It didn't matter now. Georgina didn't matter now.

Later, of course, they would question how she had survived. There would be no body at the base of the tower, as they finally made their way down, helping Sir Marcus down as they went. He would sway in and out of consciousness, but he was in command enough to tell the guards who finally managed to break into the tower not to shoot Sarah and Jack, as they were the heroes of the situation. And there would be no sign of Georgina when word got out to search London high and low for her. Her escape had long been planned.

But, as it has been said, none of that mattered now.

All that mattered was that Jack had caught Sarah. And he would never let her fall, ever, ever again.

Twenty-nine

"WE are going to miss it!" Sarah cried, worrying at her fingernails.

"We are not going to miss it," Lord Forrester replied, as Bridget reached over and took Sarah's hand, forcing her to stop her nervous picking. "We have timed this perfectly. It's high tide, after all."

"Exactly!" Sarah cried. "It waits for no man! Nor wife."

It had been a tumultuous three days since the events at the Horse Guards. There were messes to be cleaned up, in both the attic room of the Horse Guards and the Duke of Parford's study (not to mention an alleyway a few blocks removed from Somerset House), and Sarah and Jack had to sit inquisition for those messes.

Marcus required surgery. He had feinted around the knife when Georgina had stabbed him, but not enough it seemed, as he was stuck through a fleshy bit of his side. Phillippa had said she was never so happy as to realize that the bit of weight he'd gained in marriage had saved his life. But before the surgery, he made it clear to any agency that asked that Jack and Sarah were above reproach in this matter. Luckily, no agency really questioned the new head of the War Department, and with

Marcus's secretary's help, as well as Phillippa, they were sent home, free of any charges or scandal.

Of course, once they got home, they had some explaining to do.

First, they explained to Sarah's parents. Contrary to Jack's fears, the Forresters were delighted to welcome him to the family as a son-in-law-to-be, and gave their blessing for a union between them fully and completely. While Jack and Sarah might have glanced over some of the more unusual aspects of their romance—Blue Ravens, false moustaches, that Sarah's room is easily accessed from her window—the way they held on to each other was plain enough that further explanation was decidedly unnecessary.

It was also unnecessary to explain the circumstances to Bridget, who shook her head, and sighed, "Finally."

Amanda simply wanted to know what color her bridesmaid dress would be.

It was gold, as the best they could do on such short notice was to let down the hem of one of Sarah's ball gowns.

Sarah herself wore white, and walked down the aisle of their church and married Lieutenant Jackson Fletcher under special license (which Lord Forrester had moved heaven and earth to acquire, once he saw his daughter's insistence, and guessed the reason for it) and under a blue sky, a mere twenty hours before the *Dresden* was meant to depart.

But for those twenty hours, Sarah and Jack reveled and loved, and if either of them worried over the upcoming separation, or the wait that would be their only comfort for the next two years, neither allowed the other to see it. Indeed, they acted as if they had all the time in the world.

But that didn't mean they had all the time to make it to the London docks to see the *Dresden* off!

"We will never make it," Sarah breathed, once again angling out the window to see the traffic.

The roads were surprisingly cramped for dawn. But the *Dresden* was a large ship, with a sizeable crew and cargo. And everyone had to get on board, or wave good-bye to those who were.

Jack had left her bed hours earlier, to come to the *Dresden* and familiarize himself with her decks and holds, captain and crew before they set sail.

She didn't want that to be the last time she saw him—her half-asleep, him tiptoeing out the door. They had to get there before the *Dresden* set sail. They simply had to.

"You had to do your hair just so, didn't you?" Sarah shot Bridget a look. Bridget blinked back innocently at her.

"How did I stall us? You are the one who changed gowns twice."

"I was ready to go in the carriage ten minutes before you came down—"

"Girls," Lady Forrester said calmingly. "Blame does no good at this point. Sarah, why don't you hop out and run for the docks. You'll move faster on foot."

Sarah didn't have to be told twice. She was out of the carriage before the driver could even draw to a complete stop.

She wove her way in and out of the fisherman setting up their stalls, the men hauling heavy cargo over their heads. As she got closer and closer to the ship, to the dock where the *Dresden* stood, proud and tall, she couldn't help feeling a sense of dread. People were no longer standing and blocking her path . . . they were moving in the opposite direction.

Suddenly, she burst out of the maze of buildings and onto the clearing of the docks. She was there! She made it!

Just in time to see the *Dresden* fade in the distance, moving down the Thames.

"No!" she cried, her breaths coming in heavy gulps from running. The crowd of people had given up on waving good-bye to their loved ones and begun dispersing, making it easy to run right up to the edge of the dock.

"No! Jack!" she yelled out, waving like a madwoman, any pretense that she was once (and still was) the toast of the ton now officially dropped. "Good-bye, Jack!"

"Well, thank goodness you're saying good-bye," a familiar gruff voice drawled next to her. "I thought for a moment you were about to dive in the water, and I would have had to jump in after you."

Sarah turned abruptly, and stared right up into the face of Jackson Fletcher himself.

Her entire body jolted at the sight. Her head whipped around, to the ship, receding in the distance, to Jack standing tall and proud before her, grinning like a fool.

And in civilian clothes.

"But how . . ." she stuttered. "Why . . . Jack you've missed your ship!"

"Interestingly enough, it's not mine anymore." He took her arm, and turned her away from the edge of the docks, making them seem for all the world like just another strolling couple. "I had a conversation with Phillippa at the wedding yesterday. She gave me a letter from Marcus—he's doing much better and recuperating with Phillippa as his nursemaid. By the bye, you might want to call on her and get her out of the house, she's likely to drive Marcus mad. Anyway," he continued, when Sarah shot him a look, "he wrote that they need someone to follow up on Georgina's employers. See if the bits of information the Comte let spill would yield any fruit. And since he is still recuperating, he needed someone familiar with the situation to head it up. And it would also help if this person had some experience in espionage."

"You mean . . . you're working for the War Department?" Sarah asked.

"At a remarkably high pay grade, with a rather, er, colorful pseudonym," Jack returned, winking at her. "Of course, this means I'll now be based in London."

"Will you?" Sarah smiled as her heart soared.

"Yes, a fact your family thought you would approve of."

Sarah looked to where Jack indicated. There, in the middle of the docks, stood her family. Her mother looking teary, her father proud. Bridget looked smug, and Amanda simply bounced with the anticipation of what was to come next.

Truth be told, Sarah was bouncing, too. But . . .

"Jack, will you miss it? The sea?" She asked, tentatively, looking to her toes. "You've been a navy man your entire life, and now. . . ."

"Now, I'm something else," he nudged her chin up with a gentle hand. "A life of adventure and service to the Crown need not be found at sea, I've discovered." When she still seemed skeptical, he sighed, and took her hand. "I was a child when I joined the navy, looking for honor and adventure. But it didn't satisfy me. Not really. Now, I want a different kind of adventure. And I want it to start right away."

Sarah's eyes went wide as Jack slowly dropped to one knee.

Her eyes never left him, even though she could hear her mother's gasp and her sister's squeal.

"Sarah Forrester, Golden Lady," Jack began, taking a ragged breath. "I've loved you since before I knew what love was. We may have been married yesterday, but I realize I was remiss. It was always assumed you see, and so I never even asked the question. But you do need to be consulted, considering recent events."

"I do, indeed," Sarah managed through the rapid beat of her heart.

"You may decide you would rather not be married to a security section man, rather than a naval lieutenant. After all"— he gave a nervous laugh—"at one point you had been expecting a Duke."

"I don't want—"

"I may not be a Duke," he continued, "we won't be able to live that high, but I will keep you in comfort, and better still, I'll be by your side the whole time. But I only want to go on this adventure with you. So . . ." His face split into a grin, as Sarah felt tears of happiness stain her cheeks. "Would you like to go on an adventure with me?"

It was not a ballroom in front of a thousand glittering people. It was not elegant, or by any means refined. Instead, it was on the docks, somewhat after the fact, in front of only her family as dawn broke against the sky that Sarah found herself proposed to. By the man she had fallen in love with and married not the day before.

They arrived at it crookedly. And by no means perfectly. But it was perfect for them.

And so it was in those golden moments, lit by the rising run against the London docks, as men and women milled around them, going about their day's work, and her family cheered and cried, that Sarah Forrester accepted Jackson Fletcher's hand, and said yes to an adventure.

Epilogue

THE summer sun faded into autumn late in the south of France. Indeed, it barely faded at all, which was what Georgina preferred. The months spent in England, through a wet, chilled spring and a tumultuous summer, all in the pursuit of a goal that was just now coming to fruition had taught her an appreciation of the more temperate climates she had grown up with.

A little over a month ago, the Burmese had taken the island of Shapuree, which the British had claims to. All of those weeks of whispered words in the right ears were now bearing fruit, as the Burmese were no longer seen as a nuisance, but a threat to the growing British Empire. The desired war—and the desired profits from it for her employers—would soon follow.

Granted the mess in England had put a slight damper on her reputation, and she bitterly regretted being unable to deliver the coup de grace she needed to send the English into a full Protestant fury, but surely her employers would see the right of the situation, recognize her hard work, and pay her the remaining sum they owed her.

And if they didn't . . . well, she had other means by which to take what she was owed.

Thinking about the mess in England set Georgina's face to a scowl, which did not mesh with the symphony of beauty that was Montpellier in October. She forced her expression to clear, careful that anyone that chanced to look at her face would not know her true feelings. Not that it was likely that anyone would look at her. Even if her arm hadn't hung limply, loosely at her side, rendered useless by twisting it free from Sarah's grasp, and then landing badly in her fall, Georgina knew she would be outshone by her newly chosen protégée. Chloe, nineteen, lithe, and French, possessed all the charm and beauty of Jean de Le Bon as well as the more fluid moralities of Mrs. Hill, making her the perfect specimen for this line of work. She was young, moldable, although not yet entirely controlled—but they would work on that. Above all else, Georgina relished control.

She glanced over her shoulder, where Chloe was testing her wiles on the clerk of the grand hotel they were staying at, overlooking the deep blue Mediterranean. If she succeeded, Chloe would be purring with pride, and perhaps their rooms would be gratis that evening. If she didn't . . . she was very likely to make the clerk feel as bad as she did. Georgina hid a smile at the thought. Impetuous child, but really the best Georgina could have possibly found, and on such short notice.

Green eyes and golden dresses flashed across her memory. It really was too bad that Sarah Forrester had managed to break through the brittle shell of the Golden Lady. Sarah would have made a fantastic student. The right mix of anger and mischief, an internal person who understood the ladders one must climb. And she seemed to take instruction well. Unfortunate that she had to become besotted by a common navy man . . . even if he turned out to be rather uncommon. Likely shackled to him by now, turned around completely from bold to insipid in love.

Lieutenant Jackson Fletcher. He had ruined a great deal. Not just her arm, which even now tingled as if it still had feeling. Making her want to twitch and scratch and rage. But Georgina was not one to hold grudges. They took up too much time. After all, she had a business to operate. When people of means needed things done quietly, they called her. It was no place for personal malice . . . no matter how much the man's existence irked her.

Oh well, she thought, as she turned her face to the setting sun, letting its last rays of warmth wash over her. It was of little consequence, as Georgina had every intention of minimizing her work in London, and pushing forward with her European ventures. If she ever happened to meet with Jackson Fletcher again, well, she would smile, extend her hand . . .

And slit his throat.

It really was all about timing.

And Georgina always had a knife at the ready. And one steady, patient hand.

Dear Reader—

Research is part of the lifeblood of an author. It takes us directly into the world we hope to inhabit; it inspires us with ideas for plot and character, even though sometimes we have to fictionalize things. Just a bit.

The first Anglo-Burmese War was officially declared in March of 1824, but action began in the fall of 1823 when Burma took the island of Shapuree and attacked British soldiers stationed there. The war between British India and Burma lasted until 1826 and deeply weakened Burma (after two more wars, Burma was eventually taken into the British Empire in 1885). Obviously, the characters of Georgina Thompson and the Comte de Le Bon never (to my knowledge) existed, nor did their actions in any way facilitate anti-Burmese sentiment in Great Britain. But tension between British India (and, therefore, the British Empire) and Burma did exist, due to Burma's extreme expansionist philosophies, and, therefore, in my fiction, Georgina Thompson is tasked with helping the inevitable along.

It may seem odd to say that there were not enough commissions in the Royal Navy to satisfy the number of officers it had. After all, after 1815, a great era of Pax Britannica was ushered in, where Britain, due to its maritime might, was able to peacefully hold and control trade routes and greatly expand its empire. Indeed, Britain had a larger fleet than any two other nations combined. But it was still far fewer ships than they had previously. According to Dean King, author of A Sea of Words: A Lexicon and Companion to the Complete Seafaring Tales of Patrick O'Brien, *"In the years that followed [the wars], Britain dramatically reduced her naval forces in a long period of peace but still remained unchallenged as the possessor of the most powerful navy in the world."*

Since Britain didn't need all of its ships, it didn't need all of its officers. Thus, Lieutenant Jack Fletcher is rightly very worried about the future of his naval career when his ship is brought limping into the London docks.

Hans Holbein the Younger (1497–1543) was a German Renaissance Era artist known for his portraiture, and upon his travels to England, he became a favorite of the Tudor Court, painting many of the court's most illustrious figures, including Sir Thomas More, the Archbishop of Canterbury, and King Henry VIII himself.

In If I Fall, *my heroes are able to tell that the Holbein on the wall of the Duke of Parford's library is a reproduction because "it's still a bit wet—[they could] practically smell the linseed oil." Oil paintings vary in drying times, depending on how thinned the paint was by additives such as linseed oil, but even then, oil paintings are often not dry to the touch until weeks after completion. (Sometimes, a painting is not considered completely, thoroughly dry until several years have passed!) Hence, they would be able to tell by touch if the work was recently done. (Full disclosure: Holbein's chosen paints for his portraits were oil and tempera. Tempera, being made from eggs, is incredibly quick-drying. But it was used as an under layer and would have had no effect on the drying time of the thicker oil top layers.)*

The Horse Guards in Whitehall was home to the offices of the general staff of the British army, and still houses some minor army commands to this day. In my fictional world, it is also home to the War Department, and the secretive Security Section thereof. The interior geography of the building, with its attic rooms, is entirely of my own invention. (Although there is a ceremonial archway, which Jack erringly rides through, as only the monarch is meant to pass through it.)

There are a great many other aspects of the story that benefited from research (the naval offices are located in Somerset House, officers without a commission must sign an affidavit, allowing them meager half pay in exchange for not taking up other work, etc.), but in the end, it is just that—a story. And hopefully one you have enjoyed reading as much as I did writing.

Many thanks,
Kate Noble

**Keep reading for a preview of
the next historical romance by Kate Noble**

Coming soon from Berkley Sensations!

February 1824

AT last, Bridget thought, her body vibrating with excitement, *Italy*.

But not just Italy. *Venice*.

Although, she thought, wrinkling her nose in the salt air as they sailed into the port of this miraculous city, Venice was not necessarily Italian at all.

While on board the *Tromba*, the Italian-owned merchant vessel which the Forrester ladies had boarded in Portsmouth nearly a month ago, Bridget had been without what usually took up most of her time—a pianoforte on board an ocean-going vessel was pure folly. Or so she was told.

Thus, she and Amanda had taken to wandering around ship, pestering the *Tromba*'s (which meant 'trumpet' in Italian, which Bridget took as a good sign) captain. Well, Amanda was pestering. Bridget could not pester, as she couldn't get a word in edgewise.

"But it says in my guidebook"—when they had decided upon this trip, Amanda immediately devoured every travelogue of Italy she could find in their family library, not to mention in London's bookshops—"that Venice is not *really* Italian!"

Captain Petrelli, a kind man, scoffed at the notion. "Venice, not Italian! That is like saying Rome is not Catholic!" Then, humoring their lack of knowledge about the world stage, he took out his maps.

It seemed the wars at the beginning of the century had turned what had been a conglomeration of kingdoms that most Englishmen thought of as "Italy" into a bit of a redistricted mess, and Venice, at the very northern edge of the Adriatic sea, was no longer Italian at all, but part of the Kingdom of Lombardy-Venetia.

"And since Lombardy-Venetia is ruled by Emperor Francis of Austria," Amanda concluded, "one could argue that Venice is . . . Austrian!"

"But, do not worry," Captain Petrelli had said, his eyes crinkling to superior Amanda and the blinking Bridget from behind his bushy beard. He must have been smiling in there, somewhere. "The city of Venice has survived the assault of Turks and pirates and raiders for a thousand years. One little Austrian government does little to change it."

"I think what my sister means to ask is," Bridget had said while Amanda sputtered in frustration, "who owns Venice?"

"The Venetians, my little *uccello canoro*," he said and tweaked Bridget's nose then, a gesture that in England would have earned him a strong reproof (not to mention the possibility of a duel for disgracing her so), but on board an Italian ship, the rules of Italy seemed to apply. And Italians *touched*. Even sheltered English ladies, who had their mother, three maids, and three footmen travelling with them for protection.

While Lord Forrester had plead business as his reason for not accompanying them (although Bridget quietly suspected his motives had more to do with his abhorrence of traveling farther than his library), he had refused to allow his girls to travel to Europe with anything less than a maid and personal bodyguard each.

Italians also apparently called people by pet names. It took one of Amanda's Italian-to-English translation books for her to figure out that *uccello canoro* translated to "warbler," or "songbird." Apparently Bridget, without a pianoforte on board, had taken to expelling the melodies that crowded her head by singing them under her breath. All the time, according to Amanda, who shared a stateroom with her, and had to beg her to stop humming as she fell asleep.

The pet names, Bridget could get used to. The constant touches were more disconcerting.

Really, between the little tweaks to the nose and the *uccello canoro*, Bridget could half believed that Captain Petrelli was in love with her. If he wasn't old enough to be her grandfather, one who showed off the miniature of his wife of thirty years to anyone who showed the slightest interest, that is.

She was sorry to say goodbye to Captain Petrelli when they docked in Rome. Indeed she was sad to say good-bye to the entire crew. (Their mother was less sorrowful, as she spent the first week of the journey "getting her sea legs" and never fully adjusted to them, practically kissing the ground as they disembarked.) But she was far too excited for what was to come to mourn for long.

It was as if she, with each passing league away from London, felt herself shedding the old Bridget, as a bird molted feathers in the summer. The closer she got to the warmth of the Mediterranean, the further she was from the wretched, scowling thing she had become over the course of the past year, watching her sister Sarah's success at the expense of having any herself. The Bridget whose fingers failed her when anyone other than her family watched her play.

It was a second chance. She could be new again.

And, she had thought determinedly, with the help of Signore Carpenini, she would become the player she was meant to be.

They had stayed in Rome for two days. Not long enough for their mother, who, after weeks at sea, was loathe to board a ship again, and not nearly long enough for Amanda.

"But the Pantheon!" Amanda had cried, flipping to the appropriate page in her guidebook. "The Colosseum!"

"We will get to them," Bridget had tried to placate her sister. "After Venice."

As they had planned their trip in those frantic days in London, Bridget had done her best to steer her family into the opinion that it was best to go to Venice first. "It will be much easier to start at the top and work our way down. That way, we will have less to travel on the return trip," she had said, as un-affected as she could manage.

This logic looked sound on paper, and therefore it was agreed upon at the time. But now, having already docked in Rome, less than two days travel by sea around the island of Sicily and up the Adriatic to her intended destination, Bridget could not let something as little as her mother's weariness and her sister's sightseeing enthusiasm stop them.

"But Venice will be crowded," Amanda warned. "It says right here in my guidebook—" but Bridget cut her off with a wave of her hand.

"Yes, yes, the carnival. I don't know why that worries you so, I think a carnival will be fun," Bridget said smoothly. "And of course it will be crowded, Venice is supposed to be the most beautiful city there is, and the most pleasant in temperature."

Amanda frowned a little and flipped pages, looking for any information that might relate to Venice's weather.

"Well, hopefully it will be warmer than Rome," Lady Forrester replied. "Their winters may be milder than England, but one could hardly call this gray atmosphere balmy or exotic."

Bridget nodded and hoped that neither her sister nor her mother would realize that, being to the north, Venice's weather was likely similar if not slightly cooler than Rome's. And since the English winter had been the excuse given for their escape, Bridget's fragile fiction could fall apart at the seams.

"Besides, we've already arranged for rooms in Venice, haven't we Mother?" Bridget said finally.

Thankfully, this last bit of persuasion did the trick, as Lady Forrester sighed, and rang for the footmen to come and make sure their trunks were ready to be loaded onto the smaller ship that would take them to Venice in the morning.

Because it was in Venice that Signor Vincenzo Carpenini, master musician and composer, currently resided. And thus it was to Venice that Bridget would go.

❧

"I told you we should have stayed in Rome."

Amanda puffed out the words on a sigh, low enough so their mother wouldn't hear her frustration. Although, their mother was already frustrated enough.

"What do you mean you have no rooms for us? We sent a messenger ahead to arrange for them!"

"Si, Signora, you did," Signor Zinni, the proprietor of the Hotel Cortile, located right off the serpentine Grand Canal, stammered, wringing his hands. His English was very good, (and not surprisingly, his German), which was likely why the establishment was recommended to them as being very friendly to travelers of the Forrester's station and nationality. "But you arrived too quickly to receive our reply. The hotel is booked months in advance for Carnevale!"

Carnevale—not a carnival, as Bridget had been quick to dismiss it—was the festival of indulgence that preceded Lent. And it was something that Venice, according to Amanda's guidebook, was known for.

For the months of January and February, before Ash Wednesday descended and ushered in forty days of penance, Venetians took it upon themselves to make certain they had something to repent. Well, at least they *had*, before Napoleon and Austria took the stuffing out of the city. Now, the custom was limited only to those who had the funds and the time for it, i.e., the wealthy and the tourists. Which seemed to make up the entirety of the Hotel Cortile's clientele.

White masks, faces blank and frozen, made to hide the sinners from the consequences of their sins, had stared back at them from other gondolas—some made out of plaster, some heavy ceramic, some embellished with paints and gold, some austere and staring. Yet all were strangely beautiful and grotesque. People danced in the streets and on the footbridges that arched over the narrower canals. And the music! There was music pouring out of every window, on every corner. No matter their exhaustion at travel, it made Bridget's senses awake with wonder, her body vibrate with melody.

"Just wait until my husband's friends at the Historical Society in London hear about this," Lady Forrester was saying in grand, tragic tones. It had taken three ships and a gondola to get them to this hotel, and Bridget knew her mother was not about to set foot on another water-bound vessel without putting up a fight. "They are the ones who recommended your establishment, Mr. Zinni. And they travel. Quite often."

Zinni blanched, as was appropriate. "Signora, Carnevale

will be over after this Tuesday," he replied, thinking quickly. "Indeed, in three days' time, you can have an entire floor of the hotel to yourselves." Lady Forrester squinted, and then raised one imperious eyebrow at the little man. "At no additional cost, of course," he murmured.

Their mother, who relished negotiating more than was seemly for a lady of quality, preened a bit at winning that battle. But then she steadied herself, and raised her eyebrow again at the hotelier. "That is all well and good, but what do we I and my poor daughters do in the meantime?"

"I . . . I know not, Signora." Zinni shrugged. "Perhaps some of our gentlemen customers can be convinced to share a space for a time? But it would take some lira . . ."

While their mother metaphorically rolled up her sleeves, and set about haggling for a room like the very best fishwife, Bridget turned to Amanda, who was had wandered to a window, trying to stay out of the way of the numerous people passing through the hotel's main entrance, as she flipped pages of her guidebook.

"How long do you think mother will haggle?" Amanda asked, her eyes never leaving the guidebook, except to occasionally peek out the window, as if confirming something she read.

"We have not yet reached 'haggling.' We are still at 'intimidate.' " Bridget threw her eyes over to her sister. "What are you reading about now?"

"Where we are," Amanda said. "Did you know that there are no carriages in Venice? No buggies? The narrowness of the streets and all the steps on the bridges don't allow for it. If you rode a carriage, you'd never get anywhere." She nodded to the window, which opened up on to a smaller canal. "Everything has to be transported via those little flat boats. That or walking."

"Mother will be so pleased," Bridget said under her breath, and Amanda giggled. "You have certainly done your research, haven't you?"

But Amanda just shrugged in return. "I like to know things. You and mother and Sarah never tell me anything, so I have to figure it out on my own."

Bridget blinked, surprised. Although, upon reflection, she

supposed it was true. Last season, Amanda was not yet out and therefore shielded from most of the dramatics, which drove Amanda crazy with curiosity. And when she had decided to convince her parents to take them to Italy, Bridget had simply told her sister to follow her lead, not giving her any more information than that. Surely, she deserved a little more consideration.

"So," Bridget exhaled, seating herself next to Amanda. "Where are we? Precisely."

Amanda flipped the pages in her guidebook, and found one with a detail map of the streets and canals of the main island of Venice. The Grand Canal bisected the picture, and Amanda pointed to a small canal just to the east of it. "Here. Rio di San Marina."

Bridget dutifully looked to where Amanda's finger pointed, but her eyes found themselves falling on another Rio, just a few canals away.

Rio di San Salvador.

Her breath caught as little pinpricks of awareness spread across her scalp. In the letter they had received from Carpenini's friend Mr. Merrick, regarding taking lessons with the Signor, he had given his direction as the Rio di San Salvador.

And Mr. Merrick would know where she could find Carpenini.

Bridget peered closer at the map, her nose coming close enough to touch the pages.

"Good heavens, Bridge, do you need to borrow Mother's spectacles?" Amanda said, startling Bridget out of her reverie.

"What?" Bridget asked, her focus blurry as her head came up from the page. "Oh, no—ah, may I borrow this for a moment?"

Without waiting for an answer, Bridget grabbed the guidebook from Amanda's hands and quickly crossed to their haggling mother.

"Mother!" Bridget said breathlessly. "Look, we are on the Rio di San Marina."

"Yes, my dear, that's lovely. But I am trying to deal with our arrangements, as you see . . ."

"But, look how close we are to the Rio di San Salvador!"

Bridget could not keep the excitement out of her voice. "We could go there this very afternoon, and ask Mr. Merrick to help us find Carpenini . . ."

"Bridget," her mother said on a sigh. "We just arrived. Surely it can wait."

"But we could walk there easily—"

"I don't think so, my dear. Now, Mr. Zinni, surely such a sum would be by week, not by night . . ."

"But mother!"

"Bridget, I said no!" Her mother turned to her fully then. Her gaze was straight and focused—albeit slightly squinted. She had once again left off her spectacles. "It would be utterly unseemly for us to impose upon the man, without any notice." Then, with a little more kindness, "I know you are excitable, but do keep in mind this holiday is not solely for the purpose of your musical instruction. We are in Italy to . . . take a respite. And I personally think you would do better to show more of an interest in our surroundings than in the prospect of being taught by Carpenini."

The words stung. "You . . . you don't wish me to study with him?"

"I did not say that, my dear." Her mother laid a hand on her daughter's shoulder. "Once we are settled in, we shall send a note to Mr. Merrick. I promise. You've waited this long. What's another day or two?"

A day or two. Her mother wanted her to wait a day or two, when Mr. Merrick, who knew where to find Signor Carpenini, was a mere two canals away? Bridget clamped down on an automatic, panicked reply, instead taking a deep breath, and settling on what she needed to do.

She had waited this long, as her mother had said. But that was precisely why she could not wait another minute longer.

"I'm sorry, Mother. You are right." Bridget said meekly, once she found her voice. "I think the madness of travel and this busy room has unsettled me."

Her mother smiled at her daughter, but then turned to Zinni. "You see that? Your Carnevale madness has unsettled my daughter."

"Signorina, you are pleased to rest in the dining room, surely it will be less crowded . . ."

"No, thank you. Mother, if it is all right with you, I think I shall stand outside the front door. Take in some fresh air."

Her mother looked worried for a second. But since all of her attention was on Zinni, it was possible her focus was on her next counter offer. "Do not leave sight of the door. And keep Molly with you," her mother said finally. Bridget slid her glance to where Molly, the girls' ladies' maid, was chatting with one of the footmen and gesturing toward the trunks. Likely trying to ascertain which one should go where. "And," her mother continued, "do not let your reticule off your wrist. Tie it twice if you must. Now, Mr. Zinni, about that dining room—is it private?

"Oh, and wear our bonnet!" her mother called back, as Bridget headed for the Hotel Cortile's entrance, grabbing Molly on her way. "If you get any more freckles you will be one big spot!"

❧

"All right, miss, it's that one," Molly said, pointing to a red brick structure as she rejoined Bridget on the path that ran alongside the buildings on the north side of the Rio di San Salvador. They could not walk on the Rio itself, as the buildings abutted the water, but there were footpaths on the other side of the houses.

"Are you certain, Molly?" Bridget asked nervously. The house looked very plain from this side. Very nondescript.

"Well, frankly, no, miss, I'm not. But I went over to that chap and said, 'Signor Merrick?' and he said a string of Italian I didn't understand and then he pointed to this house. And then he tried to pinch my bum," Molly finished darkly. "I still canna believe your mother let you to go off on your own like this and find the letter-writing gent."

"She was busy with the hotel proprietor, and said I should take a walk," Bridget lied smoothly.

It had not taken long to get here. With the help of Amanda's guidebook, she and Molly had made their way to from the Hotel to the Rio di San Salvador. They could have taken a gondola, but the crowds of Carnevale had over taken them. Besides, Bridget did not have much money, and none of the local currency at any rate. So, they walked. Molly had expected to get lost, but Bridget had always been able to read a map. Music, maths, and maps were all things that she excelled at, and all things connected in her mind somehow. After all, finding where you were going in music was akin to finding where you were going on the streets, wasn't it?

One minor flaw in the plan, however, was she hadn't know which particular house was Mr. Merrick's; thus they had spent a considerable length of time walking the footpaths on the other side of the canal, crossing back and forth when there was a bridge, asking people in the crudest of Italian if they spoke English and consequently if they knew which home was Signor Merrick's, and getting Molly's bum pinched.

But she was finally here, Bridget thought, as a thrill of anticipation went through her. It was better, surely, that she came here herself, not sending a note, and waiting days to hear a reply. And it was better that she came alone. Her mother, Amanda, they did not understand. None of her family really understood how she felt about music.

She *must* play again—because without the music, what was she? The melodies in her head would dry up and the silence would be intolerable.

And she must play better, too—because she knew she could. Knew it in her bones that she had it in her.

And Carpenini had seen it. Four years ago, before her nerves overcame her, before the tortures of the London Season, he had heard her play one song, and seen that she had it in her.

With that surety giving her strength, she squared her shoulders, and went to knock on the little door on the side of the brick house.

彩

"Federico, get the door, would you?"

Oliver Merrick stamped down the stairs of his house, his eyes on the papers he carried, running one hand through his dark, disheveled hair. Bills, bills, a letter from his father, more bills. Damn it all, but none of this was ever going to be under control, was it?

Oliver reached the landing just as another tentative knock came from the door to the street.

"Federico?" he called again for his erstwhile valet/butler/footman/occasional cook. But Federico did not respond, lazy bastard. Indeed, the only sound Oliver heard was the same phrase of music, repeated over and over again, coming from the main sitting room. It would stop between playings, a scratching of a pencil could be heard, and then it would start again.

Oliver knew this was a bad sign. If his friend were on a good streak, the music would never stop.

"I'll just get the door myself, shall I?" he grumbled under his breath in his fluent Italian. Even if his mother had not been the classic dark-haired, olive-skinned (both of which he'd inherited), passionate firebrand that typified the race, he'd spent enough of the past decade in Venice to speak like a native.

Strange, he thought as he crossed to the door, it couldn't be a caller. His friends from the theater and any prospective students for Vincenzo would come by gondola via the canal.

The only people who ever came by the street door were the grocer and . . .

Oh no. Not again.

He knew what he would find. "God damn it, Vincenzo," he breathed, as he threw open the doors. "You are out to drive me insane with your whores, aren't you?"

But his mutterings were cut short when he found himself staring down into the greenest eyes he had ever seen.

Like the lagoon when it caught the sun just so, making the water turn jewel toned and alive, those eyes stared up at him, wide and trembling with nervous resolve. Freckles danced over her nose and cheeks like someone had reached down from above and sprinkled them there. Freckles he found oddly familiar, but could not place. Dark curls were tucked up in her bonnet, but a tendril behind her ear had escaped. She had a kind of delicate prettiness rarely seen in the streets of Venice, where bright colors and extravagant beauty seemed the fashion.

Oliver was halfway to enchanted in the space of a breath. But then he remembered he was supposed to be annoyed.

"Sorry, ladies," he said in Italian, his face as stern as he could make it, "he's not taking visitors today, nor is there coin to pay for your services." When those green eyes just blinked, and then looked nervously back at the older, more practical looking woman behind her, he let out a breath.

"Look, Carpenini might have sent for you, but I'm sending you away. I'm sorry, but the best I can do is pay for a gondola to take you back to your establishment."

"Carpenini!" the green-eyed enchantress finally said, her accent coming out decidedly English. That was shocking enough. What was more shocking was what she said next. "That is exactly why I am here!"

English. She was English. He blinked twice. And by her cultured tones, she was a lady. One, considering what he had assumed her to be, he fervently hoped did not know the Venetian dialect.

For someone whose profession was assisted by his ability to notice things, why the hell hadn't he noticed she was dressed neatly, respectably? Or that her face lacked the paint of those ladies of the evening.

Perhaps it was because it was the middle of the day. Perhaps it was because of those green eyes.

"Er . . . can I help you, miss?" His English, so rarely used here, felt thick and awkward on his tongue. He suddenly became very aware of the fact that he hadn't put shoes on yet that day.

"Yes," the girl replied, unable to keep the excitement out of her voice. "I should like to see Mr. Merrick, please."

"You are seeing him," Oliver replied, in shock enough to only wonder where this conversation would lead.

"I thought you looked familiar," she said, and smiled.

And she had one hell of a smile. Seemed a bit rough though, somehow. As if the muscles in her face had briefly forgotten how to arrange themselves. But smile she did, and Oliver again found he was losing himself in her impish countenance.

"Might we come in, sir?" the practical one said from behind the green-eyed one. "My lady has been traveling for weeks, after all."

Oliver shook himself out of his reverie, and stepped back to admit them to his foyer. He felt immediately awkward about the surroundings. The rugs were threadbare and the plaster was crumbling in a way he found charming, but he supposed young ladies of good family might not.

"You seem familiar too," he finally blurted. "Er, your freckles."

A delightful blush spread across her cheeks, and Oliver found himself wishing it would happen again. And again, and again.

"We have met before, briefly, Mr. Merrick," she said, her eyes meeting his. "I am Miss Forrester, and you wrote me a letter."

As she worked at the fierce knot of a reticule, and then began to rummage in it, a sense of the familiar began to mingle with a sense of dread. "Miss . . . Brittany Forrester?"

A small frown flashed across her face. "Bridget," she replied tersely, and then handed him a piece of paper from her reticule. A letter written in his own hand.

Oh, hell.

"You wrote me on behalf of your friend Signor Carpenini, who heard me play some years ago, and wondered if I would be amenable to taking instruction from him when he—you—came back to England. Unfortunately I learned that you would not be coming to England after all, so . . ."

"Miss Forrester," he interrupted her. "Please do not tell me that you came all the way to Venice because of this letter?"

"No." The word came out weakly, and Oliver knew it was a lie. "My family is taking a holiday . . . and since we were in Venice and you were here, we thought . . . I thought, that maybe . . ."

Oliver wanted to let his head come down into his hands. Oh hell, oh damn and blast. He cursed profusely under his breath in Italian, which was a language much better equipped for the current predicament.

"Miss Forrester, I am afraid there has been a terrible misunderstanding. You see, I did write this letter, yes, but Vincenzo—Signor Carpenini, that is—is in the middle of a composition. And when he's composing, he does not take on stude—"

But Miss Forrester was not listening to him. Instead her face had taken on a dreamy faraway look, and her fingers began to twitch in time to the music, as if playing imaginary keys.

The music.

"Is that," she finally asked, "the Signor? Is Carpenini here?"

Her face lit up with the possibility, and she took a few unconscious steps towards the door to the drawing room.

"Miss Forrester, please do not disturb him," Oliver cried, and he reached out and grabbed her arm just as she reached the closed door.

"I won't," she replied, stilling beneath his touch. "I just wanted to hear better. Is that an A minor key?"

"I don't know," he began to say, and pulled her back a little. But, unfortunately, the damage had already been done.

It could have been the sound of voices in the hallway, especially female ones, that drew his attention. It could have been Oliver's doing, speaking too loudly or too near the door. It could have been the gentle touch of Miss Forrester's hand on the drawing room door latch. But in any case, the music abruptly stopped, footsteps sounded crossed the room, and the drawing room door was flung open from the inside.

"What the hell is going on out here? Don't you realize I'm composing?" the grouchy bear who emerged from the drawing room said in grunting Italian.

"Signor Carpenini," Miss Forrester breathed.

Oliver straightened, and kept his hand on Miss Forrester's arm. Then, his mind remembering better manners than he'd known he had, he turned to the girl at his side. "Miss Forrester, this is Signor Vincenzo Carpenini. Vincenzo, this is Miss Forrester."

Miss Forrester—and the woman with her, whom Oliver had to guess was her maid—dropped to a curtsy. He still kept his hand on her arm—for some unknown reason, he knew that touch was the only thing keeping her from flying away—and he could feel her shaking.

"Signor, this is a great honor," she began, but was cut off by Carpenini crossing the room and grabbing her under the chin.

"Vincenzo!" Oliver cried, drawing Miss Forrester away.

"English, eh?" his friend said, his dark eyes going cold. And then, in his own English, he turned to Oliver. "If you are going to import a whore for me, Oliver, at least make sure she is real woman. This one is too small to be of any use."

And with that, the great composer stepped back into the drawing room and slammed the door, rattling the dusty chandelier in the foyer.

"I am so sorry; he's a bit—" but as Oliver looked down into Miss Forrester's face, he knew his apologies would be for naught. She was utterly and completely shattered.

"Molly," her voice shook. "We should go."

The maid—Molly—nodded, and before he knew it, she had whisked Miss Forrester out the door to the street.

"Miss Forrester, wait!" he cried, jolting out of his shock. He ran after them, into the street, heedless of his lack of shoes. "At least let me see you home—this is no city for a lady alone!"

But it was too late. Miss Forrester and Molly moved quickly from the alley into the main street, disappearing into the crowds of pedestrians going about their day.

"Damn it all," Oliver breathed, as he walked tentatively on his bare feet back to his house. *No*, he thought, his vision going red. *Not damn it all. Damn Vincenzo Carpenini*.

He walked straight into the drawing room, any tentativeness about disturbing his friend gone.

"Vincenzo, you bastard!" he growled, and his friend looked up from the score on the pianoforte. "Do you have any idea who that was?"

"No," the composer blinked at him. "Should I care?"